Obviously, he knew he was being followed. So why be so careful? He thought about it as he walked from room to room and decided there was only one explanation: something had been put in the apartment. Two possibilities came instantly to mind. Number one was a bug. Number two was a bomb. The Mossad in particular favored the quick explosion as a method of termination.

The question was: what was he going to do about it? It seemed to Malone that a bug was far more likely than a bomb—but this was not a matter about which he could afford to be mistaken. Neither could he take the time to be certain. If it *was* a bomb—well, if it *was* a bomb, he'd already be dead. Probably . . .

"For fans of sadistic bad guys and deathless James Bond heroics."
—*Kirkus Reviews*

"The fast pace and runaway ending make for good reading."
—*Library Journal*

The
Last Goodbye

MALCOLM BELL

St. Martin's Paperbacks

To Frank,
wherever you are
R.I.P. or ¡Hola!

Copyright © 1999 by Malcolm Bell.

All rights reserved. No part of this book may be used or reproduced in any manner whatsoever without written permission except in the case of brief quotations embodied in critical articles or reviews. For information address St. Martin's Press, 175 Fifth Avenue, New York, NY 10010.

Library of Congress Catalog Card Number: 98-28822

ISBN 0-312-95889-7

Printed in the United States of America

St. Martin's Press hardcover edition / January 1999
St. Martin's Paperbacks edition / May 2000

10 9 8 7 6 5 4 3 2 1

Acknowledgments

FIRST OF ALL, WHILE CERTAIN IMAGES AND SEQUENCES IN THE book may have been inspired by actual events, such instances served only as springboards for the author's invention and are now submerged in the entirely fictional realm of this novel.

Thanks to Jim for all his help; to Daisy for insightful comments; to Eric, Deidre, Jean, Linda, and Marilyn for valuable editorial suggestions; to Sam and Elisabeth Johnson, with thanks for their unflinching support and for throwing me first a flotation device and then an entire lifeboat; to Sam Cohen for fighting the good fight; and to Elaine, for hangin' in while I was barely hanging on.

In addition, *The Last Goodbye* acknowledges a debt to a number of printed sources for either inspiration or information.

Among the books that provided valuable background are: Tatsuichiro Akizuki's eyewitness account *Nagasaki 1945*, Lionel Davidson's novel *The Night of Wenceslas*, Herman Moll's (with Michael Leapman) *Broker of Death*, Sadakat Kadri's indispensable *Cadogan City Guides* volume on Prague, and Peter Townsend's excellent *Postman of Nagasaki*.

Articles and newsstories which served to inform the author were too many to list in their entirety, but especially helpful were the following: Reuters, November 11, 1992: Anton Ferreira, "Mystery Mercury Link to South African Murder," *Washington Post*, July 26, 1994. R. Jeffrey Smith and Bradley Graham: "U.S. Officials Clash Over Science Experiments That Create Tiny Nuclear Blasts." Aug 28, 1994: Rick Atkinson "Official Says Contraband Not A Threat." and Dec. 21, 1994 "Prague Says Uranium Found in Czech Auto Could Trigger Bomb;" *The Washington Quarterly*, Vol. 17, No.4: Igor Krhipunov: "Russia's Arms Trade in the Post-Cold War Period;" *The Guardian* (London), December 31, 1992: Martin Kettle, "The Year of Living Dangerously." *The Times* (London) September 21, 1993: Michael Evens: "Ex-KGB Agents Ply Trade in Weapons"; *Russian Press Digest*, April 30, 1993: Yevgeny Anisimov, "The Color of Mercury Is Identical with That of A Party Membership Card"; *Moscow News*, April 15, 1992: Vladimir Gubarev, Vladimir Orlov "Limited Warfare on Nuclear Market" and August 11, 1993: Vladimir Orlov, "Black Holes in Red Mercury": *Current Digest of the Post-Soviet Press*, March 3, 1993, Reprinting from *Izvestia* Aleksei Tarasov, February 2, 1993: "Myths and Reality of Nuclear Smuggling—Strategic Raw Materials Are Flowing Out of Siberia by Land and by Air, Wholesale and Retail;" May 19, 1993 reprinting of *Rossiiskaya Gazeta*, April 23, 1993 " 'Red Mercury': Criminal Proceedings Have Been Instituted. Burbulis and Employees of the President's Staff Will Be

Questioned." *Sacramento Bee*, February 28, 1993: Andy Zipser, "Red Alert—This Tale Gets Slippery"; *Forbes, December 21, 1992;* Craig Mellow, "The Metals Queen of Tallinn."; *Wall Street Journal* (date not noted), Adi Ignatius, "Red Mercury Is Hot, but the Question Is: What Exactly Is It?" *Defense and Foreign Affairs' Strategic Policy* December, 1992: "Croatia Acts as the Nexus of a New Arms Trade": *The Warsaw Voice*, April 25, 1993: Cynthia Durcanin, "Nuclear Smuggling in the Czech Republic: Cracking Down on Loose Nukes."

Broadcasts or transcripts thereof also contributed to the author's knowledge, especially: BBC Summary of World Broadcasts, May 2, 1992; *Broadcasts*, May 2, 1992, quoting *ITAR-Telegraph Agency of the Soviet Union World Service* in English 29 Apr 92: "Paper Alleges Sale of Nuclear Weapons Chemicals Against IAEA Rules;" July 16, 1993: Text of Report by Gwynne Robers and Peter Winterberg from *Mainz ZDF Television Network* in Germany 13 Jul 93: "Report on Illicit Trade in Russian Weapons-Grade Red Mercury."

Prologue

YOTARO WAS IN A TREE WHEN HE HEARD HIS MOTHER'S VOICE calling. The day's heat waited in the heavy air, but in the shade of the woods it was still cool. The sun came down through the pine branches in misty shafts of light.

"Yo-ta-ro!" his mother called. "Yo-ta-ro!"

He shouted back that he was coming and climbed down the tree. He got some sticky pine sap on his knuckle and sucked on it. He liked its spicy resin taste.

He raced toward the house, stopping in the field to pluck some *tampopo*. The round clouds of dandelion heads broke into a thousand white feathers under his fat little fingers.

Yotaro's mother looked at his hands where the white shreds of dandelion seeds were stuck in the pine sap and shook her head with a smile. He stood on the little stool. She ladled water over his hands and made him rub them with sand until they were clean, then rinse and pat them dry.

The two of them began the walk down the hill into the city to take lunch—packed in a box—to Yotaro's father. There had been so many air raids and extra duties that for the past few nights Yotaro's father had been sleeping right at the sub–post office where he worked. Right on a tatami in the middle of the big floor! Yotaro's father complained that he missed his family, but to the boy it seemed exciting to think of sleeping on the floor of a big building with a hundred other people! It must be fun!

The way was so steep that every now and then the path turned into steps. Yotaro hopped first on one foot, then on the other. His mother smiled at him although she herself walked carefully and deliberately because she was fat with the coming baby. He began jumping down the steps so as to land on two feet together, shouting, one syllable to each step: "I! Am! Yo! Ta! Ro! The! Boy! Of! The! Moun! Tain!"

His mother laughed, her musical trill gliding through the morning air. Overhead, buzzards slid through the sky. The road flattened out for a stretch, and Yotaro could see all the way down to the bay. The hills rolled down and down and ended in the bright shimmer of water. And then the quiet morning was pierced by the distant whoop of the air-raid siren.

His mother made him crouch down just there on the road. He stayed in the fragrant, warm shelter of her body, her arms folded over him, but after a minute or two the all clear sounded and they began walking again. Yotaro sang in his high, clear voice as they walked, a popular patriotic song from the radio:

"Air raid siren
  Whine like mosquito
  Enemy airplane
  Buzz like fly"

When they got to the post office, Yotaro's mother
bowed and smiled and asked one of the young men who
rode the red bicycles and delivered mail to fetch Yotaro's
father. Hideo emerged from the building. Grateful for the
food he thanked his wife. They talked for a few minutes
while their son, Yotaro, played postman, collecting rocks
and delivering them to the various pine trees planted
along the sidewalk. Yotaro's father accepted a small rock
with a grave, "Arigato." Then, in a smooth, rapid motion,
he picked up Yotaro, holding him with his two strong
hands around the boy's waist, hoisting him high overhead.
It was a game they played, and Yotaro held his arms
stretched out like a bird's wings and his father swooped
him through the air for a few moments. At the end was a
sharp dive toward the ground, and Yotaro's face came de-
liciously close to it before his father plucked him upward
at the last moment.

Yotaro giggled and hooted as his father set him back
on his feet. He begged his father to do it again, but Hideo
had to return to his duties. He told Yotaro to be a good
boy and to help his mother, and then, as he headed back
inside the building, the air-raid alert blared again. The
three of them went inside, and the adults stood next to
the wall. Used to the sirens now, if anything Yotaro's parents seemed grateful for a few more minutes together. The
boy sat on the floor, cross-legged, humming a tune and
marching his fingers over the terrain of his feet and legs.

3

He was pretending his fingers were soldiers, marching up over the hill of the knee, down the valley, up over the rock. . . .

The all clear sounded and the three of them walked outside. Yotaro looked up to see that the sky was getting cloudy. He hoped it did not rain. He heard the drone of an airplane. His mother was saying something about Ji-san, Yotaro's grandfather. His father looked at his watch and said that he must go. They all smiled and said good-bye. Yotaro and his mother began to walk, his small hand curled into hers.

The street went down a little hill, and when they were half a block away Yotaro stopped and turned to wave to his father. It was a game from when Yotaro was a very little boy—the "one more good-bye."

His parents told him how he used to cry when he did not get his way and how the first words ever to come from his mouth were *one more*. One more story, one more sweet, one more game, one more minute before he went to bed, one more good-bye when his father was leaving. And so, the "one more good-bye" became a family custom. They had a special way to do it, mimicking the way Yotaro waved good-bye as a baby, just opening and shutting the hand. When Yotaro looked back, his father was smiling, his hand moving, open and shut. And then it happened—the flash boom.

The world burst into whiteness. Yotaro's eyes felt as though they were being smashed by a brilliant white hammer. At the same time, there was a sound so loud and so huge that it seemed to be exploding inside his own head.

A monster's breath picked him up and blew him through the air, and the whiteness faded and it got dark.

Something blotted out the sun. A pine branch, a bicycle, a man in a white shirt flew past him in the air. It was as if they weighed nothing, as if they were *tampopo* seeds driven by the wind. And then the wind slammed him into the ground and he lost consciousness.

When he woke up and opened his eyes, a woman stood over him saying, "Yoto! Yoto!" He only really knew it was his mother because of her voice. What he saw was a woman whose hair had been singed off, whose face was burnt and bloody, whose clothing above the waist, save for a few shreds around her neck, had been vaporized. The skin of her hands had been scorched off and dangled in shredded frills from her fingertips, like some kind of lace. The skin on the front of her chest had been flayed from her flesh and hung down from her waist like an apron.

It was dark. The sky was full of dust and smoke, and somewhere behind it the sun glowed red as an ember, as if it were sunset rather than noon. His mother reached down to pull him to his feet, and he saw that his own hand looked like hers, with the skin hanging from his fingertips in long ragged shreds. His mother dragged him toward the spot where his father had stood moments before.

His father was crumpled over in a pool of blood, his charred face looking up to the sky, several big shards of glass around him, one stuck in his neck. Yotaro knew that he was dead.

The little boy looked away and happened to focus on the wall of the post office building. On that wall was the imprint of a silhouette of his father, standing, waving.

Years later, Yotaro would read about the phenomenon. The light created by the bomb's explosion was so bright that there were many instances of this bizarre photographic effect. The bomb-shine, impeded by some obstacle on its path to a wall—a human being, a tree, a ladder—created a permanent shadow. In the silhouette on the post office wall, the hand of Yotaro's father was raised, his palm open in the gesture of the "one more good-bye."

It was the sight of this silhouette, and not the charred remains of his father's body, that made Yotaro scream. He thought the silhouette on the post office wall was his father's ghost. When some foundation timber gave way and the wall began to buckle and crash, his father's silhouette seemed to take a step toward him. The hand seemed to move a final time in the "one more good-bye." Yotaro screamed in fear.

His mother snatched him up and cradled him against her ruined chest, and they staggered away from the post office. His head bounced against her raw chest.

Yotaro was numb until his mother stumbled. She tried to protect her son, but when the two of them fell, the pathetic stub of raw burnt flesh that used to be Yotaro's ear met the pebbly ground. Pain erupted through his entire body, and he lost consciousness.

He awoke inside his own house, having been carried all that way up the steep hill by his mother. Now she got out a pair of large scissors and, wiping them clean, cut away the skin that hung from his waist. He lay there in silence, his eyes on the ceiling, not making a sound. Finally, when she began to rub some kind of oil into the skin of his destroyed face, he again fainted dead away.

1

SOUTHWESTERN TOWNSHIPS (SOWETO), TRANSVAAL, SOUTH AFRICA

TOO BAD THE MERCEDES WAS SUCH A WELL-MADE CAR, CONstable Nobbie Mtetwa was thinking. Otherwise, the boys would have smelled the body in the trunk. And never stolen the car in the first place. And saved him all manner of trouble.

The constable stood a distance from the white Mercedes—as far as he could without relinquishing his dominion over it—while he waited for the arrival of the Johannesburg Murder and Robbery Squad. He was a small, compact man with a burr of graying hair and a fastidious appearance. Periodically he tugged down on the two points of his starched collar or brushed at a khaki cuff to remove a smudge of dust. He stared morosely at his new shoes—now hopelessly dirty. They were beginning to pinch.

A crowd of onlookers—mostly women and children—was craning and gaping toward the car. They kept their distance, too, either because of the constable or because of the stink.

It was one of the boys' mothers who had first dragged them to the little cinder-block station house. The two boys were obviously frightened—hysterical, really—and it was some time before Constable Mtetwa could figure what they were saying.

"We didn't do it!" one of them kept yelling. "Swear, I swear, I swear on—" And then he began shaking his head wildly and breathing too fast, frustrated that he could not come up with anything sacred enough to guarantee his truthfulness. The other boy was even more unhinged but, in his case, subdued and weeping, snuffling like a small child.

"I believe you," the constable said—although they hadn't told him anything yet.

The mother was a large woman who—despite her many unruly children and a husband who drank too much—normally had a big, quick smile and a teasing way about her. There was flour on her fingers and a little dusting of white where she had touched her hair. Now she shook her head grimly. A little puff of flour came off her head into the air. She looked as if she might never smile again.

"These two fools stole a car from the city," she said.

"I thought they said they didn't do it."

"They do that part all right." She glared at her son, who stood ashamed, head hanging. His friend snuffled in the corner. The constable had no idea what was going on. Clearly, this was not about stealing a car.

"And?"

It was the mother who told him how the boys drove the car to an isolated part of the township, near the chain-link fence that served as a boundary. She got to the part where they opened the trunk, to see what might be inside, and then she drew in a sharp breath and put her floury hands out in the air, as if she were pushing something away from her. "And they find a dead body in there!"

"We didn't do it!" her son shrieked.

The other boy wept harder.

"Ummmm," Constable Mtetwa said. His mood sagged. He saw the trouble ahead as a kind of squalid cloud that (he knew from experience) would settle over him for the next few days. Now he would have to be calling the Murder and Robbery Squad. There would be all kind of strangers poking around in his patch.

"One more thing," the woman said in a voice that seemed to leak out of her. "The body cut up."

"We didn't do it! I swear!"

She glared at her son.

"You mean stabbed?" the constable asked.

She hid her face in her hands, and when she took them away her face bore the pallid imprint of her finger-tips. "I don't believe them. I go to see myself. I mean *cut up*. I mean his arms and legs cut off, his head cut off, even his behind cut off."

The constable hesitated. "White man or black man?"

She squeezed up her face. "The body parts were all smeared up."

"With what?"

"Black stuff."

"And what would that be?" the constable asked.

9

"Well, I don't know that, do I?" she said forcefully, but then she shuddered, and when she spoke again her voice had shrunk to a whisper. "I think I saw a bit of yellow hair."

The smell from the trunk of the white Mercedes had been almost enough to make the constable sick. A look at the jumble of body parts inside pushed him over the edge. The sour taste of vomit still remained in his mouth. The sight of the body—a tangle of limbs, the decapitated head, a severed penis—would likely stay with him much longer.

The detectives from the Johannesburg Murder and Robbery Squad arrived, finally. They would take their time.

They had not yet touched the glove box to look at the papers. The short one was in his car—calling in the Mercedes plate numbers. The plates were from Natal—although, as one of the detectives pointed out, they did not necessarily belong to the car. "Still," he said in a surprisingly cheerful voice, "might as well get a start."

The tall detective was busy with the crime-scene photographer—waiting for him to finish so the collection of evidence could begin. Of course, this was not the crime scene. Whoever did the poor bastard in the trunk had enjoyed plenty of time and space and privacy.

The constable had secured the scene. A square area was now fenced in with the help of some poles jammed into the earth. Bright red-and-yellow tape stretched between the posts. The Mercedes stood in the center of this square of gray dust, illuminated by a bright swatch of sunlight. Light bounced off the car's flawless paint with such brilliance and dazzle, it was almost as if the scene had been staged for some advertisement. The constable could imagine one of the detectives, in some glamorized form, lifting an expensive piece of luggage from the trunk.

The photographer finished up just as the medical examiner, Colin Ridgeway, arrived. It was a warm day, but Ridgeway wore his usual black trench coat, dandruff sprinkled on the shoulders. He tossed the constable a smile—showing bad teeth—and the constable volleyed back a grin. They walked together toward the white car. The constable stopped just outside the the tape while the ME ducked under it and joined the detectives. Ridgeway pulled on some examination gloves and then bent over the trunk to take a look. "Well, he's dead, all right," the ME said. The detectives managed to laugh.

The ME crouched over the car for some time. Eventually he stood and, accompanied by the two detectives, strolled toward the perimeter of the taped area where the constable waited. Crowds of people stared at the car. Someone was selling soft drinks. The ME tapped out a cigarette.

"Any idea about cause or time of death?" one of the detectives asked.

"Dead at least forty-eight hours, possibly longer. No evidence of bullet wounds, although frankly, in the state he's in, I'll know more tonight. I'm half afraid he died of what it looks like."

"You mean he was hacked to pieces?" the tall detective asked.

The ME exhaled a large plume of smoke. "Yes."

"You don't mean he was *alive* when that happened?"

The ME shrugged. "If not alive, not long after. Still kicking, certainly."

A flood of sensation rushed through the constable's chest, and the vision of the jumble of body parts came back to him. He fought down a surge of nausea.

"Wherever he was killed," the ME continued, "there would have been *a lot* of blood. The blood spatter would have been just terrific. The femoral and subclavical arteries were fully severed. With the heart still beating, blood would have shot out of him like a fountain."

The short detective took a step toward the constable. "These boys of yours, Mtetwa," he said. "Any history of this kind of thing?"

The ME interrupted. "Forget the *boys.*" He dropped the cigarette and twisted his foot and put it out.

"It's not so easy to dismember a body. Takes anatomical knowledge, a certain amount of skill." He shrugged. "Well, I mean you *could* manage it—sawing and hacking— but not like this poor soul was done. Whoever did this knew what he was about."

"You're suggesting—what? A doctor?"

The ME laughed. "I cut people up all the time, and I couldn't manage a job like that, particularly if the subject was alive." He jerked his head back toward the car. "My guess? I'd say the body was restrained. Under all that gunk I couldn't see abrasion marks, but I'm sure I'll find them once we clean him up a bit. I'd wager the job was done by a butcher—a real butcher. I'd put money on it."

The short detective turned back to the ME. "What's that black stuff all over the body?"

"It's not mud and it's not excrement. It has a strong— oh, an industrial smell, a metallic smell of some sort." The ME sniffed. "I'd get some of that into an evidence bag and to the lab right off, if I were you." The ME patted his pockets and then stuck another cigarette in his mouth. "There's another thing that might be of interest. Whatever it is, something's jammed in his bloody mouth. I might do some damage if I try to pull it out here. When you're all finished crossing your t's and dotting your bloody i's and you get him over to my shop, I'll retrieve it. Metal thing. I could only see the edge of it, caught between the teeth." He tossed his cigarette aside and strode away.

"Could you be taking my statement now?" Constable Mtetwa asked the remaining detective, shifting from foot to painful foot. He was beginning to lose feeling in his small toes.

The detective sighed. "Yeah, sure," the man said. He looked around. "Let's go around to your station house," he added. "I might as well talk to those boys and their mother while we're about it. I'll just have a word with Nik."

Constable Mtetwa's mood surged. He followed the detective toward the unmarked sedan, his feet already feeling better—just on the promise of relief. But it was not to be.

"I'm just off to the constable's shop to take statements," the tall man said.

The second detective jumped from the car, scowling. "Forget it," he said. "We're off the case."

"*What?* Why?"

"DNI."

"DNI? How do they know—?"

"When I called the plates in, the motor vehicles computer went ballistic. Stars and pinwheels. Flashing lights. Turns out the plates *do* match the car. And if the victim turns out to be the *owner* of that car—well, they've been looking for him. 'Scouring the earth,' they said." The detective turned to Constable Mtetwa. "You're not to collect

13

any more evidence or ask any more questions," he said. "DNI will be in touch. Until then, you don't know anything." The detective issued a bitter laugh. "The spooks are on their way."

The constable's mood crashed. Once before, he'd been involved in a case that fell under the jurisdiction of the Directorate of National Intelligence. What he remembered of the experience was hours and hours of answering the same few questions put to him dozens of different ways. He stared gloomily at his feet.

2

ZAGREB, CROATIA

"Fuck."

Joe Grant stood over the body and repeated the word, softly, to himself. He looked up. "How'd it happen?"

The liaison officer from the Croatian Ministry of the Interior shrugged. His stood with his hands jammed into the pockets of his black trench coat and shook his head. He'd grown up in Cairo, Illinois, and his English was perfect.

"The guy came back," the government officer said.

"Whattaya mean, he came back?" The American agent was losing patience.

"Delicay went *out*. The cop thought it was all clear, went in and started tossing the room. And then Delicay *came back*. I guess he forgot something." He shrugged.

"So the cop *shot* him?"

"It happened very fast."

Grant shook his head.

"The cop was looking for drugs," the Croat said defensively. "The Turk had a reputation."

"No shit," Grant muttered.

The Croat wagged his head sadly. He had large brown eyes and the baleful expression of a dog. "I'm sorry," he said.

Grant nodded. The Croat was unhappy because his own service, the unpronounceable Croat intelligence service—the service everyone called the UNS—had performed flawlessly. They'd spotted the fugitive Delicay at the train station and followed him to the Inter-Con. They'd put a man outside and a second in the lobby. They'd called the CIA then sat down and waited, just as they'd been told to. Unfortunately for Joe Grant, and even more so for the Turk, the police had spotted Delicay as well.

The hotel room was a bloody mess. Chairs and cushions were upended; drawers had been pulled out, and the contents of a suitcase were strewn across the double bed. The Turk lay on the floor like a beached whale, with one arm flung up behind him, as if he were doing the backstroke through a pool of his own blood.

Joe Grant wondered if the cop had really been looking for drugs and, if he had, whether his intention had been to make an arrest—or a killing. All Grant could be sure of was the dead man's identity.

The victim (though no one had ever thought of him as "a victim" before) was a Turk named Hakki Delicay. His features were firmly imprinted in the CIA officer's mind: the high cheekbones and prominent nose, receding hairline, acne pits, and scars. He was, by all accounts, a very bad man. Grant had been carrying around his photograph for nearly two months.

The Agency had been looking for Delicay since February, though Grant couldn't say exactly why—he didn't have a need to know. There'd been a flash-cable from the Capetown station putting Delicay at the top of the Agency's lookout books—so it probably had something to do with South Africa's DNI.

In any case, they'd been looking for Delicay everywhere. And always with the proviso that if the Turk should be be spotted, he wasn't to be touched—just followed, until the cavalry could arrive.

Someone had wanted to talk to him. Bad.

And now the Turk had fallen to earth, or at least to the carpet, in room 312 of the Zagreb Inter-Con. And he wouldn't be answering any questions.

Not only was he dead; he was dead on Joe Grant's watch, and that was not good. Among other things, it meant that Grant would spend the weekend talking to police, talking to his superiors at Langley, and writing a report—rather than skiing.

Grant looked into the Turk's empty eyes. His terminal expression—a look of mild surprise—seemed a serious underreaction to the condition of his abdominal region, which resembled raw liver. "I was supposed to go to Kitzbuhel this weekend," Grant said.

The Croat smiled. "Sucks to be you."

The CIA man heaved a sigh, turned, and surveyed the room. "He leave any paper?"

The Croat nodded. "Wallet on him," he said and then rolled his head toward a desk in the far corner of the room. "And there's an attaché case," he said. "I saved it for you."

"What's in it?"

17

"Pictures. Papers. Some satellite photos."

Grant flipped open the case. There was a stack of folded papers inside. Clipped to each one was an envelope holding a single photographic slide. He unfolded one of the papers and saw a grid of city streets.

This was a digitized, high-resolution image from one of the brand-new birds—as good as anything the Agency could produce. Maybe better.

Grant could tell the shots had been specifically tasked—no one had much archival stuff with that kind of resolution. There were about twelve of the folded sheets in the Turk's attaché case, each one with its own slide for screen projection. The collection would have cost the Turk a small fortune. Grant flipped the case closed.

"You find anything else?" he asked.

The Croat crossed the room to a large armoire, opened its doors, and stepped back.

"This," he said. The armoire held a pair of stainless-steel containers. Thermoses or something like them.

"What's in 'em?" Grant asked.

The Croat shook his head. "I don't know. Anthrax? Plutonium? Binary explosive? Cocaine? You want me to open them? Have a sniff?"

Grant pretended to weigh the idea for a moment, then shook his head. "Nah."

The Croat laughed.

"Tell you what," Grant said. "Why don't we just pack everything up and I'll have someone escort it to Langley? Let them worry about it."

"Works for me," the Croat replied.

3

THERE WERE FEW PEOPLE IN THE WORLD MORE CONCERNED about Hakki Delicay's fate than Curtis Willoughby, the director of Central Intelligence. And so, although it was late on Easter Sunday and the vast parking lots at CIA headquarters in Langley, Virginia, were almost entirely empty, the CIA director sat behind his desk on the top floor.

He was not happy.

Earlier that day, he'd been sipping *caiparinhas* with his wife on the terrace of his villa at Half-Moon Bay, Jamaica. The sky was blue, the sand white, the music soft and amusing—much like his wife. And then there'd been a jangling noise in the closet, where he'd stuffed the oversized attaché case that accompanied him everywhere. Inside was a digital telephone, hard-wired with a 128-bit encryption device that made eavesdropping useless. Not that Willoughby would ever say anything interesting on the telephone. You might as well ask a cat to swim. Even so, the Office of Security insisted that he take the phone with him wherever he went.

To his credit, he'd ignored the ringing. He'd let it go on and on until, unbidden, one of his aides retrieved the phone from the closet and brought it to him. With a sigh, he'd picked up the receiver, muttered, "Willoughby," and listened to the voice at the other end.

There'd been a cable from Zagreb. The Turk was dead. And he'd left some things behind—including a pair of stainless-steel thermoses with an unidentified liquid inside. A full report was on its way to Langley. The thermoses were being pouched to Technical Services.

Willoughby took a military transport back to Andrews Air Force Base. His wife refused to sit near him on the plane, and when they arrived in Washington she took a cab to the Willard Hotel rather than go home.

He'd beaten the report to Andrews by an hour and was already in his office at around nine when it arrived, encased in a gunmetal gray attaché case that was handcuffed to the wrist of a young man. He was a special courier—not the usual circuit rider who ferried documents and money in the Agency's equivalent of a diplomatic pouch. The young man had dead white skin and black hair that did not seem to reflect light. The lock that secured the attaché case to the courier's wrist was a biometric device that opened at a touch from the index finger of Willoughby's left hand. He dismissed the courier, closed his door, locked it, opened the attaché case, and removed the report.

Even though he knew the subject of the report, the sight of the cryptonym—*Quicksilver*—was enough to make

Willoughby's heart sink. This clichéd expression came true inside his body. There was a falling sensation in his torso, as if his heart were diving toward his feet.

He spent a long time reading. And then he spent a long time thinking. And then he waited for the report from Technical Services about what was in the two thermoses.

Now it was nearly two in the morning. The rain was pissing down outside, and Willoughby still sat behind his great carved desk. He tapped his fingers on the desk and tried to make a decision.

Those who didn't know the CIA director would have been surprised to see him at the office so late. He was sixty years old, six-five, and so good-looking that throughout his life he'd been subject to the narrow prejudice that can bedevil men and women with theatrical good looks. People assumed that his success was a fluke of nature, owing more to appearance and charm than to intelligence and hard work.

Not that he minded. On the contrary, he sometimes found it useful to be underestimated. Among other things, it encouraged his adversaries to overplay their hands.

Quicksilver. The cryptonym nagged at his attention. He swung round in his chair, gazing, unthinking, at the rain streaming down the bulletproof windows.

It was the very first thing Willoughby had been briefed on as CIA director. In fact, the session had taken place in this same room, and his predecessor had conducted the briefing personally. At the time, Willoughby had been caught up in the exhilaration of being confirmed. When called into the office that would soon be his own, he'd assumed it was for a ritual handshake and the passing of the torch. He remembered thinking, *I hope this won't take too long.*

His predecessor was a small, fidgety man with compact features and sharp little teeth, known around Langley as "the Rodent." Willoughby, a career CIA man, thought the man was a lightweight and had never taken pains to mask his disdain; the Rodent wasn't a fan of his, either. And so there they were, the Rodent sitting behind the huge desk for the last time, his replacement, the director of Central Intelligence, sneaking a look at his watch.

The Rodent seemed to be having trouble getting started, so Willoughby began saying something designed to ease the way. Something about big shoes. Something about responsibility and earning the trust placed in him.

But the Rodent cut him off with a guttural snort. "This isn't some kind of farewell do-si-do," the little man barked. "There's a matter I have to brief you about." He slammed his hands down on the desk. "The code name is Quicksilver and it's one of the reasons I'm not too broken up about leaving this job. It scares the shit out of me. It will do the same to you." And then he went on, talking too fast in his high-pitched squeak, telling Willoughby about something so shocking that the new DCI's jaw literally dropped open.

"What do you mean—'a catastrophic breakthrough in weapons design'? *Red mercury?* I heard that was a joke, snake oil, nothing but a hoax the Russians dreamed up."

The Rodent released a small, tight smile. The man did not have lips. "I guess that was a *very* successful disinformation operation," he said in a smug voice, "if even you bought it." He allowed himself a little rat-a-tat-tat laugh.

Willoughby struggled to contain his shock over what the Rodent had just told him. He'd been the deputy director of Operations for six years, serving under two different directors—and he'd been out of the loop! The clearance level for Quicksilver was beyond Q-level; it was a level Willoughby hadn't even known existed.

And then the Rodent was telling him about a place called Object 51.

"The Russians change its name every few years. Now it's Arzamas–16. Used to be a great city. One of those towns with a bag over its head. Great demographics. Population: 30,000. Advanced degrees: 25,000. And they all lived at the same address."

"What do you mean?" Willoughby had asked.

"All their mail was routed through a two-room apartment in central Moscow. It was like a post office box, except it was an apartment with a family in it. But all that's in the past. Now we've got joint experiments going on, so they call the place Los Arzamas. You know—like Los Alamos—except Russian."

"I get it," Willoughby said.

"I'm glad," the Rodent replied, exposing his teeth in what Willoughby supposed was a smile. And then the man leaned forward and started talking about red mercury. Russia and the United States had each synthesized the material at about the same time, he said, in the midsixties, and they'd been collaborating ever since in a secret and ongoing effort—called Quicksilver—to put the genie back in its bottle.

"When I say it was a catastrophic breakthrough in weapons design," the Rodent said, "I mean catastrophic."

"How so?" Willoughby asked.

"There are two things that make it hard to construct a nuclear device. The first is that you need a big hunk of plutonium or uranium. The second is that an implosion bomb requires a nuclear trigger. Constructing such a trigger is very difficult. This red mercury stuff addresses both these difficulties at once. You need but a few grams of plutonium. And with red mercury, the trigger is a snap to make. You end up with a small bomb with a very big bang. A bomb the size of a coffee cup could level Washington."

Willoughby didn't know what to say.

The Rodent went on. "Well, it was totally unnecessary. We didn't need it, and we didn't want it. For Christ's sake, we already had more nukes than we knew what to do with—big ones, little ones, and everything in between. So did the Reds."

"So what was the problem?" Willoughby had asked.

"The problem was simple. *We* didn't want it. *They* didn't want it. But plenty of would-be members of the nuclear club *would* want it. So the problem *is* very simple. Red mercury is not hard to make. And it's like a virus. Once it gets out, the nuclear club expands exponentially. I'm not talking Third World countries. I'm talking about subnational groups. About Hamas and the Aryan Nations. Hizballah." His hand spiraled up through the air. "I'm talking about anybody with a half-million bucks and bachelor's degree in physics being able to make a nuclear bomb. The problem is *containment*," he said, getting up and indicating the desk with an it's-all-yours gesture. "And that's Quicksilver."

Willoughby thought the Rodent was exaggerating, but then a scientist from Sandia Laboratories was summoned into the office. He came with a tray of slides and a pointer, and he spoke for half an hour about fissile masses, uranium tampers, and neutron fluxes.

"There is one more thing your potential bomb-maker's going to need," he said, toward the end of the spiel.

"What's that?" Willoughby asked gloomily.

"Some ultra-high-temperature explosive to detonate the device. There are a few different kinds. The best of the bunch is called TRX."

"I thought this red mercury stuff was the trigger."

"No, no," the scientists said patiently. "We're talking about an implosion device. The trigger is one thing—it's what squeezes the fissionable mass. The detonator is another—it's what *causes* that squeeze. With a red mercury bomb, the detonator has to supply a lot of heat."

"And this explosive—this TRX, for example—it's hard to get?" There was a hopeful tone in his voice.

The scientist winced. "Well, I will say this. In the last four years, we've made it much *harder* to get."

Willoughby sighed. He didn't even bother to ask about the difficulty of obtaining a few grams of plutonium. He already knew the answer to that one. Given the state of affairs in the former Soviet Union, with a couple of old soldiers "guarding" some of the weapons stockpiles, with workers in nuclear plants going unpaid for months—that would be no problem. Just a week before, two *kilos* of plutonium had been recovered from a train station locker in Prague.

"Look," the scientist said. "The TRX, the plutonium— we can only do so much about them. They're around;

25

they're out there. The key thing here is the red mercury. We've got to keep that in the hole. Because if we don't?" He shrugged his way into his sports jacket. "I mean look, sir, I don't want to overstate it. I mean I guess it's not the end of the world—but let's just say the Fat Lady might be getting to her feet. And if I were you? And this was *my* responsibility? I'd put a bell jar over Arzamas 16 and fly every scientist in the city to western Montana—and then I'd put a bell jar over *it*."

4

WILLOUGHBY WATCHED THE RAIN SLIDE DOWN THE WIN-
dows, then turned back to his desk and glanced at the
heading on the top file: "Van Dyne, Pallo." He'd read the
file a dozen times. Van Dyne was director of security for
Springbok Metals, one of the largest mercury recyclers in
the world. He'd been found, dismembered, in the trunk
of his car, his body smeared with a mercury gel. This would
normally have been a police matter, but Springbok Metals
had sensitive contracts with South Africa's Atomic Energy
Agency—and so when he went missing the DNI was called
in. They were already looking for him when his body sur-
faced; apparently some kids stole Van Dyne's car and got
more than they bargained for when they opened the
trunk.

The DNI was efficient. They looked at Van Dyne's current case files and learned that Springbok's security direc-

tor had, some months earlier, become worried at discrepancies in the company's inventories of certain critical materials. Small quantities of transuranic actinides, such as californium 252, were missing. Quantities of enriched mercury. Quantities of antimony. The missing amounts were not in commercial quantities, and while normally such losses might have been put down to "shrinkage," these materials were on the list of substances whose sale was governed by international agreement. So Van Dyne took a look at Springbok's employees.

Credit checks and liquid-asset searches were undertaken on more than a dozen technicians and scientists who'd had access to the missing materials. Only one record seemed be unusual. A Russian metallurgist named Andrei Lasky had recently repaid more than thirty five thousand dollars in credit-card and casino debt. Van Dyne began a surveillance of Lasky; the daily logs were in the file, along with the memo.

A week prior to his murder, Van Dyne's logs noted that the Russian had not showed up at work. Nor, according to an informant in Lasky's building, had the Russian been seen at his expensive flat for several days. Van Dyne had been allowed to "take a peek" by the building's supervisor and noted in his log that Lasky's apartment had been tossed, was in fact a *wreck*. Neighbors reported that a dark-skinned man had been nosing about, asking questions about Lasky.

Van Dyne's mutilated body was found some three days after the last log entry, in which Van Dyne noted that he'd seen the "dark-skinned man." There were notations about said man's rental car (a Volvo) and his hotel (the Jo'burg Hilton).

When the DNI had a look at the murdered security chief's files, the memo about Lasky was the *only* document that suggested a reason for his death. The DNI asked to see Lasky and learned that the Russian had still not reported for work.

Lasky might have been anywhere. He might have been dead. But in light of his affection for casinos and his newfound solvency, the DNI faxed his photograph to the local police in Sun City. The Russian was to be approached cautiously. First, he was a suspect in the brutal murder of Pallo Van Dyne. Second, he was to be charged with several violations of statutes governing breaches of national security, the sale of material constrained by international treaty, and the trade in weapons of mass destruction.

Two hours later, the Russian was found, dead drunk, at a roulette table on the city's east side. He had $50,000 in chips and a belligerent attitude that disappeared when he was shown a police photograph of Pallo Van Dyne in the trunk of his Mercedes. Sobered up, Lasky submitted to the DNI's interrogation. The transcript of that interrogation was now on Willoughby's desk. He looked it over.

According to newly wealthy Russian metallurgist Lasky, he'd done nothing wrong—unless Springbok Metals wanted to prosecute him for misappropriating the chemical equivalent of office supplies. Yes, he'd manufactured and sold 3.65 kilos of irradiated mercury-antimony oxide—to a Turk named Hakki Delicay. Yes, he'd been paid £300,000 for his trouble.

And so what? He'd *burned* the Turk. Yes, yes, yes—he'd supplied the Turk a *sample,* one sample, a few grams of *viable* red mercury. But that was some months back. When it came time to produce the stuff in the quantity the Turk required, when it came time to fill Delicay's *order*—well, the Russian's pilfered store of californium had gone off.

"Gone off?" the DNI agent asked. What did Lasky mean?

Just what it sounded like. Gone off, like milk. Californium 252 was a very unstable isotope, its half-life no more than a few months.

And this affected the red mercury?

Yes, it for damn sure affected the red mercury! That was one problem with the stuff: not much of a shelf life. If you made it with californium, which was the best neutron transmitter, you had to replenish the stuff every few months. Otherwise, as the californium broke down into its decay products there were—at some point in the process—no longer enough free neutrons to sustain the chain reaction.

What did that mean?

What did that *mean?* It meant the red mercury wouldn't *work.* It meant a device made using it would never achieve critical mass. It meant the red mercury wouldn't trigger a *car alarm,* much less a core of fissile plutonium.

So if Delicay made a bomb using the stuff Lasky had sold him?

Delicay? The Turk couldn't make a firecracker! The man was a *butcher* by trade, Lasky believed.

All right: if Delicay's *principals* made a bomb. If they made a bomb using the red mercury Lasky sold to the Turk—

It was *not* red mercury; that's what Lasky was telling them. And if they tried to make a bomb with it? That bomb would be a dud, a nothing, a fizzle. What Lasky sold the Turk? It was no more than metal sludge. It was toxic waste.

Bring him up on those charges. Because making what he made . . . that was not a crime.

And who had killed Pallo Van Dyne? And stuffed a transponder in his mouth?

Well, not Lasky! He didn't like to kill spiders. He didn't even eat meat! He was a vegetarian. Maybe it was the Turk. He was a rough customer. Lasky himself was a "little scared" of Delicay. It worried him "big time" that once the Turk found out he'd been burned, he'd come back for Andrei Lasky and chop *him* into little bits.

But Lasky took that risk? And sold him bogus red mercury?

What could he do? He had a pressing need for the money. And he couldn't get his hands on any fresh californium or anything else that might serve.

Did Lasky know that someone fitting the Turk's description had been nosing around his apartment? Had it occurred to Lasky that maybe the Turk had taken the red mercury to a jump lab, tested it, discovered it was no good, and come back for the Russian?

Of *course* it had occurred to him. Indeed, he was *still* scared of the Turk. He hoped the DNI found Delicay. He hoped they locked him up good and tight.

Who *were* the Turk's principals? The DNI interrogator pressed.

Well, the Turk didn't tell him that! And Lasky didn't ask! Why would he want that kind of information? Did they think he had a death wish?

Why would the Turk kill Van Dyne?

Lasky didn't know; he *really* didn't know. Once or twice the Turk had mentioned a tail, had threatened dire consequences if Lasky was setting him up. Maybe he thought

Van Dyne was part of Lasky's team? Or maybe Van Dyne had been following them?

The DNI knew that this indeed had been the case. Perhaps the surveillance had been too clumsy. The Russian hadn't noticed, but the Turk was far more alert. Perhaps Van Dyne had approached the Turk. Perhaps the Turk had caught Van Dyne trying to put the transponder on his car. Perhaps the Turk had come back from the jump lab and, unable to locate Lasky, had "questioned" Van Dyne about the Russian's whereabouts. Perhaps he'd become impatient when the Springbok security man couldn't answer his questions.

They might never know. In any case, the Turk's substantial dossier showed that he'd grown up a butcher's son in Izmir and as a young man had developed something of a name for himself due to his signature habit of leaving his victims in pieces.

Once Willoughby had digested all this, he'd breathed a sigh of relief. No real damage had been done (except to Van Dyne). With the exception of the sample, which would no longer itself be viable, the metallurgist had concocted a casserole of mildly radioactive garbage—which he'd then sold for a fortune.

The matter was not without its consequences, however.

How Delicay had first found Lasky was anyone's guess, but it was a serious worry. While the Turk's file was a thick one, there was nothing in it to suggest a prior acquaintance with the Russian metallurgist. It was possible that Delicay had somehow obtained a list of the thirty-seven Russian scientists who'd participated in the red mercury experiments at Arzamas 16.

Since Van Dyne's death, every one of those scientists

had been located, his or her life subjected to close scrutiny. Some were dead, others retired; a few were teaching, and a dozen more—like Andrei Lasky—were working in laboratories in various countries around the world. Apart from Lasky, none of the others seemed to be depressed or have substance abuse problems, gambling addictions, expensive mistresses or boy toys, serious illness, or unexplained sources of wealth. Given what had happened with Lasky, however, their lives—and the lives of their U.S. counterparts—would continue to be subject to close scrutiny for the foreseeable future.

Keeping a lid on red mercury was one problem. The other, more pressing concern was that the Turk clearly had a client who wanted to construct a nuclear device. No one knew the identity of that client.

Around midnight, the call came from Tech Services. The lab tests. They'd isolated each of the thermoses in a clean room and opened them through a glove box. The contents of the thermoses had been analyzed at a cost of $12,000, and it was determined that one of them contained 1.32 liters of coffee. And the other: 1.21 liters of cognac. Willoughby would have laughed, but he was too worried, and besides, that wasn't all. The exterior of one of the thermoses bore traces of what the tech boys had identified as a marker chemical in a binary explosive, a highly classified, state-of-the-art explosive developed by the High Explosives Working Group at Los Alamos: TRX.

And that's where the matter rested. Someone was building a bomb. He almost certainly had the plutonium. It looked like he might have the TRX. To complete the package, he needed the red mercury. It was sheer luck that Lasky had failed to provide it.

Thanks to the satellite photos, there was no need to guess the target. The ballpark. Sea World. The zoo. Mission Bay. Coronado. *San Diego.*

The Turk was dead. Lasky was under national-security house arrest in Natal. And Curtis Willoughby was still sitting behind his desk in CIA headquarters, doodling. Outside, the rain was relentless.

He looked at what he'd drawn—a fat woman in a Viking helmet, complete with horns—and scratched it out. He was now so tired that a seam of fatigue had opened inside his head and he worried that if he closed his eyes to think, which was a habit of his, he might fall asleep.

It wasn't as if he didn't have a plan. He did. It was just a question of choosing the right man. Or *person.* But as it happened, it had to be a man because, even if he'd wanted to, he couldn't find a woman who was, on the one hand, so *very* experienced and, on the other, so completely fucked up.

The fucked-up part was important. Indeed, it was essential. What he had in mind was an off-the-books operation. An operation that was absolutely black and totally deniable. A suicide mission, of sorts. (Thus the fucked-up part.)

There were half a dozen folders on his desk beside Lasky's and the Turk's, and each of them contained the details of a life that had gone out of control. Willoughby sighed.

If a fucked-up domestic life and the specter of bankruptcy were the only criteria, any one of the former CIA men profiled in the folders in front of him would be perfectly suited for the assignment that Willoughby had in mind. But the matter was more complex than that. A Judas goat wouldn't do, if that was all he was. Willoughby needed someone who was an operator, and not just any operator. He needed a point man, someone who enjoyed working close to the edge, or, failing that, a suicide case who'd do his job and self-destruct in a way that wouldn't leave a mess.

As Willoughby grazed the files, he reminded himself that the intelligence business had always operated along the fault lines of the human psyche. Find someone with trouble or something to hide—money problems, a drug habit, hidden homosexuality—and there you might find an asset to exploit.

But nothing too strange or too obsessional. In Willoughby's view, an obsessed agent was inherently unreliable. He picked up a file, glanced at it, and set it aside. Benton was a nut who spent his weekends dressed in latex and a mask. He'd nearly killed a woman in a hot tub at Vail. Willoughby wouldn't work with him.

Rodriguez. Rodriguez had been a talented agent, but now . . . Rodriguez was a drunk, and he just couldn't be trusted. In any case, his physical decline was such that it was doubtful that he'd last long enough to finish the assignment. Ditto Gary Dobbs—who was HIV-positive and beginning to cough a lot.

Carlson was more interesting. Willoughby fingered the file with Carlson's name on it. In some ways, Reid Carlson was perfect. Former station chief in Belgrade and Bucharest. No wife, no kids, a lot of debt that he couldn't possibly pay off. He'd even done a turn as an arms dealer. Unfortunately, Carlson suffered from the one affliction that absolutely disqualified him from Willoughby's consideration: he was unlucky. None of the difficulties in which Carlson found himself (and they were many, diverse, and considerable) could be honestly said to have been of his own making. Carlson was living proof of the dictum that shit happens, and Willoughby would have no part of him.

Which left Marcus Malone. He, at least, was not unlucky. To the contrary. He'd had more than his share of good breaks, but in the end, he'd turned out to be an absolutely terrible businessman—the kind who "didn't like to fire people." His business affairs were in complete disarray. He had a dozen unpaid parking tickets and at least three collection agencies threatening foreclosures of one kind or another. By the looks of it, he'd lose his car within the month.

His personal life wasn't in much better shape. His marriage hadn't survived the double whammy of his son's death and the unfortunate business with Halaby in Beirut. When the divorce came, it seemed that Malone had been overly generous to the wife. She was still living in their house in McLean—a big house that the IRS was likely to grab. As for Malone himself, he'd taken up residence in an apartment-hotel in Foggy Bottom.

Malone's life was coming apart at the seams. And not only that: he was free as a bird. No wife, no kids—not even a steady girlfriend. His money problems were chronic and, at the moment, acute. All of which made him a very good candidate. But what persuaded Willoughby that Malone was absolutely the right man for the job was the tour he'd served with the Foreign Operations Group.

An autoworker's son from Morrisville, Pennsylvania, Marcus Malone had enlisted in the army at eighteen. While in Vietnam, he'd done a turn as an LRRP (Long Range Reconnaissance Patrol). "Lurps," as they were known, came in all shapes and sizes and dispositions, but they shared one quality: they were guys who loved risk. They went into the jungle for long periods of time, alone, and essentially functioned as snipers and scouts. As Willoughby thought about it, he realized that a "Lurp" was exactly what he needed: someone who didn't mind being alone and liked working in enemy territory.

The young Marcus Malone had performed this task admirably. At one point, scouting enemy positions in the Delta, he'd stumbled upon a Vietcong encampment where several Americans were being held in a temporary bivouac—en route, no doubt, to some place secure enough for interrogation and then, at best, to tiger cages. Malone single-handedly broke them out. He took a bullet in the arm as he covered their departure; he killed or at least wounded a number of the enemy. Malone was awarded a silver star and eventually a battlefield commission.

It was this particular exploit that earned the Agency's attention—along with Malone's high I.Q. He was just the kind of kid the Agency liked: a nice smart Catholic boy (he'd already hastily married his high school sweetheart) who was both "good from the neck up," and fast on his feet. And unlike many Lurps, who were often shy loners, Malone was a big, easy-going guy everybody liked. He just happened to have high-wire reflexes and a knack for prowling around in hostile terrain.

The Agency recruited him, promising to get him through Temple University, which was near his hometown. After he got through school, he was earmarked as a candidate for the new Foreign Operations Group.

FOG was to be an elite commando unit of about fifty operatives available to participate in crash operations all around the globe. It was modeled on the Israeli commandos who had so spectacularly rescued that planeload of hostages from Entebbe Air Field in Uganda. Someone at the Agency had scratched his head and thought: "Gee, we oughta have a group like that." The army had Delta Force. The navy had the Seals. The Agency would have FOG.

In fact, Willoughby himself had been part of the team that designed the training and selection procedures for FOG—and he often sat on the selection board. He actually remembered Marcus Malone distinctly, a black-haired, blue-eyed man, notable because he'd finished near the top of the heap. Those competing against him in training exercises always complained that Malone was "just lucky." During debriefing, Willoughby recalled, that seemed to hold true: Malone usually had stumbled upon some unforeseen shortcut or received some unexpected help.

Willoughby slid the surveillance photos out and shuffled through them, looking to see what fifteen years had done to the man. The answer was: quite a bit. Malone was still good-looking you might say, but he was not looking good. He looked worn out, almost haggard. And in a society which put such a premium on youth that "looking good" and "looking young" were often synonymous, Malone looked every one of his forty-one years.

But the key point about Malone's selection to FOG was that the training was so arduous and the selection process so nightmarish that Willoughby knew Malone *had* to be an essentially stable person—or he never would have made the cut.

Recruits were generally flown to an isolated base in

Nevada and put through a process calculated to break them—if they could be broken. It began with a trek through the desert carrying a sixty-five-pound pack. Each candidate was given an azimuth, a set of coordinates, and a rendezvous point twenty to forty miles away. He was told to get there as soon as possible and when he did, he was given a new set of coordinates and sent on his way. After two weeks of this—burning by day and freezing by night—some candidates had fallen away and a new phase of the selection process began.

Once the survivors had finished wringing the blood out of their socks, they were handed copies of two books: *The Red Badge of Courage*, and *A Rumor of War*. They got two hours to read them both and report on their contents. Usually, they could hardly focus.

If they got through that, candidates were driven to Las Vegas and ordered to "penetrate" the MX-missile site at Nellis Air Force base and then report on the location and security of the missiles. They had no I.D. or money and if caught at Nellis, would find it extremely difficult to bullshit their way out of it. Nellis was not warned beforehand of the training; it was certainly not impossible that the candidates would be fired upon if spotted. Quite a few were cut at this juncture.

Those that made it in and out of Nellis without detection gave their reports and then were "arrested." Thrown into what amounted to a dungeon for twelve hours, they then endured hostile interrogation to see if they would break their cover. Some did; Malone didn't.

The survivors of all this were brought one at a time into a kind of star chamber, seated in front of a panel of psychiatrists, military brass, and intelligence "advisers" such as Curtis Willoughby. The candidate was given a series of hypothetical scenarios. For instance, he was told he was involved in a crash operation in a denied area. The idea was: he only had so much time to get from one place to another and he ran into a couple of kids and the kids *knew* he didn't belong. The kids would tell . . . their parents, their teachers, the cops, the army—whoever they *could* tell. What did he do? Shoot them? Don't dismiss it: remember, many lives were at stake. Or just tie them up, maybe? Hit them over the head? Let them go? Take his chances? Quick, what did he do?

There were no right or wrong answers in these scenarios; everything was situationally dependent. Each candidate was put through a dozen scenarios, and the psych-board liked to boast that getting by them was the hardest part of the whole ordeal. They weeded out the trigger-happy and the secretly suicidal, and separated the mentally quick and agile from the merely fast. In the end, only one out of ten recruited—and they were optimal candidates to begin with—made it through the process. The idea was to find loners who were leaders, tough guys who could dance.

And Marcus Malone had been one of them.

After his stint in FOG, Malone became an agent-handler—just like Willoughby himself. He'd spent time in the Middle East and elsewhere in Asia. There was a stint on Cyprus, another in Karachi. Then Colombo, Bangkok, and Beirut. He'd done well everywhere he went. And then, when the Agency let him down, or, more accurately, when the CIA was forced to cut its losses (in this case, one of Malone's agents, Hussein Halaby), Malone had quit. Just packed a suitcase, locked the door, and flown home.

No complaints, no explanations, nothing. One minute

he was running an import-export front on the rue de Paris in Beirut—and then he wasn't. Suddenly he was in an office on K Street three blocks from the White House, with a sign beside the door that read: "Malone Associates."

He'd done all right for a while—but then almost *anybody* could have made money as a security consultant in the eighties. There was that much money rolling around. But the mistakes he'd made were structural—a long lease with too much space in an expensive building, an unnecessary investment in countermeasures equipment. The company was designed to self-destruct at the first whiff of a downturn. By now, Malone Associates was all over but the bankruptcy proceedings.

A small smile composed itself on Willoughby's patrician features. When you came right down to it, Marcus Malone was just about perfect for what Willoughby had in mind: a bad, but not unlucky, businessman who felt at home in the company of trip wires.

He glanced at his watch. It was a terrible hour to call, but he tapped out Bill Diamond's telephone number anyway. Diamond's wife, Alicia, answered in an annoyed, sleepy voice, then passed the phone to her husband.

There was a weary, "Hello," and Willoughby said, "Bill . . . I'm afraid I need your help."

5

―――――――――

MCLEAN, VIRGINIA

MARCUS MALONE DROVE TOWARD NATIONAL AIRPORT ON the George Washington Parkway, which ran along the bluffs overlooking the Potomac. His dark hair was still damp from the shower. A cup of black coffee perched on the dashboard of his Saab. His briefcase sat on the passenger's seat, stuffed with Malone Associates brochures and catalogs, some of them so expensively printed that, five years later, they still smelled of ink.

The aroma reminded him of better days, when he'd been flush enough to spend money without thinking about it—on plush office space, state-of-the-art equipment . . . and overpriced brochures. The smell of the ink even brought the graphic designer's face into his mind: her slicked-back hair, eyes behind some weird glasses that made her look like an insect. "Quality," she'd told him earnestly. "After all, these brochures are the face your company presents to the world. It's an investment." Even at the time, it had struck him as funny—a twenty-five-year-old woman who resembled an insect counseling him about quality.

The river was narrow, north of the city, raging and brown with spring rain. The sky was a brilliant, painful blue—the color of ballpoint ink. On the grassy shoulders, tulips and daffodils seemed too bright, almost lurid in the sharp light, as if they'd been colorized. He put on his sunglasses. The brochures, the equipment, the long office lease—all that was killing him now. He tried not to think about it.

The shuttle to New York was packed, a cattle car stuffed with power-suited men and women hunched over their briefcases, portable computers, *Wall Street Journals*. People without a minute to waste. Malone did not join them in their busy industry. He leaned back and closed his eyes and wondered what had prompted Bill Diamond to bring his security concerns to Malone Associates—rather than to a big firm like Wackenhut or Kroll.

Diamond & Bliss was a brokerage firm, and Bill Diamond, partner and cofounder, was a true captain—make that a bird colonel—of industry.

Malone's mind wandered into the dangerous terrain of wishful thinking. He began to spend the money he might make, settling his debts. And, when that was done, there was enough left over to take care of the small things. Bonuses for his employees. A new suit. A car and—*fuck!*

He caught himself. The truth was: hardly anything ever came of these meetings. The client wasn't really a client. He was just window-shopping. And doing it on Malone's time and dime.

Which reminded him: was his Visa card still good or was it, like everything else, the victim of financial entropy? Maybe he'd better stop at an ATM and get some cash. But no: they were having lunch in Diamond's club, which meant that Diamond would have to sign for it. *Lucky me*, Malone thought. *I can have a fucking appetizer.*

He killed half an hour walking around and arrived at the Century Club precisely on time. It was elegant and a little shopworn. The polished wood gleamed, but the carpets and upholstery showed wear. The lounge and dining room had a seedy feeling, as if old money was holding out against a new generation of television producers and software tycoons. Even so, it was a comfortable place, with subdued lighting and a sea of cracked leather chairs, their seats sagging from the remembered weight of too many well-fed men. Glancing around the dining room, Malone noticed that the youngest waiter appeared to be about sixty years old. The staff moved with deliberation and respect. And, almost in spite of himself, Malone was impressed: he was in the citadel of American capitalism.

Nearby, an older man got to his feet with a generous smile and gave a little wave. "You must be Marcus," he said, offering his hand. "Good of you to come."

Diamond was sixty, with silver, rather than gray, hair. He had a strong face—a long, straight nose and wide mouth with big white teeth. Jet-black eyebrows and sharp eyes. He wore a blue blazer and charcoal trousers and regarded Malone with the kind of flattering, intense focus that was a hallmark of many successful men—and not a few predators. He paid attention in a way that suggested

Bill Diamond would rather be sharing the next hour with Marcus Malone than with anyone else in the world, that gave no hint he had other things on his mind—the Nikkei index, for instance, or aluminum futures, a wife, a troubling HDL level. They sat down.

When lunch finally arrived—snapper for Diamond, a BLT for Malone—Malone was still waiting for Diamond to get to the point. So far, the talk had been confined to current affairs. They'd discussed the prospect of an interest-rate raise by the Fed, the troubles in Asia, the market, the religious right. Diamond was insightful, charming, and very funny. Malone was surprised to find that he was enjoying himself. Then he took a bite of his sandwich and a sharp pain rocketed through his lower jaw.

"Something wrong?" Diamond asked with what seemed to be genuine concern.

Malone shrugged it off even though it felt like someone had stuck a knife into a nerve. It seemed unwise to discuss *dental* problems with a potential client. The pain feathered away and subsided to a dull throb. "Good sandwich," he managed.

While they waited for coffee, Diamond excused himself to go to the men's room. Malone downed three aspirin and wondered again why he was there. Obviously, there was a problem at Diamond & Bliss—but what? A hostile takeover? Or something to do with the SEC? Maybe. But an internal threat was more likely, especially since Diamond was taking so long to get to the point. Missing stocks, an unreliable employee, a partner sliding over the edge into drink or women or God. Insider trading. It could be anything.

It was Malone's policy not to rush clients but to let

45

them cross the uneasy bridge to disclosure. The truth was he was not adept at making the move from conversation to business. A reluctant salesman, he was tempted too often by the truth, telling clients what they didn't need— rather than selling them whatever they might be able to afford.

What he should be doing was selling as many systems and services as possible: a shredder for every desk, bug detectors on every phone, and psychological stress evaluations, once a month, for every employee. He should be recommending countermeasure surveys, labor-intensive surveillances, and background investigations on everyone from the janitor on up. That was how you made money in the security business: you fed the client's paranoia. But if you were Marcus Malone, you heard yourself saying, "I think you ought to get a couple of smoke detectors and stay off the cell phones. That ought to take care of most of your problems."

He took the opportunity of Diamond's absence to fetch a brochure from his attaché case. He put it on the table, a visual aid. When Diamond came back, Malone nudged it toward him with the words: "I brought along some material for you to look over."

Diamond put the brochure in his inside jacket pocket but never looked at it. He just stood up and asked, "You wouldn't mind a little voyage, I hope?"

Malone contained his surprise when Diamond told the driver to take FDR Drive down to the Battery.

They rattled along the FDR. The plastic barrier separating them from the driver was so pitted and scarred it was nearly opaque. The taxi bucked and shook on the dilapidated roadway. Malone looked out the window.

Along the FDR, away from the scrutiny of pedestrians, most of the street signs and traffic signs were entirely obliterated by graffiti. Layer upon layer, the relentless imprinting of self. It was territorial, he supposed, like dogs pissing on each other's scent. The graffiti seemed almost Arabic, the letters curlicued, sensuous. "HOOLIGUNS. RAJ 72." Or maybe it was that old tactic when the residents of a city uprooted street signs or painted them over to confuse the enemy. But then who, exactly, was the enemy?

Finally they curved off the highway, then wound through the narrow streets of lower Manhattan and rolled to a stop near the terminus of the Staten Island Ferry.

Malone had no idea why Bill Diamond wanted to take a ride on the Staten Island Ferry. On board, he took up his place next to the banker, forward, at the uncrowded rail. Diamond appeared to be studying the filthy water. After a minute, the engines surged, the wind rose, and the ferry began to move.

"I have a proposal for you," Diamond said, raising his voice to the pitch of the engines.

Malone nodded, trying not to look too interested. And thought: *Nice tradecraft.* Obviously, Bill Diamond knew something about secure meetings. It was cold in the wind, and after a few tourists posed for their obligatory photographs against the dramatic Manhattan Skyline the two men were left alone.

They stood at the rail in an envelope of white noise, their conversation muffled by the throb of turning engines, their eyes fixed on surging gray water. They might have been talking in one of the communications vaults at the Agency, except this was oddly intimate. They had to stand close in order to hear each other over the racket. Malone's head was inches from Diamond's. He could feel the man's warm breath.

In February a man was killed in South Africa," Diamond said. "And then, a little while later, another man was killed in Croatia. . . ." Diamond paused and waited for a comment. When it didn't come, he added, "This is difficult. . . . It's a sensitive matter, and until I know you've taken it on . . ."

"It won't go any further," Malone stated. "Whatever I do or don't do."

Diamond nodded, as much to himself as to Malone, and fell silent, gazing at the gray smudge that was Staten Island. Malone copied his gaze. He saw another orange ferry in the distance, beginning its return voyage to Manhattan. And he remembered making the same trip years ago, with Fay and Jeff. A trio of amateur bluesmen had played for quarters on the open deck. He remembered the ride as leisurely, but it was not: the ferries charged across the harbor at surprising speed.

Diamond took in a lungful of air and said, "You may have heard about the man in Croatia. Turkish national. Thug named Hakki Delicay."

Malone thought about it. Finally, he replied, "Yeah. I know who you mean. Fat guy. Ran errands for people in Baalbek. He'd do anything for a buck. We had him on the lookout list in Karachi, but he never showed up. Who'd he work for?"

"Just about everybody. Gadhafi, Jibril, Nidal—an equal opportunity employee. If you could pay, he was your man. I don't suppose it mattered what you wanted."

"Sounds about right," Malone said. "And now he's dead?"

Diamond nodded. "Mmmn."

"Not mourned by many," Malone said.

For a while, both men fell silent. A seagull floated in the air in front of them, drifting on a thermal. Finally, it slid away with a cry, and Malone turned to Diamond. "So . . . who was he working for when he died?"

"Ahhh," the older man said. "Now that is the question, isn't it?"

"I don't know," Malone replied. "You haven't asked me anything."

"Let's take a turn around the deck," Diamond suggested, bunching his lapels close to his throat. "I want to tell you about something that doesn't exist—something the Russians made, a long time ago, in a place called Object 51."

Malone let Diamond take his elbow, and together the two men began to circumnavigate the deck. Diamond kept his head down, as if to avoid the wind. He began to talk.

"It's called red mercury."

6

WHEN DIAMOND FINISHED HIS RECITATION, THE STATEN Island docks were clearly visible. "What do you think?" Diamond asked.

Malone was trying to figure out what something called red mercury and a dead Turkish arms dealer had to do with Diamond & Bliss. He didn't really want to know, because no matter how much he needed the money, he felt honor-bound to be up front with Bill Diamond. "I ought to tell you—we don't have a lot of resources in Croatia, or in South Africa either, for that matter."

"Pardon?"

"I could probably find subcontractors, but me—I'm sort of a one-man band. To be honest, something like this? I think you might do better with a larger company."

Diamond looked at him, uncomprehending. "What do you mean, 'company'?" he asked.

"I mean Malone Associates. What are we talking about?"

"Oh," Diamond said, suddenly abashed. "Of course. Your company. I see what you mean." For a moment he looked embarrassed, and then: "Listen; I'm sorry, but I think I may have brought you here under false colors, because . . . well, it isn't actually your *company* that we're interested in, Marcus. It's . . . *you*."

"I see," Malone said, though he didn't.

"And since I'm making a clean breast of it, I'm not here on behalf of Diamond & Bliss. Not exactly."

Malone frowned. He didn't know where the conversation was going, but it wasn't going well. The possibility that he'd be stuck with the cost of the shuttle tickets was looming large. "I don't get it," he said.

"Well, in point of fact," Diamond said, "I'm more or less standing in for Curtis Willoughby."

Malone groaned, and Diamond jumped right back in. "He speaks very highly of you, Marcus—"

"I'll bet he does."

"—and he thinks the two of you could be of help to each other."

"I doubt that very much," Malone said, rocking back on his heels. He looked at the sky. Of course! The fucking *director!* There'd been an article in *People*. And a picture of the two of them playing, Diamond and Willoughby, throwing a football back and forth in Harvard Yard. Circa '55. They'd been roommates or something.

"Then you're mistaken," Diamond said, resting his hands on the rail.

"The *director's* forgetting something," Malone replied. "Or maybe it didn't make my dossier."

"You mean that business with Halaby?" Diamond asked. "I don't know anything about it, but Curtis said you might bring it up. He thought the whole business was a shame—"

"A *shame?*"

"—but he said to remind you that it happened on someone else's watch. Different administration. Not his fault."

An old photograph flashed through Malone's mind: It was a Polaroid snapshot of Halaby, taken just after he'd been found on the road to Beit Mary, in the mountains above Beirut. The Syrians had shoved the agent's face in boiling acetone and then allowed it to cool—so that it looked as if his head had melted in midscream and the scream had then exploded. After that, they had killed him.

Yeah, Malone thought, *that was a shame and a half, and what made it shameful was that it had been unnecessary: we left the man behind because someone at Langley wanted to teach him a lesson.*

"Do you want to hear me out?" Diamond asked. "Or . . ." He stirred the air with his hand and waited.

"Go ahead," Malone said. "It'll give us something to talk about on the way back."

Diamond sighed and flexed his hands on the rail. "Delicay was shot to death by a policeman. In the Inter-Con. So it wasn't as if he died in a vacuum. He left things behind—including a letter of credit from the Banque de Paris et Pay Bas."

"How much?" Malone asked.

"Fifteen million."

"Dollars?"

"Yes."

"That's a serious amount."

"Not just that. His gear had traces of an unusual explosive, a classified material called TRX."

"What's that?"

"It's an ignition agent for red mercury. It gets it very, very *hot*."

"So—"

"So someone's building a bomb. A small one. And we want to know who."

Malone nodded, thoughtfully, wondering where he was supposed to fit in. "What else did they find?"

Diamond sighed. "The Agency found some satellite photographs, high-resolution tasked shots of San Diego. Sea World. Mission Bay. The Eleventh Fleet. The baseball stadium. I'm told they would be useful to a terrorist—in terms of analyzing placement for . . . maximum effect."

A man stepped out on the deck to smoke a cigarette—below the NO SMOKING sign—and Diamond fell silent. Malone moved to the side and looked back at Manhattan. His tooth was throbbing, and he tried to suppress the pain. He used a technique he'd taught himself in Vietnam, where he'd learned to transform any sensation—pain, an itch, a desire to cough—into a tiny black dot inside his head. He focused his attention on the dot and made it dissolve.

By the time the man finished his cigarette and left, more people were on the deck. The engines had slowed, and the ferry was pulling into the docks. Malone followed Diamond into the terminal building, where they bought some coffee for the return. Reboarding the ferry, they found the deck clear of tourists. No one seemed to want to be photographed with the glories of Staten Island as a backdrop.

When they were under way, Diamond resumed the conversation. "Delicay had a notebook. We think he had a schedule. The notes indicated he was working back from a deadline: August 9." He paused and then continued. "Mean anything to you?"

Malone thought about it, then shook his head. "Could be anything. Could be nothing. Maybe it's an anniversary. Founding of Black September. Something like that." Malone paused. "Though I don't see how San Diego fits in." Once again, the two men fell silent. Finally, Malone asked, "What about the letter of credit?"

Diamond shook his head. "The banking end's impenetrable. We chased the letter of credit back to a Liechtenstein *Anstalt* called Real Impex—and that was that. The *Treuhänder* told our people, very politely, to fuck off."

"That's what a registered agent's for."

"I know. But it isn't helpful. We still don't know—we don't even know if the goddamn thing is pronounced 'reel' or 'ray-ahl.' Let alone who's behind it."

"Sounds to me like you need a bag man. Someone to go inside."

Diamond shrugged. "Maybe. I suspect there are a number of efforts under way to identify Delicay's client. But . . . I'm only involved with one."

"And which one's that?"

"You, Marcus. Curtis thinks you can be very helpful. In fact, he sees you as a sort of secret weapon."

Malone frowned at the metaphor. Weapons blew up. That was what they *did*. That was what they were *for*. "What does *Curtis* have in mind?"

"Delicay's client has a problem. His purchasing agent's dead, and he can't do anything without the red mercury.

Eventually, he'll find someone who can deliver what he wants—or worse, he'll get someone to reverse-engineer the shit from his sample. Curtis would like to get there first."

"And how does he intend to do that?"

"He wants to create a man for all seasons," Diamond said. "An arms dealer who can provide anyone with anything—including red mercury—for a price. We'll provide you with samples—the real stuff—and put you on the street. With luck, Delicay's client will find you."

"There's a little problem, isn't there?"

"What's that?"

"Well, Customs, to begin with. ATF. The police. It seems to me the authorities will be an obstacle. I can see Boardwalk, but how do I pass Go without landing in jail? Guys willing to provide 'anyone with anything' end up like Ed Wilson—who, as I recall, is doing consecutive life terms, *underground*, in Marion." He paused. "A little cell with a big light that shines every minute of the day . . . and night. Buried *alive* as an example to all those who might follow. Does the director's plan give any consideration to that particular detail?"

"Indeed it does," Diamond said.

"And what's the solution?" Malone asked.

Diamond's smile was grim. "Well, it should be obvious. If all goes well, we'll drag your name through the dirt, ruin what's left of your life, wreck what's left of your business. You'll be indicted on various counts of arms-trafficking and export-control violations. You won't stand trial, of course. You'll jump bail, flee the country, become a fugitive."

Malone laughed. "And here I was thinking bankruptcy might be rough."

"You'll have to give up everything you have, of course;

that's essential. Hearth and home. Reputation. And there's a substantial amount of danger.''

Malone stared.

Diamond made a vague rolling gesture with his hands. ''That's the essential picture, anyway. I'm not asking for a decision this moment, of course, but . . .''

A shadow slid through the air just at the edge of Malone's vision. It startled him. He looked up and saw that it was only the seagull. It was so close to them, he could see the individual feathers. ''Well,'' he said in a jokey voice, ''that sounds just great. Why would anyone ever say no?''

Diamond spoke again. ''The stakes are high, Marcus. Once that bomb is built, we've lost. He can carry it around in a bowling bag. With a lead liner, there won't be enough radiation for anyone to detect.'' He paused. ''We're talking about millions of people.''

Malone nodded thoughtfully as the ferry slid past the Statue of Liberty. Finally, he asked, ''Why me?''

Diamond shrugged and looked away. ''You're the best man for the job.''

''Really? And why is that?''

Diamond looked uncomfortable.

''Don't bullshit me.''

After a moment, Diamond said, ''All right. You're the best man for the job because you're very good at what you do . . . and because Curtis says you don't have anything left to lose.''

Malone stared at the water, which was developing a little chop. Finally, he laughed out loud. ''Well, he's got that right,'' he said.

''And your country will be grateful for—''

''Oh, Christ, here comes the flag.'' He took a deep

breath. "Appealing on behalf of the *government*? Ask Hussein Halaby's wife and children about that. Leave that out."

Diamond tapped his foot. "What I'm getting to is that there will be a lot of money in it for you, Marcus. And a new life."

Malone said nothing.

"Actually, it's important—in operational terms—for your cover that you spend some money. Rather a lot of money, I should think. We'd like you to be conspicuous about it. Ill-gotten gains. Plenty more where that came from. That sort of thing. I know you're not a wealthy man, at least not at the moment, so we'll have to make it possible for you to seem so. Of course, what we're talking about here is a fairly crude exercise; the money won't stick. It's all for show; think of it as play money—"

Malone interrupted. "What do you mean?"

Diamond hesitated and then met his eyes. "We'd like to work with your files for a couple of days. Make it look as if you've been keeping a double set of books—with a *sizable* chunk of unreported income. When you're arrested—"

"When I'm *what*?"

"When you're *arrested*, what happens to drug dealers and the like will happen to you: the government will seize your assets. Eventually, the IRS will auction them off for back taxes."

"On profits from deals that never happened."

"Exactly."

Malone deadpanned, "This is the best offer I've had all week."

"You may have forgotten: at present, your liabilities ex-

57

ceed your assets, anyway. In any case, thanks to your divorce, you're actually quite unencumbered for a man your age. But you'd lose your car. Office machines. *Cuff links.* Everything. But of course, in the end, we're prepared to pay you very well indeed."

"Now would that be real money or play money?"

"Real money."

"*How* much, Mr. Diamond?"

"Please. *Bill.* Well . . . *enough*, Marcus, to allow you considerable freedom—"

Malone shook his head. This was one of the reasons his business was failing—because he hated to talk money, because he shied away from nailing down the details. He forced himself: "How *much?*"

Diamond looked at him with a cold, bottom-line stare. "Plenty. We'll liquidate your liabilities and, on the back end, see to it that you get a new identity and enough to make you comfortable into your golden years."

Malone really was a shitty horse trader. He couldn't look at Diamond. "How comfortable?" he managed.

"Let's say a million."

Malone thought about it. And he knew that he looked like he was thinking about it. Finally, he said, "Let's not. Let's say three."

"There's only so much available, Marcus. . . . It's a discretionary fund."

"Lemme see," Malone said. "I seem to recall, ah, 'drag my name through the dirt,' ah, 'ruin what's left of my life, wreck my business.' "

"Well—"

"Do I remember talk of *indictments?*"

"All right," Diamond said, and hurried on. "You do

understand that the Agency has to be totally deniable? This isn't something that would fly before an oversight committee. So other than the director and me, no one else will know about the arrangement."

"And when the operation's over?"

"You'll be dead."

It was Malone's turn to raise an eyebrow. "It gets better and better," he said.

"*Figuratively*, Marcus. What I mean is you'll be walking away from the life of Marcus Malone, forever." Diamond hesitated. "We'd *advertise* your death, get that news around. Meanwhile, we'd set you up in a new life. Like the witness-protection program—except first-class." Diamond emitted one of his high-wattage smiles.

"And if I say no?"

Diamond gestured to Malone's attaché case. "I'll take the security system of your choice. Actually, I'll take it anyway. It will give us an excuse for future meetings."

"What makes you think this client is going to find me?" Malone asked. "The person that's making this bomb? It seems like a hell of a long shot."

"I already told you. We're going to make you famous. And you *are* a long shot. There's no question about that. And as I said, I'm sure there are other efforts under way. But considering the stakes? The phrase *no stone unturned* does come to mind."

"So I might trash my life . . . for nothing."

"Not for nothing. You'd still have the money."

"If I agree to go ahead, I want to be briefed—fully briefed, about *everything*. I can't go blundering around—"

"That's understood."

"When do you need an answer?"

Diamond sighed. "We haven't got a lot of time. Tomorrow night." He thought for a second, pulled a business card out of his wallet, scrawled a number on the back, and then handed it to Malone. "I'll be in your neck of the woods." Malone looked at it. It was a Maryland number. Potomac, he thought. "Eight o'clock," Diamond said, "one way or the other."

It had been a strain for Malone to catch every word Diamond that had been saying. He'd listened so intently that he hadn't noticed the engine change its pitch. Looking up, he was surprised to see the Manhattan terminal building looming just beyond the bow. His judgment of the speed of the vessel was distorted by his surprise, and he thought for a moment that they were going to crash into the concrete embankment. He spoke exactly when the engines cut back, his voice suddenly much too loud.

"How bad would I look?"

"As bad as we can make it," Diamond said, without a trace of a smile. "Unredeemable."

At the airport, he stopped for a drink, waited too long to board, and ended up with a middle seat, wedged between a fat, bald man sweating in the hot air and a tiny old woman with a bad cough. As the plane hurtled down the runway, the pain in his tooth intensified, as if synchronized with the jet's engines. Malone shut his eyes.

He knew he should be thinking about red mercury, about San Diego, about innocent people and nuclear terror. But he couldn't. He kept wondering how many other disintegrating lives Willoughby had studied before he'd settled on Malone's. They went looking for someone willing to toss his life on the junk heap—and the best candidate they could find was . . . him. It was flattering in a way. He was, in the informed opinion of the CIA, the uncontested King of Fuckups.

The plane began to climb, and Malone opened his eyes. His tooth throbbed; he'd have to see the dentist in the morning. In the meantime, he hoped it wouldn't be too long before the stewardess came down the aisle with the drink cart. A double scotch would definitely help kick the pain into the background.

He looked past the fat man, out the window. No one else bothered. The bird's-eye view had become humdrum. He watched New York shrink. From the air, the city gave no hint of its dilapidation. In fact, it was quite beautiful and appeared tidy and organized—the neat rows of streets, the orderly streams of traffic, the clever network of bridges linking the landmasses. In the same way, the planet, from a distance, gave no sign of its turbulence, its famines and wars and epidemics. From space it was a gorgeous ball, a serene blue-and-green jewel, swirled with milky cloud.

In the end, it was all a matter of perspective.

He could try the trick on his life. Step back, view it as a construct. If he looked at it that way, was it really so bad? Were his current troubles just a temporary downturn—or was his life, in fact, so fatally flawed, so permanently wrecked, that he should abandon it and hurl himself toward what Diamond had promised, that almost irresistible temptation: a new life?

7

"OPEN WIDER, MARCUS," DR. PRATT SAID. THE WORDS drifted through the gas-borne euphoria. Everything filtered through a kind of wonderful rhythmic buzz.

They had squeezed him in around noon: Malone, flat on his back in a dentist's chair. Emergency root canal.

"See that, Karen?" Dr. Pratt continued. "You'll rarely encounter a worse example of a molar inlay than that. *Inviting* substructural decay. I told you last time, didn't I, Marcus? I warned you that this tooth was living on borrowed time."

Malone shifted his gaze to Karen, Dr. Pratt's assistant. She wore a name tag shaped like a little tooth. Her suctioning device produced a liquid rasp as she lowered her head to peer into his mouth. Her breast pressed against him. He concentrated on that warm blur of sensation as the discussion of his dental problems continued.

Years of substandard overseas dentistry throughout the Third World had taken their toll, and he'd been spending a lot of time—and money—in the past few months getting his teeth fixed. Now Dr. Pratt spoke as if reclaiming Malone's mouth from decay was a project worthy of the Army Corps of Engineers.

"Open wider, Marcus."

He experienced the pain obliquely, through the wall of anesthetic, as if it were happening to someone else.

"Good," said Dr. Pratt finally. He hummed a few bars of "Yesterday," jammed something down on the stub of Malone's tooth, and took away the rubber gas mask.

"Bite down hard, Marcus. Time it, Karen—five minutes."

The euphoria faded. Malone could feel his mood collapsing as the effects of the gas retreated.

It was a measure of the condition of Malone's life that this root canal might be the high point of his day. He wanted to stay there, reclining in the dental chair, anesthetized, immobile. He did not look forward to contemplating Bill Diamond's proposal—which seemed by turns alluring and insane. Was he really ready to toss his life away? To ruin his good name? To leave the country? To give it all up? Never to see his friends again? It seemed like a hell of a decision to make, and it had to be made in the next few hours.

He certainly didn't want to go back to his office, where a blizzard of yellow Post-its were stuck to his computer screen, memorializing the telephone calls he'd received—of which, he was sure, a disturbing number had come from creditors. Not that going home was that much more attractive.

The thought of his impersonal rooms at the Guest Quarters being home brought a strange smile to his face.

"I'm glad you can smile," Karen said. Then she told him he could stop clamping his teeth together and began grinding off excess cement. He studied her from his vantage point—inches away. She had dark red hair, an unusual color that reminded him of an expensive cognac. He studied the faint array of freckles on her cheek.

"I actually had a dream about you last night," she said as she finished up, patting his face with cotton balls. "That's a bad sign, isn't it?"

"What? You mean dreaming about me? I hope not."

She laughed, an open, reckless giggle. "No. I mean—you've been here so much lately, you're now showing up in my dreams."

"What was I doing?" he managed. "In dreamland." The words came out mushy and inarticulate. After the multiple shots of Novocain and the long procedure, he felt as if he'd been punched in the mouth.

"It's a little boring," she said, with a charming smile. She unfastened the paper thing from around his neck. "We were at Disney World. You were on an island on one of those little lakes." She peeled back her gloves, revealing small hands. "You were fishing."

"I hate fishing."

"You were catching huge fish, enormous fish. I wonder . . ." She pressed a button and the chair whirred and tilted him upright.

He swung his feet to the floor. "What?"

"I wonder if all my dreams are slowly going to become more like ads. I mean this was pretty much like a Disney

64

World plug. I'm worried that next I'll have a Toyota dream or something."

"Have dinner with me," Malone heard himself say. Numb-mouthed, indistinct.

"What?"

What? was his own reaction. The gas must still be affecting him after all. Still, he crashed on. "Let me take you to dinner. We can discuss the invasion of your dreams by corporate images." Suddenly he had a moment of panic. Tonight he had to call Diamond. He couldn't just excuse himself and decide his future between the appetizer and the entrée. Tonight, he really ought to be alone. "How about . . . tomorrow night?"

Small sharp instruments glinted from the surfaces around them. A huge model of a set of teeth rested on the counter. The mammoth gums were the exact color of bubble gum. Karen gave him a look and then shrugged and smiled. "Sure. Why not?"

There was an awkward moment while they both came to terms with the formality—that he had actually asked her for a date. He felt suddenly embarrassed, clumsy. And now he had to nail down the details—get a phone number, an address.

She wrote them on the back of an appointment card. No schoolgirlish rounded letters, he saw. A surprisingly forceful hand, an executive scrawl. Her last name, he saw, was Faulkner.

"Well," he mumbled without much enthusiasm, "see you Saturday. Seven-thirty?"

"OK." She smiled. She had—what were they called?—dimples, he saw, and a slightly opaque look in her eyes, as if she was thinking that maybe she'd just made a mistake.

———

His mood deteriorated as he drove through the dense traffic. His office was in Tyson's Corner, amid the concrete and glass sprawl of northern Virginia. Twenty years ago, Tyson's Corner was just farmland; now it had more office space than Miami. His own suite was on the fourteenth floor of a huge building that looked like a brick shopping bag.

His secretary sat idly at her desk, twisting a lock of hair around her index finger as she talked on the phone. Seeing him, she was moved by some vestige of the work ethic to hang up.

"Gotta go. 'Bye."

Evelyn was thirty-two years old, and she was not very good at anything a businessman might ever need. Her spelling was imaginative, her memory porous, and her eye for details myopic.

If I had any guts, Malone thought, *I'd fire her.* She wore a short flowery dress and too much mascara and lipstick. A strategy to distract attention from her squarish body, a matron's body, really, which resisted the ferocious aerobics that she inflicted upon it.

"Hi!" she said brightly. "How's the mouth?"

"Numb."

She giggled and turned her attention to her nails, holding her hands in such a way that she could admire them. He saw that she'd had them done again. They were long, gleaming with white polish. In the center of each was painted the tiny pink shape of a bunny.

He went into his own office. To the left of his computer was an array of personal stuff. A small lapis elephant from Sri Lanka. A lucky rock from Switzerland. Two photos of Jeff. One as a child of six—no front teeth. The other a candid shot of the twelve-year-old Jeff in a yellow life jacket on a raft in the Colorado River—arms akimbo, a goofy smile on his face. The thought of Jeff, as always, sent a brief arrow of pain through him.

He rifled through the stack of opened mail. Many bills, most with insistent Day-Glo reminder stickers. "This payment is seriously overdue."

Evelyn came in and stood by the windows, looking out, steadily chewing her gum. "It's raining," she said.

"Look," he started. "Evelyn—you might want to start looking around for another position."

"Oh, no. I'm sure things are going to turn around."

"I may have to put you on half-pay."

"Oh, no. You can't do *that*. I couldn't pay for my condo."

Malone shrugged. "I'm sorry, but . . . it's blood from a stone, y'know?"

She looked puzzled. "It's *what*?" she asked. "Blood from a—oh, I get it! That's cute. But maybe Sam will come up with some new clients."

"Yeah, right: Sam the Rainmaker. Just to be on the safe side, you might want to start looking."

"Hmnf," she said. "Well, on that happy note, I think I'll take off . . . *just* a little early."

Malone looked at his watch. Quarter of four. Evelyn was supposed to stay until five. He was about to insist that she stay, but he stopped himself. What was the point? Apart from answering the telephones, there was nothing for her to do.

The phone rang and he waved good-bye.

His other remaining employee, Sam Pedicini. Sam was a fifty-five-year-old former army investigator, a good man, unspoiled by ambition. His style was fifties: chinos (which he called chinos, not khakis), button-down shirts, hair in a brush cut slicked up in front.

"Hey, Boss."

"He interested?"

Sam had been demonstrating the beauties of Malone Associates' fully equipped surveillance van to an Iranian named Waddy.

"Nah. This ain't goin' nowhere."

"You offer him a deal?"

"Hell, I offered to throw in Evelyn. Bottom line: he'll give us twenty grand."

"Twenty grand! The van is worth more than that just as a car."

"I know it."

"What if we cannibalize it?"

"Kind of a buyer's market for every damn thing, know what I mean?"

If he didn't take the deal for the van, Malone was thinking, there was almost no money due to come in, except for the Springhill check. And he knew that Springhill had its own financial problems.

"Boss?"

They almost never used the surveillance van. And twenty grand would cover costs for a little while—pay Evelyn, pay Sam, pay the rent. "Take the deal," he said.

"You sure?"

"We need the money."

"Yessir."

Sam always called him Boss or sir. It was his military

training, Malone thought. He was comfortable, Sam was, with the inhibitions of rank.

He drove home behind a Lexus with vanity plates that read: "BIG DOG." Stopped at the light at Swink's Mill Road, he watched some kids practicing soccer in the fading light. A blond kid went up for a header, nailed it. Malone followed the trajectory of the ball until the blast of a horn behind him made him jump. He looked at the road in front of him; the Lexus was easily a hundred yards ahead.

All day, he'd been operating in a fog of distraction. The decision he had to make was forcing him to think about his life from the strange perspective of someone who was thinking of leaving it. His concentration was gone. It was as if he'd decided to commit suicide and was just hanging around to get laid, one more time.

"Home" was a two-room suite in Guest Quarters, and when he got in the door he yelled, "I'm home, honey!" It didn't seem funny.

He popped a beer and sat down in the couch in his "living room." He watched the news.

It got dark outside. He grabbed another beer and looked at the array of take-out menus held by magnets to the refrigerator door. *Maybe Chinese,* he thought, and dialed up Wok 'n' Roll.

He sat back down on the couch and flicked through the channels. He felt curiously hollow, as if he were pretending to be himself. He put the remote down and fingered the pencil holder Jeff made him in third grade, a lumpy cylinder of coiled clay painted a gaseous yellow. People on the television were speaking very earnestly to one another, but he couldn't seem to pay attention to what they were saying. He sat there on his Guest Quarters couch, feet up on the coffee table, in the dark, suffused with memories.

Fay.

Jeff.

After a while, he flicked the television off and watched the oblongs of headlights slide up the wall and across the ceiling. When the phone rang, he couldn't bring himself to answer it. He couldn't seem to move at all. The machine clicked on, and he heard his own recorded message and then Sam's voice floating through the dark room.

"Hey, Boss. Just checking in. Listen. . . . We're all set with Waddy. Got some cash out of him, and the check on Monday. You know where to get me."

Malone sat in the chair. Thoughts and memories wove in and out of his mind, while behind them some surge of emotion was building. He was thinking about his friends and family. At this point, the truth was that Sam was his closest friend. Family? He had no family. Fay? Any chance for the two of them had died along with Jeff. One thought in particular seemed to circle his brain a few times before it cohered into meaning. How had Diamond put it? "You'll be dead." Maybe he was better off dead.

"Fuck it," he said and reached into his jacket for the card that Diamond had given him. Finding it, he tapped out the number and waited. When he heard the banker's distracted hello, he took a deep breath and pulled the trigger. "I'm in," he said, and hung up the phone.

8

KAREN FAULKNER TOSSED AND TURNED FITFULLY ON HER bed.

She would not have been surprised to learn that the discovery of a body in the trunk of a stolen white Mercedes in South Africa some two months earlier had inaugurated a series of events that would soon transform her life. She believed in the mysterious interconnectedness of all events. She really believed, for instance, that when that little old lady in Dubuque sneezed everything changed: stock prices might fall; Bill Clinton might reverse his stance on Cuba.

It was what kept her from sleeping soundly—the thought that an avalanche of unpredictable events might follow from a single small decision. Finally, she gave up, got up, headed into the kitchen. Might as well make a cup of tea. Sleepytime. One of her roommates—Aimee—was a great believer in Sleepytime tea.

What nagged at the edge of Karen's consciousness and kept her from sleep was this question: why did she say yes when Marcus Malone asked her to dinner? She'd kept to her resolution—no men—for so long she'd shocked herself by accepting this mumbled invitation. After she had said no so many times, suddenly "yes" fell out of her mouth. Why? She knew next to nothing about this guy. Most of the time she'd spent in his company, he was groggy with gas and, in any case, unable to speak because his mouth was full of dental instruments. He could be a total loser, and she'd have no clue.

The kettle shrilled; she poured water into the mug. She could call him tomorrow and tell him to forget it. His number would be on Dr. Pratt's computer.

She shared the town house with two flight attendants, Millie and Aimee. Millie was a forty-four-year-old divorcée from Texas who was just under six feet tall, had long blond hair, and called everybody "darlin'." Aimee was thirty, a brooding woman with a rosebud mouth and a shy manner. She had never in her life, Karen would bet, called anybody "darlin'." They were seldom home, but they were the ones responsible for the decor, utilitarian beige set off with what Millie called (not without sarcasm) decorative accents. These mementos of their travels included ebony heads from Africa, a crudely carved Mexican chess set, a tray composed of butterfly wings pressed under glass, Guatemalan wall hangings, and a staring lurid mask from somewhere in the South Pacific. It looked as if someone had gone berserk shopping at Pier One.

Karen sipped her tea. Maybe she'd sworn off men for too long and that "yes" had escaped her despite herself. She was bored and she was impulsive. A bad combination.

She'd been known to endure even deep boredom and un-happiness for long stretches, but suddenly, when her misery reached some kind of critical mass, she was likely to leap off the next available cliff into the unknown. Often— and this was what worried her about that "yes"—by falling in love. And then getting married. She was thirty-one years old, and she'd been married three times. At the rate she'd been going, she was in danger of reaching grotesque, even *tabloid* numbers. Liz Taylor numbers. Millie on the subject: "God, darlin'. Don't you ever say no?"

And so Karen had put herself on the Two-Year Plan. The Two-Year Plan had only two rules: (1) no money from the fam and (2) no men.

No money. That was clear enough. She didn't blame *them,* of course, but she believed that her wealthy family and their willingness to bail her out over and over again had deformed her life. She seemed to coast along with the attitude that if something didn't work out, well, she'd do something else. One day she had realized that she was *deferring* her life, her real life, her *only* life—while she figured out what to do with herself.

And so, for the first time, she refused to let her parents rescue her from yet another bad decision. No, rule number one—the no-money rule—that was not the problem. Her parents had almost stopped offering money, although she knew it caused them actual pain to answer the question: "What's Karen up to?" with the truth. Which was that their only daughter, Harvard-educated, with "so much promise," worked as a dental assistant in suburban Virginia.

She could picture them, her mother's rueful smile, her father's little shake of the head. They wouldn't make too much of it, though. Among their friends there was plenty of offspring failure going around. They'd be vague: "Oh, Karen's still . . . struggling." Funny that it wasn't the disastrous marriages or her absolute failure to do anything useful with her life that bothered them the most—it was the tackiness of her job. A *dental assistant*. Karen suspected they'd like it better if she were a drug addict or the victim of some serious—but curable—disease.

The second rule: no men. What did that really mean? She told herself it meant no serious relationships. It meant no falling in love. It meant no marrying anybody. It might even mean no sex. But did it mean she couldn't have dinner with someone?

She finished the tea, put the cup in the sink. She had to get some sleep. Her own room was plain, a bed and matching dresser of curly maple, which she had found at a secondhand store, a small desk, a bookcase. There were no knickknacks, only an alarm clock and a single framed Japanese print. When she left Clay, she left everything behind, and she didn't have the money to accumulate clutter. The furniture would look better on polished wood floors, but the whole place was carpeted in beige wall-to-wall. The dresser was placed to cover a nasty, resistant stain that to Karen looked unpleasantly like blood.

The mirror on the dresser was deteriorating, the silvered backing spotting slowly into ruin. Her reflection was always slightly unsettling, as if she were glimpsing herself through the fog. Or as if she herself might be fading away. She looked at her mirror image now and automatically rearranged her thick hair, combing her fingers through the tangled curls. *"Go to sleep,"* she said out loud.

Back in bed, she stared at the ceiling. Maybe she had said yes because the night before Marcus Malone asked her to dinner Millie had come home from the store with jelly beans and little chocolate bunnies. Which led to the realization that it had been in April, the year before, around Easter time, that Karen had moved into the town house. Which meant that she had been there for a *year*.

A whole *year*—when she saw this as a temporary state, a buffer zone between chapters of her real life. Yes, she was proving something to herself. But still, in a year's time you'd think she would have done some soul-searching, made some progress, some plans. Instead, she was exactly where she was a year ago, floundering *on her own,* it was true, floundering *alone*—but still floundering. Inertia was a powerful factor, she saw, not to be underestimated.

There was nothing temporary about a year.

She looked up at the ceiling, completely awake, but too exhausted to get out of bed and turn off the light, which she'd left on.

There was a crack in the ceiling, a meandering riverlike crack that started near the light fixture. A tributary ran into one corner. In that very corner was a small black spider. A committee formed in her head, ready to weigh in about this "date" with Marcus Malone. It advised her to resist the impulse of change for the sake of change, to stick with her rules. A subcommittee recommended that she stop obsessing; it was only dinner; don't make such a big deal of it; go to sleep.

She stared at the spider for a long time before she realized what she was thinking: *If the spider moves, I will call and tell him I changed my mind.*

Ridiculous. If the spider moves . . . You couldn't do that, make deals with the future on the basis of a *spider moving*.

Get a *grip*.

She got up. Turned off the light. She had once written a paper called "Freedom, Fate or Choice?" The paper had explored Heisenberg's principle of uncertainty, quantum mechanics, chaos theory, abductive logic, and implications for the question of determinism and free will.

And now she was relinquishing her future to an *insect*.

It's not an insect, insisted a fussy voice in some forgotten corner of her mind. *It's an arthropod*.

She was tired of everything, tired of thinking, tired of herself. But it was not until the first light began to brighten her small window that this tedious self-reflection finally gave way to exhaustion and she fell asleep.

When she woke up, the spider was still there.

9

LAKE BLED, SLOVENIA

YOTARO KAWAI WAS ANNOYED. NOT AS ANNOYED AS HE would have been if he'd known that the Turk had been so stupid as to write things down. That would have turned his irritation into anger. And if he'd known that what the Turk had written was now being studied by CIA analysts in Langley, Virginia, his anger would have shifted into outrage. And if he'd known each of those things and also that the Turk was dead, his fury and disappointment would have turned incandescent.

Even so, his expression would have remained impossible to read.

The keloid scarring that disfigured his features effectively froze his face into a expressionless mask. Only his small black eyes—buried in the puffy scar tissue like raisins in bread dough—had any mobility. When he laughed, which he did rarely, the entire mass of his face rose and fell, the maze of lines in the mutilated flesh wobbling with the vibration.

The best plastic surgeons that money could buy had not been able to help. Indeed, initial efforts when he was a child, they told him, had only made matters worse. And so his face was only one of the things for which he sought revenge. He remembered his father, his mother, his unborn brother.

Most of the time, Yotaro preferred to keep his features hidden behind a mask. The mask was attached to a bamboo wand, and he held it an inch or so in front of his face—just far enough to keep the humidity in his breath from building up and causing condensation. The mask was molded of transluscent plastic, modeled into the handsome and benign features of a Japanese mannequin. It had tinted rosy cheeks, elegant elongated eyebrows, painted lashes around the eye openings. Its pinkish open lips were forever poised around the mouthhole, frozen in the disposition of imminent speech.

It was not that he was ashamed of his face. That was, after all, the result of a criminal act. Since he was entirely innocent of responsibility for his monstrous appearance, he was not embarrassed by it. He had come to see it as a distraction and preferred to conduct business free of its distorting effect.

It was not always so.

As a younger man, he had often used his disfigurement to his advantage, utilizing the moment of shock the first sight of him caused, which put an adversary off balance, or exploiting the soft seam of pity that often presented itself. It amused him to think that in other circumstances he might have been a celebrity. In Shanghai, for instance, in the twenties and thirties the most spectacularly deformed beggars grew rich beyond belief, were delivered to their chosen spots by limousine, and had bodyguards and mansions in the French Concession. His own deformities were different, however, and did not inspire awe at nature's bizarre power or even the disgust that was a form of awe. His hideous bread-dough face, the clotted, twisted flesh that swirled around the opening that was his ear—these were disfigurements that during his youth were far too common to be worthy of awe. There were hundreds, there were thousands, scarred like himself and worse.

When he was a child and youth, his deformities were hallmarks of national defeat. They were badges of disaster. They were the indelible reminders of surrender.

But as the years passed those injured like himself—the *hibakusha* of Nagasaki and Hiroshima, the explosion-afflicted, the man-made monsters—were no longer shunned and considered objects of disgrace and dishonor. They became something else, something worse. They got special benefits. They were pushed forward; they were celebrated; they were displayed to the world—not as casualties of war, but transformed into a new role, that of martyrs. They became emblems of the new Japan: not the proud, if vanquished, country, the divine Land of the Gods—but poor little Japan, the shuffling victim of U.S. brutality.

Yotaro himself followed the code of Bushido, the ways of the warrior. Were not the Japanese the divine people, the race of the gods? It was beneath their dignity to moan about being mistreated.

To Yotaro's mind, there was no shame in losing a battle or even a war; one could recover from that. But there was shame in this latter-day insistence that mighty Japan, instead of being an aggressor in the war and a worthy and brave adversary, had been nothing but a poor, pathetic victim.

So he held the mask in front of his face. That thin shield of plastic protected him from being cast in the victim's role he so despised. After a while, in any case, he had grown weary of witnessing the range of reactions to his face. He knew them by heart: the indelible if disguised recoil, the pity—always corrupted by a sense of superiority, the voyeur's fascination, the attempted indifference. The universal reaction was best expressed by the German word *Schadenfreude*—the pleasure human beings take in another's misfortune.

Yotaro Kawai lived in paradisiacal splendor in a sprawling villa whose Mediterranean exterior concealed a traditional, if palatial, Japanese home. The villa was tucked in the hills overlooking Lake Bled, Slovenia. Behind it were the snowcapped peaks of the Julian Alps—not always visible, due to pollution, but glittering white today under a clear blue sky. Below the villa was the lake, set like a diamond amid the crumpled emerald of the surrounding forest.

From the teahouse perched on a small rise near one of his streams he had a perfect view of the lake and its little island.

The waters were famously still, protected from wind and chop by the surrounding mountains. So still that the little lake had been the site of many international competitions. As it was, rowers practiced daily, and it was one of his pleasures to watch the slender sculls with their perfectly synchronized oarsmen skim across the shimmering water. Often there were regattas on the 2,000 meter course.

Best of all, he liked to sit and watch the tourists from the Grand Hotel Toplice row the varnished wooden boats to the small island. On the island was a Baroque tile-roofed church with a tall gray spire. Sometimes he took out his binoculars and followed pilgrims up the broad stone steps. Many went into the church itself, but it was the rare pilgrim who did not first proceed to the famous Bell of Wishes. Kawai's binoculars were powerful, and he spent many hours observing individuals in the interesting process of making a plea to providence. Most stuffed a few coins in the metal receptacle and then yanked several times on the dangling rope. Some looked to the heavens; some crossed themselves; some squeezed their eyes shut as they pulled. He amused himself imagining the nature of these urgent petitions. On a fine day such as this one, the bell rang all day long.

He himself had made the pilgrimage earlier this year. It was in February, a brutal day, and the long ascent up the steps had tired him. He had arrived at the church perspiring and shaking. He had pushed into the receptacle a bulky wad of currency.

He had set his hands one atop the other on the bell's rope. He could still remember how it felt, the hemp stiff with the oil of thousands of hands, the loose threads spraying out under his grip. He remembered the way the backs of his hands looked. Through the shiny scar tissue he could see a sprinkle of the small reddish spots that had begun to appear only a few weeks before. Given the disaster of the rest of his person, most would have not noticed them, but he knew what they meant. Just as today's AIDS victims feared the purple lesions of Kaposi's sarcoma, all *hibakusha* lived in dread of these tiny surface hemorrhages. They were the harbingers of death. They were the beginning of the end. Medical science was still not sure of why it was so, but one of the effects of radiation on the body was interference with the body's ability to produce blood cells. It caught up with many of them, sooner or later. Radiation-induced leukemia. That was what the spots meant.

At the Bell of Wishes, he had pulled the rope only one time. He had only one wish.

And it had seemed that his wish was about to be granted.

It is a cliché that the Japanese have a talent for revenge, a talent that is enhanced by an ability to take the long view, a capacity for patience. A cliché, yes, but not untrue. Many, for instance, saw in the millions of Toyotas and Datsuns and Hondas rolling over American roads or in the VCRs and camcorders that U.S. citizens used to record and watch their very life events, their birthdays and weddings, a delicious kind of reprisal against the former conquerors.

But no matter how many Hondas purred at U.S. stoplights, Yotaro Kawai was not satisfied. He was after a purer and more pointed vengeance, an exact and undiluted retaliation, an arrow through the back of time. In Yotaro Kawai's mind, the bombing of Nagasaki constituted a criminal act, one so dishonorable and contemptible that it demanded retribution.

The bombing of Hiroshima was a separate matter. As

a student of history and military scholar, Kawai could agree with the reasoning that had led to the bombing of Hiroshima. If the Allies had continued to wage conventional warfare against their Japanese foe, the war might have dragged on for weeks, maybe even months. The Japanese leadership was arrogant. Honor demanded a willingness to fight on in the face of great odds. More fighting, more suffering were required before an honorable defeat could be acknowledged. Little Man, the nuclear device that the United States dropped on the city of Hiroshima on August 6, 1945, left a powerful impression, destroying nearly two-thirds of Japan's seventh largest city and killing more than a hundred thousand of its citizens. Hiroshima had been considered a beautiful city, and many of its inhabitants, having mentally surrendered the war, had believed that city would not be bombed because they thought the Allies likely to choose it as the center of the occupation administration.

They were wrong. Approximately half of Hiroshima's 250,000 citizens were killed or seriously injured in the blast. The lucky were vaporized, the less fortunate scorched, melted, irradiated—much like Yotaro Kawai. Even worse than the initial blast, perhaps, was the firestorm that followed. The screaming citizens of Hiroshima, desperate with thirst caused by the superheated air, threw themselves into the rivers and were boiled alive. Hiroshima: it was terrible but not, to Yotaro Kawai's mind, criminal.

Nagasaki was a different matter.

Surrender is not a simple thing, especially when a country has various military leaders, a civilian government, and an emperor thought to be descended from the gods.

After the bombing of Hiroshima, as military leaders and political leaders and diplomats squabbled over the details of surrender, the United States promptly dropped a second nuclear device, this one called Fat Boy, on the city of Nagasaki.

Why? Why just three days? Why not wait a week? Ten days? But no—with Japan reeling from the bombing of Hiroshima, with the dead uncounted, the city still in flames, military leaders of the United States could not wait a week, could not agree to a cease-fire, insisted on unconditional surrender. And then they dropped their second bomb, not on its primary target, but—ironically—on Nagasaki, the most Christian city in Japan and the city most opposed to Japanese militarism.

Why did they not wait a few days more? Historians hired by Kawai supplied an answer, drawing information from classified sources, from evidence in back-channel chats between the U.S. military and its engineers and scientists at Los Alamos.

The second bomb, Fat Boy, was a far more sophisticated device than the Little Man bomb dropped on Hiroshima. Fat Boy was the prototype of the other bombs in the U.S. arsenal, the advanced form of what the Los Alamos scientists called their "gadget." And the terrible truth was that they dropped it so hastily on the city of Nagasaki, before Japan could organize a surrender, because they *wanted to test it*—not on an isolated island, not in the desert, but on a real city. And they were afraid that the Japanese would surrender before they could do so. They wanted to test it on a real city, Yotaro Kawai's city, the beautiful Nagasaki.

Through his binoculars Kawai watched a woman in a lavender shirt pull on the bell. What was she wishing for? .Her face was earnest, not at all lighthearted, as they often were. After she finished, she embraced her husband, who waited for her against the wall. A baby? He thought so. He hoped she was not from San Diego.

Although why should he care? Had any thought been given to him? Or to the deformed child lifted from his dying mother's womb? Had any thought been given to *that* baby, his dead brother?

And in any case, perhaps she would be quite safe even if she lived in San Diego. Because despite the tremendous sums he had promised the Turk for timely performance, Delicay was late. *Days* late. True, there was no exact timetable, but both the red mercury and the satellite photos were necessary before the device could be constructed and plans finalized.

The photos would be up-to-date and full of valuable detail. Kawai's experts were anxious to plug what they could learn from the photos into their computer studies of prevailing winds, geographical features, and time-variable population densities—with a line toward optimal placement.

Kawai reminded himself that there was still plenty of time. Perhaps Delicay had run into some perfectly reasonable delay. Perhaps.

Still. Yotaro Kawai put the binoculars down and stood up. It was time to make some inquiries.

10

ALL DAY, KAREN WAS EDGY AND IMPATIENT. IT WAS THIS
weird dinner date; she was wrecked about it. Although
maybe Marcus Malone wouldn't even show. Finally, it was
time to leave the office. Saturday hours: another one of
Dr. Pratt's innovations. At home, she unlocked the door,
picked up the mail from the floor, and put it on the hall
table. Looked through it. Nothing for her. She was glad,
which gave her a twinge. She remembered the days of looking forward to the mail.

She removed the name tag—a gold-colored, tooth-
shaped thing that said: KAREN—and threw it on the
dresser. She hated that tag—it made her feel like an animal, or a child on a field trip, incapable of identifying
herself in an emergency. She pulled off her green scrub
suit. She *did* like wearing a uniform. It exempted her from
choice, from selecting a persona for the day, a way of pre-

senting herself. She liked pulling her hair away from her face; she was happy to dissolve into anonymity. Patients liked it, too. They didn't want to see large earrings, ornate hairstyles, flashy clothes—anything that might hint at unreliability. Not when people were messing with their teeth.

She took a shower, wrapped a towel around her head, smoothed moisturizer onto her legs. Rubbed her hair with the towel. Brushed her hair, fluffed it, arranged it, put on lipstick, swept mascara onto her eyelashes. Her pale face leaped into focus in the disintegrating mirror. The transformation startled her—because she rarely bothered with makeup anymore. She'd relinquished the power of her face, of her body. She'd come to prefer the pale, unembellished Karen—in the baggy scrub suit. She looked at herself in the mirror again. So why was she doing this?

She reminded herself how it was that she had ended up here, in Annandale, Virginia, working as a dental assistant.

Clay Moody. The thought of Clay was almost enough to make her scrub off her makeup, turn off the lights, hide in her room.

She looked into her closet. Not much there; it wasn't hard to decide what to wear. She put on the olive silk blouse, the brown nubby silk skirt, the black linen jacket. She threaded on her only pair of good earrings, heavy gold hoops. She had come close to selling them after her abrupt departure from her life as Mrs. Clay Moody.

In fact, technically, she was still Mrs. Moody. The divorce wasn't final yet. In fact, she hadn't spoken to Clay since that day in Washington, when they were staying at the Hay Adams. While he attended his conference, she looked up her old friend from Harvard, Robin Lawler. She and Robin ate bagels and salmon spread and observed in each other the visible changes wrought by the eight years since they'd seen each other.

Suddenly Karen was talking about her life with Clay and she realized she couldn't stay with him for even one more day. Something about seeing Robin sprang this loose in her. Karen refused, absolutely refused, to ask for help from her family, and Robin reluctantly offered refuge in her tiny Capitol Hill efficiency for a few days—which turned into three weeks. Karen looked for a job, any job. Very quickly, it came down to a choice between being a waitress and working as a (no experience necessary) dental assistant. Once she had the job, she found the house share in Annandale (cheaper than D.C. and closer to work).

By that time, getting up at dawn in an anonymous town house and putting on a uniform did not seem strange. What seemed strange, what seemed impossible to grasp, was how she'd put up with Clay for as long as she did. It was inconceivable that she'd *married* him—how could she have made such a mistake? She had misread his stiffness as dignity, his arrogance as nonchalance, his possessiveness as love.

She looked in the mirror and studied her reflection. She had to be careful. She had this extravagant red hair; she was pretty enough; in anything but the scrub suit, the body was kind of over the top. If she used a little bit too much makeup, if she wore shoes with heels a little too high or a skirt that was a little too short, she had a tendency to resemble a Barbie doll. It would have been worse, she told herself, if she'd been a blonde.

Still. She licked her finger and rubbed off half the lipstick. She looked at herself again and shook her head.

What was this guy going to think, anyway? He didn't know she had a brain in her head. He didn't know about her family, her squandered "potential," her disastrous taste in men, her abandoned academic dreams, her whole tortured history. He didn't know about the Two-Year Plan. He'd asked out: a dental assistant who looked a little bit like a Barbie doll.

She sighed and flicked on NPR. She looked around the living room and shook her head. When she was fifteen years old and dreaming about her future, never for a second would she have imagined herself living in some bunker in suburban Virginia. Never would she have imagined for one moment that she would wear a name tag or spend her days in an aqua scrub suit suctioning spit. She sat down to wait.

Marcus Malone drove through the unfamiliar streets of Annandale, Virginia, wondering what the hell he was doing. It seemed easier to go through with it than to cancel, but now he couldn't recall the frame of mind that made him blurt out his dinner invitation. It must have been the gas. Or the panic about what he was going to tell Diamond. What was he going to talk about with this woman?

He turned right, checked the number, pulled up. There was a birdbath in the yard next door, an amazing structure, three tiers of sea horses supporting a circular basin. It was white, stippled with electric blue, and blindingly clean. Didn't look as if a bird had ever been near it.

Karen opened the door with a tentative smile. "Come in."

He was shocked by the change in her. He'd thought

she was cute. Clothes instead of the scrub suit, a little bit of makeup, and she was beautiful.

"Drink?"

He smiled and gave an offhand shrug. "Sure." Looked around the room. She followed his glance as he took it in. She had an urge to show him her own room, to demonstrate that this interior decoration was her roommates' taste.

"You have a choice between beer," she said, "or Aimee—one of my roommates—has some wine coolers in the fridge." She giggled. "Peach, I think, or maybe blackberry."

"I'll go with the beer."

"Wise choice."

He followed her into the tiny kitchen. The counter was dominated by a huge microwave.

"I had a wine cooler once, when I was fishing," he said. "It tasted like Kool-Aid."

"I thought you hated fishing."

He laughed. His laugh was big, generous. She liked his laugh.

"I do. But periodically, I'm forced by circumstances . . . it's a male thing," he said.

She laughed. Her laugh was a delighted, reckless giggle. They moved into the living room, sat awkwardly with their drinks, then both started talking at the same time.

"Well—"

"How—"

A mutual laugh. "How's your tooth?"

He was a big man—six-two, she guessed. She liked big men; there was something reliable about them. She tended to trust them, as if their size obviated the need for guile.

"It's dead," he replied, "but it still hurts."

"Well, you're almost done with all that," she said. "You almost have a whole new mouth." *Brilliant*, she thought, *brilliant conversation. I have forgotten how to talk about anything but teeth.*

"How long have you lived in Annandale?"

A knock at the door interrupted this terrible conversation. She looked startled, almost frightened, and he wondered momentarily if she had some dangerous secret. A stalking ex-husband, a jealous boyfriend.

"I don't know who that can be."

She opened the door on a short Oriental man holding a book.

"You come see," the man said in an urgent voice. "May never believe me." He spotted Malone, stiffened his back. "Oh, sorry, Ka-ren. You have guest."

"It's all right. Mr. Kang, this is Marcus Malone. Marcus—Mr. Kang."

Mr. Kang bent slightly from the waist. *"Northern Oriole,"* he whispered in a hushed, exalted tone. "In the backyard. In my tree. You hurry."

Malone followed them through Karen's kitchen into her small backyard, a plain square of grass. Across the chain-link fence, the adjoining yard was floodlit and elaborately landscaped. And there it was, in a small tree, a bright orange-and-black bird. It looked unreal, a jewel illuminated by Mr. Kang's back porch light.

"How did you ever see it? It's dark."

Mr. Kang nodded and pointed to his face. "Good eye."

———

They ended up at a Thai restaurant called Bangkok Cafe. Over Singha beer and *satay,* the awkwardness suddenly evaporated. They talked for an hour and a half straight, about everything except certain matters that they seemed to avoid by mutual consent. His past. Her past.

"I once went to a dentist in Sri Lanka who called himself a dental mechanic."

"Oh, God," she giggled. "It sounds like . . . taking your mouth in for a brake job."

"It was meant to be reassuring. The implication was machinelike efficiency. Of course, when he approached me with the crowbar I was worried."

She laughed, her delighted giggle. "What were you doing in Sri Lanka?"

"I was in the CIA."

She took that in, nodded. "And now?"

"Now I'm a security consultant."

"What does that mean?"

Malone shrugged. "Mostly, it means a lot of catalogs and brochures."

He didn't mention that the catalogs listed things other than locks and alarm systems, that apart from encryption and decryption devices, electronic eavesdropping equipment, he could also supply Zodiac rafts, small arms, and even some fairly sophisticated weapons systems. Available as well were binary and plastic explosives, remote fusing devices, specialized transmitters, spectrum analyzers. In short, providing the purchaser had the right letters of credit and end-user certificates, Malone Associates sold everything that might be needed to take over or defend a small country.

Or it used to. Soon it would be selling even more. Or

seem to be. Items of interest to *large* countries. Restricted substances. Controlled technologies. TRX explosives. He heard Diamond's voice in his ear. How bad would he look? Unredeemable.

They ordered two more Singhas.

"I don't believe in that," Karen said. "I mean as a concept."

"What? Consulting?"

She laughed. "No. *Security.* I mean how can anyone ever feel *secure?* There can be an earthquake, a stock market crash, a nuclear accident. In one second everything can change. I mean there's no *Soviet Union* anymore. There's no Yugoslavia. Think about it—you're in a coma for ten years. You wake up. The whole map of the world is different. And who the hell is Bill Clinton? And there are ATM machines, something called the Internet . . ." Her hands drifted out to the side and then came back, a little self-consciously, to the table. "I mean *security;* come on."

"You're absolutely right," Malone agreed. "No one can ever feel secure—and as someone in the security business, I'm grateful for that. I was wondering," he said, "how you ended up working as a dental assistant. I mean—"

"Don't wonder," she said. "I mean it sounds like a simple question, but . . ." She looked up at the ceiling, and when she looked back at him the bright teasing expression was gone and her eyes looked hard with sadness or some other expression he couldn't quite read. "I mean my life story," she said, recovering. "We'd be here all night."

Karen was in trouble. All the time they'd been sitting there, between bites of Pad Thai and Ginger Chicken, between interesting facts and anecdotes, he'd been accumulating in her mind: the way his dark hair curled at his temples, the angle of his jaw, the way his eyebrows lifted and his eyes widened when he was surprised.

Something else was happening, too, a molecular shift inside her: desire. She felt it in the space between them—a thickness in the air, a humid longing. She was beginning to imagine things they might do together.

Abruptly she excused herself. In the ladies' room, she contemplated her face in the mirror. She looked rosy, an alcohol flush on her cheeks. She washed her hands; she splashed water on her face. This was the longest she'd gone without sex since she lost her virginity to Donald Darrington in the backseat of his father's Buick when she was sixteen.

Sex itself was not the problem. The problem was separating sex and love. There she was not to be trusted. There and in that assumption she always made—that someone who was a good lover was also a good man. That someone expansive and generous in that most intimate situation could not be a shitty person. Several times already that supposition had proven false.

She drifted back to her seat, sat down, looked straight into his eyes. He reached his hand out for hers and held it, awkwardly, across the table. Languor overtook her. Her arms and legs felt heavy; she was breathing too fast. Thirty-one years old and she still heard her mother's voice in her head: "Surely not on a *first date.*"

"Want to go to a movie?" he asked.

She looked at him. "No."

Her mind moved to practical matters. She was still taking birth control pills—she'd heard it was bad to stop and start, so she had never stopped—but what about condoms? They could stop at a 7-Eleven. Then she remembered—

the image jumped into her mind—that Millie, or maybe it was Aimee, kept some in the medicine cabinet. A small tidy box of Trojans, next to the Tampax.

The waiter hurried up to the table, put down the bill with a little crouching bow. Marcus slapped his credit card down on top without looking at it, and the waiter took it away.

In the car, she did something that shocked her. It just happened, a spasm of the libido or something. She reached across and ran the back of her hand along the inside of his thigh. Knuckles gliding along the smooth cloth. Her hand rolled over his crotch and away. Marcus made a strange sound, a throaty gasp, something like clearing his throat.

Her mother's voice spoke in her head again: "He'll think you're a slut."

They pulled up to the curb in front of the town house. The sea-horse birdbath gleamed from Mr. Kang's front yard as if lit from within. She'd fallen silent during the ride, giving herself a pep talk: *It's not too late. Get out of the car; say thanks; run to the door. Don't do it.*

But it was too late. It was probably too late when she said she'd go out with him. It was almost certainly too late the minute he walked through the door of the town house. She sensed it then, some urgent swerve within her. She'd forgotten what this was like, being with a man, the lack of self-absorption, the lunge for contact, the achy, insistent yearnings of her body. And then she made the mistake of turning toward him, and she was kissing him, a long, wet kiss. A little moan welled up in her, and there was that sinking, swoony feeling. And she knew she had to have it, that deep comfort between men and women, the comfort of flesh.

Inside the town house, he pushed her against the wall. A deep kiss, a kiss that involved their entire bodies. She was collapsing. She was half gone already. She could barely stand up. She opened the door of her room for him and then forced herself into the bathroom. There they were, thank God. She ripped a condom from the segmented roll.

They had trouble with their clothes. After a few minutes, while she still had the presence of mind to do it, she pulled away, tore open the condom package with her teeth. It was difficult, unrolling it onto his penis; small motor control was gone.

She was dying for it—she really was—she'd forgotten how it felt, this sweet familiar ache, this deep wilderness of need. She was lost, dissolving. She closed her eyes. It didn't matter where he touched her. It almost didn't matter what he did. Everything was too much to stand—she was wild; she was frantic with desire. Suddenly he was inside her and she thought she might pass out from the sweet shock of the sensation.

When it was over, she was pinned to the bed, obliterated in a kind of hazy exhaustion. "Thank you," she said finally. "I mean you just don't know."

11

THIS TIME, MALONE'S LUNCH AT THE CENTURY CLUB WAS followed by a walk. Diamond stuck to subjects like the weather and the economy until they reached a blue-painted plywood walkway flanking a construction site.

It was noisy—a pervasive thudding din, interspersed with the warning beeps of heavy equipment backing up. And it was messy. Pedestrians pretty much stayed on the other side of the street. Good tradecraft again—between the traffic noise and the racket of machinery, the conversation would be hermetic.

They stood beside a mesh window that gave a view of the construction in progress. The pit was four or five stories deep. At the bottom, hard-hatted figures toiled, operating crude machines.

"Memorize it," Diamond was saying. He meant the number typed on the plain white index card he'd just handed to Malone. Malone glanced at the string of numerals and pocketed the card. "That's your account at Credit Suisse. We'll be moving a million into it this afternoon."

At the word "million," a little jolt zipped through Malone. He struggled to keep the giddiness off his face. "This is the 'play money' you talked about."

"Yes. And right away we want you to start spending it. You'll want to settle some of your immediate debts, of course, but that won't take much of a chunk. We want you to become a conspicuous, even a *lavish* consumer. Buy a Mercedes. Start looking for an expensive condominium. You'll pay in cash." Diamond stopped, shrugged. A truck wheezed noisily to a stop nearby. "Well, I guess most people don't need advice on how to spend money, but don't sink it into something... invisible, you know.... I'm thinking of..." He paused and gave Malone a cold smile. "... well, gambling, for instance."

Malone smiled back. So they knew about his habit of betting on sporting events and his occasional poker game. His "gambling habit" costs him maybe fifty bucks a week, but it had always been a sore point with his ex-wife.

"Chinese porcelain, for instance, would also be a bad choice," Diamond said. "Or baseball cards. We're after *visibility.* Indulge yourself; have fun with it. You might as well. It won't last long."

A high-pitched metallic whine rose up from somewhere, and Diamond leaned closer, raising the volume of his voice. "You'll want to fly over immediately and bring back some cash to get started. A couple of trips to Switzerland will look right, anyway. While you're over in Europe, I'd suggest setting up a dummy corporation and running the money through that. If you really were what we're going to make you out to be, that's the way you'd do it."

He handed Malone a business card. An address on Artillery Square in London. "There are a dozen of these firms advertising in the *Herald Tribune*," Diamond said. "Or you can do your business in Liechtenstein, Cayman Islands, whatever you prefer."

"What about the other money?"

Diamond smiled patiently and withdrew another index card from his pocket. Canary yellow this time. Malone looked at it: Banque Generale de Luxembourg. Urs Birchler. "While you're in Zurich, go see Herr Birchler. We've deposited half a million in the account. You can take it all out if you want; you can move it; it's entirely up to you."

"And the rest . . . ?"

"Another half a million when you're arrested. The remainder in a year."

"I'm a little curious—I guess I'm trying to imagine my immediate future—but . . . where do I *go*? I mean after I'm arrested, to set up shop."

"Well, quite a bit of thought's been given to that. The director is leaning toward Prague."

Malone let the idea of Prague settle into his mind. It made a certain amount of sense. Throughout the Cold War, the city had been a safe haven and crossroads for arms dealers and political factions of every sort—not least of all because Czechoslovakia itself had a well-developed arms industry.

Diamond shrugged. "Even though the Czechs gave away their weapons-producing facility during partition—I mean it went to the Slovaks—still, people are used to meeting in Prague. And I do mean everybody—Sendero Luminoso, Armenians, Sikhs, Tamil Tigers, you name it. Every nonscheduled lunatic fringe and liberation movement in the world seems to swing through Prague. And if they have to go to Bratislava or Brno, they don't actually have to *stay* there. The PLO, I believe, still holds an annual conference in Prague, and any number of rejectionist groups still maintain offices in the Old Town." Diamond took a quick look at his watch and continued. "Another point in Prague's favor is that the 'velvet divorce' from Slovakia is keeping all the legal and judicial talent busy trying to figure out how to divvy up the resources."

"So?"

"So they haven't got around to revising their legal code. What you've done, what you're *going* to do"—he pushed his hands down in a dismissive gesture—"that's not against the law, not an extraditable offense. Not yet, anyway. And there's one more thing to recommend Kafka's city."

"What's that?"

"The place is jammed with Americans. You won't be conspicuous to the wrong people."

Diamond adjusted his tie, smoothed his hair, took another glance at his watch. He rested his beautifully manicured hand briefly on Malone's shoulder. Malone was floating in a fantasy of spending money, but Diamond's hand somehow brought him back to earth. He hadn't won the lottery. He'd agreed to abandon his life, to destroy his good name.

"Don't wait," Diamond said, fastening his eyes on Malone's. "If you have any second thoughts, have them now.

We've got to get this rolling. I think you should plan on being in Zurich by Wednesday or Thursday."

At the airport, Malone pulled out Karen's card. Already it was creased and messy, looking like an important memento. He shouldn't be calling her; he knew that—the last thing he needed in his life right now was another distraction.

Karen was finishing up for the day, filing some patient X rays, when the receptionist told her she had a telephone call. Dr. Pratt frowned—personal calls were discouraged—but said nothing. It seemed awkward to refuse the call; she'd have to explain too much. So she took it—at the front desk, standing next to Doreen, the receptionist. The only other phone was in Pratt's private office.

"It's Marcus. I'm in New York." He sounded nervous. He was calling from a pay phone. She could hear the noise—public, chaotic—in the background.

"I knew it was you," she said.

"I tried to call you yesterday." He paused. "And last night."

In fact, he'd called several times, but she wasn't answering the phone; she let the machine do it. She'd been thinking.

Thinking that she just wasn't going to do it again. Fall for some guy because she was suddenly sick of her life and he happened to be around when she was in the mood for a change. Time to wise up—call it a terrific one-night stand and forget it.

"I got your messages, but . . ." Her voice trailed away.

"I want to see you. Maybe tonight, if you're free." God.

She felt like a teenager. Even his voice did something to her.

"I don't think so."

"Tomorrow? After that I'm out of town for a few days."

"No, what I mean is . . . I don't think it's a good idea."

"What's not a good idea?"

"You and me."

"But . . . I thought . . . I mean . . . *why?* Why not?"

Suddenly she became aware of Doreen next to her. The spicy sweetness of Shalimar. The sound of Doreen scribbling industriously. But how could she help listening? Karen felt self-conscious and embarrassed. Even worse, Dr. Pratt was striding toward them.

"Look; I can't talk. I really have to get back to work."

"I don't get it. I thought—I mean I can't believe you're blowing me off like this."

"I really have to go."

"Wait." First his voice had sounded bewildered; now he was actually angry. "If I call you tonight, will you at least talk to me? Will you answer the phone?"

She hesitated. Dr. Pratt busied himself by glancing at the appointment book, but she didn't miss his disapproving look. "Yes," she said finally. As soon as she said it, she knew it was a mistake.

They both stayed on the line for a moment, not speaking. She could hear the noise from his end. A man shouting. The sound of an amplified voice. The train station, the airport. She couldn't seem to move; she stood there with the phone pressed to her ear even after he hung up. Finally, she gave the receiver back to Doreen.

"Guy trouble?" Doreen asked, even though Dr. Pratt was right there.

Karen nodded. "Sort of. No big deal."

"Karen, you know as far as the telephone is con—" Dr. Pratt started.

"I know." She put her hands up: *I surrender.* "No telephone calls. Look; that's fine with me. I don't even want to get telephone calls here. I mean . . ." She turned to Doreen. "Just take a message next time."

"He said it was important," Doreen said defensively.

"Oh . . . I . . . well, I'm sorry." Shit, now she was going to get Doreen mad at her.

"It's just that the patients . . . ," Dr. Pratt began in a conciliatory tone.

She nodded, listened to him, managed to smile, and then returned to filing the X rays, wondering how much longer she'd be able to last at this job. She took three deep breaths and reminded herself: *Suck it up.* She had forbidden herself to quit a job, no matter how irritating it was to be treated like a ten-year-old—not until she had another job anyway.

Dr. Pratt was generally fair and had given her two raises. And her job history was a joke. She'd started back to school in January, taking a couple of courses at George Mason. It was all she needed to finish up her degree. And then she'd have a B.A. in philosophy! Job offers would roll in!

She must have laughed, because Dr. Pratt asked, "What's so funny?"

"You kind of had to be there." She shook her head. "If you know what I mean."

"You have a nice smile," Dr. Pratt said in a strange voice.

Oh, no, Karen thought. *That's all I need.*

———

Two minutes after she stepped inside the door, the telephone rang. She knew it was Marcus, so she let the machine answer—even though once she heard his voice it was all she could do to keep herself from lunging to pick up the receiver.

No matter what she'd promised about answering the phone, he was trouble.

An hour later, the phone rang again. This time, he left his number. "C'mon, Karen. C'mon. Call me." There was actual discomfort in resisting the impulse to pick up the phone. She felt uncomfortable, hollow, edgy, as if she needed him in a physical way—like air or food or water.

Need him? He was exactly, she told herself, what she didn't need.

He called twice more before she finally unplugged the phone. Maybe if he got a busy signal for a few hours, he'd get the message: *Forget it.*

12

A GRAY MORNING, THE AIR HEAVY WITH IMPENDING RAIN. Malone checked into the Opera, a four-star hotel only two blocks from the river.

The narrow corridors were full of housekeepers whose nationality he could not guess. His room was tiny and disappointing, considering that he was paying more than two hundred dollars for it. One large window, fogged up with moisture, faced the street. Tired wooden furniture. An ersatz wood minibar crouched under the desk.

He stripped down to his underwear and by moving the desk chair created enough space to do his push-ups and sit-ups. He had to get into shape, and he knew that a simple regime of running, push-ups, sit-ups, and stretching would do it. He used to be able to do 500 sit-ups at a pop, 200 push-ups. He used to do dips using two chairs. He used to be able to walk on his hands. His resting pulse used to be under 40.

He stopped at thirty sit-ups and managed exactly nineteen push-ups before his arms began to quiver. He put on his old running shoes and a T-shirt and shorts and forced himself out the door. A maid in the hallway looked at him like he was out of his mind. He ran for twenty-five minutes along Limmatquai, beside the river where there was a pedestrian/bike path neatly striped in yellow. Every step of the way he felt uncoordinated and clumsy. There was no smoothness or grace in his choppy stride. But he knew it would come back.

Something else was already returning to him, something he thought he'd lost permanently: what he still thought of as "driving the horizon."

Most people, even as children, are dependent on a predictable routine for a sense of security. Some, however, and Malone had been one, could learn to thrive in a precarious environment.

As a Foreign Operations officer, he took a course in high-speed driving. The instructor told them that good drivers were born and not made, that it was all instinct and reaction time. If they had it, they had it; if they didn't, he couldn't teach them. He explained that the normal driver's instinct, when confronted with danger, is to put on the brakes, stop, freeze, assess. What the good driver does is the opposite: stay in motion; maintain maximum flexibility; accelerate through danger. He couldn't teach them that instinct, the impulse to go rather than stop. Most of them had it, or they wouldn't have been in FOG. What he could teach them, he said, was to "drive the horizon," to train the eyes and mind to scan the road all the way ahead, as far as visibility allowed, leaving their instincts free to operate in whatever immediate conditions arose with the benefit of maximum information.

Perhaps it was because Malone was in this mode that he noticed the blond man in the lobby. The man turned aside as Malone came through the door, a rapid swivel of the head, covered flawlessly by a look at his watch. But still, the quick glimpse of the man's face bothered Malone, nagged at him. He'd seen the face before, but he couldn't remember when. Or where.

After he showered and dressed, he inquired at the desk for the main office of Credit Suisse. The clerk offered him a small map of the city; she made a little "x" on the site of the hotel and another on the location of the bank and looped an efficient oval around the two. "On the Bahnhofstrasse, just here."

It wasn't far. He decided to walk.

Pedestrian traffic in Zurich moved briskly. Malone, jet-lagged, fatigued from running, had to will himself to match the hurried pace. Three blocks from the hotel, the first drops of rain spotted the pavement; within moments, it was a downpour.

He ducked into a shop, which turned out to be a boutique. Expensive clothes, objets, pottery, jewelry—and a selection of pricy umbrellas. He picked one out and then some earrings for Karen, simple gold balls with inlaid rings of blue stone. Lapis, the clerk told him. She wrapped them in what looked to him like butcher paper and tied it with a shred of straw. He understood that this was supposed to be stylish.

———

Credit Suisse. Malone was surprisingly nervous. He imagined a dozen ways this visit to the bank might be awkward. Somehow he couldn't quite believe it was possible to walk into a bank with nothing but a number and emerge with a large sum of money. But once he entered the bank itself, his anxiety evaporated. The Swiss banking industry knew just how to smooth the way for edgy patrons. Soon he was sliding into his pocket an envelope containing $40,000. No questions irrelevant to the transaction were asked. They didn't want to know his name. Discretion was absolute. Discretion, he believed, was a constitutional mandate in Switzerland.

He stopped first at a leather-goods store and bought a hand-crafted leather attaché case for an insane amount of money. Then he found a jewelry store on the Limmatquai and purchased a Rolex Oyster Perpetual Datejust—for which he paid a little more than eleven thousand dollars in cash. The man who took his money didn't blink an eye; he was accustomed to selling these ridiculously expensive watches for cash.

A Rolex was almost de rigueur in the Agency, and for years Malone wore one of the less expensive ones—until a few months back when he'd sold it to pay bills. The Rolex was a kind of unofficial global currency. Of course it was crazy to have a watch that cost so much, but the truth was you could sell a Rolex anywhere in the world and get a decent price for it. It was portable and had the additional advantage of being unaffected by the currency restrictions that so many countries imposed on their citizens.

And it also told the time more or less accurately.

The jeweler directed him to the Banque Generale de

Luxembourg. Herr Birchler was a foot shorter than Malone. A redheaded man with elfin features, he made Malone think of a leprechaun. He ushered Malone into his office. They spent twenty minutes discussing how to structure Malone's account, and Herr Birchler carefully explained how Malone could get to his funds without "bringing your person to Switzerland."

Malone left with another $200,000 in his new attaché case. He headed back to the hotel, thinking, *I have almost a quarter of a million dollars on me!* For a moment he felt a jangly exhilaration. But then he just felt very tired.

And as he turned the corner near the Fraumunster Church, he thought he caught the sight of a vaguely familiar blond head—the man from the Opera's lobby?—bobbing in the crowd.

Fatigue made the act of putting the cash into the small safe inside the closet slightly surreal, as if he were watching himself on television. The key was attached to a chain designed to be worn as a necklace. He slipped it on. It reminded him of his childhood, when he was required to wear the key to his house on a chain around his neck—along with his Saint Christopher medal. He remembered the key, bouncing on his chest when he ran. He stretched out on the bed; within two minutes, he was asleep.

London. The Hyde Park Hotel.

Malone dipped his glass into the ice bucket. Opened the minibar, took a miniature bottle of Glenmorangie, and tipped it over the ice. The ice cracked, a sequence of soft fractures. Malone went to the window. Down the street,

Harrod's—its architectural outlines strung with lights—twinkled and glowed, like some enormous cruise ship in a harbor.

He hadn't even thought about it when he'd looked at the itinerary. That Evelyn had booked the Hyde Park Hotel.

He rattled the ice in his glass, thinking about Fay and that disastrous London vacation. She'd been moody, tired of living in the backwaters he'd been assigned to throughout his career. Tired of the heat of Luanda, sick of the second-class status State Department types tended to confer on anyone connected to the Agency.

So: meticulous arrangements for the care and feeding of Jeff, lavish arrangements for "a fabulous week in London." Plays. Dinners. Shopping. The Hyde Park Hotel.

And the fabulous week had quickly dissolved into days of misery. That embarrassing shouting match at Langan's. That terrible night back at the hotel, *this* hotel, Fay crying for hours.

He didn't understand; he didn't *understand* how miserable she was.

What did she want?

She didn't *know*. She didn't *know!* She didn't want whatever it was that she had.

And while he and Fay argued and Fay wept, Jeff was back home in Luanda suffering the first symptoms of what would turn out to be bacterial meningitis. Learning that he was ill, they rushed back—only to find they were too late. Jeff was dead.

Jeff was dead and Fay blamed him. Blamed him, blamed the Agency, blamed Angola, blamed herself, blamed everything but misfortune and bacteria.

Malone stood up. He couldn't stay in the Hyde Park Hotel. He drained the scotch, splashed some water on his face, grabbed the minibar slip and his belongings, and headed downstairs.

The lobby was decorated with clutches of people in evening dress; the bright luster of the women's dresses made them seem like night-blooming flowers. The clerk raised an eyebrow. "Checking out, sir?"

"Plans have changed, I'm afraid."

As he walked out the door, he caught in the corner of his eye an anomalous motion, a man ducking his head as if speaking into a cellular telephone; then he did not so much see as sense the man hurrying after him at a pace so quick as to be almost frantic.

The doorman opened the taxi door, and he got in, asking to be taken to the Hilton. Nothing of importance had ever happened to him in a Hilton.

He was probably imagining things again, as he had in Zurich, but he turned around and looked out the back window as the taxi pulled away. A man was getting into another taxi behind him. He caught a glimpse of a squarish face, a short, blocky physique.

When the taxi pulled up at the Hilton and he got out, he entered the door but, instead of proceeding to the desk, sidestepped, attaching himself to the periphery of a group standing there. He bent down and fiddled with the latches of his suitcase, obscured by their bodies.

The man didn't burst through the door; he walked in nonchalantly. The giveaway was in the eyes—that wide-angle assessing gaze shared by secret service men, body-

111

guards, security details. Malone observed the man's face, his clothes, his shoes, his slightly pigeon-toed walk, and then straightened up and went to the desk.

In his room, he thought about what it might mean, that someone was following him.

1. Money. He was carrying over two hundred thousand dollars. Maybe someone had seen him pay cash for the Rolex and was extrapolating from there.

2. Diamond and Willoughby were "baby-sitting" him, making sure that he did what he'd been told, behaved as expected.

3. There was a part of the plan he knew nothing about. And in that part, he was a patsy. He could hear himself now: "But they *gave* me the money." "Right, Mr. Malone. . . ."

He flipped on the TV. Someone on the screen was rattling on about "Thatcherites." He rotated his neck to release the tension in his shoulders. He'd just started this operation and already he was looking over his shoulder; already he was certain he was being followed. What was it going to be like when he was on the lam? When he was doling out samples of something he couldn't ever deliver?

In Zurich, he'd persuaded himself that nobody was following him; it was just the natural nervousness of getting back in "the life." It was the jitters that came with the territory—as useful as an athlete's pregame nerves. Now, however, he *knew* he was being followed and he had to deal with it. It made him tired, and if Diamond turned out to be the source of the surveillance, it made him angry.

———

In the morning, he set out for Artillery Square. Took the tube to Bank Street and with the help of his A to Z guide walked through the small, old streets of the financial district, the ancient city of London. Square-face was with him all the way.

The address he was looking for turned out to be a tiny row house, hunched between two other slightly larger houses. If the outside was quaint, the inside was all business—fluorescent lighting, metal furniture, computer terminals. A huge building directory dominated the first floor reception room. It displayed a list of at least two hundred firms that claimed this puny building as their corporate headquarters.

A girl with bleached hair emerged from one of the cubicles and showed him upstairs. Lionel Cowhig leaned forward over his massive oak desk, and the two men shook hands. Cowhig was in his late twenties, a reed-thin man with bad teeth and quick eyes. He placed his palms on the desk in front of him. "First of all," he said, smiling, "it's not really necessary that I know your name."

Malone shrugged.

The whole matter took less than half an hour. As Diamond suggested, Malone purchased his corporation "off the shelf"—legal entities already prepared by Cowhig and ready to roll. From a half-dozen computer-generated identities he chose the name Towson Hall Industries, Ltd. He signed a bank signature card. There were no other documents to connect Malone by name with the corporation. Towson Hall Industries, Ltd., would be controlled entirely by bearer shares, anonymous pieces of paper. Cowhig would see to the nominees and the necessary paperwork;

he'd hold the mail and respond to any telephoned re-
quests by Malone. It would then be ten days before the
corporation would be able to receive and dispense monies.
Malone had no need for his corporation to be listed on
the notice board, a service that cost an extra seventy-five
pounds per year. Cowhig handed him a slim folder containing some documents, and he handed Cowhig £378 in
cash. They exchanged an efficient handshake.

He had an idea about how to confront the man following
him, but he needed darkness. He headed toward Turnbull
& Asser, where he thought he might as well order a dozen
custom-made shirts while Square-face cooled his heels.
Measurements were taken, fabric and style samples displayed, selected. The clerk was a young man named Jeremy, a kid with an upper-class accent, impeccably dressed.
Jeremy entered Malone's measurements into Turnbull &
Asser's permanent register. The shirts cost over seventy
pounds each.

Malone offered his American Express card. Might as
well leave a paper trail for some of these extravagances.
Jeremy shot his cuffs as he presented the slip for signature,
and Malone saw that the kid's wrists were tattooed. Blue
dotted lines circled them and the message: CUT HERE.

Jeremy caught his glance and tossed him a merry grin.
"Well," he said with a shrug, "it seemed quite witty at the
time."

Malone waited for night and then walked out behind the
hotel and through the Albert Gate into Hyde Park. There

were few pedestrians, and in the damp night the street-lights gave off soft halos of light. He walked a few hundred yards, then sat on a park bench and waited. The compact form of Square-face nudged through the gate a few moments later, sat on a park bench perhaps a hundred yards away, and lit a cigarette. A plume of smoke from his mouth. Malone got up and resumed his stroll, stopping at another park bench. This little cat-and-mouse game went on for two more sets of benches. Then Malone glanced at his watch and reversed direction, as if he were returning to the hotel. Square-face was trapped and bent to fix his shoe, waiting for Malone to stroll by. Instead, Malone sat down on the bench next to the man, so close he could smell the man's sweat and the stale odor of cigarettes on his breath. In a motion so sudden the man had no time to react, Malone stood up, stepped behind the bench, and wrapped his forearm around Square-face's neck in a choke hold. The man was older than Malone, perhaps fifty, but muscular and powerful. His hands clawed at Malone's arm, his body bucked and thrashed, and for one moment Malone was afraid he would break free, but Malone had a terrific advantage in leverage and eventually the man's efforts subsided and all that remained was a sickening staccato choking sound as he struggled for breath.

"Why the *fuck* are you following me?"

Malone relaxed the hold just slightly to allow the man to breathe and then felt like a chump when Square-face took advantage and nearly ducked his head down under the choke hold.

Malone regained his purchase and increased the pressure. "I'll kill you," he said in the cold voice of his youth.

And it made him slightly queasy that he meant it. A quick snap of the arm was all it would take.

A pair of lovers had appeared a couple of street lamps away, and Malone had not quite decided what to do about them. But they stopped and embraced. He released the pressure again, and this time Square-face choked and sputtered for a few moments but no longer had the strength to struggle.

"... the *fuck?*" Square-face squeezed out. "Just keep an eye on you." He was an American. Chicago or thereabouts. "Not do anything."

"For who?"

"Don't know," the man sputtered. "Just a baby-sitting job. Faxed your photograph," he coughed. "Itinerary." He choked and took a rattling breath. "You could have killed me," he whined.

The lovers had resumed walking toward them. Malone came around and sat down on the bench next to the man and threw his arm around his neck, placing his thumb on a pressure point in the man's neck and his fingers in front of the throat. The lovers averted their eyes as they passed from what they could only assume was a homosexual encounter. Malone waited until they were out of earshot. He and Square-face did not part company until he had the man's wallet and his gun, a Glock concealed in a shoulder holster. Of course, the wallet might be pocket litter, although not from the squawk Square-face raised about it. That, too, could have been cover. Malone gave the man his money and let him go. Let him go because he had a good idea this was Diamond's little game and he was furious.

13

MARCUS RETURNED FROM LONDON CERTAIN THAT DIAMOND was responsible for the surveillance on him—and mad as hell about it. Diamond admitted it with a sheepish look.

"Yes, well, Marcus . . . we weren't *sure* you wouldn't just take the money and run, for one thing, so we took the— I think entirely reasonable—precaution of baby-sitting you. Also, you've been out of the game for a long time. We wanted to see how you'd react, if you'd notice the surveillance, what you'd do." Diamond grinned his million-dollar grin.

Marcus shook his head and quoted John Lennon: " 'Thanks very much, and I hope we passed the audition.' "

"It wasn't unreasonable," Diamond said.

"I could have killed him."

"He's not very happy. He thought it was a nothing job,

and then you fracture his windpipe. He's looking at a cer-
vical collar for two months."

"Tough."

Diamond apologized more earnestly. "You are right,
Marcus—that you need to trust us and we need to trust
you. It won't happen again, I assure you."

And then, on to the next order of business.

The fine-tuning of the files Malone was to salt among
his legitimate records.

A further briefing on red mercury and TRX.

And finally, Pauline Weeks. BATF.

Malone was to place an ad in the *Washington Post;* Diamond even provided the exact wording on an index card.

"But I don't need more office help," Malone pro-
tested.

"Yes, you do."

"I do?"

"You need Pauline Weeks. She'll apply; her résumé will
be perfect. In reality, of course, she works for the Bureau
of Alcohol, Tobacco and Firearms. They've become very
interested in you, Marcus—as well they should."

Aimee talked Karen into going with her to the Alexandria
Waterfront Festival. "They have bands, food, even
fireworks. Please? I don't want to go alone."

The two of them bounced around the place for awhile,
had some chili, listened to some bluegrass. When it began
to grow dark, they joined the other festival goers and
staked out a spot on the parched, stubbly grass near the
river. Most of the people had come prepared with coolers
and blankets, and a large area was covered, blankets

square-to-square, like a giant quilt. She and Aimee settled down right on the grass, sat back on their elbows, and stretched out. Across the river, heat lightning shook the sky over the city. A little girl in a pink romper cruised the edges of everyone's blankets, making sharp turns at the corners.

"Evangeline, will you sit down?" said a harsh voice. Evangeline said "No," in an absolute, matter-of-fact voice and continued her restless marching.

"I'm just crazy about fireworks," Aimee said. "I really am."

"Me too," Karen said. "One of mankind's higher achievements, I always thought."

Behind them, someone's beeper went off; its shrill staccato nagged the air.

"I *mean* it Evangeline," the harsh voice said. And then the sharp slap and the child's outraged wails.

"Clay Moody," Karen said suddenly in a voice that sounded very loud.

Aimee gave her a puzzled look. "What?"

"Clay Moody. My last husband," Karen said. She felt her face getting hot.

Aimee looked puzzled and concerned. "Excuse me? Are you all right, Karen?"

"He used to hit me," Karen said. She felt her face instantly get hot.

"Oh, Karen," Aimee said and put a hand on her arm. "I wondered. . . ."

The mother's voice behind them: "I warned you, young lady."

There was a rumble of thunder. Someone said: "I told you to bring the umbrella."

Behind them, the little girl wailed on. The woman's voice again: "You want something to really cry about? You just keep that up."

To Karen's surprise, the usually reserved Aimee turned around and glared at the mother of the little girl. "If you hit that child again, ma'am, I can promise you that I will slap *you* just as hard as I can."

"Heyyyyyyy," a man said. "Now a complete stranger is telling us how to bring up our kids. Mind your own business, lady."

Aimee touched Karen's arm, a consoling gesture, then handed her one of the canned daiquiris she'd stuck in her purse when they left Annandale. It tasted warm and metallic.

Clay Moody's face came into Karen's mind: his elegant, silver-haired head, the little smile playing about his lips. She remembered sitting there, back to him, waiting for it. She even remembered saying things to provoke him.

The first time, though, it was a complete surprise. No one had ever raised a hand to her in her life; her life was without any personal violence. The thing was, Clay drank too much, something she had come to realize only gradually because it was so hard to tell. There was no slurring of the speech, no maudlin storytelling, no loss of small motor control. His mood shifted and that was all it took for a sudden swerve toward hostility. Maybe for a long time, she did her best not to notice.

But nothing prepared her for the first time he hit her. His hand coming toward her, connecting with the side of her face. She was more astonished than anything; she did not experience it as pain so much as shock.

"The thing is," she said slowly, "why did I let him?"

"Let him?" Aimee said. "That's brainwashed thinking, Karen. You know that, don't you? You don't *let* someone hit you. It's not like it's your fault."

"Still."

"But you did the right thing. You left him! You did a hard thing. You didn't have any resources, but you up and left the sucker." It was almost dark. Someone set off a string of small firecrackers. Children shrieked and squealed. "You left," Aimee said. "That's the point."

"Not right away," said Karen.

Her mind drifted back to mental terrain she'd been successfully avoiding for a long time: the Clay Moody days. This alone was telltale, wasn't it? That she thought of the different periods of her life in terms of the men she was with.

Clay had retired at fifty, although when they weren't traveling, he spent nearly a full work week handling his paperwork. In between trips, they lived a life of leisure in Clay's big house in Atlanta, a gracious place with white pillars out front, stiffly decorated by Clay's first wife, Hannah. Each week was sprinkled with cultural evenings and tended to be capped by a charity event, dinners at round tables with men and women whose names Karen struggled to remember. The women treated her with chilling Southern courtesy, a superficial friendliness that never went any further. She was a good twenty years younger than most of them; they resented her youth and her displacement of the former Mrs. Moody. She accumulated a considerable wardrobe of cocktail dresses and evening wear. She was always getting her hair styled, her face tended, her nails done. She took golf lessons; she was polishing her tennis game. It seemed like a life worth trying out for awhile.

And if she didn't have any friends in Atlanta, Clay was enough for awhile. He was stimulating company—extremely well read and better educated than any man previously in her life (Emory, University of Virginia Law. A Rhodes scholar, too.). Maybe because of her own premature departure from academia, she'd been a sucker for all that. His slow Southern voice and good manners coupled with a quick mind and a ready wit; the combination was hard to resist. That was what she'd fallen for, maybe. She'd been inordinately impressed; when she first met him, he was "re-reading" Camus in French. Admittedly, she'd been tired for a long time by then of the aimless existence of the yacht set. She'd put up with too many assholes in too many crowded quarters.

But what was she thinking the first time Clay hit her? That it was some kind of aberration? That it was a mistake? Immediately after it happened, he stared at his hand, appalled, as if it belonged to somebody else. And for days afterward, he was extra tender, extra thoughtful, genuinely attentive.

But that first time broke something loose in him, his restraint of himself. It happened again, and then it started happening more often. In an odd way, she began to provoke him. There was a pattern to it. They'd be out and he'd drink too much, but he'd charm everybody as usual. All the way home, she could see it building. It was around them in the air, a dangerous silky feeling, the rising expectation of violence. Even the second time, she knew it was going to happen before it did.

She could remember it perfectly: sitting there at the

vanity table, in an emerald-green velvet dress with a sweet-heart neckline.

Clay behind her: "You were flirting with Jimmy De-meth."

She sat there. Her hair was piled up on top of her head, an artfully arranged bloom of curls. She was removing a drop pearl earring. She saw him in the mirror. There was something pugilistic in his stance, some perfectly balanced aggression.

"Right. I just naturally go for guys with big bellies. It's—"

"You think I can't tell." That Southern fullness in his voice: *cay-un't tay-uhl.*

"Come on, Clay. I'm tired."

In two steps, he was there, his hard palm smacking against her cheek. She didn't move. She didn't utter a sound. Instantly, she discovered something many in her position had discovered before: the only power in a situation weighted so badly against you is not to give the satisfaction of pain. She watched her cheek grow red in the mirror, flush an angry mottled pink. It burned hot, like a bad sunburn.

"Whoa," she said. "Macho man."

She tilted her head slightly, started to remove the other earring. He hit her again. Tears shot into her eyes, but once again, she didn't make a sound. The earring tore her flesh slightly. A bright spot of blood.

She stood up. He looked at his hands again. It was a dangerous discovery for him. If the first time was like taking a drink after a long abstinence, then doing it again was a more deliberate step into forbidden territory. She could see the exhilaration on his face.

"Is this some new kind of foreplay?" she asked shakily. "Because if it is, it's not working for me."

Of course, he hit her again.

It was almost six months later—*six months*—that she found herself sitting across from her old school pal Robin Lawler and suddenly realized there was no way she was going back to Atlanta. In fact, she never even went back to the hotel. She made Robin take a note to the Hay Adams.

And that was how she ended up inventing the Two-Year Plan. Clay Moody. And that was why she had to stick to it.

The first firework exploded, a soft rose-colored one that bloomed like a giant peony. The crowd expressed its approval in an appreciative "Ooooh." Karen drank the rest of the canned daiquiri and leaned back to watch.

They finally found a parking place—nearly two blocks from the town house. She and Aimee were talking, and were halfway up the walk before Karen saw them: Millie sitting on the front stoop. And next to her, Marcus.

"Hey, darlin'. Look what I found. He said, 'You must be Millie.' I hesitated a second, and then I said, 'I must be.' So I offered the man a drink." She held up what looked like a gin and tonic. "Oh this is Marcus, by the way. And that's Aimee."

There was an exchange of smiles and "nice to meet yous." Aimee tossed a worried look at Karen.

"So how 'bout you two?" Millie said. "A drink? Brought some Tanqueray back from the Duty Free."

Aimee declined the offer and excused herself, saying

she had to get some sleep. Karen said *sure* in a hesistant voice, not looking at Marcus. "How was the trip?" she asked Millie.

"Ooooh. Don't ask. It was all right until the last leg from Heathrow. Four hyperactive toddlers running up and down the aisles and the New Zealand All Blacks rugby team. Huge men, honey. Huge men in black blazers. Some *serious* drinkers. I'll be right back," she said.

Karen stood there. Marcus made a "what can I say?" gesture. "I was in the neighborhood," was what he said.

"Right." She tapped her foot.

"I don't know you well enough to tell," he said, "but is that a bad sign?"

"What?"

He tapped his foot.

"Well, that's right—you don't know me. And . . ." She felt something building up in her, a mood to tell him about her childhood, her parents, her marriages—the whole messy picture. A confessional urge that must be resisted.

"What?"

"I don't know."

He took her head between his two hands, tilted it, lowered his head toward her, and kissed her. It started out as a sweet kiss, a mere touching of the lips. That was what he intended, but it immediately got out of hand—but then they heard Millie humming a tune, coming toward the door, singing, and they pulled apart.

Karen's face was hot; her skin burned where his beard had abraded her; she was breathless. *Watch out,* she told herself. Because it was definitely there, that primitive, almost cellular attraction, what Millie called the DNA sizzle.

"It's when your body's saying, 'Let's have a baby,' " Millie said. "That's when you really want to keep yourself in hand, darlin'."

"Millie," Marcus said, "you'll want to watch that."

"What?" Puzzled and offended.

"That thing you're humming."

"Oh, my Lord! You're right!" Millie had been humming "I Got You, Babe." "Where on earth did that come from?" She handed Karen a drink and set a basket of chips and a bowl of salsa on the steps. "How does something like that go gettin' in your head?"

"I've heard it called an auditory virus," Marcus said.

"You mean . . . like *infectious* tunes?" Millie laughed. "I like that. And now I've gone and put Sonny and Cher in your brains."

For a while they tortured one an other with terrible songs, shrieking and laughing, trying to out do one an other.

"And Windy had *stormy* eyes. . . ."

"Don't. Stop."

"Jingle around-the-*clock*. Mix anda . . ."

"Stop."

And Marcus realized that he was happy, happy in a way he hadn't been in a long time. Out on the stoop, with these good-natured women. This was something he'd almost forgotten—a smooth, glassy feeling, a nonchalant exhilaration.

After a while, Millie couldn't stop yawning and excused herself and went off to bed.

They sat there for several minutes, not talking. A damp, hot wind rustled the leaves in the trees. The moon slid under flimsy clouds. The pale light caught on surfaces: the curved hood of a car, the stiff little leaves of Mr. Kang's azalea bush, the ridged wire arches of the low fence. In the house, behind them, lights snapped on and off. Karen tried to remember her mood at the fireworks. She tried to remember Clay Moody and the Two-Year Plan.

Marcus put his arm around her. Karen felt herself sinking into him. Immediately she lost the sense of the border between them, exactly where his body stopped and hers began. Everywhere they touched was a blur of sensation.

She tried a return to the world of talking. Even though he'd called her fifty times, she heard herself whine, "You said you were going to *call.*" Her voice sounded like she'd borrowed it from someone else.

"Yeah, well . . ." His hand caressing the base of her neck, fingers in her hair, swirling. His hands under her T-shirt, his tongue in the hollow of her collarbone. Explosions of pleasure radiated from his touch. His mouth drifting down. Through her T-shirt, he took her nipple lightly between his teeth and then began to suck it. Her head fell back, as if the stalk of her neck couldn't hold it up. She was out of control with this guy, she thought, as they lurched to their feet and headed inside. She was out of her mind.

14

YOTARO KAWAI'S GARDENS WERE EXTENSIVE. REALLY, THE Slovenian soil and climate were wonderful. The microclimate of the lake was far milder than one might have imagined in the foothills of the Alps. He employed nine gardeners; on his better days, he himself often spent hours weeding and digging, separating and transplanting, mulching, and diagramming improvements. His gardens were arranged as a series of outdoor rooms, cascading down the hillside.

He had a walled garden, with serpentine brick walls modeled on those of Thomas Jefferson. He had a knot garden, with its intricately planted hedges. He had an old-fashioned cottage garden, a rose garden, a perfume garden. He had a white garden, where only white-blooming flowers and shrubs and trees were permitted. He had, of course, a Japanese rock garden where the gravel was combed twice daily. He had a night garden, full of evening-blooming plants.

And, of course, he had the pipe garden.

There were two planted in the pipe garden at the moment. He was inclined to keep them there for a few more days. He was in most ways a patient man, and it was amazing what a little time underground could accomplish. Just when you thought you had obtained every possible bit of information out of someone, you would hear his voice, rising up out of the soil, oddly hollow, amplified as it was by the lengths of PVC pipe. Promising revelation. Promising the goods. Promising the keys to the kingdom.

They were nothing but hustlers, the two in the ground. Kawai knew that. They had promised him "red mercury," and that's what they had delivered: mercury colored red. They had disappointed him. Still, they provided him moments of pleasure. Just the night before, one of them—the Irishman—had sung truly the most poignant version of "Danny Boy" that he had ever heard. The Irish. The Irish were so romantic, but so impractical.

For most human beings, pain is either a useful signal, a warning that the body is endangered, or the dying spasm of a doomed organism—in which case the pain is quite useless. Pain for pain's sake.

Yotaro Kawai understood pain, because he was a student of terror. And pain, he knew, was one of the two great vectors of terror, which he liked to define as a state of mind generated by the convergence of pain and fear.

The men in the pipe garden were also students of ter-

ror, but of a different kind. Theirs was a practical, ad hom-
inem study, whereas Kawai's interest was at once abstract
and professional. By burying the men in the garden Kawai
hoped to accomplish several things at once: to punish
those who'd tried to steal from him; to set an example for
others; and, finally, to entertain himself. In each of these
objectives he'd been successful. The men in the ground
were contrite. The people with whom he did business were
increasingly sincere. And the garden gave him hours of
pleasure at a time.

In the end, the men in the ground had been naive.
That was their sin, to think that they could fool him—and
the scientists who worked for him in laboratories that he
owned. He knew that red mercury was real. He'd even gotten his hands on some. A few grams. The Turk's sample.
The metallurgists had tested it, and yes, they said, it would
work as claimed. And then the Turk had been killed and
the connection broken.

The timing could not have been worse. He had two
plutonium pits, extracted from weapons that had been retired in the Ukraine. They had been extremely expensive,
but worth it. Even now, they were down below, in the lab,
in their protective cases, waiting.

If there were only more time on hand, Yotaro Kawai
would have built a factory to enrich mercury himself, would
have acquired scientists capable of directing the manufac-
ture of the stuff. Or he would have acquired more plutonium and built a conventional trigger—although that
would present logistical problems because the device would
then be so large, so much more difficult to transport and
conceal. Still, it might have been done. The problem was
that in both cases the enterprise would take too much time.

He left the pipe garden and shuffled up the steps toward the house. He did not think he would be able to eat, so he went instead to his media room.

He watched the local San Diego news broadcast taped yesterday. There was an arts festival in the Old Town. There were shots of the old mission building. There was a piece on a new baby giraffe born at the San Diego Zoo. He enjoyed particularly watching the small children— there were many small children, laughing and having a fine time. Laughing children with balloons, children eating ice cream. The Old Town, he was told, would certainly be destroyed. The zoo also, since it was centrally located. The fallout would destroy Sea World specimens.

After the news broadcast, he watched a tape of the previous night's home game between the San Diego Padres and the Saint Louis Cardinals. He enjoyed the game. Baseball is a game of precision and concentrated skill, and this combination had an innate appeal. Here again, however, he enjoyed even more the crowd shots and human-interest close-ups. The little boy pushing a hot dog into his mouth, the smear of mustard, the licked finger. The kids in their too-big Padres caps. The toddler clapping on his father's lap.

Kawai imagined himself sitting amid this crowd, in daytime, under that famous California sun. Would they shrink away from him, his fellow fans? Of course. Would he see fathers and mothers duck their heads? Would he know that they were whispering in their children's ears that it was impolite to stare? Of course. Would he mind? Certainly not. For one thing, his terrible deformity was finally to serve a useful purpose. It was how he was going to get into the country.

The irony was almost too perfect. American chagrin over its wartime internment of those of Japanese ancestry had combined with residual guilt over the bombings of Hiroshima and Nagasaki to produce a gesture designed to "heal" old wounds. Summer of Peace, they called it. Oh, how he loved that. He could not turn the phrase over in his mind without a smile coming to his lips. Summer of Peace. There were to be ceremonies involving the Japanese who had been interned in U.S. concentration camps and others for bomb survivors and joint ceremonies for both. Japanese-American groups had scoured the lists from internment camps and with the help of Japanese organizations sought out the names of *hibakusha*.

Initially, his name had not been among these, of course. For one thing, he was supposed to be dead. However, his agents had managed to insert a false name onto the list—the identity actually belonged to an employee of his, an out-islander of his own approximate age. This man had, in fact, been born in Nagasaki but chanced to be in Kobe on the fateful day. An invitation had duly been received. And who would question him? The *hibakusha*'s passport was imprinted on his face. Already a list of planned of activities had been sent and a letter from the family in La Jolla who would be his special "sponsors."

Was it luck that "his" set of ceremonies was to take place in San Diego? It was a city with a population nearly equal to that of Nagasaki. It was a city with hills rolling down to the sea. It was a city that offered the pretext of a military target, in this case, the Eleventh fleet. Was it luck that after the ceremonies scheduled for the day of August 9 he had a "free" afternoon? Was it luck that the Padres had a home game on that day? He didn't believe in "luck." He believed in fate. He was Japanese, a warrior. A criminal act must be repaid in kind. Revenge must be exacted before there could be any "peace." Time and circumstance had delivered to him this opportunity for justice and the wherewithal to build the perfect reciprocal device. His whole life had been constructed to focus him toward this very end. He was certain of that.

He was still considering a number of sites, although he had nearly decided to settle on the stadium. It offered him the delight of a plentiful array of companions for the final moment. In the faces around him he hoped to see the parallel souls to his father, his grandmother, his friend Ito, the grocery man, the lost ones. And then all of them would dissolve, together with him. Into the *pika-don,* the flash-boom, the eternal flame.

On the screen, the game was in the bottom of the ninth, Padres down by four. It was pleasant to let his mind wander. Where in the stadium would he sit? Somewhere in the cheap seats, he'd been told, up high—although his engineers were not yet in full agreement about the most advantageous placement in terms of blast dynamics.

When would he detonate the device? He thought that should be left until the day itself, until it struck him that the perfect moment had arrived.

The last batter stepped up to the plate. There was a shot of dejected players waiting it out in the dugout. The camera panned the stands. Many were beginning to move toward the exits, but the camera focused on a little blond boy, both fingers crossed, his face intense with hope. He was to be disappointed: The batter flied out to left. The outfielder plucked the ball from the air with an ease that Yotaro Kawai appreciated, as if he were picking a flower.

He clapped his hands once, and the woman came in to bring him some tea and to change the videocassette. For his evening's entertainment he planned to watch the movie *Some Like It Hot*. Dated, of course, but filmed at the famous old hotel in Coronado. The bridge joining the island of Coronado to the city of San Diego was known as "Big Blue," and it had been given serious consideration as a site for the detonation. Jumping—whether off a cliff, into a volcano, or off a skyscraper—was a very popular suicide method in Japan. There was a certain aesthetic pleasure to be derived from imagining the elongated moment of the fall. He had imagined it many times, his trajectory off "Big Blue," the spectacular midair explosion. It had an aesthetic appeal, yes, but he thought the stadium, on balance, was the better choice.

The bridge would not survive the blast. The Hotel Del Coronado would be leveled, along with the many comfortable homes on the island. The golfers would be incinerated, the tennis players irradiated. Most of the U.S. Pacific Fleet, which was housed in the great natural harbor of San Diego Bay, would sustain irrevocable damage, along with the many aerospace and electronic concerns headquartered in the city. This thought gave Yotaro Kawai considerable pleasure, even more than "Danny Boy" had.

On the screen, Jack Lemmon came out, in drag, wobbling along in his high heels. Yotaro Kawai laughed.

15

PAULINE WEEKS HAD BEEN WITH THEM FOR TEN DAYS NOW. Evelyn, of course, was working twice as hard as she'd ever worked in the history of her employment by Malone Associates. It was almost enough to make Malone believe in the virtues of competition.

He waited for the office to be empty so he could tinker with his files in privacy. It was nearly seven-thirty. Evelyn and Sam were long gone. Finally, he heard Pauline Weeks shut off her computer. A few moments later, she materialized in his doorway. She wore a stylish navy blue suit; her short reddish hair framed a sweet face. There was an unblemished innocence about Pauline, a kind of Pre-Raphaelite beauty that made it hard to remember that she was an undercover agent for ATF. Sam—whose bearing toward women had not significantly changed since he was a teenager—didn't know this. Of course, he had a terrible crush on her.

"She's *gorgeous*," Sam said, popping his eyes, when Pauline left after her initial interview. Sam had since taken her out to dinner. Malone imagined these two out on the town: Sam with his hormones jumping, Pauline trying to weasel information out of him.

Now she stood across from Malone's desk, trying to read the paper he was looking at—upside-down—and the effort gave her a perplexed, cross-eyed look.

"Well," she said in her high-pitched voice. "Aren't you the busy bee!"

"Yeah, well," he said with a shrug. "I've got to put some quotes together."

"If I can help . . . ," she replied, leaning slightly forward.

He folded his arms over the paper, obscuring it—despite the fact that it was nothing, just a copier maintenance contract that Evelyn had given him to sign.

"Oh, no, I'm just about done."

Annoyance momentarily marred her sweet features. Well, she wouldn't have to worry much longer. Once he'd salted the files with the material that Diamond had given him—a chore he hoped to accomplish tonight—he'd see to it that Pauline had a set of keys to the office. Then she'd be able to peruse all the damning evidence at her leisure, ransack his files to her heart's content.

Now Pauline heaved a little sigh and hitched up the really enormous thing she carried as a purse. Malone wondered what she had in there. A gun? Certainly.

"Well, I'll see you Monday," she said brightly.

He picked out several different pens and began labeling file folders in his messy printing, dog-earing the tabs to give them the right look. The folders would hold papers detailing a dozen illegal transactions involving Marcus Malone, hard evidence of widespread and long-standing violations—offenses that would be of profound interest to the Bureau of Alcohol, Tobacco and Firearms, to the U.S. Customs Service, and, once the numbers were added up, to the IRS.

Into a folder marked "Triad Trading Co." went a sheaf of papers revealing his extensive dealings with a thinly disguised proprietary of the Libyan government's intelligence service. In large red letters at the top and bottom of each page was the predictable word: *SECRET.* Much of the prose featured the misspellings and tortured syntax so common to clerical staffs of Third World countries. The imperfect English only added to the documents' air of authenticity.

There were contracts for the sale of explosives, detonators, "rasdio transmitters," "special weapons," "electronic survalence equipment," and "termination equipment." The "termination equipment" turned out to be a list of poisons, identified by numbers and letters. Descriptions included the method of administration (oral, for the most part), time of action (everything from "instantaneous" to "72 hours"), and effect (ranging from heart failure to the even more ominous "internal organ decomposition"). All in all, the contract with Triad was for almost 4 million.

Those documents alone, which revealed violations of the arms embargo to Libya, trading in sanctioned matériel and banned substances, and falsification of end-user certification, would have been enough to put him away for some time. But there was more. Much, much more.

There was, for example, a deal with the Iranians. To them, the papers showed, he'd sold everything from "high-explosive fragmentation shells for A-44 cannons" to "quadruple antiaircraft machine guns" to "engines and spare parts for F-4 aircraft." The lists of weaponry were on sloppy photocopies, splotched with gray.

Next file: The Iraqis. Mortar-locking radar. He was beginning to see what Diamond meant when he said that Malone's reputation would be "unredeemable."

It was an odd exercise, filing evidence of violations he'd never committed, sowing the seeds of his own destruction. When he finally finished, he put the files in his desk and locked the drawer.

He rubbed his neck. His back ached. He stood for a moment and looked out the window. A smoggy night—he could just make out the Washington Monument amid the sprawled glitter of the city across the river. He poured himself a drink and continued to stand there. His moods had become unpredictable. Sometimes he was caught up in a giddy buoyancy. Other times, a bleak gloom settled over him, as it did now. And behind it he was tired, a ragged, adrenaline-pushed exhaustion.

The bust was going to come down soon. A week or so. He'd already had the initial meetings with the agent of his demise, a smooth little Iraqi. There would be further meetings, and at the final one the FBI and BATF would bust in. Diamond had warned him not to carry a gun.

"I never carry a gun anymore," he had told Diamond.

"Even a Swiss Army knife," Diamond had said without smiling, "would be a bad idea."

Of course, there had been second thoughts. What was he doing? Why did he agree to this? He could have filed for bankruptcy; he could have looked for a job. He could have put his arm around Karen, hopped into his car, and driven away into the sunset. There were a thousand ways he could have turned his life around.

But it was too late; there couldn't be any sheepish interview with Diamond, any clumsy attempt to push the toothpaste back into the tube. His bridges were on fire, burning brightly.

In Diamond's opinion, considering the short time frame, Malone was doing a good job of spending money lavishly. He'd sublet a place at the Watergate. He was driving an E-class Mercedes for which he'd paid cash. He and Karen had flown to the Virgin Islands one weekend. He was amazingly well dressed. And as he'd become such an avid consumer, he'd realized the beauty of Diamond's plan. Not only did the spending back up his legend as an arms dealer; it all but eliminated any possible change of heart.

He turned off the lights, locked up. A maintenance crew worked down the hall somewhere; he heard the industrious hum of a vacuum cleaner. As he waited for the elevator, the machine stopped. The trill of a woman's laugh. It reminded him of Karen. The security guard nodded to him as he went out the door into the garage.

Karen. Every day he thought about how to end it. The longer he waited, the harder it got. He knew that, but still he did nothing. He'd tried to break it off three or four times. Once, he actually kept away from her for five days. But he couldn't seem to help himself where she was concerned. His hand moved to the telephone as if by remote control; he found himself pulling up to her town house without ever having consciously driven there.

He maneuvered around the last concrete piling and out through the gate. Maybe tonight he'd tell her. It was all prepared in his mind; he'd even rehearsed the lies.

"I'm not the right person for you. I think for your sake . . ."

"There's someone else . . ."

Sometimes he tried to talk himself out of his feelings for her. It was the novelty. It was because he knew it had to end that it was so intense. He was infatuated. He was having a midlife crisis.

Sometimes, he half-believed himself, but never when he was with her. Never then, looking at her face, touching her arm, listening to her talk as she cooked in her tiny kitchen. Never when he heard her laugh, sitting next to him in the movies. Never when they made love. And there, in the car, rocketing along the Beltway toward her house, he knew that he was not going to tell her tonight. He made a deal with himself, like any addict. Just this last time.

She was not expecting him. She looked out through the screen door, her face composed into its public look, a suspicious if not unfriendly sizing up. Her hand never let go of the doorknob behind her, and there was a certain physical tension in the way she stood that made it clear that she was ready to slam the door in someone's face if she had to. Malone wondered what had happened to her, why she was so vigilant. There was still a lot about her that he didn't know.

"Marcus! I thought you weren't coming tonight."

"I—"

"I have to study. My exam is tomorrow."

She barely got the door closed before he began kissing her; immediately he wanted her. "Wait," she said. "I have to turn off the rice. We don't want the smoke alarm—

"Now," she said, closing the bedroom door behind her and actually diving onto the bed, a blue wrapped condom between her teeth. Then she pulled off her T-shirt, arched her back slightly and undid her bra, got out of her jeans.

Eventually, she would be the one to put the condom on him, a task she addressed with earnest concentration. "It's the only way," she'd told him in the beginning, "to do it every time—like a seat belt. I mean seat belts are restrictive and uncomfortable, too. But you put up with it because you don't want to go through the windshield. You know?"

Even this, with her, had become an erotic moment—the way she straddled him, the slight swing of her breasts. He knew from what little she'd told him that her sexual history was complex and not without its dark corners. But to him, her unblinking attitude toward sex had an innocent quality, and her straightforward pursuit of their mutual pleasure came as a revelation. He had remarked on this once—her passion. She said, "Well, not everybody likes it so much, I guess. Although it is hard to figure out why not."

When it was over, he watched the shadows crawl over

the ceiling. Karen propped herself up on one elbow, stir-ring the hair on his chest with her finger.

"What are you thinking about?" she started, then shook her head. "Don't answer that. I used to hate it when . . . someone asked me that, which they do all the time. I always lie, no matter what I'm thinking. I mean you could be thinking, *God, we're out of toilet paper,* or something like that. And you don't want to admit it. You want people to think you're always having important thoughts." She put her head down on the crook of his arm.

"I'm thinking that I have to tell you something," he said, in a voice that was too loud and clear and dropped into the room like a bad joke.

"Oh?"

"I'm not a nice man," he heard himself say.

Karen cocked her head like a dog who had picked up the first faint warning of an intruder. All along, Marcus had left her with only vague impressions of his work.

She looked at him. *"What?"*

"Remember when I told you that I was a 'security consultant'?"

"Ummmhmmm."

"Well, you might call it that." He looked not at her but at a space slightly above her head. "Mostly, I sell guns. Guns, bombs, poisons, ammunition, rocket launchers, grenades, mortars. You name it. I sell it."

His voice faltered. But he was going to be arrested. *Soon.* In a public way. It would just sandbag her. At least this way, she'd be a little prepared.

"I sell them to anyone; I sell them to the worst people in the world. I sell them to men who use them against innocent people. I sell them illegally."

"Marcus . . . what are you saying?"

"I'm saying I'm nothing but trouble and you'd be well-advised to tell me to get the fuck out of your life."

"Don't tell me this," she said. Her face was blank, stunned.

For a second, he considered telling her the truth: "I'm working for the CIA. In a couple of weeks, I'm going to be arrested. It's a setup so that I can track down a nuclear outlaw." Even to him, it sounded insane.

A decent man would leave now, he thought. *A decent man would stand up, get dressed, leave right now.* But he was not a decent man. He took her in his arms; he kissed her on the lips; he told her he was crazy about her. And he did not have the strength to walk out the door.

16

MARCUS MALONE LOOKED INTO THE APPEALING BROWN EYES of Akmed Akmadi. He had this considerable problem with Arabs: he trusted them. There was something about moist brown eyes and flowery manners that absolutely leveled his normal veneer of suspicion.

Arabs were often portrayed in American popular culture as fierce-eyed, merciless men with exaggerated Semitic features. Frequently they had facial hair or sinister eyeglasses. Sometimes they were turbaned; in more extreme examples, they clenched scimitars in their teeth.

To say that Akmed looked nothing like this was a huge understatement. He was a small man with baby-smooth skin wearing an expensive slate blue silk suit. He smelled of some spicy aftershave. He looked as if he wouldn't hurt a fly. With his bright brown eyes and eager expression, he reminded Malone of a small animal. A chipmunk.

This chipmunk had, however, asked Malone to supply guns, Stinger missiles, and destructive materials of all kind. His shopping list had included an explosive whose use was largely for detonating nuclear devices—TRX. And then there was a direct plea for "something my principals are really keen on—this nuclear trigger material, this red mercury."

If it was hard for Malone to remember that Akmed was supposed to be the envoy of a despicable regime, it was even harder to remember that Akmed was actually setting a trap for him. Improbable as it seemed, Akmed was, in fact, *The Man*, and in about an hour his heavily armed friends would be arriving and Malone would be handcuffed and headed for some place a lot less pleasant than room 601 of the Plaza Hotel.

"Plees," Akmed said. "Before we start, you would like something to drink? Tea, perhaps, or coffee?"

"Coffee."

"If I can call room service? And then we can talk." A really sincere smile.

While they waited for room service, Malone heard himself embellishing for Akmed the details of one of the bogus cases in his files—picking up a thread from one of their previous conversations.

"So I had a line on these Bell helicopters. And this guy wanted them so bad he was practically drooling." He heard himself go on, sounding like an American blowhard. "We're just about to close the deal. His whole office is littered with antiquities. Very valuable—which I knew because the guy told me about them, one by one, in detail. You know"—he mimicked a proud, high-pitched voice with an Iranian accent—" 'This is from Persepolis, and it's *hundreds* of years old. This is from Isfahan, and it's *thousands* of years old.'

"So I don't know what gets into me . . . but I hesitate. 'There's only one thing,' I say. 'What?' he says in a eager voice. 'What is that thing?' Well, I tell him, 'I really need a present for my wife's birthday—no time to shop, you know—and what I'd really like is one of those vases. You throw in one of those babies, and we've got a deal.' You should have seen him. His face seized up. Absolutely seized *up*." Malone made a miserable, stricken face.

Akmed rewarded him with an endearing, if tentative, chuckle.

Malone laughed. "I had to let him off the hook in the end, though. Settled for a rug. *Beautiful* rug. In my dining room to this day."

Room service arrived. Akmed served. It was very much in character. Arabs do not rush anything.

While they drank, it struck Malone as bizarre that over the entire course of his relationship with Akmed—they had suffered through two meals together and several hours in each other's company—nothing about it had been genuine. Malone was not the blowhard American arms dealer he sounded like, indifferent to the niceties of Arab culture. Neither was Akmed the pleasant but canny businessman, intent on acquiring weapons for a divinely inspired regime of terror. Malone was not really selling anything; Akmed was not really buying anything.

It was a strange dance.

When they finished their tea and coffee, Akmed glanced at Malone's briefcase.

"You have prepared the contracts?"

146

"All set. Oh—but first, I have a little something for you."

A pleasant, quizzical look.

Malone fumbled in his pocket. A frisson of worry crossed Akmed's face. People in the arms business get jumpy when men start fumbling around in their pockets. "Now where did I put that thing?" He'd been laying it on, ever since he met Akmed, acting like just the kind of dumb-ass arrogant arms dealer stupid enough to get busted. Finally, he opened his briefcase and extracted the videocassette. He held it up and looked around the living room of Akmed's suite.

"Jeez, you do have a VCR in here, don't you?"

"In the bedroom," Akmed said, a little worried. Probably no cameras in there.

"Want to show you what the Stinger can do, and I got a demo of a red mercury bomb, TRX detonated. Show you what it can do."

Akmed looked expectant and happy. Malone slipped the cassette out of its sleeve. Diamond had supplied a typewritten sheet with detailed information about the operation of the Stinger missile and a briefing paper to prep him for the TRX section of the video also. Malone had spent several hours studying, then destroyed the papers according to Diamond's instructions. He also screened the videotape several times and actually wrote and then rehearsed his own narration. All he lacked was a TelePrompTer.

They retreated to the bedroom. Akmed opened the doors of the video cabinet. They sat on the king-size bed, perched on the edge. The tape was video only, no sound.

It began with a one-minute clock, which swept around to zero. When the actual film began, there was an establishing shot of a few dozen Stingers. They were dull red in color, lined up on a patch of dirt. Malone rattled off the statistics: weight, explosive power, range, et cetera. Suddenly there was a shot of empty sky, a pure wash of blue. After a long time, maybe an entire minute of blueness, an aircraft drifted into view.

"That's the drone," Malone said. "The targeting system is essentially heat-seeking. A single man—not even a particularly strong one—can hold one of these things comfortably. That's the beauty of it. Here we go." There was a shot of a GI in desert camouflage, standing on a patchy desert floor, holding a launcher. The soldier pulled the lever. A long shot showed the ascending missile. "Now this is slow motion," Malone mentioned. "Otherwise it all happens so fast, you can't tell fuck-all."

The missile headed straight and unerringly toward the helpless drone.

"Flies right up its ass," Malone said.

The drone exploded in a bright asterisk of fire and smoke. Akmed giggled. Pieces of twisted metal and debris floated out from the center.

"Bingo," Malone said. "It's for relatively close-range stuff, of course. But not so close your man doesn't have some time to maneuver—you know, leave the area."

They watched the screen, which reverted to black and white. Another one-minute clock, the second hand sweeping around. A white flash as the needle touched the zero and then the actual footage began. A close shot of a spherical object, perhaps nine inches in diameter, dull gray, on a blue field. Alongside the object, for the sake of comparison, were a coffee cup and a metric ruler.

"That's the explosive device," Malone said. "The shell is a titanium sandwich around the red mercury. Inside that is a plutonium pit, recycled from a retired warhead. As you can see, it's fairly compact." In the video, the camera pulled back from the bomb. The room was revealed as a laboratory, and a man in a suit entered it. He picked up the bomb and carried it rather ostentatiously out of the room.

Malone felt weird. Whoever he was being staked out to trap was never going to see this footage. And it didn't matter fuck-all to Akmed either. Nevertheless, they both watched it as raptly as men on shore leave watching a porno show.

There was a break in the video, and the subsequent footage was in black and white and rather grainy. A long, trembling tracking shot showed an unfamiliar vehicle driving along a road in a gray landscape, featureless except for the undulating ridge of a low mountain on the horizon. There was a split in the ridge just about in the middle of the screen.

"That's a Lada," Malone said. "Russian car." On the screen, the Lada stopped. A dark-haired man held a spherical device in his hand. He said something to the camera, smiled, and then passed the device to a bald man, who seemed to weigh it for a moment. He attached some kind of suction cup to it, out of which ran two wires. These were stuck into a white ball of what looked like Play-Doh.

"That's the TRX," Malone said.

The other man held something in his hand that looked vaguely like a garage door opener.

"Radio control device," Malone said. "For remote detonation."

The bald man stooped and placed the bomb on the ground. The two got back into the Lada and drove off. There was another break in the footage, and when it resumed the camera was obviously much farther away.

"Same piece of real estate," Malone said. "As you can see by the shape of the mountain." The split in the ridge was still there, but now perhaps one-tenth the size it was in the earlier footage. Suddenly the screen went white, a shaking incandescent white. There followed the slow, roiling formation of the familiar mushroom cloud. Somehow it seemed even more horrific without sound. The explosion went on for a long time. The cloud began to collapse back into itself, and Malone tapped the button to stop the tape.

Akmed was beside himself with happiness, wagging his head back and forth. Malone rewound the cassette and ejected it from the machine.

"Can I have this video? My principals . . ."

Akmed's voice faded out on a tone of absolute wistfulness. Akmed Akmedi was quite the brilliant little actor. Malone winced. "Sorry. I've got to hang onto it."

They returned to the living room. Malone extracted the paperwork from his briefcase and replaced the video. The contract involved some C-4 and Tovex explosive, five Stinger missiles, 3,000 submachine guns of Chinese origin, a grab bag of rocket launchers, some C-4 and TRX explosive. There were many pages to the contracts, specifying delivery dates, locales, and the details of final payments. The total amount came to slightly more than $7 million.

They signed the contracts with a Bic pen, after which Akmadi produced a British Airways travel bag.

This would contain the down payment. He and Diamond had argued about this. Malone insisted that it was extremely rare for cash to change hands; deals were more realistically done on the basis of letters of credits, final payment by direct bank transfer. Diamond was insistent about the cash. "They just don't feel comfortable without it, Marcus. You see, they want to arrest you *right there*, red-handed. The other way, they would most likely be unable to subpoena the bank evidence—unless you were planning to do your banking at Citibank or something, which would be even *more* unrealistic." In the end, Malone had agreed.

Akmed unzipped the bag to give him a look at what was supposed to be $500,000 in cash. Malone nodded and worked to remain calm. But as soon as the contracts were signed, his body was on full alert, a revved-up anxiety he worked to control.

He had a trick with fear, a way of grabbing it and turning it back on itself, but maybe he was rusty, because it wasn't working. He was so extremely restless, he was forced to stand up. He worried that he'd suffer what actors called flop sweat. He plastered an "it's a deal" smile on his face. Akmed returned a "satisfied customer's" grin. Neither one of these smiles was persuasive.

Malone stepped toward the door, knowing that Akmed would surely detain him. He could read Akmed's mind: *Where the fuck are they?* Akmed looked pale and an alarmed expression seized his features.

"You are not leaving?" he said desperately. "I have ordered some champagne."

Malone glanced at his Rolex. "Mind if I use your bathroom?" Akmed looked relieved.

In the bathroom, for some reason, Malone washed his face and then looked at himself in the mirror. He smoothed his hair. Wanting to look his best? The sole sign of Akmed's occupancy was a fluorescent pink Reach toothbrush, some toothpaste, and a cheap blue nylon toiletries bag. Malone opened the bag. It contained shampoo, a disposable razor, and a bottle of Advil. So the Bureau was willing to pop for the silk suit and the hotel suite, but their largesse did not extend to providing an agent with a top-of-the-line shaving bag.

He looked at his watch and waited another two minutes, despite the fact that he felt claustrophobic. He enjoyed the notion of Akmed sweating it out in the other room.

Akmed was placed so that he could see Malone come out through the bathroom door. His hand was in his pocket. He removed his hand from his pocket and picked up the telephone, making a little motion to Malone as if to say, "I'll be right with you."

"Room service?" he said into the receiver. "We are still waiting for our champagne in suite 601. Thank you."

As they always say, it happened so fast. Malone took two steps toward Akmed, and then there was a knock on the door, followed by a loud smashing noise. Bodies exploded into the room, and the next thing that crossed his consciousness was that some cold metal was jabbed into his neck and he heard a voice say, "That's a shotgun behind your ear, motherfucker. Don't move."

17

HE DIDN'T. SOMEONE FRISKED HIM, AN ODDLY INTIMATE PROcedure. The man didn't just pat him—a hand lifted up his balls; fingers gouged between his buttocks. Even without moving he could see nine or ten men, all of them dressed in blue warm-up suits, with FBI and BATF emblazoned on their backs in huge letters. They brandished shotguns, rifles, and pistols. They wore baseball caps; they looked like a football team with guns. Akmed's flowery manners had disappeared, and he sat across the room, smirking.

"Akmed, did you order enough champagne for everyone?" Malone said.

"Shut up, you fuck," the man holding the gun into his neck ordered. They cuffed him.

"I hope you burn in hell, asshole," Akmed said.

Someone read him his rights with exaggerated care, and then he was hustled into a service elevator. The walls were lined with quilted gray material. They pushed him toward the back, continuing to treat him roughly, to inflict whatever routine pain they could pass off as incidental. He had the impulse to joke with them, to make them like him, but he resisted. He was barely human to these men, and it wouldn't take much to provoke them.

They put him in the car, shoulder to shoulder with two beefy guys, two more guys in the front. The car stank with everybody's nervous sweat.

"Where are we going?" he asked.

"Shut up, fuckhead."

Malone looked at the agent and then understood. They didn't know what he would do. They were afraid of him. They were whistling in the dark.

The driver knifed through the knots of traffic with the occasional use of the siren. The city floated by. Malone couldn't see very well; he was left with the impression of crowds, humidity, fumes. They took him to the Manhattan Correctional Center, where he was fingerprinted, photographed, and allowed to call his lawyer. He'd been over that with Diamond, the question of a lawyer, so he was prepared.

"Why do I need a lawyer?" he'd asked. "In my case it shouldn't matter."

Diamond had sighed, a disappointed sound. "Because, Marcus, you can *afford* one. And a good one. But mostly because you need to get out on bail. It's not automatic."

The recommended lawyer agreed to represent Malone and explained that while people on television were instantly sprung from jail by their lawyers, in his case it would take at least a week.

He spent the night in a cell with a huge man named Calvin Bigelow. Bigelow was an ugly white guy who had the bulked-up look of the ex-con. He sported a whole panorama of crude tattoos, including a swastika and a skull and crossbones and an eye spilling a trail of tears. He couched his comments in such a way as to make them useless as testimony against him. He was accused of murdering a clerk and wounding two policemen in a 7-Eleven holdup. Bigelow seemed less concerned about the charges against him than he was put out that the 7-Eleven clerk was armed.

"That little gook squeak pulls a gun, you fuckin' believe that? The fuck he care, man? A fucking 7-Eleven. You believe that?"

Malone's lawyer was an African-American and wore little round glasses that gave him a very focused look. He confided that he was hearing things he didn't like hearing about a client of his.

"Like what?"

"I'm hearing 'snake in the grass.' I'm hearing 'fucking traitor.' I'm hearing 'make an example of him.' "

"I see."

He gave Malone a steady look.

"Marcus." He smiled. "I'm very good at what I do, but unless something unpredictable comes up—and who knows what we'll find in discovery—I see nothing but some serious time. So if you've got anything to trade . . . well, you know that tune. Think about it."

Marcus promised that he would.

They shook hands.

He received visitors in a cubicle, separated from them by a thick panel of scratched and fogged Plexiglas. He wore a bright orange jumpsuit and understood that he did not look good. Calvin Bigelow had turned out to be quite the restless sleeper.

Communication was by telephone. Talking into these particular telephones was the reverse of normal experience—when someone called from very far away and sounded as if he were next door. This time, while you could see who you were talking to, it sounded as if they were in Indonesia.

Malone had only two visitors.

Sam. All spruced up, in a suit, and relentlessly cheerful. "Hey, Boss! You look like hell." That rat-a-tat-tat laugh.

"Thanks."

"Don't even bother going to one of those color consultants. Orange definitely ain't your color."

"You're cheering me up no end. Hey, I'm sorry about this."

But Sam wasn't quite ready to let go of his joke. "You must be a 'winter.'" He cleared his throat. "You ever figure *Pauline*? A snitch? Shit. And you should see the office. Jesus *Christ*. Crawling with feds." And then he broke into a heavy whisper, as if all of this were somehow private. "They're asking me a lot of questions."

"Just answer them. Don't worry about it. How's Evelyn taking it?"

"She ain't been so thrilled since her car was stolen. She even got to be on television!"

When time was up, Sam suggested that they get smashed together when Malone got out, gave a little salute, and walked jauntily away.

Karen had the look of a Sunday school teacher who had stepped into a parallel universe. She wore a floral printed dress with a big white lace collar, a garment Malone was sure she'd borrowed. He understood her motives and was touched. This was the way a killer's girlfriend would appear in court. And if the killer herself were a woman, this was the way her attorney would tell her to appear in court: wholesome, a visual testimony to innocence.

She said something and he pointed to the telephone. She looked at it, surprised, and picked it up.

"I saw you on the news," she said. Her voice was thin and broke up into static; still the sound of it started something up in him, a longing. For the first time he really felt imprisoned, his lack of freedom real.

"Karen."

"They make you sound like a monster. I don't even recognize you, to tell the truth." Her eyes kept straying away from him. It was hard, it was unnatural, to look directly at someone while speaking into a telephone receiver. "Do you need anything?" she asked.

"Only you," he said before he could stop himself.

She tried a smile, which threatened to break up into a sob, then hung up the phone. She leaned forward and pressed her right hand against the Plexiglas, fingers splayed. He fit his hand up against hers. And then she was gone. He stayed there for a minute, watching the humid imprint of her hand evaporate until it, too, had disappeared.

Farewells.

First Fay, his ex-wife. Even though what had happened between the two of them was not entirely his fault, he felt he still owed her something. And it was going to have to be money, because he had nothing else to give.

She met him at the door and did not ask him in. Whitey barked and jumped in excitement, and Marcus leaned down to pet the dog. He saw from the startlingly bright brass disk and small nicks in the wood that since the divorce Fay had changed the locks. She wore a pale pink linen sheath, white hoop earrings.

"You look terrific."

She raised an eyebrow and smiled, although she was not happy to see him. Tapping her toe. Tight as a violin string.

"So . . . how are you, Marcus?"

"I'm . . . gettin' by."

"Where are you staying? It's not an idle question. My lawyer has some"—she rolled her hand through the air—"I don't know, something about the alimony."

"I have an apartment at the Watergate."

Fay raised an eyebrow. "Oh. And how's the girl-friend?" He shook his head. She couldn't resist. "What's wrong? She finding you less attractive now that you've been indicted?" A little laugh. "Aren't we all."

"Fay. Could we just step inside?"

She gave only a little ground. They stood in the flag-stone foyer. Whitey collapsed in front of the door, as if to block Malone's exit. "I'm not sure you understand . . . uh . . . what's in store."

"Marcus, if you have something to say . . . *say* it."

"The way the government sees it, not only have I violated some laws about selling various things—"

"I am not interested in your legal troubles. Not remotely."

He ignored her. "But also the income was unreported. I failed to pay taxes. What that means is that everything of value that I own . . . is subject to seizure."

He had her attention now. "You mean your fancy car, your apartment? All this new stuff my lawyer is so pumped about?"

"I mean everything. I may not be able to come up with the alimony for a while."

"But—"

Her face hollowed out; he was afraid she was going to cry. He took the fat manila envelope out of his pocket and pressed it into her hand. It contained $300,000.

"What's this?"

He didn't answer. "Don't spend it for a while or they might come after it. 'Ill-gotten gains,' you know. What you want to do is hide it somewhere—maybe the folks—you'll know who to trust. Tough it out for a a while." He bent down to pet the dog.

He was going to miss Whitey.

A certain giddiness was coming over her face. He knew that she'd count the money as soon as he left. He would have done the same.

From the car he looked back. She stood in the doorway and raised her hand in a little salute as he drove away.

———

White lines furling away underneath him. Through Balti-
more, over the Delaware Memorial Bridge, up the New
Jersey Turnpike, across the river to Morrisville, where he
wound through the familiar played-out streets until he
reached the Shady Grove Cemetery. A pallid old man in a
forest green uniform looked at him curiously and pointed
to his hand and nodded at the baseball gloves that he carried. "No ball playin' in here, mister." Marcus nodded.
The man's pallor was so great, it would not have been hard
to believe that he'd just scrabbled his way up from one of
the graves. "Respect for the dead!" the man said in a so-
norous voice. "Yessir!"

Hazy sunshine. Ninety-four degrees. Air quality: un-
healthy. The sun glared, a bleary ball behind the poisonous haze. The vegetation was prostrate, exhausted, the
grass withered and brown. By the time he reached the
grave, the shirt Marcus wore was plastered to his back;
drops of sweat slid down his spine.

JEFFREY ANTHONY MALONE
Much Beloved Son and Grandson
1974–1987

He ran his fingers over the engraved letters. The granite was warm from the sun. The grave was neat, tended; a
wreath of plastic flowers, garishly blue and pink, lay on the
brown grass. Fay's parents, no doubt. He stooped and
placed the gloves against the stone. His own and Jeff's,
kept all these years in his desk drawer. In Jeff's glove he
put the ball Jeff had caught at a Phillies game, a ball

fouled off by Mike Schmidt. It was just possible that catching that ball was the high point of Jeff's life.

Playing catch was certainly the spine of his relationship with Jeff. Jeff was so competitive, so driven, that it was only when doing something like playing catch that he remained free of the terrible pressure he put on himself. The ball looping back and forth. Nothing to win or lose. No way to measure yourself against anyone else. Even so, Jeff often tried to impose a structure: "Let's see how many we can do in a row!"

But Malone had always resisted, insisted on the open-ended ritual. "Nah! Let's just toss it around." They had played catch in Colombo, in Larnaca, in Karachi, in Luanda, in Morrisville, in Arlington, in dozens of other spots. Malone ran his fingers over the stone, over the incised letters. "Jeff-o," he said out loud. His baby name, a name he'd forbidden them to use once he was five or so. Malone turned and walked away.

With Karen, he wanted to avoid a scene, so he decided to tell her in a public place, a restaurant, where the presence of other people would buffer their emotion, or at least turn down the volume.

He told her he was in the mood for steak and took her to a place in Arlington. She sat across from him in the viciously conditioned air. It was one of those modern places, no thick rugs or draperies to absorb the noise. Marble, an open kitchen, uncomfortable bistro chairs. A rackety hubbub bounced off the hard surfaces.

Karen sipped a gin and tonic, looked at the menu.

Malone wanted to wait until their food was in front of them, until they were actively eating. He didn't want Karen to rush out of the restaurant. But suddenly, he couldn't wait; he had to get through it.

"I have to tell you something."

She looked up, concerned, alerted by the strange tone in his voice. His throat constricted; he took a sip of beer, leaned toward her.

A male voice behind him said, "Is it fucking freezing in here or is it just me?" Malone had the impulse to turn and engage this voice in conversation but forced his attention back to Karen.

"I'm guilty, you know. I'm not quite the shit they're making me out to be, but I won't get off. My lawyer tells me ten to fifteen years. Not as a sentence. Ten to fifteen years that I'll have to do. That's the best-case scenario. That's if they don't decide to make an example of me."

Karen's face went blank, smooth as a mask. This was something he knew about her now, the habit of hiding behind that blankness. "Maybe he's wrong," she said.

"I don't think so. And I can't do it." He paused a second, gulped some beer. "I *won't* do it. I'm going to leave the country."

The sentence drifted into the air between them. The man behind Malone said, "You can't feel bad for the Knicks. They're fucking brutes." Once again Malone wanted to turn around and discuss the NBA play-offs with this stranger rather than proceed with Karen. He felt marooned, perched on his chair.

"You mean you're going to become a fugitive?" Karen said. The word sounded strange, old-fashioned somehow. "Where will you go?"

"I don't know. Some place an arms dealer won't make too much of a stir. Maybe the Middle East." There was that sense, becoming familiar to him, of ... not lying ... but leaving a false impression. "That's one of the things I wanted to talk about. I want to come up with some way to stay in touch, some way we can communicate." His voice was gaining velocity. He was talking faster and faster, as if by getting through it faster the meaning of his words might have less impact.

Karen winced, as if in a glare. "Some way short of telling me where you are."

"No. It isn't that—"

"No. Nothing like that." She pushed a lock of hair away from her face with the backs of her fingers.

Malone was heartened. This was going as well as he could have expected. Karen was angry, but she wasn't falling apart on him. The waiter arrived behind her shoulder. Malone made a circle with his finger, another round of drinks.

"The thing is," he told her, "if you know where I am, either of two things can happen: I can get into trouble, or you can get into trouble. Because they *will* subpoena you."

"You assume I'd tell them."

"They will *order* you to tell them. The whole truth and nothing but the truth. They'll put you under oath. You can't refuse. Either you'd have to perjure yourself or ... they'd cite you for contempt."

"Well, I *would* perjure myself. Elementary ethics: in a coercive relationship, the ordinary obligations don't hold. All those Nazis, you remember, just following orders, that didn't cut it, because in ethics there's always a hierarchy. And in my hierarchy, your well-being would come ahead of the state's request for information. And . . ." She stood up. "It's time to go home now," she said.

She sat on the bed, resting her head against the head-board, her knees hunched up to her chest. She kept her lips pressed together. He could hear the television, faintly, through the wall, from the Kangs', a rolling mumble. He sat down next to her, took her hand in his, kissed her knuckles. She kept staring straight ahead, wouldn't look at him.

"Karen." A moth batted against the window, the soft thump of its body like an erratically beating heart. "What am I supposed to do? Plead guilty, do the time, ask you to wait for me? I can't do that."

"You could *ask* me to go with you. You could at least ask."

"I couldn't ask you to get into all that. I mean for your own good."

"Oh, I see. For my own good! You know, of course, you would know that—what's good for me."

"Look . . . Karen. I wish—you know how much you mean to me. This is as hard for me—I wish it wasn't this way." He fumbled with these clichés. His voice stumbled and faltered.

"So when are you going?" Her voice sounded almost conversational. Outside, a car door slammed. "Or wouldn't that be good for me either . . . to know that?"

"Karen . . . look . . ."

"What if I want to come with you?"

"No. I don't want—"

"Do you have any idea how patronizing this is? I mean what have we been doing here, Marcus?" She shook her head and spit out what was supposed to be a laugh.

"I can't let you come with me."

"Listen to you. You can't 'let me.' I don't believe this. You can't *let* me. You can't *allow* me."

From the Kangs' came the muffled sound of canned laughter, a giddy ripple of programmed merriment.

"Maybe in a year or so," he whispered. "Maybe—"

"I get it," she said suddenly. "We're in *Casablanca* land. You're Bogart, I'm Bergman, and you're sacrificing 'our love' for my safety."

He was startled. Without consciously thinking about it, that was exactly what he had thought; he had couched his whole departure in those grandiose terms.

She turned toward him. "It's not the forties, Marcus. What if she had an opinion about it? What if she wouldn't get on that plane? What if I would?"

"Karen," he said finally, "I'm going to be on the run for the rest of my life. I'm going to be one of those guys on the post office walls. With a price on my head. Chances are I'll wind up broke and crazy in some fly-blown dust bowl like Khartoum. Unless someone kills me for the reward, in which case maybe I'll get lucky and die in a good hotel."

"You," she started, but then her voice faded.

She leaned in to him and then she kissed him and he realized after a moment that she wanted to make love. He felt that her face was wet, that even as they made love she was crying, but that didn't stop him.

When it was over, they just rolled apart and stayed there

in silence for what seemed to be a long time. Her head was on his shoulder. He turned toward her. "Karen—"

She sat up. She pushed her hair back from her face. "Please don't talk, Marcus. Please don't say one more word. Just get out."

18

VIENNA

JUST AS SWITZERLAND TOOK THE POSITION THAT A CLIENT'S financial affairs were none of the government's business, Austria was famous for not keeping too close an eye on exactly who came into or out of its territory. If you could launder your money in Switzerland, you could launder your footprints in Austria. In addition to its lax border controls and its popular policy of not stamping passports, Austria had an enviable geographical position, Czechoslovakia, Hungary, and Yugoslavia on one shoulder, Germany, Italy, and Switzerland on the other.

Diamond had supplied Malone with four passports and pocket litter for each. Of course it wouldn't do to be caught with this wealth of identification, but there, too, Diamond had been helpful, supplying a state-of-the-art Agency suitcase with a truly ingenious false bottom.

Today he was flying as Keith Wald, a sporting goods

importer from Reston, Virginia. Arriving in Vienna, he was not nervous, only tired from the bad air and worse food.

The bored young man at passport control barely glanced at his passport before nodding him on his way. In training Malone had been taught methods to control nervousness—meditation, deep breathing, biofeedback to lower the pulse—but today there was nothing to be nervous about. His own name and passport number would have been tagged into the computer, but since he wasn't using them, that wasn't a problem. The terms of his bail required him to check in by telephone twice daily (between nine and eleven and again between three and five). He'd called in at five. His flight had taken off at seven-thirty. Because of the time difference, he'd be in Prague before anyone would realize that he was missing. Only then would the U.S. marshals' service begin to move, calling, then *knocking* on doors: his office, his friends, his ex-wife, his lawyer.

His girlfriend.

The bail bondsman would be put in the picture. Malone's name and fingerprints and photograph would be sent to Interpol, and a red alert would be issued internationally. If Diamond was playing it straight and the Agency did not know about him, his picture would appear on any number of lookout lists. But by then he'd be in Prague.

An hour after his arrival in Vienna, he flew out on CSA using the name of Fielding Hart.

At the Prague airport, he stopped at one of the travel kiosks to make hotel arrangements. It was the way he liked to operate when he was "driving the horizon"—last-minute arrangements, decision by intuition. It was more difficult to keep track of someone who didn't have plans.

The agent asked him where he wanted to stay in the city and how much he wanted to pay. He knew that eventually he'd put in a good deal of time at hotels like the Inter-Con—the preferred chain for arms dealers—but he wanted to lay up for a day or two, get oriented, recover from jet lag. A hundred dollars, he guessed, and the Old Town.

"Oh, you can be very nice for a hundred dollars." She opened a loose-leaf book. "Well, let me see. There is the possibility of this one." A plastic-covered sheet displayed a building with arched doorways, a front entrance crowned with a thatch of flags, and a room that looked spacious. In fact, it appeared to be a suite, and that was what he liked about it: its size.

They say everybody's afraid of something. General de Gaulle, that old warrior, had once been asked what he feared. "The shipwreck of old age," the general replied. But that was a reasonable fear. For many, there was a more direct terror, irrational, something that fastened one wriggling and powerless as if at the end of an entomologist's pin. Malone was claustrophobic. And although he had learned to subdue it, to ride in elevators when absolutely necessary and to move easily in crowds, it was always there.

"Looks fine," he said to the agent.

She was surprised by his hasty agreement. "This is not my only possibility," she said in her charming voice, anxious to show him the splendid variety of modestly priced accommodations in the Old Town, but he had made his decision.

After securing his hotel room, he went out—with his map—to get the lay of the land. In Vietnam, in the Delta and in the Highlands, the ability to pass through the world without being noticed had been a question of camouflage, of Malone knowing how to disappear in plain view. Among other things, it required a keen sense of place, an acute awareness of the world outside—and a stillness that came from the inside.

But he wasn't in the Delta or the Highlands anymore, and now his survival depended upon his ability to pass unnoticed in a room, in a crowd, on a bus, in an elevator. It was no longer a matter of camouflage but one of disguise. The truth was: people noticed Malone. They always had. When he entered a room, heads turned and conversations drifted—just for a moment, but it was there. You could tell. People were curious about him. They always had been.

This was hardly an ideal trait for a spy, much less for a spy on the run. Still, even if it were impossible not to be seen, there were things that he could do to limit the attention that he received—or, failing that, to leave a false impression. It was only a question of tradecraft.

It was particularly useful to project an appearance of stupidity—this on the principle that stupid people are less interesting (and less threatening) than intelligent ones. Operatives in the field also found it useful to eliminate the appearance of alertness, because the condition of alertness is contagious. A worried or suspicious man, a fidgeting man, makes other people nervous: what does he know that they don't? And then a person who seems interested in what he is doing is always less noticeable than a person whose interest is directed elsewhere. Which is to say that if you don't want anyone to notice that you're waiting for someone, read the book in front of you—don't keep looking up at the door.

Malone spent the evening walking through the crowded streets. The town was absolutely stuffed with tourists. Every street corner had a perplexed visitor grappling with a foldout map. Malone fit in perfectly.

It was unbearably hot in most of the restaurants, and he ended up at a sidewalk café where he ate a sturdy plate of trout and potatoes.

At one end of the square was a huge art nouveau statue of Czech religious reformer Jan Hus, familiar to Malone because of a photograph Diamond had shown him. Diamond's photo had an arrow pointing to the spot on the plinth, directly below the feet of Jan Hus, where Malone was to check daily for a yellow chalk mark. The presence of the chalk mark would tell him to listen to his shortwave radio (a Sony, bought at the duty-free shop at Dulles for about $250) at 10:00 P.M. He would tune to a specific frequency and wait for his call name—which would always be read by a woman speaking Spanish.

Very few people knew anything at all about the numbers' stations. There were dozens of them on the shortwave band, broadcasting messages encoded by numbers, and/or by the phonetic alphabet. The broadcasts went on for hours on end, with the letters and numbers transmitted in groups of five and in languages as diverse as Serbo-Croat and Hindi. The only people who heard them were spies and ham radio operators, and the latter didn't understand a word.

The hands-on work was, in fact, the responsibility of

the Army Security Agency, or ASA, working out of secret facilities such as the one in Warrenton, Virginia. While virtually every intelligence agency in the government had recourse to the Vint Hill Farms facility in Warrenton, the CIA and DEA were the regular customers.

The lion's share of the broadcasts were in Spanish because most the communications were directed at agents inside Cuba or, for the DEA, operatives in Central America, Mexico and Colombia. Since Malone spoke Spanish well enough and since it would make broadcasts to him blend with the large numbers of broadcasts in Spanish, his call was also in that language.

"Atención, vagabundo. Atención, vagabundo."

This would be repeated several times before Malone's message started, the numbers in Spanish, the letters phonetic.

The key to the message, in Malone's case, was the *Cadogan Guide to Prague*—chosen because it was unexceptional and would be easy to replace, although Malone had to be sure to buy the same edition.

The first number in the message identified the relevant page of the book—albeit inverted. Therefore, if the first number was 47, the page in question was 74. If the initial number was 702, that meant 207.

After the first number, there was a pause. The second number corresponded to the line.

Then Malone was to open the guidebook to the proper page, find the line, and configure the code. The code had to be reconfigured each time. It was a simple system. The first letter in the line—which might be a *T* or a *K* or an *F*—became *A*, the second became *B*, and so on, until an alphabet was constructed. When you arrived at a letter that had already been used, you went on to the next new one. *Q* and *X* were exempted from coding and were to be used in plaintext. Zero remained in plaintext. A numerical progression was established in exactly the same way as the alphabet. If the first number appearing on the key page was "2," "2" became "1," and so on.

Telephone numbers were always preceded by the word *hello*.

So once he heard his call name, the first group of characters would be the inverted page number, a pause, the line number. Then the Spanish word *repeto*. The page and line numbers would then be repeated three times. Then the message, which consisted of five-letter groups, a pause between each, until the end, when the voice said: "Final. Final. Final." The message would be repeated, every hour on the hour for two days.

Once he constructed the alphabet, it was simple, if tedious, to decode the message. And as long as no one knew the book, it was secure enough. The best thing about it was that Malone had no incriminating equipment or paperwork. No keypads. No transmitters. Only the shortwave radio, which was also a regular radio and otherwise unremarkable. As for the guidebook—it was a guidebook. Half of the tourists in Prague had one just like it.

In front of the plinth of the Jan Hus statue a guitarist had set up. He was singing—badly—"Blowin' in the Wind." Malone edged through the crowd to get closer. Not that he expected it, but there was no mark. A woman stood and watched, and something about the set of her head reminded him of Karen. He walked away.

He walked past the point where *he* was to leave a mark if he had a message to send. This was at the intersection of Husova and Liliova Streets, and he found it without any problem. His messages would use the same code, but this time written on a flimsy paper and hidden in a drop device.

A chalk mark is delivered by taking a chalk stub from the pocket, grasping it between the knuckles so that it barely protrudes, and simply brushing the back of one's hand against a surface. In a crowded venue, such as the Jan Hus statue or Malone's street corner, even with photographic surveillance it would be difficult to pinpoint who had left a mark.

Chalk marks and dead drops. These were the old methods, clunky and antique. They seemed almost quaint in an era of computerized communication and NSA satellites so powerful that overflights above the North Korean nuclear site were capable of monitoring not only the number of people present but—just about—their cranial measurements. Still, the old methods had the advantage of a small footprint—virtually no paper trail and compartmentalized access.

He looked on his map for the large patch of green representing Stromovka Park. He took a tram across the river and up the hillside. He was running four times a week now. He had his mileage up to about twenty-five a week, and for the first time in a long time he was feeling fit. The heat was oppressive, and he saw no other runner. The photographs he'd seen, and then burned, had been in a series. One, the entrance to the park. Two, a shot of the paved path and the elegant, but boarded-up, building half a mile along. The building sat on an overlook, and there were benches provided for those who wished to look at the view. The final photograph was of a trash receptacle, one of those old-style metal ones, with the bands of metal curving out to make a wide opening.

A drop could be anything—a pencil, a cigarette lighter—but the most popular items were trash. For years, beer and soda cans had been used. They were ubiquitous, more or less impervious to the weather, and a fairly lengthy message could be left inside. The age of recycling had put an end to that.

When it had been established that Malone would be in Prague, Diamond had decided on the cigarette package. Czechs were still smokers, so empty packets were common litter. A message could be concealed on flimsy paper secreted between the interior foil and the stiff paper of the pack itself.

The arrow in the photograph pointed to the ground, near the stone wall—as if someone had tossed an empty packet of cigarettes toward the bin and missed. There had also been a close-up of the packet in question—the most popular brand in Prague: Petras.

Malone stopped, leaned up against the railing, stretched his calf muscles.

On the way back, he got off the tram in Mala Strana to visit a third site. Because it was important to know if your messages were received, there was a mechanism for that as well. In Malone's case, if he received a radio message, he was to leave a chalk mark on a concrete abutment near the Charles Bridge.

When Malone left a message for Diamond in Stromovka Park, the radio would signal its receipt at 10:00 P.M. with the words: "Atención vagabundo. Receto," repeated every hour on the hour for forty-eight hours.

The next day, he had more business to attend to. First, a safe house. Apart from his actual residence, it was important to establish a place to go to ground, a place to hole up if and when things got rough. He consulted an estate agent, presenting himself as a businessman who would be in and out of Prague. He was after one room, with a kitchen and bath, what the British called a bed-sit.

He slipped the agent an envelope with $300 in it—"for your help." She blushed and said the fee was included. He insisted. The next day he took the first place she showed him, a large, pleasant high-ceilinged room in a section of Prague called Vinohrady. The word meant "vineyard" and the area had been planted with grapes for centuries. His room was in the back, on the ground floor of a dilapidated nineteenth-century mansion. He met the stiff old couple who owned the room, which they had divided off from their own apartment. They insisted on giving him a beer in the garden. He gave them $2,200 for six months' rent. They seemed embarrassed to take it.

He asked the the realtor to explain to them that he would not be there often but that he disliked hotels. "That suits them," she told him. He waved good-bye. The key he received was large and old-fashioned.

He spent the afternoon at an outfit called the Business Club on Karlova Street, a concern that serviced the capitalists who had descended on Prague in the years since the Velvet Revolution. Malone was shown around by an aggressively friendly American named Mike, well under thirty, who delighted in showing Malone the yuppie gizmos at his command—fax machines, computers, copiers, printers, scanners, telephones.

Two hours later, Malone had acquired a beige cubicle, a telephone number, a fax number, the services of a Czech receptionist named Vlasta, and, thanks to the miracles of desktop publishing, a passable letterhead and a stack of business cards:

MALONE ASSOCIATES, PRAHA.

He was ready to go.

19

_____

THE ALARM WOKE HER, YANKING KAREN FROM HER DREAM. She almost screamed out loud. In the dream, she was with Marcus. In fact, they had been walking along a beach, side by side, and somehow his penis had been inside her. Impossible, of course, but . . .

It was Tuesday. She called in sick. She was pinned between the sheets, exhausted, glued to the bed. She was sick. This was love as the ancients depicted it, not a blessing but an affliction. Shot through the heart. Lovesick.

She felt inundated by yearning, wave upon wave of longing that was going to have the gradual but eventual effect, like surf crashing against a rock, of eroding her substance. There was nothing attractive about this state; this was not the forlorn and romantic woman pining for her lost love, looking out to sea, hair whipped by the wind.

This was ugly, a beached fish in a gasping frenzy, the wild eye, the desperate writhing for the lost element.

Marcus gone. Forever.

By Friday, she only got out of bed to brush her teeth, drink water, and pee. It was that terrible listlessness she'd sunken into once before, that dead torpor.

She began to be nostalgic for the initial days after Marcus left—when she was heartsick, lovelorn. Now she would have welcomed anything as acute as pain; now there was nothing. A meaningless series of days stretched out endlessly in front of her.

She came to see that Marcus had been her last chance. She'd put it all on black and the ball landed on red. She would never recover this time; she was permanently disabled. In the soul.

How could she have capitulated so easily? She'd let him go like a child releasing a helium balloon.

But there was one chance. There was one thing he hadn't counted on—how nosy she was, how observant.

She knew where he was.

Or at least she thought so. She'd only caught sight of it for an instant—it was when she'd unexpectedly returned home for lunch one day to surprise him. He'd been in the kitchen when she came in, and there on the clunky table was a book—splayed open—and along its spine was the word: *PRAGUE.*

It barely registered at the time, but a few nights later, when he told her he was leaving, it came back to her. She saw it in her mind's eye, watched Marcus casually cover the book up, setting a newspaper on top of it. It was that smooth but anomalous motion of deception, maybe, that made the image stick.

Prague.

In the bank she had $2,300. Pathetic enough for a year and a half's scrimping. All in all, she told herself, it was probably cheaper to go to Prague than to pay for a shrink. At least she wouldn't have to spend the rest of her miserable life—assuming she ever pulled herself out of the stupor—wondering. At least she would have tried.

If Malone had wanted to disappear from the face of the earth, he might easily have done so. The passport blanks that he carried and the sizable bank balances that he maintained made his identity changeable and his range unlimited. But that wasn't the point.

The point was that the right people needed to know where he was and that he was back in business. Malone had to display his wares in order to get the attention of whoever had hired Hakki Delicay to buy the ingredients of a nuclear bomb.

Diamond instructed Malone to contact Salim Petrovic, a commercial attaché at the Consulate of Bosnia-Herzogovina in Prague. It was Petrovic's mission to defeat the ongoing arms embargo in place against his country. This job had been made more difficult by the recent arrest of a German arms dealer. The German had been about to make good on a large part of Petrovic's shopping list. Now the German was locked down in a cold prison on the outskirts of Hamburg and the matériel that he'd hoped to deliver was sitting in a Rotterdam warehouse in containers for which Malone held the bills of lading.

Malone bought a phone card at the tobacco kiosk and went to the pay telephone around the corner from his hotel. His conversation with Salim Petrovic was oblique and vague, but in the end they agreed to meet the following night at the bar in the Inter-Con. "I'm tall," Malone said, "and I'll carry a copy of the *Financial Times*." This British newspaper was a favorite identifier. It was available everywhere and was printed on distinctive salmon paper.

Arms dealing is a circuitous business. In the normal run of it, there were two intermediaries involved in putting the buyer and the seller together. The first intermediary was the person with access to goods (in this case Malone); the second (in this case Salim Petrovic) had access to funds, usually contacts within a government.

Arms were an enormous business globally, and not surprisingly the commercial sectors of the exporting countries were inclined to be helpful. The dicey part came when the would-be buyer was under restraint—an embargo, for instance, or trade sanctions. Or when the seller was restricted by treaty. It was forbidden, for example, to sell anything that might assist a country in developing a nuclear capability because doing so would violate the nonproliferation treaty.

Of course, there were ways around these difficulties. When Saddam Hussein, for instance, needed hardened maraging steel to make centrifuges for the uranium enrichment process, he'd simply bought the shares of a

German company that produced it. From there, it was an easy matter to get the steel to Iraq. The Germans had been *shocked*, of course, when all this came out in the wash, but in the meantime, they'd turned a nice profit on the rise in the shares' price.

Even more blatantly, it was sometimes necessary for everyone to pretend that something was not what it so clearly was. The Emperor's Clothes strategy. If no one blinked, it worked. Men like Marcus Malone came in handy in turning such a trick because they could blur the route and destination of interesting goods. They were able to provide, among other things, end-user certificates with hygienic destinations—not Bosnia, for instance.

The country of Bosnia had barely been recognized as an entity before the UN slapped an arms embargo on it, forbidding anyone to sell weapons to the new nation. This was too bad for the Bosnians because, in the breakup of Yugoslavia, almost the entire military establishment—weaponry, tanks, and soldiers—had stayed with Belgrade and the Serbs. UN spokesmen talked airily about how allowing Bosnia to arm itself would further destabilize the region. Predictably, the Bosnians were besieged, returning artillery fire with handguns.

At the moment, there was a cease-fire. But how long would it last?

And while the Bosnians were not themselves rich, there were Muslims in the Middle East who were, and they contributed generously to the cause. The Serbs warned that this was part of a grand conspiracy to reinvent the Ottoman Empire, creating a foothold for Islam in Europe—but the truth was more mundane. Muslims everywhere were aghast at the tepid reaction of the West to "ethnic cleansing" and the mass rape of Muslim women.

So the Bosnians had bucks. And, thanks to Diamond, Malone had what they wanted, sitting in a Rotterdam warehouse: Cymbeline mortar-locking radar, frequency-hopping Jaguar radios, and a brace of "Stalin organs." There were other items on Petrovic's shopping list—night-vision equipment, helicopter parts, various light arms, and a startling quantity of ammunition—and Malone was going to see that Petrovic got them.

Malone would have preferred to walk. But the Inter-Con was a good two miles from his hotel and it was hot, so he took a cab.

He wore a gun-barrel gray suit from Aquascutum, a Turnbull & Asser shirt, a Hermés tie that might have been hanging in the Louvre, and calf-skin brogues that had been hand-crafted on Jermyn Street. His price lists were equally well dressed, reposing in a $600 leather portfolio that he carried in his right hand.

The Inter-Continental, which at one time had surely been the only Western-style hotel in town, was an uninspired example of seventies architecture in the throes of an aggressive renovation now that it had newer competitors in Prague. Various plywood barricades and numbered slabs of marble attested to the fact that the renovation was incomplete. Malone stepped into the air-conditioning with an instant nostalgic recall of the climate-controlled life he'd left behind. The cocktail lounge was on the top floor and offered a stunning view of Prague's spires and rooftops. He entered the room—decorated in English hunt style—grasping his *Financial Times*. Hardly necessary. It wasn't difficult to spot Salim Petrovic. There were only five people in the large room, and the other four were two middle-aged couples.

Salim was a short, balding man with bright brown eyes. He beamed upon spotting Malone, stood, and beckoned. They shook hands, and Salim cast an admiring eye on Malone's expensive clothing and gestured to the seat across from him. The table demonstrated that he'd been there for a while. A tall glass of something, nearly empty, and a package of Sparta cigarettes—the ashtray held three crumpled stubs. The waitress teetered toward them on extremely high heels and took Malone's order—a gin and tonic that would no doubt cost as much as his entire dinner: pizza, grabbed on Wenceslas Square.

"Mr. Malone," Salim said.

"Marcus. Quite a view."

"It is the view that brings me here, this and, I must confess, the air-conditioning. We are not used to this appalling heat." He lit another Sparta.

On the table in front of them was a sealed cellophane packet of pistachios, Prague's substitute for a bowl of snacks. "Your English is so good," Malone ventured. "I bet you went to school in the United States."

"Bingo," Salim said with a hearty peal of laughter. "Syracuse University. I am an Orangeman! And you," he said, revealing that he'd done a bit of research, "graduated from Temple. An Owl. I still follow the Big East basketball. You had a good team this last year."

Malone laughed and nodded. Salim tore open the packet of pistachios and spilled them out on the table. A trio had taken its place on the tiny bandstand. The vocalist was a woman in her forties, of uncertain nationality and substantial girth, who wore a sequined dress. Improbably, she launched into a rendition of "Raindrops Keep Falling on My Head." She had some trouble wrapping her tongue around the English words.

"You've been checking."

"But of course. And only to find you are quite . . . famous. Tell me, when did you arrive in Prague?"

"Recently."

Salim laughed and then, although his cherubic face did not lose its smile, his eyes narrowed. "And how did you happen to hear of Salim Petrovic?"

Malone dismissed the question with a shrug. "What's important is that I have a copy of your shopping list. And I think I can help you with a number of items. I've added some other things that I have available, in case they are of interest."

He took out the list and handed it to Petrovic. It showed the items, the price per unit, the extension costs, the country of origin. It included the field guns and 50,000 rounds of HE (high explosive) ammunition and the Cymbeline mortar-locking radar, as well as the communications and night-vision equipment. It also included red mercury at a cost of $500,000 per kilo—not that Malone expected Salim Petrovic was going to bite on that; he was just putting out the word.

The trio launched into "If I Fell," and one of the couples got up to dance, soon joined by the other.

"FOB Trieste or Koper," Malone said. "Or even Dubrovnik. You would have to arrange land transportation."

Petrovic glanced at the sheet, then folded it in half and then in half again. "Your prices are high."

"They include Philippine or Belgian end-user certificates."

"One thing worries me—I see you list this matériel I have been hearing about, this 'red mercury.' This, I have heard, it is nothing, a joke. This makes me worry that the rest of your goods, too, are—"

"Don't believe everything you hear," Malone said. "You take some of this stuff, about a pound of plutonium, and a grad student in nuclear engineering, and you could bounce half of Belgrade back to the Stone Age."

The vocalist was singing a strange and impassioned version of Michael Jackson's "Man in the Mirror." It was lousy dance music, but the two couples were doing their best. The woman spun around and for a moment Malone saw the delight on her face, the absorbed happiness, and he was struck with a sensation of envy. Karen. He sealed the thought of her away.

"It's all we can do to defend our borders," Salim said a bit stiffly. "I don't think we're in the market for nuclear materials." He stuffed the folded list into his jacket pocket. "I'll have to consult my principals, and then I'll be in touch."

"Suit yourself," Malone replied. The waitress sashayed toward them with his second drink. "But don't wait too long. Other parties are interested and the warehousing fees are killing me."

"The items are ready for immediate delivery?"

Malone nodded. "I'll need a letter of credit from your bank, of course."

"Not my bank," Salim giggled, a high, whinnying noise. "My principals' bank."

"Of course." Next came a delicate bit of business—how to get Salim Petrovic his cut of the profits.

Malone followed his usual pattern.

He leaned forward. "Salim, do you think you could provide me with the name of a local agent in Bosnia to handle things from that end?"

"Of course," Salim said with a smile, and drew out a pen. "My cousin . . ."

The sequined chanteuse sang "It Had to Be You." The couples glided and dipped on the dance floor. Again Marcus pushed the thought of Karen aside and looked out at the gaudy sparkle of city.

Two days later, he had a remarkably similar meeting with Sadi Mosaghedi. This time the mating dance of capitalism took place on the rooftop terrace at the Adria. Was there something about arms deals in Prague, Malone wondered, that negotiations required a view? He elbowed his way through a polyglot throng of would-be diners waiting impatiently for a spot on the veranda.

The Iranian was portly and worldly, his skin a gleaming and robust café au lait, his hair so black it gave off a bluish sheen. He ate and drank extensively and expensively. It wasn't until they'd reached the coffee—accompanied by the Czech liqueur Becherovka—that the business at hand was discussed.

"I have studied your list," Mosaghedi said in clipped English, "and my people might be interested if we can come to terms." He did a fairly good job of transmuting what must have been his "people's" slobbering enthusiasm for some of the items Malone was offering into a nonchalant "just browsing" stance. It was an old game, familiar to anyone who'd ever bought a used car—not disclosing one's ardor for the deal before a price was struck.

"I have marked the items of interest," Mosaghedi went on, "and some price adjustments." He waved a carefree hand. "You will look it over and we will see.

"Oh," the Iranian said casually, flicking a crumb from his sleeve, "and I was asked to inquire about this 'red mercury' and its assistant, this TRX." He enunciated the syllables precisely and then frowned. "Frankly, we had heard that red mercury was nothing but bullshit." He turned his head up to watch the waiter set down two new glasses of Becherovka. "So . . . ?" He curled his forefinger through the air in Malone's direction.

Sadi Mosaghedi was leaning forward, his finger still curling lazily through the air as he waited for Malone to answer.

Finally, Malone shrugged. "I don't make it," he said. "I just sell it. Personally, I have no interest in constructing nuclear weapons, but for those who do, I understand it's useful." He shrugged again, caught the waiter's eye with an upward motion of his head, scribbled in the air to indicate he wanted the check. And tossed the ball back to Sadi Mosaghedi.

20

———————————

THE CHARLES BRIDGE HAD BEEN BUILT IN THE FOURTEENTH century, and for a very long time, according to Karen's guidebook, it was the only bridge to cross the river, linking the castle with the Old Town. A pedestrian bridge, most of the time it was crowded with people. Along its sides were thirty statues of saints, most of them black with soot. Below, white swans cruised the dirty water.

Each day, when Karen arrived in the morning to take up her post on the Charles Bridge, she went to the spot where, hundreds of years before, Saint John of Nepomuk had been cast into the river for refusing to betray the confession of his queen. The spot was marked with a bronze relief that was black with oxidation and age. The sculpture was of the bridge itself and showed a crowd of helmeted soldiers, with poles and staffs, standing at the parapet, gazing at the bright figure of Saint John as he tumbled from the bridge, his outstretched arms reaching for the water. That the figure was bright—that it actually *glowed*—was owing to its reputation for conferring luck upon those who touched it. Over the years, the gentle touch of a million hands had burnished the dull, blackened metal to a brilliant gold. For the sake of superstition, Karen might have set up right there, except that huge lines congregated, waiting in turn to touch the lucky scrap of shining bronze.

She'd taken a room at the Europa Hotel on Wenceslas Square—which was not a square at all but a broad boulevard. The Europa was a beautiful art nouveau hotel, with a plush velvet-draped lobby. Some of the rooms were said to be pleasant, but hers was an airless cube with furniture that seemed to be made of plywood—which was why it was so cheap, forty-two dollars per night.

She'd flown to Paris on a charter airline and taken a train to Prague. She read, cover to cover, the *Cadogan Guide to Prague*—which she recognized as the book that Marcus had so smoothly covered with a newspaper so long ago. She'd debated about the best place to station herself. She had considered the statue of Jan Hus or the astronomical clock in the Old Town Square. In the end, the bridge seemed to be the best bet. She was counting on the fact that Marcus was tall.

Each morning, she got up at seven, purchased a croissant for breakfast, a baguette and a piece of fruit for lunch, and a bottle of Mattoni water, and walked to the bridge. And then she stood and looked. When she got too tired or the crowds became so thick that she couldn't see, she hopped up on the wall. Even though it was capped with a pediment in an inverted *V* shape and sitting there was both precarious and uncomfortable. Even though it scared her and there was nothing to rest her back against. Even though one false move would send her the way of Saint John of Nepomuk.

The first day, she had suffered a bad sunburn. Her skin was pink and peeling, her lips flaking and sore. She bought some sunblock and a white cloth hat from the Kmart on Narodni. She had been shocked to see that familiar logo: Kmart.

Life on the bridge was interesting. Early in the morning, it was peaceful and easy to keep the vigil. Few pedestrians, the first vendors arriving and setting up. The rule was that only licensed vendors could sell things on the bridge, but anyone could play music. In the morning, there were no musicians—except, occasionally, a young violinist in tails and top hat, playing Mozart, Smetana, Dvořák. The vendors began arriving at seven, carrying their clever fold-up tables and stands, displaying their permits and laminated photos of themselves. The vendors sold postcards, photographs, drypoint etchings, woven barrettes, bad oil paintings. Down on the embankment, old women threw scraps of bread to the swans.

There were other, unauthorized vendors, and they usually stayed just near the beginning of the bridge so they could leave quickly if they had to. Three American boys with a hand-lettered sign reading: YOUR NAME ON A PIECE OF RICE set up a little stand most mornings. The snake man was another regular, a blond Norwegian giant with a rust-and-white-patterned boa constrictor named Bobo. You could drape Bobo around your neck and stand in front of the statue of a saint, and the blond guy would snap a Polaroid.

By noon, the musicians were out in force. There was

the man who played tunes on an arrangement of thirty wine glasses glued to a board and filled with varying amounts of water. He got an amazingly clear tone and played everything from "Edelweiss" to "Bridge over Troubled Water."

By late afternoon, the bridge was nearly impassable. Rock bands tuned up, attracting huge crowds.

A hundred times a day, at least, she thought she saw Marcus. A glimpse of black hair, the set of a pair of shoulders, a familiar gait. Each time her heart jumped in her chest, and each time it was someone else, although more than once she struggled through the crowd in pursuit of someone who, in the end, looked nothing at all like Marcus. Sometimes she had the panicked thought that she'd forgotten what he looked like, that he might walk right in front of her and she wouldn't recognize him. Or that he had somehow changed his appearance—bleached his hair, grown a beard. He was trained in that sort of thing.

She went to the McDonald's—just across the bridge in Mala Strana—to pee and sometimes to get a cup of coffee, worrying all the time that it would be that moment he would cross the bridge and she would blow it; she would miss him. It stayed light until quite late—nine-thirty or so—and she remained there until it was dark. Her eyes twitching and burning, her legs and back aching, her feet sore. She staggered back to the Europa, grimly satisfied that at least she was doing her best. Ten more days—that was all the money she had.

Already people were beginning to nod at her with gestures of recognition and some of the other denizens of the bridge had tried to strike up a conversation. She just smiled and nodded as if she didn't understand the language they spoke—though usually it was English. The number of Americans in Prague amazed her.

Her life had come down to this. She waited. She watched. And if Marcus never walked across the Charles Bridge? She might just lean back a little too far; she might just let gravity do its work.

Marcus was beginning to have vague fantasies that it could go on forever like this: Diamond had forgotten him and he was part of a bizarre behavioral experiment.

He'd received a good deal of money, willingly submitted to arrest and humiliation, and then abandoned his life. Apart from the trumped-up deals with the Bosnian and the Iranian, transactions involving the exchange of matériel and money he never saw—and which therefore seemed almost illusory—he had done nothing but wander around Prague. Well, there had been the calls to Diamond's "hello phones" to set those two deals in motion, but in neither case had Marcus actually spoken to a human being.

But then he took his morning stroll past the Jan Hus statue. A pigeon sat on top of the great reformer's head. And there it was—on the plinth—the telltale smear of yellow chalk. It seemed enormous to him, and garishly bright, although of course it was barely noticeable.

The radio message that night instructed him to pick something up at the dead drop in Stromovka Park.

When he jogged past the dead drop, there were two women sitting on the bench, taking in the view, so he ran a couple of miles farther and then doubled back. He seemed alone now, but he checked for surveillance. Stretched his calf muscles. Dangled to stretch his hamstrings. Picked up the Petras package and stuffed it into his waistband. The stiff cardboard dug into his skin. At the tram stop he put the cigarette package into his fanny pack.

In his room at the Jedna, he opened the cigarette package and pulled out a claim ticket and a small slip of paper with the penciled notation: "Naradzi Holesovice." The train station.

Malone spent half an hour idling on the bench, pretending to read an Italian edition of a Prague guidebook. He approached the left luggage office casually, glancing at his watch. It was a black soft-sided Samsonite, which the uniformed attendant—a wiry man with the unnaturally thin physique of a heavy smoker—heaved up onto the ledge with a grunt of effort. He said something in Czech that must have been the equivalent of: "Whatcha got in here? Lead?" To which the proper answer would have been, of course, "Yes." Malone paid the small fee, tipped the man an unexceptional ten crowns, and smiled and nodded his assent that it was heavy indeed.

The suitcase was one of those with a pullout handle and sturdy wheels—for which he was grateful. A taxi took him to the Jiri Hotel on Wenceslas Square, where he had taken a room for the day. He opened the case. Nestled between a layer of clothing and some white towels were the samples: twelve cylinders about the size of Mont Blanc fountain pens. He transferred them to his attaché case— and walked to the Jedna, where he continued to stay in the same spacious suite he'd taken the day he arrived in Prague. He worked hard to keep his gait casual and his shoulders even, despite the fact that the case must have weighed forty pounds.

Tomorrow he would take it to the safe house in Vinohrady. He had been there only once since renting it, making a point to wear a suit and carry an attaché case. He stocked the tiny refrigerator with beer, wine, Mattoni water, cheese, ham, olives. Put some crackers and instant coffee in the little kitchen area. He made a point of stopping in to see the Galushkas, presenting the wife with a bouquet of flowers. They gave him a beer. Since they spoke no English and he no Czech, their get-together consisted of smiling and nodding. All three of them were relieved when he nodded and smiled and indicated that he had to go. He did sleep there that night, however. He didn't want them to worry.

Karen's last day. She had exactly eighty-two dollars left. She'd already checked out of the hotel. They were keeping her bag behind the desk. She had her plane ticket, and the eighty-two bucks ought to just be enough for the train to Paris, the trip to de Gaulle, and then the bus and metro from Dulles. And then? And then she would throw herself on Millie and Aimee's mercy.

She sat on the bridge. She no longer believed she would see Marcus; it was just a kind of religious observance, to see it through to the end.

The glass harp man finished "Bridge over Troubled Water" and waited for those who were leaving to throw change in his hat. He then told his little joke: "And now for that Austro-Hungarian hit: 'Edelweiss.'" He said this every day, many times, delivering the word *Edelweiss* after just the slightest hesitation, with perfect comic timing. She overheard him tell one woman that he was a student at Charles University. This was just for the summer. Actually, the crystalline sound produced by the glasses was quite beautiful. Sometimes, when he played "Plaisir D'Amour," tears came into her eyes.

Her eyes. She'd had to buy sunglasses. The fourth day on the bridge, her eyes had turned as red as tomatoes. Sunburned, the pharmacist told her, and gave her some drops. Now her eyes never stopped stinging, itching, burning. Sometimes her right eye twitched, an annoying and uncontrollable flutter. Her back hurt. Her feet throbbed. Her heart ached.

What she did: she looked; she craned her neck; she scanned the crowd. It was very hard, *looking* all the time. It was exhausting.

She believed that every single person in Prague must go across the bridge at least once each ten days. So either she'd missed him or Marcus wasn't even in the city. Even that certainty she'd had—that memory of Marcus smoothly covering up the Prague guidebook—had disintegrated as the days went past. She wasn't even sure anymore. Maybe it had said "Poland" or "Portugal." Maybe it had said "Paris."

So she sat there, perched on the railing, grimly attentive to the passing crowd.

Marcus might not have seen her at all. She was perched on the stone edge, leaning forward, sunglasses in one hand, rubbing her eye with the other. She wore a hat, for one thing, and her face was obscured. It was the color of her pants that caught his eye, a distinctive slate blue. She didn't have many clothes, and she'd worn those pants a dozen times since he met her—and he'd taken them off her a dozen times, peeling them down over her hips. When she looked up, her eyes had that indirect gaze of secret service men, that scanning wide-angle sweep. Clichés came true in that moment she lifted her head: he couldn't believe his eyes; he froze in his tracks. The crowd buffeted past him.

He was on his way to meet the Iranian at the Three Ostriches—right on the other side of the river in Mala Strana. In his attaché case he had one of the lead tubes containing a sample of red mercury.

He was transfixed. She could not be there, but she *was*. "Karen!"

Her eyes fumbled around wildly and then finally focused on him. Her body gave a lurch, and her hat fell off. It seemed for a moment that she was going to fall.

His heart lifted, a light floating feeling in his chest. *Karen.* She closed her eyes, pressed them shut, and then opened them again, as if she thought she had suffered a hallucination. Then they were running toward each other through the crowd. A woman in a yellow T-shirt said, "Hey, watch it." Karen staggered and fell against him. Her skin was warm through the thin blouse, her face covered with a thin sheen of sweat. The crowd flowed around them as if they were a rock parting the flow of a stream.

Karen. The sudden shock of her in his arms released a surge of emotion so powerful that he was rolled over in it—like a bodysurfer caught in a wave. For a moment he felt obliterated, and then he recovered enough to kiss her. Her lips tasted of salt. They kissed long enough to inspire a smattering of applause.

"Oh, Marcus."

He fumbled out questions: "How did you get here? I mean what are you doing here? Karen? What? How . . ."

But she was shaking her head, crying, unable to speak. She leaned against him heavily as he led her down the steps to a café on Na Kampa—the island just below the bridge. They sat down at a tiny table outside the café, and immediately a waiter approached, regarding them almost with an air of suspicion. He lifted his head, waiting for their order.

"Champagne," Marcus said. "Bring us your best bottle of champagne."

The waiter's diffidence evaporated and he smiled. "You celebrate?" he asked with querulous expression. He looked at Karen, who sat fiddling with the stems of her sunglasses. The sun lit up her hair like a nimbus. The light caught on her cheek, and Marcus could see the bright, wet streak of a tear. "I'm thinking you are sad," the waiter said. "I'm thinking you are fight."

"No," Marcus said. "We're celebrating. Celebrating a miracle."

On the way back across the bridge, Karen stopped and waited in line to rub the little figure of Saint John of Ne-pomuk. Marcus didn't understand, and while they waited their turn she explained a little bit of the story.

"So it's for luck," she finished.

"Well, for luck," he said. "Absolutely. Can't have enough luck."

But when Karen got to the figure and pressed her fingers against the warm brass, she closed her eyes briefly. *"Thank you,"* she whispered.

21

"AUGUST 9," WILLOUGHBY SAID GLOOMILY. "BOMBING OF Nagasaki. It has to be him."

They were in Willoughby's family room, and Willoughby's dog, an ancient Labrador, limped through the door. The director rubbed the dog's head and ruffled his ears, and then the dog retired to the corner, collapsing arthritically on a round plaid dog bed.

Diamond sat across from Willoughby, peering through his half-glasses, first at a bar graph of city populations and then at the Xeroxed pages that showed, in reduced form, the satellite photos of San Diego found with Hakki Delicay. All of the pieces of paper were now stamped with various security markings, including the red *C*-in-a-square that stood for "COSMIC." And then there was the dossier on the Japanese, the long and bloody list of terrorist activities attributed to him, the two extant photographs of the man. Diamond looked at Yotaro Kawai's image and winced.

"The annoying thing is knowing who it is," Willoughby said, "and having no proof, no evidence, not even a trail to follow. But it's got to be him. Supposed to be dead, *confirmed* dead. But either he's done a Lazarus number or that was a very clever bit of business. Known bank accounts fallow all these years, then this letter of credit is found with the Turk."

The banking end had eventually yielded to pressure—which had surprised Bill Diamond—and information about the letter of credit pointed to a Japanese national. And the only one who fit the picture was thought to be dead: Yotaro Kawai. When Diamond asked what Willoughby had needed to do to get the banking information, his old friend had said, grimly, "Don't ask."

Now Willoughby shook his head, stood up. "No word from him, not since '86, not a sigh, not a *whisper*. All the more amazing because you can't miss him! Just four and a half feet tall. Face like Silly Putty. How can someone like that hide for *twelve fucking years!*"

The dog looked up from the corner.

Willoughby, whose calm demeanor was legendary and who rarely used profanity, was as close to rage as Diamond had ever seen him.

"Well, do you actually need to send me over personally to brief Malone?" Diamond asked coolly.

"I know! It's beyond the call of duty. It's too much to ask; it's risky as hell. Malone ought to be under surveillance by now. But the stakes, Bill." The director was falling into incoherence. "He's my last card."

"How can you be so sure it's Kawai? Why not some other Nagasaki survivor?"

Willoughby shook his head. "It has to be. He has the motive for bombing on that date and the wherewithal to do it. It's *perfect.* He has a taste for that, the impeccable response, the exemplary revenge."

"You'd better tell me everything."

The director sighed. "Yotaro Kawai. We tangled, you know, years ago. He's always been anti-American. Can't blame him, really. He was three years old when Truman bombed Nagasaki. Yotaro and his family were caught outside, near ground zero. His father was killed. His mother, who was pregnant, died a few months later. The baby—a boy—was taken by cesarean section. He was misshapen, apparently, with multiple birth defects, and survived only a few days. Yotaro was severely burned—his face and hands particularly because they were exposed—and of course he was badly irradiated."

The dog emitted a muffled bark. His paws twitched, and his muzzle quivered. Chasing something in his dream.

"So . . . Yotaro Kawai," Diamond summed up. "He was weakened, stunted, disfigured. He was orphaned and his home, I take it, destroyed." Diamond looked at his friend. "Then what happened?"

"After the war, he was sent to an orphanage on one of the out-islands. It was a cold, miserable place, more a factory than anything else. A hundred of these kids made Cracker Jack prizes in a great windowless room."

Diamond grunted, remembering the prizes.

"He was eight when his uncle came for him and took him away."

"This uncle—after five years, he just shows up?"

"He'd been in prison. A war criminal. He'd run the Japanese army's procurement operations in China. Which meant, basically, that he stole everything on the periodic table from Shanghai to Ulan Bator—along with any old masters that he came across. Paid for everything in scrip—totally worthless. And when the war ended, the uncle was one of the richest men in Asia—though most of his assets were untraceable."

"So what happened?"

"There was a lot of blood on the floor in Shanghai. A war-crimes tribunal sentenced him to death."

"But—"

"We got his sentence commuted. We needed him. The Cold War was gearing up and, whatever else he may have been, the old boy was rabidly anticommunist. We reached an understanding with him in Sapporo, let him out, and—lo and behold—two months later the Liberal Democratic Party was founded with a $10 million war chest. Bulwark against communism ever since. And it didn't cost us a dime."

"So he adopted Yotaro?"

"Mmmnnnnn. And then he started something called the Chrysanthemum Study Society—which, after a year or two, fell to Yotaro."

"We're not talking about flowers, are we?"

"The Chrysanthemum Study Society was sort of a paramilitary group. They studied traditional Japanese values, Bushido and all that, in a military setting. Over the years their agenda evolved, and they started showing up at demonstrations. The idea was to establish a Chrysanthemum Republic—a so-called Greater Asian Co-Prosperity Sphere—from Tokyo to Kashmir."

"One continent, under the emperor—"

"Exactly. But first they had to get American troops out of Japan. And that meant a strategy of terror. There were kidnappings, hijackings, half a dozen bombings at servicemen's clubs and military installations.

"Kawai was on the run for years, and . . . we were given to understand that he was in killed in Italy. Car bomb."

"You don't think it was him."

"I *did*. Until now there was no evidence that he was alive. And I don't understand why he stopped what he was doing. But now I think he's gone to ground somewhere. I believe that in red mercury he's seen his chance. I can't imagine anyone else having both the money and the motive and the . . . desire for pure vengeance."

"So you take this entirely seriously. You don't think there's a chance somebody was just fantasizing."

"Well, I might be tempted to think that—except for that letter of credit. Fifteen million dollars."

"Kawai has that kind of money?"

"Far more, I'd say."

"Well, what about time? The guy's only got a couple months."

"Not really," Willoughby said. "He's either got a couple of months, or he's got a *year* and a couple of months. The point is that once he gets the materials it's essentially over for us. These bombs are small. They don't give off telltale radiation. We have *tons* of drugs coming into the country every week, and we're talking about something the size of a softball. How hard is that going to be to sneak in here? He gets the materials; we've got no point of access."

"At least we know the target."

"But that doesn't help us! Not really. And we can only

hope he doesn't give up this idea of the perfect revenge—a nuclear device. Because if he decides what the hell, why not anthrax, we're fucked! You understand?" He clapped his hands together. "What are we going to do? We can't prove anything. It makes sense, but it's all supposition. We're going to evacuate San Diego on August 9? Just in case? I don't think so." He rolled his fingers through the air, the palm falling open in a gesture of loss. "And that's why it's worth going over to brief Malone."

"What can Malone do?"

Willoughby sighed. "Maybe nothing. Maybe everything. He's a worm on a hook. If we get lucky, Kawai finds him . . . and bites."

"And then what?"

"We bite back."

22

MALONE HAD LIVED IN THE HOTEL JEDNA SINCE THE VERY
first day he arrived in Prague, but he'd remained just a
guest until Karen joined him. She made friends easily and
immediately charmed the fiftyish ladies who ran the hotel—who in turn practically adopted her. They brought
her flowers, pears from the country, paper-wrapped slabs
of home-cured ham.

It wasn't easy to find an apartment in Prague, but with
the ladies helping Karen located one. It was a two-bedroom
flat in the Mala Strana, on the third floor of a beautiful
old building near the apricot-and-white French embassy. It
wasn't perfect, of course. It had swooping and ancient gray
moire drapes that disintegrated into dust if you pinched
the fabric between your fingers. It had nice old plaster
walls, wedding-cake molding on the dining room ceiling,
but it was painted a poisonous green. The furnishings were

a bizarre collection of comfortable old furniture and the kind of stuff available at Kmart: mass-produced plastic garden chairs, for instance, around the mahogany dining table.

Still, it was a great place with only one serious problem, a strange smell, something like burned cabbage. In fact, when they first went to look at it, they'd assumed someone in one of the apartments *had* burned cabbage. But it turned out to be permanent.

When they moved out of the hotel into the apartment, Karen took the ladies to dinner at a plush riverside restaurant with a view of the castle. Malone would not forget this: the two ladies, in their lacy finest, giggling and girlish, eating lobster and veal and getting slightly tipsy on champagne. With much blushing and pride, they presented Karen with a fine lace tablecloth. Karen still went to visit them every few days.

Life was ordinary and at the same time deformed by the constant tension of waiting. Marcus felt exposed simply walking down the street. Seeing things where there was nothing to see. Hearing things when there was nothing to hear. A subtle change in the light, a barely perceived movement in the shadows—his heart galloped.

Worse was his fear for Karen. Apart from the sickening responsibility he felt for putting her in danger, her presence also doubled his exposure.

Lying next to her in bed, listening to her soft, almost inaudible breathing, he contemplated the perversity of the situation. In his heart, he had abandoned any hope of love. He would have settled for much less: the day-to-day small pleasures like a good cup of coffee. A job that didn't make him hate himself at the end of the day. Then it happened, a gift from the gods. He fell in love. She loved him. A miracle. Not a day went by when he didn't thank the incredible largesse of fate. And he was also, as it happened, doing something important. His life meant something and he had someone to share it with. And yet . . . this left out the pain of love, the terrible responsibility for another human being.

A dozen times he pressed her to leave. He begged. Threatened. Pleaded. Just for a month or two. She flatly refused. "For my own good? I did that once before, Marcus," she said.

"For me," he insisted.

"No."

The simple fact was he couldn't scare her into leaving without telling her the truth. And the truth would only compound her danger.

He came home from a jog, and as he opened the door it occurred to Marcus that he was beginning not to mind the burnt cabbage smell; it was beginning to smell like home.

A while later, when Karen came in—her arms full of groceries—he was talking on the telephone, arranging to meet a German named Karl Obst later that night. She headed for the kitchen. Marcus finished with Obst and followed her in.

"You're not going to be here for dinner?" she said. "And I was going to make chili. Another meeting, huh?" The reproachful tone was hard to ignore.

Karen still thought he was an arms dealer—and she disapproved. From her vantage point, it was death that he was selling. It didn't help that, as far as she could tell, he was a *hardworking* arms dealer, selling just as much lethal equipment as he could.

And business *was* good—the successful deals with the Iranian and the Bosnian had seen to that. He'd become known as a man who came through. By now, he'd dispensed four of the dozen samples of red mercury that Diamond had sent, and he was already stalling would-be buyers with stories about delivery problems.

Occasionally, Malone traveled by plane; he couldn't always get the mountain to come to Muhammad. He'd been to Moscow, Budapest, and Damascus, delivering samples, flogging his wares. It was risky, transporting the samples, but they had been made to look like fountain pens in silhouette and he let them ride in the baggage compartment.

Diamond had cautioned him that they would not bear close scrutiny, and Malone believed him. They looked about as much like "writing instruments" as Cuban cigars looked like tampons, and besides, they weighed about a kilo each.

And there was plenty to keep him busy right here on the home front, too. Given his mission, he couldn't afford to reject a meeting with any new client—although almost all the meetings were a waste of time. But anyone might be fronting for the would-be nuclear bomber Diamond had briefed him about, and it was impossible to weed out likely prospects in advance. Most of them weren't even interested in red mercury, but it always took some time to get around to that fact.

So he'd been spending a lot of evenings in the sleeker hotels and restaurants, buying meals and drinks for people he didn't really know. Karen wanted to come along. He wouldn't let her, and he told her why: While most of the men he met (and they were *always* men) were Third World bureaucrats, military attaches, and diplomats, some were political fanatics—and some were criminally insane. They might be dangerous, but they were *often* bumptious—as men are when the only women they know are their mothers, their wives, and whores. So Karen took the advice, but his description of his colleagues didn't do much to improve her opinion of him.

The meetings? For the most part, they were fishing expeditions. Some of the men were looking for this kind of equipment, some of them wanted that kind of ammunition—and some them just wanted to make any kind of deal. They wanted to trade yellowcake uranium, maybe, for whatever they could get for it. RPGs? Submachine guns? Field telephones? And while they were discussing these matters, most of them wanted to have a good time. Apart from the restaurants and hotels, Marcus had spent more hours than he cared to remember in clubs with girly shows, his guests drooling over the parading Czech pussy.

"So what's it tonight?" Karen said. "Bombs? Bullets? Body bags?" Her face was flushed red; she pouted. For a moment he could see what she must have looked like as a little girl.

He put his hand on her shoulder. "Karen."

"It doesn't even sound like you," she said, "when you're on the telephone with one of those creeps. It sounds like someone *related* to you, the sleazeball in the family, the one who was always going to turn out to be no good."

"It's what I do."

"You don't have to."

"Maybe I *am* no good."

Suddenly her mood changed. "Oh, Marcus. That's not true." She came over and kissed him on the lips. She was like that, very quixotic; she rarely stayed angry for long. Unlike himself; he could carry a grudge from one lifetime to the next.

"Thanks for that vote of confidence."

"Explain to me," she said suddenly. "I don't understand it. Why is someone like you even necessary?"

"What do you mean?"

"Well, if the Czech Republic wants to sell a bunch of weapons to"—she waved her hand in the air—"I don't know, Germany, why don't they just *do* it? Where do you come into it?"

He explained to her that countries didn't make weapons; *companies* did. But . . . countries did do most of the buying. "So let's say Germany wants to buy ammunition from the Czechs. That *might* happen, straight military procurement, but probably not, not without an agent."

"Why not?"

"Because German manufacturers would be ragged that their own government bought military supplies from a foreign source and not from them." He paused and thought for a moment. "You have to understand that the sale of arms—and even boots and tents and things like that—from one country to another, even if private companies are the producers, is always a political act."

"Why?"

Malone smiled at her curiosity.

"When one government sells—or allows the sale of military equipment produced in its country to another government, basically, it means that the country buying the

211

weapons has the approval of the country selling the weapons."

"The approval to do what?"

"To use the weapons. Selling military equipment to a regime is considered a tacit endorsement of that regime. Because, of course, you're providing that regime with the means to defend itself . . . and even to extend its borders."

"I never thought about it that way."

"So, if Heckler & Koch wants to sell 50,000 submachine guns to—well, let's make it easy and say the IRA—that sale is not going to be very popular with Germany's common market partner Great Britain. So Heckler & Koch—who still want to sell their product—need an intermediary."

"And that's where you come in."

"Right. They sell it to me. I tell Heckler & Koch I'm selling to—I don't know—the Swiss army. The Germans know that's bullshit, but . . ." He shrugged.

"They didn't know."

"Right. And it's even more convoluted than that. Let's say the Germans wanted to sell those Hecklers not to the IRA but to . . . India. Now the Germans are not in some regional knot with the Indians as they are with England—but they do trade with Pakistan. Maybe the Pakistani government buys 100,000 widgets a year from Germany. Well, why should the Germans get the Pakis mad at them when they don't have to? They can just as easily sell the guns to an intermediary, who will then sell them to India, and no one's mad at anyone; it's just business."

" 'Just business.' " Karen shook her head. "So you're saying that arms dealers exist in order to enable countries that produce arms to *pretend* they care who buys them. But really to sell them to whoever wants them."

"That's capitalism. It's called diversifying markets."

Karen shook her head.

"There's another reason arms dealers exist," Malone said. "Probably a bigger reason."

Karen was sitting cross-legged on the couch. "What's that?"

He made the universal gesture: his thumb striking softly against two of his fingers.

"Bribery?"

"We prefer the word *commission*."

"To the *seller*?"

Malone shook his head. "No. It's the *buyer* who gets the 'incentives.' The seller has his own profit margin. But the buyer—well, a *hell* of a lot of money changes hands in an arms deal. And if you're the guy in, say, Iraq, and you're in charge of acquiring 50 million dollars worth of battlefield computers for your army . . . well, shouldn't you get a little reward, a little something for your patronage? One percent? Two? Just a taste?"

She pushed her hair back from her forehead and frowned. "Like a rebate when you buy a car or a smoke alarm."

"*Exactly*. Manufacturers reward buyers for choosing their product or entice them to choose the product. Selling guns is no different—because almost always the buyer has a choice. Our hypothetical Iraqi, he can buy his computers from the French, the Brits, the U.S.—not *directly*, of course, but still . . . he can get them. He has alternatives. So he's going to see which middleman can give him the best price and the biggest commission."

"A kickback."

"Well—there you go again. A *fee*. And that fee is one of the biggest reasons for people like me. Because the buyers can't pay commissions to their own people. That would be a scandal. That would be *corruption*. I mean the U.S. government isn't going to allow General Bigwig, their procurement officer, to take a percentage of the deal he cuts to buy 20,000 pairs of soldiers' pants. The general might be tempted to take—not the best deal for the army, but the best deal for himself. On the other hand, when arms deals go through an *intermediary*, someone like me, a cut is always part of the transaction."

"I don't get it," Karen said. "How does it work?"

"I simply point out to the customer that I'll need a local agent, someone to handle the liaison at his end. Does he know someone?"

"I guess he usually does."

Malone laughed. "He *always* does. And that's his fee, his cut—what goes to the 'local agent.' "

"And it doesn't bother you," Karen said, not looking at him but at the ceiling. "I mean it doesn't bother you that these weapons are going to be used. I mean"—and this time she looked at him directly—"it doesn't make you feel like you have," she put her hands in the air, "blood on your hands."

"Karen."

She stood up, walked stiffly into the kitchen, and started washing some glasses. He came up behind her and put his hands on her shoulders. "You don't have to do it," she said. "You could do something else." She laughed, a little bitterly. "I could get a job. I'm so versatile."

He wanted to tell her the truth, but he couldn't; it

would be self-indulgent. Telling her the truth would be like giving her a grenade. An unreliable one, which might blow up in her face.

"I'm going to change the subject before we get into another fight." He wrapped his arms around her from behind, his crossed hands each taking a breast. He rubbed his open palms over her nipples. He kissed the back of her neck, then moved forward, his lips sliding along her collarbone. A minute later, they were on the bedroom floor, and his job description was entirely beside the point.

Karlovy Vary, better known to English speakers as Karlsbad, was about seventy miles west of Prague. Malone took a train.

The arrangement was to meet in the steam room—the one with the sign indicating that it was temporarily out of order. Diamond was already there when Malone arrived. They sat in their towels in a large tiled room—its only occupants. The white tile was cracked here and there and reeked of eucalyptus, not a faint piney scent, but a deep and redolent stench. Malone wondered momentarily if Diamond knew he was claustrophobic and had arranged the site to put him at a disadvantage—but very soon he wasn't wondering about anything so trivial.

First Diamond was telling him that to the list of those trying to find him and "bring him to justice"—the U.S. Marshals' Office, bounty hunters working for the bail bondsman, and Interpol—he should now add the CIA. Malone sputtered and made some puny joke about the right hand not know what the left was doing.

Diamond managed a chuckle. "I know it's ironic. But

it's a deniable operation. The director can hardly call off the dogs without blowing your cover."

"Right."

"Of course, he's doing what he can—and that's quite a bit, really—I mean to see to it that the pursuit is ineffective."

"I'm touched."

"Still, he wanted you to know that it does mean that you're in the lookout books. He thinks you should burn the 'Keith Wald' identity—I guess that's the one you left the U.S. on, right?"

Malone nodded.

"And if you travel, you should probably make some effort at disguise."

Malone sat in a cloud of vapor, coming to grips with this idea—that the Agency was after him and that if he were to be caught, all knowledge of him would be denied.

"We have a little more information on the target man—we think he's a survivor of the bombing of Nagasaki, a Japanese national named Yotaro Kawai."

"That's not likely to do me too much good."

"If you could identify your clients—"

Malone objected. "How the fuck am I supposed to do that? Do I look like a private detective?"

"Well, can't you just . . . draw them out?"

Moisture dripped down the tiled walls. Occasionally a fat drop detached itself from the ceiling. The acoustics in the room made Diamond's voice oddly hollow and somehow dissociated from the man himself. It was as if the words were not coming from his mouth, but out of the steamy air somewhere behind him.

"The guys I do business with?" Malone started. "They get a little hinky when you start asking a lot of personal questions."

Diamond looked at him. Moisture collected on his eyebrows, and he swiped at them with the back of his hand. He looked old. He looked tired. He looked as if the last place he wanted to be was in a steam room at an aging spa in the Czech Republic.

"Mmmmm," Diamond said. "Well, you'll just have to do the best you can, I guess." He shrugged. He doled out the few clues he had in a grim and spectral voice. The letter of credit was from the account of a company called Real Impex. The bank? Vaduz branch of the Banque de Paris et Pay Bas. Malone should be looking out for those names on any financial instruments. And, of course, he should be particularly attentive to any approach involving a Japanese national. And whoever it was might be in a hurry.

"They're all in a hurry," Malone remarked.

Diamond shrugged.

"And I don't usually deal with principals, you know. Chances are, I won't ever know my contact's client."

"I understand. All you can do is your best."

Diamond stood up, and his towel slid off his thin white shanks. He pulled it back up and wrapped it around his waist. Diamond was supposed to leave first. Malone was to cook a little longer. As Diamond began to pad away, he suddenly turned back. "Oh," he said. "I don't know whether they covered it over here, but you've been tried in absentia. In New York."

"And?"

"It was pretty florid. If I remember correctly, they called you 'a broker of doom, a death merchant of the worst kind, a man without human feeling or conscience.' "

"Is that a quote?"

"More or less."

"Christ, now I know why people hate the press."

"It wasn't the press; it was the judge."

"Great."

"You got fifty-four years."

23

_____

KARL OBST WAS FIFTY, FAT, AND ANXIOUS TO PLEASE. AFTER
they had a drink, Obst wanted to go to U Flecku—"if you
don't mind, of course"—the 500-year-old beer hall in the
Stare Mesto. Malone had been there once with Karen that
summer sitting out in the beer garden under the stars at
long tables—while oom-pah-pah bands played and tourists
clapped and got drunk on the sweet dark beer.

U Flecku was dark and old, served delicious bratwurst
and schnitzel, and tonight, as always, it was crammed with
hundreds, a raucous crowd amid a background of polka
music. Powerful-looking waiters carried ten heavy liter
mugs in each hand. Obst beamed with pleasure when the
waiter slid two in front of them.

"To business." Obst chinked his mug into Malone's.
"Ja?"

Malone nodded his agreement. "Business."

Obst didn't get into it until he was on his second mug of beer and tucking away the last of his plate of bratwurst and sauerkraut, mopping up stray bits with a hunk of bread. Because of the noise in the place and because the seating arrangements were at long tables, Obst sat next to Marcus and spoke into his ear. Malone smelled his mustardy breath.

"Shall I be direct, Mr. Malone? My friend Salim Petrovic tells me that you can provide something my principal wishes to acquire."

"No kidding."

"Red mercury. In the quantity of four kilograms."

Malone inclined his head.

"Pending a sample and a happy result from the lab." Obst drained his beer. Malone signaled another round, although he did not intend to drink any more himself. He also pinched his fingers together so that the waiter would bring Obst a Becherovka. This was a popular combination in U Flecku—a Czech boilermaker. "This is possible?" Obst was asking. "A sample?"

"Of course."

"We've had disappointment."

Malone shrugged. "I don't think you'll be disappointed in my sample."

"Another thing of importance to my principal is the delivery time frame."

"Well, that depends, doesn't it? How long will you take with the sample? Where will you take delivery? Are there other items on your list? The financing is usually what slows things down."

The waiter slid the beers in front of them and, at Malone's nod, set the small glass of Becherovka in front of

Obst. Obst used his large, thick fingers to check off his points. "First, we do not require any other items. Second, we will take delivery anywhere in Europe—here in Prague if you wish, but we will pay a substantial bonus for delivery to my principal because, of course, we would like to test it. Third, if you will accompany the sample to where my principal is, we could test it and place the order immediately. The financial arrangements need not take long. Given all this, how soon could we expect delivery?"

Something tripped in Malone's brain. Test it? While-U-Wait? It would mean someone had a very sophisticated laboratory of their own.

"And the financing? You haven't even asked my price."

"What is your price?"

"One million per kilogram."

Obst hesitated only slightly before nodding. He tossed back the Becherovka in one gulp. "Ah. That is expensive."

Malone smiled. "Almost everything worthwhile is."

Obst laughed, a polite and robust "har-har-har." "This is true, Mr. Malone." He had now put away quite a quantity of beer yet he showed not the slightest sign of being intoxicated. "Supposing there is not a problem with money? How long do we wait for delivery?"

Malone hesitated. He'd been specifying two months—and he didn't know who Karl Obst might have talked to. He was already stalling the Iranian with stories about delivery problems.

"Six weeks if there's no hitch with the financing."

"That would be six weeks after the testing of the sample?" Obst asked.

Malone nodded.

"Mr. Malone, could you be persuaded to take a short trip later this week? Friday? A day of your time is all we will require."

"Where would I be going?"

"Ah," Karl Obst said, "there you are in for a treat. The beautiful young country of Slovenia. You can make your own transportation arrangements. Call me tomorrow at the Hoffmeister. We will meet you at the airport in Ljubljana."

Slovenia. Something tripped over in the back of Malone's mind. Something Bill Diamond had said about Hakki Delicay's various ports of call—before the Turk got his ticket punched in Zagreb.

"Actually," Malone said, following his standard procedure, "I'd prefer to take a room in a hotel in town."

"Ah, but you are welcome as our guest."

Malone shrugged. "I just never liked to stay at other people's houses. Even as a kid. Maybe I just like hotels."

"You make your arrangements and you tell us where to meet you," Obst said. "No problem." He raised his mug and waited for Malone to do the same. "How do you say? *Cheers*?"

"That's British," Malone corrected. "What *do* we say? Oh. . . ." He lifted his glass and chinked it against Obst's. "Here's mud in your eye."

They drank. "Mud in your eye?" Obst said in his heavy accent. "Mud. In your eye." He shook his head. "This I do not understand."

"Karl." Malone leaned toward him. "What do you expect when the people who are making up the sayings are crocked?"

Obst laughed, a full-throated chortle. "Here is mud-in-your-eye."

Late at night, Karen heard Marcus get out of bed. Balanced there, on the cusp between waking and sleep, she listened to him go into the living room. The scratchy sound of his radio. She had heard this before, but so far she had not asked him about it. She had to remember that Marcus had tried to keep her from coming to Prague. The fact that she had forced herself into his life meant she had somehow forfeited her right to pry or complain.

She knew that Marcus thought she was asleep, that he had waited until he was sure. She could hear the mysterious voice droning. "Tango, Alpha, Victor, Victor, Kilo." *What could this possibly mean?* she wondered. "Bravo," whispered the voice. "India. Charlie."

She stayed where she was. She was tired of fighting with Marcus about what he did for a living. But she couldn't help feeling sick at heart. She was living off it, after all: blood money. One of the problems was that she had no life apart from Marcus. She had to do something—get a job, take Czech lessons, something. She rolled over and closed her eyes and allowed the voice, which was meaningless in any case, to disintegrate into nothing but a faint noise.

In the living room, Marcus turned off the radio, emerged from the tent of the blanket, pulled out the Cadogan, and began to construct the alphabet. It took almost an hour, and when he decoded the message it was bad news. Very bad news.

"REASO/NTOBE/LIEVE/MOSSA/DINPU/RSUIT/ YOU/" quickly separated into the words "Reason to believe Mossad in pursuit you." So, to the list of those trying to find him and "bring him to justice"—the FBI, U.S. Marshals' Office, bounty hunters for the bail bondsman in New York, Interpol, and the CIA—Malone should now append the Israeli intelligence service, the Mossad. This was not good; this was, in fact, terrible. The Mossad was efficient, and it didn't play by the same rules as the others. If the Mossad caught him, they'd kill him.

Diamond had told him that the supposition was that the Israelis knew about red mercury; some of the Soviet project's scientists had immigrated to Israel in the early nineties. Israel was the single state with the most to fear from the spread of nuclear capacity. And that Israel would go to great lengths to prevent any state within reach of its borders from acquiring a nuclear capability had been demonstrated, time and again.

In 1979 Israeli commandos had infiltrated a closely guarded warehouse in La Seyne-sur-Mer, France, where French-built reactor cores were awaiting shipment to Iraq, and destroyed them before they could be loaded aboard ships. A few years later, when the Iraqis almost had a nuclear plant up and running, Israeli pilots staged a raid over the reactor site at Tammuz I . . . and demolished it.

It stood to reason that the Israelis would pay attention to red mercury, which is to say the Mossad would have noted a well-publicized arrest in New York and be more than a little interested in a fugitive arms dealer named Marcus Malone. And there would be very little downside to taking out "a merchant of doom."

Malone shredded the piece of paper and flushed it down the toilet.

24

HE WALKED DOWN THE STEPS OFF THE CHARLES BRIDGE AND left his chalk mark on the abutment to show Diamond he had received the message, then stopped at a kiosk and bought a pack of Petras and a tram pass. He'd dump the cigarettes out when he could do so without attracting attention.

Although not raining, it was a dreary day. Malone could taste the pollution in the air. Despite the fact that it was overcast, there was a sharp light off the water that made him squint. Prague. He had always pictured it a gray place, but the colors of Prague were earth tones, ocher and sand, the warm terra-cotta of the roof tiles. Today's malignant light made all the colors seem off, as if Prague were a badly exposed photograph of itself—or a movie shot through the wrong filter. The effect was of walking through an artificial landscape, a stage-set Prague. This sense of unreality was persistent and did not abate when he arrived at the Business Club and went inside. The light infiltrated the building, sharp and poisonous and false.

Vlasta greeted him, frowning and squinting. A big, robust blonde, today her complexion was pasty rather than rosy.

"Dobry den, Vlasta."

She made a sound somewhere between a whimper and a moan. "Dobry den, Pan Malone."

"What's the matter? You feeling okay?"

The moan again. "I have late night. I am drinking many drinks."

He nodded sympathetically. "I've been there," he said.

"To the Konvict Klub?"

This kind of misunderstanding was common with Vlasta, whose grasp of English did not extend to the idiomatic.

"No," he said. "I meant I have upon occasion had too many drinks myself."

"Ahhhhhh." The light dawned. Connecting the dots seemed to make Vlasta feel even worse and she moaned again.

He asked her to make flight reservations to Ljubljana and to book him a hotel room. Then he retired to his cubicle.

He had to compose a message for Diamond, after which he would have to encode it, go out, leave a chalk mark at Liliova, visit the dead drop, and leave the message. These methods were increasingly annoying. Malone yearned for a burst transmitter or even a crystal radio. He did have a number to call—a "hello phone"—but that was for an absolute emergency and this did not qualify.

But Diamond needed to know about Karl Obst and the trip to Slovenia. He needed to know that Malone had a customer with a sense of urgency—and a lab that could test red mercury on the spot.

He opened the guidebook at random to page 205, wrote down "502/9," and began to construct the alphabet. Encoding took time.

He left the mark at Liliova and walked toward the tram stop. By the time he got there, he was fairly certain he was being followed. The man in question was young, maybe thirty, with brown hair pulled back into a neat little ponytail. He wore a bulky tan jacket, blue jeans, and what seemed to be new brown shoes with thick, gummy soles.

It was the shoes that caught Malone's eye. At the stand where he bought the package of Petras he'd fumbled his tram ticket and bent to pick it up—and caught a glimpse of the gleaming chestnut footwear. He'd thought to himself, *Those won't last long.* Prague was hard on shoes. The sidewalks and streets in the older parts of town were made of small granite cobbles, no more than three or four inches square, not mortared but set in sand. There was a great deal of renovation going on, and where the cobbles were new the edges were still sharp, and the result was that shoes took a beating. All of his own shoes were scraped and scarred.

He got off the tram in Mala Strana and proceeded past the Polish embassy gardens—where a gardener was clipping the roses. He turned right up Thunovska, paused at the squat bust of Churchill near the British embassy. The street was very narrow, with buildings hemming it in—a perfect echo chamber—but he could not hear the man. *Gumshoe*, he thought. Meaning "detective." Shoes that obscured the sound of footsteps. His own loafers slapped against the hard cobbles. Turning the corner, he caught sight of his pursuer in his peripheral vision, perhaps thirty yards behind.

He headed for the New Castle Steps, which led to Hradcany Castle. Just as the "New Town" in Prague dated from medieval days, the New Castle Steps were not new but dated from the 1400s. There were hundreds of them. The grade was steep.

Let's see what kind of condition Gumshoe is in, Malone thought. He picked up speed as he ascended, taking the steps two at a time. The pace was anaerobic and after a minute he was winded. But he was in good shape now and forced the pace. The sound of his own progress was enough so that he could not actually hear the man's footsteps behind him. He didn't turn. Halfway up, his quadriceps began to ache and burn and his breathing became labored and painful. When he reached the top, he was gasping and his muscles were screaming. He turned. Gumshoe was still with him but farther back.

Hradcany Castle is not a single building but a small town, a bewildering maze of cathedrals, churches, palaces, courtyards, cottages, and towers. He pushed past the tourists lined up to buy tickets in the courtyard, hurried through the maze of streets, past St. Vitus Cathedral, made a wrong turn down Golden Lane, reversed, pushed rudely through a crowd of British tourists.

"Say," said a man in black. "Watch your bloody step."

"Rufus!" complained a woman's voice. "Watch your tongue."

Malone broke into a jog, passed the creamy facade of the Lobowicz Palace, and finally arrived at Hradcany's west gate. He emerged at the top of the Old Castle steps. He stopped halfway down, at the far side of a stand where a young woman displayed drypoint sketches of the castle. He was breathing hard and sweating, but when he looked back he did not spot Gumshoe. The woman spoke to him in Czech, quoting prices for the sketches. He smiled apologetically and resumed walking. By the time he reached the bottom, his tortured legs quivered with fatigue.

He walked quickly to the Malostranska metro station and took a taxi from the stand, asking to be let off near Stromovka Park.

Malone got out at the Hotel Splendid—a half block off the park. As idly as he could, he extracted the last Petrus from the pack, crumpled the package, and threw it at the dead drop. He was tired now and very much wanted to be with Karen, preferably in bed—preferably in Karen. But he stayed there instead, smoking, telling himself that he had to be disciplined, that he had to pay attention to tradecraft. He had to create a simple illusion: Man Smoking in the Park.

There is something about outwitting a tail that inspires a momentary but pure euphoria. A gleeful and juvenile sense of triumph that probably goes back to childhood games. But in Malone's case the euphoria quickly receded. Surveillance was a labor-intensive activity, and that was a bad sign.

After a while, he ground out the cigarette with his shoe and walked away at a leisurely pace.

The next day, Karen went off around noon to have lunch with her friend Jana. He stayed home, staring morosely at

CNN. Finally, in the late afternoon, he went out for a run. Maybe it would help him think. His form was choppy, his quads tight and sore from the chase up the steps.

Fear. That's what the episode with Gumshoe had brought to him, and that's what he was thinking about as he loped across the bridge.

In FOG Ops, it had been said of Malone that he had ice in his veins, and in a way it was true. He could turn himself off like a light switch, if he had to . . . and sometimes he did. Once, during an operation in Lebanon, in Baalbek, a sniper who'd been shooting at their little party disappeared into a hole in the ground, vanishing into the earth like Alice in Wonderland or something. And Malone—so claustrophobic that he'd walk five flights of stairs before he'd take an elevator—had gone down after him in the dark. Followed him for a mile, or maybe it was only a hundred yards. But followed him, in any case, for what seemed like forever—and captured him and brought him back. Malone remembered A. J.'s face, the big black man laughing as he reached down to give Malone a hand, pulling him out of the street. A. J.—who died in a helicopter crash the year after this happened—knew about Malone's claustrophobia; he was the only one who did. And Malone could still remember what A. J. said: "You *cold*, homes! You a mothuhfuckin' lizard!"

But that was then. And the fear he felt now wasn't something he could turn off, because he wasn't afraid for himself. He was afraid for Karen. Any one of the parties looking for him—the Agency, the bail bondsman, the Mossad, the marshals—might go after Karen. What if they grabbed her?

He ran through the narrow twisting streets of the Old

Town, turned around near the Powder Tower, and then headed back. He realized that the only way he was going to persuade her that she was in danger, the only way he was going to talk her into going away somewhere for safe-keeping, was to tell her the truth. And that wasn't going to be pretty.

"Hello!"

She was in the kitchen, wearing jeans and a green T-shirt, her hair pulled up in a messy ponytail, half of it escaping from her pins and barrettes. She was making some kind of stew. Sautéing green peppers and onions and garlic.

"Marcus!" She put down her wooden spoon. "Guess what?" She put her arms around him and kissed him. Then kissed him again. Then reluctantly pulled away. She picked up the spoon and stirred the stew while she talked. "I got a job! Jana, you know, my friend at the Globe Book-store, well, someone just quit, and I walked in and—"

"Karen."

His tone of voice stopped her cold. She stiffened and looked up at him. "What?"

He turned off the burner, took the spoon out of her hand, set it down on the counter, and led her into the living room.

"What?" she asked again.

He told her. It took a long time. Starting with Diamond on the Staten Island Ferry telling him about red mercury and ending with Gumshoe chasing him up the New Castle Steps. "So I think . . . for your safety . . . we should think about where you should go."

"I know where *you* can go!" She got up and went to the closet and threw on her raincoat.

"Karen." He put his hand on her arm.

"Let go of me."

"Where are you going?"

"I don't know! *Out.*"

She walked out the door. He gave her a little head start, and then he followed her.

Karen's head was boiling, a black turbulence. She had no destination in mind; she was after sheer motion. As if movement alone might set her thoughts in order.

She walked along Bridge Street and then through the Gothic archway of the bridge towers, stepping out into the rain and wind as it sliced off the river. She threaded through the construction near Charles University and headed down Kriznovica. She wanted to walk along the river.

At one moment, she was relieved. Marcus wasn't a criminal. And she had been through such torment about that—his arms dealing. But then that comforting thought was obliterated by her sense of betrayal.

She'd been living with a stranger and a lie. Marcus. His face appeared in her mind. "Just business." "It's what I do." "I'm going to change the subject."

She walked past the Old Jewish Cemetery. Marcus—he was a "security consultant." Then he was an "arms dealer." Now . . . The CIA? The Mossad? Red mercury? Was this for real, or was it just another lie? Maybe he was one of those men who couldn't ever tell the truth.

She remembered visiting him in jail, his hand on the opposite side of the Plexiglas. That was just for show! She'd been so worried about him. And all this time, he let her think . . .

She remembered the night he told her he was going to leave the country and she wasn't invited along. That he was going to become a fugitive and life would be too dangerous for her. He had looked her right in the eye: *"Chances are I'll wind up broke and crazy in some flyblown dust bowl like Khartoum."*

She stopped and looked out across the river toward Mala Strana. Behind the haze, the sun was sinking like a bruise in the west.

And now what? *Now what?* What was she going to do? Stopping was a mistake. She had to keep moving. Was it sharks whose gills were designed so they had to keep moving through the water in order to breathe? Had to keep moving or else they would die?

It was easy for Malone, following Karen. Her blue jeans, green T-shirt. The streets were not crowded. The rain was enough to make people choose the tram or the subway, even for a short trip. He hoped she would just eventually turn back and head for the apartment. He had no plan; he just wanted to keep her in sight.

And then she turned a corner near the cemetery and he followed her, turning the same corner—only to find that in the ten or fifteen seconds that she was out of sight she'd stopped. Dead in her tracks, thirty yards ahead, staring at the sunset, totally lost. And so Malone lingered, looking in the window of a shoe shop. Looking at the reflection in the window. Looking at the man in the reflection, the man across the street, coming to a sudden stop as *he* turned the corner. This was not Gumshoe; it was someone else. Malone had seen him before—when he'd turned away from Karen on the Charles—a man with glasses and a military-drab coat with lots of pockets and zippers.

Whoever he was, Zippers was a professional. He paused for a second or two and then marched on up the street past Karen, disappearing around another corner, as if nothing had happened. Malone was sure he'd see him again or, if he didn't, it meant the man had been replaced by someone new.

Karen resumed her angry stroll, and Malone stayed with her, thinking: *We must have been followed from the apartment.* Karen turned down Revolucni. He'd been diligent about the apartment. They received no mail there. He had given the address to no one. It was rented under the name Fielding Hart. The telephone was in the landlady's name, and although occasionally he made short calls from there, he didn't give out the number. He was careful to take different routes and to be watchful whenever he met a contact or came from the Business Club.

They were now near the metro stop at Wenceslas Square. He watched Karen go down the steps until all he could see was her head, and then he sprinted after her. His intention had been simply to follow her until she calmed down—and see where she went. She made friends easily and had collected half a dozen pals during their time in Prague. He thought probably she'd go and stay with one of them. His plan had been to see where she went and then to arrive in the morning, ambush her with flowers, beg her forgiveness before she was really awake.

For a moment he thought he'd lost her, but then he caught sight of her again, descending toward the platform. There was a rush of passengers from a just-arrived train, a crowd of people coming up the stairs. They were students, laughing and joking, spread out so that the staircase was blocked. Malone pushed roughly by on the right and was almost through the knot of them when a young man in a Chicago Bulls T-shirt stepped into his path—entirely without looking. Malone crashed into him. Hard. The young man said something in Czech: an apology, Malone thought. Malone pushed rudely by, leaving behind him a stir of Czech irritation at his rudeness.

But the delay had been just enough. By the time he reached the subway platform, a train was pulling away, and Karen was gone.

He walked, stopping every so often to look back. But there was no one. Either Zippers was awfully good or the tail was no longer with him. He should have felt good about that, but instead, it worried him. He hadn't tried to lose the tail. So what had happened to it?

Karen was headed for her friend Jana's apartment in Busevice. She got off the metro and was walking up the hill, hurrying because of the rain, when the car pulled up next to her and two men jumped out.

She heard herself say, "Hey!"

Then she was in the backseat and her face was pushed down into rough fabric. She struggled, but the car was already moving and then her arm was bent up behind her back in such a way that any motion at all caused a terrible pain. Next she was yanked to a sitting position and a piece of cloth was jammed in her mouth, tape slapped across it, and some kind of hood pulled down over her face. Then she felt a sharp pain in her thigh. Just before she lost consciousness, she realized it was a needle.

25

MALONE'S VISUAL SENSE WAS HIGHLY DEVELOPED; IT WAS why he'd been such a good Lurp. A leaf twisted the wrong way, a broken twig, a tremor of motion—even in the dark, he could spot the telltale deviation. So he knew someone had been in the apartment, although the intruder had been careful to conceal the fact. His tradecraft was good, but it wasn't perfect. If it had been, he'd have taken Polaroids before he touched anything.

It was the spoon that confirmed Malone's suspicion. Karen had been stirring green peppers and onion and garlic—which remained in their pan, curled and cold. He had taken the wooden spoon out of her hand and put it down on the counter. He could call up the image in his mind, the precise angle at which the spoon had been set down. It was different now, yet neither he nor Karen had returned to the kitchen. As evidence, the tiny pool of grease that should have rested just under the bowl of the spoon was several inches to the left. He looked up. Probably the spoon had been moved to allow someone to stand on the counter and look on top of the cabinets.

Apart from the spoon, he wouldn't have known for certain that anyone had been there. That in itself made him nervous, the care that had been taken. Obviously, he knew he was being followed. So why be so careful? He thought about it as he walked from room to room and decided there was only one explanation: something had been put in the apartment. Two possibilities came instantly to mind. Number one was a bug. Number two was a bomb. The Mossad in particular favored the quick explosion as a method of termination.

The question was: what was he going to do about it? It seemed to Malone that a bug was far more likely than a bomb—but this was not a matter about which he could afford to be mistaken. Neither could he take the time to be certain: If it *was* a bomb—well if it *was* a bomb, he'd already be dead. Probably.

On the other hand, he wanted to be there when Karen came back. The best plan seemed to be to go out the back way, leaving whoever was watching him with the impression that he was still inside. That way, he could watch the front door, intercept Karen, and check out whoever was watching him.

He left the lights on in the kitchen and proceeded to the bedroom. Opened the window and went out. He had memorized escape routes from the building the day they moved in, and in any case, there was enough ambient light outside to see the window ledges and pediments that would take him down to the street.

It wasn't exactly a staircase. The pediments, like little roofs over the windows, were in an inverted *V* shape and made of slate. They protruded some distance from the wall—about a foot—and they were also set well above the windows. If he'd been three inches shorter, he would not have been able to get a footing on the sill below while still hanging onto the pediment above. The worst part of it was that the damp day had left all the surfaces slick, almost oily.

He had one very bad moment, right at the start. Because the pediment protruded, his feet dangled into air and it was necessary to set up a slight motion to swing his feet in to the wall. But that small motion was almost enough to dislodge his grip on the slick piece of slate he was hanging onto. A rush of adrenaline rose like a plume in his chest until he felt his feet touch.

By stretching, by pushing his hands upward and his feet downward, he jammed himself into a position of stability despite the fact that the purchase of both his hands and his feet was poor. Once he felt secure, he crabbed over to the edge and got his hands down, under the pediment to the top molding of the window itself. Then his feet were on top of the pediment of the window below and he repeated the procedure.

The ground-floor doors were open arches, set into the walls and without architectural detail, so he had to drop maybe fifteen feet from the last sill. The idea was to land on the balls of his feet, knees flexing. His quadriceps, which had to absorb the impact, hurt so much when he landed that he nearly screamed.

But when he made his way around to the front of the building there was no sign of any surveillance. No van, no parked car with someone sitting in it, no loitering pedestrians, no one hiding anywhere. It was possible that they'd rented a room in the building across from the apartment, but barring that, he'd put money on the fact that no one was watching. By 2:00 A.M., he was pretty sure Karen wasn't going to show up. He stuck it out until six—when he risked reentering the apartment to get Karen's address book. Then he went to the nearby Hotel Splendid and pounded on the door until the night clerk woke up and let him in. By six-fifteen he was waking up Karen's friends. By seven he had called everyone he could think of. No one had seen her.

He wasn't worried, exactly. He called the Europa—where she had stayed before their reunion on the bridge. He called the Jedna—where they had stayed for several weeks before renting the apartment. No Karen. But she *had* grabbed her purse on her way out. Her passport was in it. She might be in any hotel. She was angry. He didn't think she'd leave Prague, but she might disappear for a day or two, if only to teach him a lesson.

But he did want to go back into the apartment, and that meant determining what the intruders had put there. If he found a bug, then he'd be able to relax about the bomb. Why bug some place if you're going to blow it up? He went to Kmart, had some coffee nearby while he waited for it to open, and then bought a cheap portable radio and some batteries. Returning to the apartment, he took a deep breath and then went in, walking from room to room with the radio in his hand, tuning from one band to another until—quite suddenly—a low howl burst from the speaker. He was getting feedback from the bookshelf, which meant that there was a microphone in the room.

He was relieved and he was exhausted. He took a hot shower and then stretched out on the bed.

In the dream, he was standing on a bridge that crossed a small river. He was looking upstream, watching a trio of round black forms float around a bend in the river. Soon it was apparent that they were people on inner tubes, and in a moment they were passing beneath him. First, Fay's mother, in an old black bathing suit with a skirt. Then Bill Diamond. Jeff was the last of the group. Jeff was yelling something at him, something he could not hear because the sound of the rushing water was so loud. There was another sound, a ringing noise, that seemed to be emanating from the water. In the dream, he thought, *That sounds like a telephone. There can't be a telephone here.*

And then he realized that it *was* a telephone, and he was out of bed and lunging toward it, hoping it was Karen.

"Hel-lo, Mar-cus," said Karl Obst, in his thick German accent. "Goot afternoon."

"Karl. I was going to call you to—"

"Mar-cus!" Obst interrupted sharply. "I think we have"—he paused—"something that you lost."

Marcus was still half in the dream. He had no idea what Obst was talking about. Had he left his attaché case with the German? His sunglasses? Impossible. Maybe he'd mis-understood. *"What?"*

241

"Some*one* that you lost."

The meaning of Obst's words sank into Marcus's head with a sickening certainty. And a moment later he realized that somehow Obst had acquired the apartment's telephone number.

"I'll fucking kill you if you hurt her."

"Mar-cus. Please. She will not be harmed if you follow very precisely my instructions. My principal—he very much wishes to meet with you personally to discuss this matter."

Marcus took a deep breath. "What are your instructions?"

"Get the first flight to Ljubljana."

"Looby-*what?*"

"Ljubljana," Obst said patiently. "It's the capital of Slovenia. And then call me with the flight number. We'll pick you up at the airport." Obst hesitated. "And don't forget the sample."

The first flight from Prague to the Slovenian capital was on Air Adria, the national airline; Malone caught it with four minutes to spare.

Slovenia. Malone didn't have a mental picture of the country—knew only that, like Croatia and Bosnia, it had broken away from Yugoslavia. He wasn't even entirely sure where it was until he looked at a map in the airline's magazine. It turned out to be the part of the former Yugoslavia in the northwest corner of what used to be Yugoslavia, just to the east of Italy.

He tried not to think about Karen. It was best to stay in the moment, drive the horizon. He looked out the window. The weather was clear; they were flying over the snowy grandeur of the Alps. By the time the coffee and snacks were cleared away, the Alps had given way to smaller mountains, crumpled and brown, and then below them was a plain. Farmland, cornfields, the ridged patterns of the fields becoming more visible as the plane descended.

26

KARL OBST WAS WAITING AT THE GATE. MALONE DID NOT greet him, merely followed him outside where a large gray Mercedes, with smoke black windows, waited at the curb. The car was driven by a rail-thin Asian man in a black windbreaker. They wound through rural villages, heading northeast. The signs read DOMZALE, CELJE, MARIBOR. About ten miles out of town, near a stand of pine trees, the driver pulled off to the side of the road.

Obst smiled apologetically. "If you don't mind, Marcus . . . My principal is very"—he smiled, considering the word—"*reclusive.*"

In his hands he held an ink blue piece of cloth and what looked like silk-covered beanbags attached by a strip of fabric. The beanbags would fit over Malone's eyes, the blue piece of suede holding them in place. The moment he realized that he was to be blindfolded, he glanced at his watch to check the time. Two-fifty. Unless the driver took a circuitous route, it might give Marcus a rough idea of the distance.

They waited, perhaps ten minutes. *Karen.* Sitting there, blindfolded, he could not repress the realization he'd had: that if she had been interrogated—thanks to his untimely confession—she'd be in the position of telling them something that in all likelihood would get her killed. She might be dead already.

He stopped himself. He couldn't afford to think about what *might* be; he had to pay attention to what was.

And then, abruptly, he was pushed out of one car and shoved into another. He noticed that the motor sounded different, not as smooth. Pebbles rattled against the undercarriage as the car swung out from the shoulder of the road.

He was struck by the amount of unconscious and automatic adjustment—based on vision—that the body is required to make in a moving vehicle. Without being able to see and anticipate the changes in speed and direction, he swayed this way and that, crashing into Obst and into the window, rocked by Newtonian forces.

He sat back, against the seat, and braced himself with his feet. On the radio, the Spin Doctors sang about a pocketful of kryptonite.

After a while, they seemed to be in a town. He could hear other vehicles, horns, the wheeze of a bus. The car stopped several times, as if at traffic lights or stop signs. He tried to remember the map of Slovenia that he'd studied on the plane. It was a small country, smaller than Switzerland, and Ljubljana was almost in the center. It seemed to him that they'd been traveling for about forty-five minutes or so. But from the capital an hour's drive could put them in almost any town in the country. With no sense of the direction on which they had gone, it was useless to try to guess where they were.

They left the town and began ascending. After a while, his ears popped. This, too, offered little in the way of directional help. Except for the valleys along the rivers, the entire country was mountainous. The turns became sharper and more frequent. The car slowed, and then it stopped. Malone heard the window whirr open. The driver spoke briefly in a language Malone did not understand, and then the window whirred shut again. A garage door creaked open.

Malone performed a breathing meditation—taught to him in long ago in training. He could not afford to let anger or anxiety build up and interfere with his ability to react and think. *I am breathing in a long breath without anger,* he thought. *I am breathing out a long breath without anger.*

When the blindfold was removed Malone was in an absolutely plain room, with sisal carpeting. He could not see at all. It was like stepping out from a matinee into a brilliant afternoon. While he blinked and squinted, he was asked to remove his shoes and escorted into another room. He looked at his watch: 4:05. The room held nothing but a rolled futon. The red mercury sample, along with his briefcase, was taken away from him and he was kept in the simple room for eleven hours. Twice, a kimono-clad woman delivered food. Twice, a bulky man escorted him to a bathroom. There was no switch to turn off the very bright light. Finally, he lapsed into a fitful sleep, and then the bulky man was shaking him, gesturing that he should get up. He was taken down a corridor and into another Japanese-style room, this one large, about fifteen feet by fifteen feet square and edged by shoji screens. Tatami mats and a low table. A small figure dressed in a traditional kimono sat at the table. His head inclined slightly toward them. Obst returned the gesture and propelled Malone toward the table. Malone's eyes were still adjusting to the light, and and it was not until they arrived at the table that Malone actually saw the figure as anything more than a blurred shape.

It was difficult not to gape at the man's hideously scarred face. "Please. Sit down, Mr. Malone." The voice was smooth and powerful. On the table was an ikebana arrangement: a sprig of pine, a white orchid, a stalk of grass. The man ran his scarred fingers up the ribbon of grass.

Malone sat down. "What have you done with her?"

"Tea?" said the man in the kimono.

Malone shook his head no, but the figure in the kimono inclined his hideous head to the side and immediately a shoji screen slid open and a traditionally dressed Japanese woman entered with a tray. Her movements were precise and graceful, a little ballet.

The man gestured toward his face with his ravaged hands. "You are wondering can you get used to it?" he said.

"No. I'm wondering who you are and, more to the point, what you've done with my friend."

The man disregarded his comments. "How *can* one live with a face like this? How does one stand it? The answer, Mr. Malone, is that the human capacity for adjustment is vast, unfathomable. I have seen a documentary about—what is this word in English?—*freaks*. Yes, Siamese twins joined here." He touched the top of his head. "And yet they go on. Then there is the boy whose father set him on fire; he sustained burns on 90 percent of his body. There is the man with no arms and legs, only flippers. And yet they 'get used to it.' Because what is their choice? The instinct is to *survive*." He smiled; the effect was unsettling. "As to my identity, that is no true concern of yours. In the case of Ms. Faulkner, I promise that you will be seeing her soon."

Even though the man seemed to be waiting for him to speak, Malone said nothing. Running through his mind was the memory of Bill Diamond in the steam room at Karlsbad, talking about a madman who apparently wanted to retaliate for the bombing of Nagasaki. What Malone thought was: *I am looking at Diamond's madman.*

"So," the madman said. "Let us go for a walk, Mr. Malone, and discuss our business."

"What is our business?" Malone asked. "The only business I want to talk about is Karen Faulkner. I have entered into a good-faith business arrangement with you, through Mr. Obst, and your response is—"

"This is what we wish to talk about, Mr. Malone," the man interrupted, "your *good faith.* As for your friend, all in good time, Mr. Malone. Her welfare, to a very large extent, depends on our discussion."

Malone followed the man out to the room where he'd removed his shoes. The little figure indicated with his head that Malone should put them back on. A woman materialized with a black overcoat and a pair of boots, which the Japanese put on with her assistance. Malone followed the shuffling figure through a door, down a set of concrete steps, and outside.

"It's quite a spectacular setting, is it not?"

Behind them were mountains. Between two forested peaks, a glimpse of the jagged snowcapped summit of a larger mountain. Below them, the hill sloped away. As for the immediate surroundings, all Malone could really see were trees—scrub oak and pine. Through the branches, he saw a bright chip—possibly light reflecting off water—but then the wind moved the branches and it was gone. He looked back over his shoulder and saw a part of the house. From the exterior it resembled a traditional European villa, stucco, with a red tile roof. The rest of the house was concealed by the lay of the land and the trees and shrubs. He couldn't even see the roofline. None of this was likely to help him locate the place again.

"The gardens are not at their best at this time of the year," the Japanese man said. "Too hot. And yet, I thought you might appreciate a tour."

Malone said nothing. The gardens were like rooms, stepped down the hillside, all of them walled—as far as Malone could see—with stone, serpentine brick, or tall evergreen hedge. Malone followed the shuffling Oriental from the rock garden, with its stern elegance and combed gravel, to the rose garden.

"What we are going to talk about, Mr. Malone, is time. Time and money. There is a saying in your country, I believe: 'Time *is* money.' In your case this is literally true." They now walked through a long covered archway, the lattice overhead twisted with heavy, leafy vines. "And time is more than just money. Time is also the fate of your friend Karen Faulkner."

"I don't understand."

"Well, it's very simple, really. You delivered a sample of a product I very much wish to obtain. The sample was quite satisfactory, incidentally. It passed its tests. But I require a faster delivery time. Six weeks. It's too long.''

"I don't know what you want me to do," Malone said.

"We are not talking about a tank, or some helicopters, or even shipments of arms. What I require you can easily transport yourself in a car or on a commercial flight. I see no reason why, if you were able to provide the sample, the shipment should be problematic.''

"The problem is not with me," Malone insisted. "The supplier.''

But the Japanese interrupted.

"I would say that this is not just your supplier's problem now; it is also *your* problem, Mr. Malone.''

"I don't follow you.''

"Time, Mr. Malone, and money. I am prepared to pay a sizable monetary bonus for the *timely* delivery of red mercury. By *timely*, I mean within three weeks from today. That should give you plenty of time.''

"But—"

The little man admonished him with a raised hand. "I placed an order; I expect that order to be filled. I am not a well man, Mr. Malone, and I simply don't have the luxury of patience—normally one of my strong points.''

"I don't—"

"Believe me, Mr. Malone, I am confident that the additional incentive provided by Ms. Faulkner's presence here will have a salutary effect on your ability to make a timely delivery.''

Marcus remained silent. He was somewhat relieved by the man's words; it meant to him that, at least for the moment, Karen had not been harmed. They walked down a few steps and through a gate. "This, Mr. Malone, is what is called a knot garden. A Victorian invention—the patterns of the hedges were thought to resemble the diagrams of loosened knots." Low clipped hedges in elaborate patterns enclosed plantings of herbs. The little man bent and pinched a thin gray leaf between his fingers and brought it to his ruined nose. Even Malone could smell it: rosemary. Then the herb was crumbled between fingers and allowed to fall.

"Are you a gardener, Mr. Malone?"

Malone shook his head. "No."

"Pity. There is much to be learned from the practice. The compost heap, for instance. Such an instructive model. There is a certain elegance, a beautiful simplicity, in the concept of transforming scraps and refuse into the engine of growth for the new plants. That what comes out of the soil goes back in to improve it."

Malone wanted to bring the subject back to Karen, but he kept silent. The little man shuffled in front of him, using his cane for assistance He stopped every ten yards or so, breath heaving, resting until he recovered the strength to go on. Malone realized that he was very ill.

"The gardener must also learn the proper balance," Kawai was saying, "in the use of fertilizer. Too much and some plants won't even bloom; they merely produce ever more luxuriant foliage. Too little and, of course, they do not flourish."

This gardening bullshit was beginning to get to Malone. They crossed a stream on an arched bridge, and he wanted to pick up the little man and toss him off it. He took a deep breath and concentrated on the feeling of the air entering his lungs. He glanced up and down the stream to see if he could spot any landmarks. It was one of the few moments during the slow walk when he did not feel hemmed in. But the bridge had been placed at a natural bend in the stream, and to either side, forty yards away, were stands of tall, tightly planted cypresses. From what Malone had been shown of the gardens so far, the sense was of enclosure. They paused on the bridge, and he looked down at the water. It burbled and rolled over the rocks and pebbles. They continued.

"Even catastrophe," the little man said, "in nature, has its purposes. For instance, the seed of the red pine does not germinate until it reaches a temperature of 1,000 degrees. In other words, it requires a forest fire to get started. So without the disaster . . ." He paused again. "And so one hopes," he said, curling a graceful hand in front of his face, "that even personal catastrophe has its own place in the grand design."

Now they walked down a slate path, past a small potting shed, and into an area enclosed by tall yew hedges. Four diagonal pebble paths converged on a wrought-iron gazebo in the middle.

"And this, Mr. Malone, is the pipe garden."

"Excuse me?" Malone was looking around, trying to make sense of the term. Maybe it was, like *knot garden*, some bit of gardener's vocabulary that he did not understand. But actually, nothing seemed to be planted in the area where they stood. He did notice that there were two big men lounging against the far gate and that both of them had submachine guns—AKs, he thought—dangling from shoulder straps. And while they did not seem particularly interested in the proceedings, they were definitely there to watch and see that nothing went amiss for the little man with the terrible face.

The ground was covered in a pine bark mulch. Then Malone heard the sound, voices, two separate ones at least, one making a keening sound, the other a deeper moan. For a moment he had the impression that the sounds were coming from behind the hedge, but then Kawai stopped and tapped his walking stick against one of the three short lengths of white PVC pipe that protruded from the brown mulch and Malone realized that the sounds were coming from the ground.

Malone had seen the tubes, but he had thought them part of an irrigation system. When he realized the meaning of the voices and the pipes, his spine froze. And when a new and louder moan came from the ground, the hair on the back of his neck began to move. He reminded himself that the Japanese man could not know that he was claustrophobic.

"Now what we have here are two men who have disappointed me," the Japanese said, leaning on his cane. "With the use of a nutrient fluid, and the proper clothing, and regular watering, and a catheter to remove fluid waste, it's possible for them to stay alive for a long time. Like bulbs." He paused and inclined his head. "A surprisingly long time, actually."

Malone said nothing.

"We layer their clothing of course. Polypropylene underwear, wool, a Gore-Tex fabric to keep the moisture out. They are in simple pine coffins, modified, of course, to accept the pipe. Then, too, once you go under the ground a certain distance, the temperature remains constant and, even in winter, surprisingly mild. As gardeners know. It is the secret of the root cellar."

"The root cellar," Malone heard himself say.

He watched as the little Japanese man pulled a weapon from the pocket of his coat. For an arms dealer it was a reflex to observe the nature of any weapon, and Malone noted absently that the small scarred hand held a Makarov. From his other pocket the Japanese extracted the black tube of a suppressor, which he proceeded to screw onto the barrel.

"And of course, once it is over," the Japanese said in his strong voice, "there is no problem with disposal." He paused. His face cracked. A smile, Malone supposed.

The sky was a pure dense blue with the exception of a jet contrail. The bright point of the plane crawled toward the sun as the trail behind it dissolved into wispy shreds.

"This, of course, is a difficult moment for our friend in the ground," the little man said as he stiffly bent over and inserted the barrel of the suppressor into the white mouth of the PVC pipe. His hand was not steady, and it took him some time. It just fitted. "He doesn't know what is coming. Is it the tube with water? The nutrient fluid? Or deliverance."

A silencer—or, more properly, a "suppressor"—does not entirely eliminate the sound of a shot being fired. What it does is contain the sound made by the gunpowder's explosion. But that isn't the only noise that a gun makes when it's fired. Unless the powder load has been reduced to lower the ammunition's velocity, the slug will break the sound barrier on its way toward the target. The trade-off, of course, is that a reduced powder load will also lessen the slug's impact and stopping power.

But in this case, the gunman didn't need to be concerned about that. His target was only a few feet away, and he couldn't miss.

Malone tried not to flinch as he heard that insignificant pop. It was followed by a muffled gurgle, a small but precise sound that Malone would not soon forget. From the adjacent pipe issued a piteous moan, equally indelible.

He watched as the Japanese patiently unscrewed the silencer, returned it to one pocket of his kimono, replaced the Makarov in the other, and then stooped to pull the length of PVC out of the ground. There was some resistance, and the Japanese grunted with the effort. The soil was heavy with clay, and when the pipe slid free of the earth a hole the diameter of the pipe remained. Malone suddenly had the thought that perhaps it was all for show. A couple of microphones in the ground—it wouldn't be hard to rig. But then his eyes fastened on the end of the pipe, where a little skirt of blood—actually gore—clung to the plastic. The Japanese tossed the length of pipe aside and heeled in the dirt over the hole.

Malone stared.

He watched as the Oriental man shuffled over to a potting shed and returned with a shovel, then walked to the protrusion of PVC pipe some distance from the other two. He jammed the shovel into the recently dug earth. Then he tapped the pipe sharply with his cane, twice, crouched down over the opening, and shouted into it. The pipe amplified his voice. In any case, Malone felt that the little man's words were being delivered not into the pipe but directly to the center of his brain.

"A visitor, Ms. Faulkner."

And then Marcus heard, unmistakably, Karen's voice curling up from the ground. "Please," she said in a slurred tone. *"Please."*

Malone's impulse was to hurl himself at the little man, and this impulse was so strong that he was unable to keep his body from lurching toward the Japanese.

But of course the little man remained crouched over the pipe, and into its opening was now pointed not his mouth, but the Makarov. Malone could easily have leveled him with one kick. He could also have kicked the gun out of his hand—and certainly before the Japanese could fire— but there were still the two bulky men to think about. They had taken a few steps toward the center of the garden, and they now held their guns in their hands. Malone took a deep breath.

"We thought it kinder to give her a fairly large dose of tranquilizer," the little man said, "but even so . . . it can only be an unpleasant experience. You will want to get Ms. Faulkner out of the ground as quickly as possible. Since you are not a gardener, let me advise you as to how to go about digging up this tender plant. The box is perhaps four feet under the ground. Concentrate your initial efforts around the end where the feet are—you don't want to disturb the pipe and the air." He put the Makarov in his pocket and handed Malone the shovel, although he did not immediately relinquish his grip. "And, Mr. Malone," he said finally, letting go, "don't disappoint me."

"Karen." He spoke into the cold white plastic. His skin crawled at the thought of her . . . buried alive. "Karen. I'm so sorry."

"Marcus?" she said in a spacey voice.

"I'm getting you out!"

He dug. It seemed to take forever before the shovel hit the wood. But the sound revived him and he worked at an even more furious pace. When he looked up, he saw the brutes in the corner standing there, impassive.

Finally, most of the coffin lay revealed. He scrabbled away at the earth around the pipe with his hands.

"Karen? Are you all right?"

Her voice was thick, drugged. "Marcus? Do you have my coat? I don't know what I did with my coat."

The shovel was a flat spade, and he used it to pry the boards apart. And then she was revealed. She looked like an astronaut or an Olympic skater, her body entirely encased in silvery material, a hood over her head, mittens on her hands. Only her face was exposed. She whimpered as he lifted her up. Her body was almost a deadweight, her arms and legs lolling. "It's all right," he said, kissing her forehead, her cheeks. "It's all right; it's all right." The two bulky men approached. One of them put a gun to Marcus's temple, and the other one took Karen from him.

They were back in the room with the low table. The woman with the kimono poured tea.

"Where is she?"

"She's been bathed and dressed. She's resting."

"I want to see her."

The man's eyes were embedded in the puffy flesh, two hard brown chips entirely devoid of compassion.

"Mr. Malone," he said, "I am a man of my word. I want you to be the same. When you return with the delivery, Karen will be there to meet you. At the airport, for instance. At the train station. At a hotel in Ljubljana. Ms. Faulkner will be there. Wherever you say. Then she can accompany you here, we will test the product, and in a matter of four hours or so—pending the results—you will both be free to depart. And you will also have a very large amount of my money."

"I want to see her."

The Japanese slurped his tea.

"And you *will*, when you return. There is a flight to Prague in less than two hours. I think you should not waste any more time, Mr. Malone."

27

ON BOARD THE AIR ADRIA FLIGHT, MALONE WROTE DOWN every single thing he could remember. The return trip to the airport had been a reverse duplicate of his trip from the airport. A twisting, turning trip with very few stops. Blindfolded. The cassette player on this time, a tape of Puccini arias played at a volume that, while not high, was enough to obscure any exterior sounds that might have provided clues. When the blindfold was removed and Malone was once again in the Mercedes, it was night. He saw that they were already on the outskirts of Ljubljana.

He studied the map of Slovenia in the in-flight magazine and realized that the villa might be anywhere, even across the border in one of the surrounding countries— although that seemed unlikely. Certainly there had been no official border crossing.

When he thought about it, he realized just how little

he knew about where he'd been. There were the mountains that he'd seen outside, behind the villa, but they looked like . . . mountains. As for the house itself, the two rooms Malone had been in were almost bare of ornament. He'd seen only that one exterior facade and had no clear idea of the building's size. From the outside the building did not look like a Japanese mansion but a Mediterranean villa. He remembered that there had been a stream and that he thought he had caught a glimpse, far down the hillside, of still water. A pond maybe. Or a lake. Who knows? Maybe a swimming pool. Or maybe just a trick of the light.

It wasn't much. The one snowcapped peak might be distinctive enough in shape to narrow the area. The walled gardens might be identifiable from the air.

He stopped at a call box in the airport and punched in the emergency number Diamond had given him so many months before. A young woman stood behind him, making impatient sounds, her phone card clutched in her hand.

He felt her, behind him, waiting with him. There was a long series of sounds. First the ringing. Then the phone was answered, but not by a person. There was an electronic bleat, followed by another series of rings, and then a sharp, staticky blast. A silence so prolonged that he was afraid he would exhaust the predetermined value of his card. He knew what was happening. The call was being patched through to Diamond, and of course Diamond might be anywhere.

More static. Another series of rings. The young woman behind him muttered something in Czech and tapped her card angrily against her palm. He tossed her a shrug. Finally, Diamond's voice, saying hello.

"I've got a problem," Malone said. "And I think it involves the party you were telling me about the last time we met."

"Excellent," Diamond replied in his unmistakable Long Island lockjaw. "Does that mean you think you've located him?"

Because there was no way to secure Malone's end of the conversation, it had been made clear to him before he ever left the States that the use of the telephone was to be kept to a bare minimum and that all discussion should be in deliberately vague language. But at the moment, Marcus didn't give a shit.

"I can give you a country, but not much more. Slovenia. I think we need to meet."

Diamond paused. "Can you send us a name? And calm down."

"A name? No. He didn't introduce himself. But he's your guy. A description? Yes. Japanese. Four and a half feet tall. Face and hands badly scarred. And there's anoth—"

"Listen for a message tomorrow," Diamond interrupted. And hung up.

Malone did not return to the Mala Strana apartment. He took a circuitous route through the Old Town, bought a short wave radio at an electronics shop, and then made his way to the safe house in Vinohrady.

He stayed inside the whole next day, not willing to expose himself in the city—by going to the Commerce Club, for instance. He had come to the conclusion that whoever had put the bug into the apartment might not be Obst. At any rate, whoever it was, he couldn't play games now. He couldn't make use of the bug in the apartment—which had been his plan—to give misleading information. He had no one to talk to, for one thing, and he could hardly mutter ersatz travel plans and red herring statements to himself.

But the main thing was that he couldn't afford to take any risks now, because Karen's fate depended entirely on him. He waited anxiously for Diamond's response to his telephone call to come over the radio. And tried not to think about her.

Tried not to think about her but failed. He couldn't get it out of his mind: the way she had looked when he unearthed her, encased in that silvery jumpsuit—the dead white skin, the dull drugged eyes. He couldn't get out of his mind the thought of her, underground, buried alive; it was his own worst nightmare.

Ten o'clock finally arrived and his signal: *Atención, vagabundo*. He decoded Diamond's message; it disturbed him. A meeting was scheduled for Wednesday, in the steam room at Karlsbad.

Bill Diamond looked tired. When Malone finished telling him about Karen's kidnapping, the trip to Kawai's villa, the pipe garden, he looked even more tired. He rubbed a hand over his silver hair, which was matted with dampness now, plastered to his scalp.

"Why didn't you tell us that you were going there? There was concern about that."

"I didn't have time," Malone said. "My contact is a German named Karl Obst. He called and told me he was holding my friend hostage—and that I should get on the next plane to Ljubljana. I made an attempt to call in, but it took too long to patch it through. I couldn't wait; I had to get on the plane."

"Hmmm," Diamond said. "This friend now . . . who is she?"

"I don't see the relevance of that."

"I don't want to offend you," Diamond stated. "It's just that . . . how can you be certain she's not implicated?"

"Forget it. Take my word for it. What happened to her only happened because this . . . *madman* . . . wants some leverage over me. He's your guy, for certain. Because he's in a major hurry."

"OK," Diamond replied. "Tell me again. I want to make sure nothing's left out."

Malone again delivered a concise account of his visit to Slovenia. Ending with the exhumation of his girlfriend and the Japanese man's demand that he produce four kilos of red mercury in three weeks' time. "Actually, nineteen days from today. So you can see that my 'problem' is not only serious but pressing."

"Hmmm," Diamond said. "I don't know; I mean—"

"That's how much time we *have.*"

They'd been in the steam room so long that Diamond decided both of them needed to get out and cool off briefly. He would go first, take a five-minute cool-off in the pool, then change places with Malone.

Diamond disappeared from view even before he reached the door. Malone sat in the dense steam, thinking about the pipe garden, thinking about Karen, and suddenly he couldn't breathe, the eucalyptus steam choking him. It was that old sensation of space itself caving in on him, of the air collapsing, a frantic trapped desperation.

He was unable to resist. He hurled himself toward the door, convinced in his head that it was locked, and then he was outside, in the cool air of the tiled corridor, gasping for breath and feeling stupid.

It was to his father that he owed his claustrophobia. When he was a small child, as a punishment—for breaking something, being rude, whatever transgression his father fixed on—Marcus was routinely locked into a storage room in the dungeonlike basement of the house. He was afraid of the basement anyway, a fact known to his father. It wouldn't be fair to say that his father was actually sadistic. He took no pleasure in it. It was a blunt show of force; that was all. Indeed, Marcus had heard his father congratulating himself on the humanity of his child-rearing methods. "I don't hit the boy, don't believe in that. I just put him somewhere so he can goddamn think about what he done."

Sometimes he remained in the basement for hours. Periodically, through the glacially slow minutes of terrified imprisonment, Marcus would become convinced that his father would never release him. Or it would occur to him that his mother and father might be killed in a car accident or the house might catch on fire and no one would know he was down there and he would die of starvation or thirst or burns. And no one would ever even find his bones.

He crept back into the steam room just before Diamond returned and, when the man came through the door, told him that he was going to the pool in order to cool off himself and he'd be right back.

The pool was ghostly. Eerily lit with old, high windows and populated by the elderly. Old ladies wearing white rubber swimming caps with straps under their chins—a sight he had not encountered for decades. Old men teetering cautiously down the steps, their dead white feet laced with blue veins.

Back and forth in the cool water, he thought about Karen but killed the thought with motion, swimming fast laps in his efficient crawl. He shook his head when he got out, like a dog.

Thirty seconds after entering the steam room, it was as if he'd never left. The sweat poured from him. Diamond asked if there was anything else he could remember.

"Yes." Malone leaned toward him. It was important that Diamond get this right. "I think Kawai has his lab there, right there, near his villa—probably underground."

"That would be some pretty sophisticated equipment."

Malone agreed. "I know that."

He hesitated. "It's just a guess—but, for instance, no one took the sample from me until I got to Kawai's villa. They could have taken it at the airport."

"I'll point that out."

"And then I want you to impress on them . . ." Malone paused, thought out what he was going to say.

"What?"

He sighed. "Tell Willoughby that when he comes up with a plan, the safety of the hostage is of paramount importance to *me*. Look—I'm planning to go back there anyway. If I have to go in with four bricks in my suitcase, at least I'll get in the door. And if I get in the *door*, I'll have a chance. So whatever you come up with has to give me a least that chance and a little bit more—I'm talking about the chance to get out."

"Well, I'm sure—"

"Let me make myself clear. The way this is set up, I

have a number to call in Vienna when I'm ready to deliver. It's an answering service, and I'm sure it's cut out three different ways so you can't walk it back to Karl Obst, let alone Kawai. I give my flight and arrival time. I'm met at the airport. I get in a car; we go a little ways. I'm blind-folded; I get out; I get in another car. At least that was the drill the first time out. So, at least two cars keeping an eye on each other—and who knows how many others? So it won't work to have some kind of tail from the airport. Anything like that is going to be detected, and if it's de-tected the hostage will be killed and probably me, too. Now I don't much like my chances of going in there with a suitcase full of bricks. But I do like them better than I like the idea of some Pentagon thugs or spooks crashing around in the dark. If I see a glimmer of that in any kind of plan . . . I'll break contact, and you'll lose contact with Kawai.''

The steam came on again, with a steady hiss.

"I'll make every effort to make that point. But, Marcus. There's a city at stake!''

"Not yet. This lunatic doesn't have the red mercury. Not yet. I'm sure he's *trying* to get it, and not just from me. I'm sure he's trying to walk his way back to the Turk's supplier, and I'm sure he's doing a full court press. But he doesn't have anything, or else he wouldn't be pushing me like this. So the inhabitants of San Diego are just fine for the moment, but there is one *real* person who's totally fucked *right now,* and the fact of the matter is that she's totally fucked because of me.''

"I'll convey your message,'' Diamond said.

28

CIA DIRECTOR CURTIS WILLOUGHBY SAT ACROSS FROM TANner Rhoades and listened to the little man utter a cliché in his Tennessee twang: "I guess the shit has hit the fayun, Curt-is. Otherwise, we wouldn't be here." This was followed by a nervous squeak that, under the conditions, did not sound like a laugh; indeed, it sounded like the noise a cat makes when you step on its tail.

There were simpler and far more pleasant ways to conduct a secure conversation. But military types usually had a fondness for gadgetry; that was only one of the reasons Willoughby had chosen to meet Rhoades in the room, one of the Agency's anechoic chambers.

The technology was first developed to protect against ever more sophisticated attempts at eavesdropping. When laser devices became capable of reading voice vibrations from walls and windows, anechoic chambers emerged as a way to defeat that technology. The technique involved intricate sets of baffles in rooms built on springs. Such chambers had been built in many U.S. embassies—to provide secure spaces for sensitive discussions within those easily targeted buildings.

Unfortunately, the elimination of vibration and echo also made the human voice sound very strange. It was as if the rooms were packed with cotton wool. Every sound stopped dead; no noises carried; syllables seemed to drop from the lips one by one. The effect was to make even simple sentences difficult to understand—as the mind was forced to connect the sounds without the normal slur and blur of human speech.

Willoughby hated the rooms—communication being sacrificed to security—and he rarely used them. But calling a meeting in one of them had three advantages. The first was compression: it was the rare person who wanted to hang around in one of these chambers for long. The second was that the strange atmosphere had the effect of lending an aura of somber importance to the proceedings. The third, and most important, was that Willoughby had spent endless hours in an anechoic chamber, practicing talking and practicing listening, until he was very effective at both under conditions that left most people tongue-tied and fuzzy-headed. The effort had seemed worthwhile to him; conversations in the chambers were often of extreme importance. But in the end it had another positive effect: his ease in the chambers gave him a huge and entirely unknown advantage. And so, when he had a meeting in one of these rooms, and he had something to sell, he almost always got his way.

Cooperation between the CIA and the Defense Department's DIA was seldom without friction and turf battles. Willoughby was going to make an outrageous request of the DIA man sitting across from him. It was going to involve—at the very least—the loss of an aircraft and a good deal of embarrassing damage control on the part of the military. And yet as he leaned toward the little man across from him he was confident that he would wind up with—not just cooperation, but enthusiasm.

"Tanner," he began, "I've got a little operation in mind, and I'm going to need your help." His voice sounded clear as a bell.

It was a week before Malone got a message. This time, a car picked him up from the front of the Penta hotel at precisely 8:45. It was a blue Skoda, driven by a jovial Czech who said his name was Frantisek. Frantisek had the radio on; he accompanied Smokey Robinson singing "Shop Around," his voice an almost perfect emulation of the Motown star's. Frantisek and Smokey sang ". . . my momma told *me* . . . ," and then Frantisek interrupted himself: "Hang on."

A moment later, the car leaped ahead away from a light, rocketing into a tunnel—where Frantisek executed what in Malone's high-speed driving course at the Agency had been called a bootlegger's turn. He remembered the way it was done: hit the brakes and spin the wheel at the same time, going into a slide as the car turns, then accelerate out of it. Ten minutes later, the Skoda pulled into a slot in a parking garage.

Bill Diamond was seated in the car next to the Skoda. Malone got in next to him, and the Skoda left.

"At least we get to wear clothes," Diamond said.

Malone didn't say anything.

"Well, the director has come up with something." He sighed. "I don't know what you'll think. Anyway, the technical people are concocting a brew for you to take back to your client. It's not red mercury exactly, but . . . I guess it has all the same components. So when it's tested . . . well, it will stand up for a while anyway."

"Go on."

"You said get me something that's better than a bunch of bricks—and this *is*, because it gives you a little time—but . . ."

"But what?"

"There's one more thing." He hesitated again.

"What?"

"They want to put a transponder in it—the ersatz red mercury."

Diamond looked almost embarrassed. He shifted his clear blue eyes away from Malone and stared at the concrete wall in front of him.

"And then what? What responds to the transponder?" Malone asked.

Diamond brought his hands together and made a surprisingly loud noise.

"They want to bomb it?"

"Not exactly. They want to dive an airplane into it, keyed in on the transponder. U.S. military craft. Pilot ejects. There's a certain amount of Yankee chagrin; we fall all over ourselves apologizing to the Slovenian authorities— craft wandered off course, engine difficulties, warn them that there was radioactive material on the aircraft, help them seal the site and investigate the wreckage."

"Jesus."

"The thing is . . . The thing is when you are . . . separated from the sample, you have to initiate the transponder."

"And how do I do that?"

Diamond ran his hand over his silver hair. He looked as if he'd rather be just about anywhere but where he was. "They're making you a watch. It works like a garage door opener. You press the button and it closes the circuit."

Malone thought about it. "You're saying that I have to press this button when I hand over the material. I can't wait, for instance, until I'm on my way out of there—assuming I *can* get out of there."

Diamond looked at him. "Well, apparently—just like a garage door opener, it only has a certain range."

"And how long, after I press this button—"

"Four hours."

Malone said nothing for a minute and then: "Well, at least I wouldn't have to worry about the pipe garden."

"Look; you were *there*. I mean *we* can't do the risk assessment. We can't know if you have a chance to get away."

"I don't think that's the point," Malone said. "I think the point is will I do it."

"You did *say* you were going back anyway. And you said no surveillance. I mean—there's not a lot of options, Marcus."

"I'm a suicide bomber."

"I don't need an answer right now," Diamond said quickly, almost as if he didn't want to know Malone's answer. "You have forty-eight hours. We need to know then because it will take some time to arrange the military end of things."

The two men sat awhile without speaking, and then Malone asked, "How will they get the material to me?"

"They didn't tell me," Diamond said. "No need to know."

They sat for another minute in silence. Malone opened the door of the car and stepped out, but instead of closing the door, he leaned in through the opening.

"Tell them I said yes."

29

THE OLD COUPLE WHO RENTED HIM THE ROOM AT THE VInohrady safe house were not inquisitive, but nonetheless, Malone went to visit, bearing a bottle of wine and a half-kilo of shrink-wrapped smoked salmon. The old lady beamed; the old man pressed a beer into his hand. Malone explained—more or less in sign language and pantomime—that he had much business in the area for the next few weeks and that he would be staying in the room most of the time. Later that night, the old lady came shyly to the door with a bowl of delicious soup.

He stayed away from Prague Center and kept to the peripheral areas for meals, to jog, to buy the paper, to make telephone calls. He no longer risked visiting the Jan Hus statue in the Old Town Square to look for chalk marks, merely listened to his radio anxiously each night, waiting to hear that the concoction of ersatz red mercury was ready.

He tried not to think about Karen, although, of course, the thought of her was almost constantly with him. It was something like what he experienced after Jeff died. At that time, he might wake up and not immediately remember that Jeff was dead—but the realization was never far off. When it occurred, it was as if a veil had dropped between himself and the world, and the rest of the day would be spent in a fog of grief and loss.

Sometimes he didn't think about Karen for a short while either, but when the thought of her returned, it was accompanied by an inundation of fear and longing. And in the swamp of emotion the knowledge of his role in her peril would revive as well, a cold blade to his heart.

He put in a call to Vlasta—about a week had gone by since he'd last visited his cubicle.

"Where you *are*, Mr. Malone? I am having so many messages."

He told her he was calling from London.

She started rattling off the messages: "Mr. Mosaghedi, please call him; Mr. Borodin, please call him; Mr. Haddad, please call him; Mr. Borodin, *again;* Mr. Mosaghedi." She went on. Apart from the familiar names, there were several unfamiliar ones as well; he wrote down the names and numbers for future reference. If there was a future.

"Tell them I'll be gone for two more weeks, that you can't reach me."

"Oh-oo-kay-ay," Vlasta said disapprovingly.

And then, finally, the radio brought the message that he'd been waiting for: "Vagabond . . . Declan Yates . . . Penta hotel."

In the morning, he extracted the Declan Yates passport and pocket litter from the false bottom of the suitcase he'd been keeping in the room and headed out. It was a hot day, overcast and polluted. The heat sifted through his clothing. He walked fast and arrived in a sweat.

He stopped at the first telephone to call Air Adria— making a reservation for the first flight to Ljubljana in the morning. He had known the schedule for weeks: it left at 11:42 and arrived a little after one. The thinking had been that once he received the material, he should wait until the next morning to leave Prague, giving the maximum hours of daylight to the military pilot with the unenviable assignment of deliberately crashing his plane for reasons that would probably not be explained to him.

He caught a taxi to the Penta and gave the desk clerk his passport.

"Yes, Mr. Yates," the desk clerk said. "Your bags beat you to Prague, sir. The airport courier brought them. They're already in your room."

Malone took the elevator to the eighth floor, where he found his room at the end of a long corridor hung with prints of Prague. The room itself was unexceptional, consisting as it did of a fourteen-by-fourteen-foot square littered with blond furniture. But the view was spectacular: the Moldau wound through a forest of blackened spires and tiled roofs, curling beneath the castle on the hill.

He went to the closet where his luggage had been stowed. It consisted of two large soft-sided suitcases, navy blue, embroidered with the monogram "DBY." Declan's middle name was Byron.

Declan Yates must have been doing overtime at the health club, because the suitcases were so heavy that Malone groaned when he lifted them—first one, then the other. It wasn't the fake red mercury itself; the problem was the lead that surrounded each container.

There were four of these, each more or less the size of a coffee can. The housings were blue and each had a small handle on the top.

Buried amid the clothes in the suitcases he found the watch that would activate the transponder. He frowned when he saw it because what Technical Services had chosen to house their activator in was a digital watch—the big, clunky kind with a confusing array of numbers and buttons and a liquid crystal display that could probably tell you how fast your heart was beating and your stockbroker's home number.

It was not the kind of watch that you wore with Turnbull & Asser shirts and Aquascutum suits. On the contrary, Malone thought, it was the sort of watch that a mechanical engineer might wear . . . at a track meet. Would Obst or Kawai notice that he'd abandoned his Rolex in favor of this black plastic thing? Probably not. But even so, he'd make sure it stayed underneath his cuffs.

Meanwhile, he searched for directions as to how to use it, and found them in an envelope in the toiletries kit. It was simple enough. There were four buttons on the watch; pushing the two on the right side simultaneously would initiate the transponder's signal.

Rain pecked against the windows with a hard, ticking sound—a break in the oppressive heat. It was tempting to make his calls from the hotel, but he pulled on a trench coat and headed out.

First he called Diamond. There was the usual delay while the call was patched through and then Diamond's voice, saying hello.

"Everything received," Malone said curtly. "Tomorrow morning. Plane arrives at thirteen hundred hours."

Then he called Obst at the Vienna number, hung up, and waited for the German to return the call. Rain needled his face, and he turned out of the wind.

The telephone rang and the German's hearty voice came over the line. Malone told him his arrival time and reminded him of their other arrangements.

First, Karen would be there at the airport or he would not claim his luggage.

Second: the financial arrangements. Malone had realized that it was essential to his credibility that he make a big deal over these, and so he and Obst had spent considerable time on the telephone hashing them out.

Normally, a letter of credit became *payable* when the seller agreed that the goods had been shipped. In the arms trade, this almost always entailed an on-site inspection at the docks. Crates would be opened at random or, in any case, at the buyer's discretion. Their contents would then be examined to make certain that what was being shipped was what was wanted—rather than what was stipulated in the contracts, RPGs, for instance, rather than socket wrenches. If everything was in order, bills of lading would be approved and copies sent to the buyer's bank. The letter of credit would then be implemented, after a telephone call from the purchaser's bank to the seller's bank.

That progression, of course, was not possible in the transaction with Kawai. First of all, Malone was required to deliver the goods himself. And, as he explained to Obst, even without the complication of the hostage, such a delivery would put Malone at considerable risk. With so much money at stake, Malone—and the hostage—might easily be made to disappear after Malone handed over the goods. It was essentially the same dilemma that a drug dealer faced—how to arrange the exchange of goods and cash in such a way that no one got burned and no one got hurt.

Malone knew that Yotaro Kawai would have been very suspicious without a good deal of prudence and vigilance on his part; certainly Kawai would expect him to nail down the money end.

After some thought and discussion, a solution was decided upon. The $4 million letter of credit from Kawai's bank, the Banque de Paris et Pay Bas, would be made payable in advance to Malone's account at the Banque Generale de Luxembourg. That is, it would be made payable upon Malone's arrival at the airport in Ljubljana. Before claiming his luggage, Malone would be able to reassure himself on two accounts. The hostage's health would be ensured—because she would be brought to the airport to meet him. As to the money, upon Malone's arrival Obst would telephone from the airport and have his bankers implement the letter of credit. Then Malone would call his banker, Urs Birchler, to confirm that everything was in order.

That done, Marcus and Karen would accompany Obst to Kawai's villa and hand-deliver the matériel—which Kawai would then have tested while the two of them waited.

The essential component of the arrangement was left unsaid: Marcus and Karen would be hostages to the test's results, and if the tests didn't go the way Kawai wanted them to go, both would be buried alive in the pipe garden.

"Ja, ja," Obst said over the telephone line. "We will take care of all that at the airport."

Malone had considered renting a car and driving to

Slovenia, arriving at the airport in advance of his arrival time. But the weather was bad and the trip through the mountains seemed like a bad idea. If his plane was delayed, all parties concerned, from Obst to Diamond, would know that. But if he had car trouble or encountered some delay in the Alps, things might get sticky. He would be arriving in Slovenia, as it was, only one day in advance of Kawai's deadline. It seemed best to play it straight.

He spent the rest of the day in his hotel room, taking his meal from room service. He watched CNN. He slept. In the morning, he got ready to go and then set out for the airport. He had his passport in his pocket and $2,000 in cash. All he lacked was a gun. And, maybe, a shovel.

30

THE PLANE DROPPED THROUGH THE THIN CLOUDS SO abruptly that his ears hurt, and then, just as suddenly, Malone was on the ground.

And there they were, waiting in the arrivals area. Obst. And Karen.

The sight of Karen took his breath away. He stopped walking, and a passenger behind him lurched into his back, cursed, pushed around him. And then Karen was in his arms, but there was something wrong. Her grasp seemed weak and tentative, and when he drew back and looked in her eyes they seemed glazed and dim. He realized she'd been drugged. Then he clasped her again and whispered something into her ear, something he'd said once before, the time he showed up at her place unasked, unwanted: "I was in the neighborhood."

Karen made a little sound that was somewhere between a sigh and a sob. Karl Obst coughed.

Marcus released her and they stood there. Karen tried a little smile. But mostly, she looked stoned.

"As you can see," the German said nervously, "we are taking good care of her. She is perfectly fine."

"I doubt that," Malone replied.

They went into the terminal, where they were joined by two powerful men—Bulgarians, by the look of them. Malone recognized them as the two brutes who had stood in the pipe garden, watching him exhume Karen. "My colleagues," Obst explained.

Then, as agreed, Obst made the call to Kawai's bankers, telling them that everything was in order. They went to the airport café for coffee, and then it was Malone's turn. He called Urs Birchler at the Banque Generale de Luxembourg, and Birchler said, "Yes, yes, Banque de Paris et Pay Bas is calling; I have them on the other phone now; everything is go, *non?*"

"Oui."

"What's going on?" Karen asked. The Bulgarians looked at him intently, as if his answer was of vital interest to them.

But Marcus didn't answer. Instead he turned to the German. "I suggest that we put Ms. Faulkner on a plane back to Prague now. Or she can wait at a hotel in the town. There's really no reason for her to return with us." He spoke in the voice of sweet reason, but the German was obstinate, shaking his head, a grim set to his mouth.

"I don't think so," Obst said. "That wasn't the arrangement. She comes along."

Malone argued, but the German was immovable, and finally they headed for the luggage carousel. Malone thought about making a break for it right then, but the Bulgarians never seemed to be more than two feet from him.

He claimed his suitcases.

The gray Mercedes sat idling at the curb. As if on cue, the trunk popped open. The Bulgarians took the suitcases from him, heaved them into the trunk, and closed it. Behind the Mercedes was a Mitsubishi Pajero with what looked like twin brothers of the Bulgarians sitting in it. He and Karen got into the front passenger seat, next to the Japanese driver. Obst got in behind him, joined by the two muscle men.

The Mercedes pulled away. Malone looked in the side-view mirror. The Pajero followed.

He held Karen's hand and thought about the situation. The Bulgarians looked like blocks of gristle, powerful and bulky, but lithe—baby sumo wrestlers, he thought. Tweedle-bang and Tweedle-boom. If they were going to play man-to-man defense all afternoon, bumping him everywhere he went, it was going to be very difficult to get loose. In fact, it might be impossible.

"Marcus?" Karen said in a small voice. "What's happening? I want to go home."

He squeezed her hand. "Just a little business," he replied, in as reassuring a tone as he could muster. "We'll be on a plane to Prague in a few hours."

They were blindfolded; they were switched to another car. Malone held Karen's hand and tried to keep his mind clear and relaxed. On the periphery of his consciousness, Obst and the unseen driver were discussing—in English—

the relative merits of German and Italian soccer players. Then they began to pick ideal teams from the entire world.

"You can have Del Piero," Obst said in his thick, low voice. "I *give* you Del Piero."

Four, Malone thought, exhaling. Inhale. *Three.* Exhale. But then he stopped himself. It was a form of meditation, but it felt too much like a countdown.

"Jurgen Klinsman," Obst said.

The driver cackled. "Too *old,* Kahl. You sen-ti-men-tal. *Grandpa* Klinsman. I'm taking Roberto Carlos."

About an hour later, the car stopped, There was the segmented creak of the garage door as it rolled open. They had arrived.

When the blindfolds were removed, they were in the same room Malone remembered—the absolutely plain one with the sisal carpet. There were six of them in the room. Marcus, Karen, Obst, the driver, and the two Bulgarians.

With the exception of the latter, everyone was removing their shoes. Malone considered doing it right then— pushing the button on the watch, grabbing Karen's hand, and bolting through the door. No one would be expecting it, and they *were* just next to a door. But that door only led to a garage. And then there was Karen, who seemed too out of it for anything abrupt and athletic.

The coats were hung by the Japanese driver on a Shaker peg rack that extended the length of one wall. The suitcases stood nearby. They were rapidly unzipped by Obst and the blue containers lined up on the floor. Malone looked at his watch. It was 3:42.

The thought had occurred to him even as he sat in the

283

car next to Bill Diamond that he didn't *have* to initiate the transponder. He could hope that the tests dragged on; he could try to squeeze out a couple more hours.

He watched the Bulgarians move toward the canisters.

"Well, go ahead then," Karl Obst said to them. They picked up the containers—effortlessly—and headed for the door. As the driver opened it for them, the thought of the pipe garden came into Malone's mind, putting an end to his fantasy. In the event that escape was impossible, better to blow up than submit to the consequences of Yotaro Kawai's disappointment.

Malone shot his cuffs and pressed the two buttons on his watch—initiating the transponder's signal. He imagined it briefly: the signal beaming to a satellite. Somewhere in Europe, a bunch of men hunched over maps and a pilot was heading for the tarmac. As for himself, he now had four hours to get out of there.

Malone watched the door close behind the Bulgarians and tried not to worry. While Diamond had assured him that everything would be fine, that it would be hours before the ruse would be discovered, suddenly he became worried. What did Bill Diamond know?

They were ushered into the room with the shoji screens and offered tea. Malone accepted. Karen shook her head no. She was clearly sedated, her eyes vacant, her pupils tiny. She yawned. After a while, he looked over and saw that she was slumped over on the table, head in her arms, asleep.

"What do you have her on?" he asked Obst.

The German shrugged. "A little Xanax is all."

"A *little* Xanax? She's practically a zombie."

"She was very . . . *nervous*," Obst said.

"Nervous?"

"Well . . ." The German shrugged. "Not cooperative. Combative. You know women."

Malone smothered his emotions. There was nothing he could do now about Karen's ordeal; one way or another, unless the military end of things failed, it was over. He turned his attention back to the table, to the ikebana arrangement: a blue Dutch iris and, on either side, two thin white-edged blades of grass, curled over in perfect parabolic arches.

Time passed in an awkward silence as everyone awaited the verdict from the lab. There was an effort at conversation, at first—and then nothing. They all sat there, deep within themselves.

Malone was good at waiting. He had the ability—like a dog—to slow down his mind to idling speed; he inhabited the period of waiting like a hibernating animal. He was not in a state of dread. He was waiting *for* something—a glimpse of light, the hint of an escape route, a new perception, a chance.

Finally, he asked to use the lavatory and was shown into the small room he remembered from the time before. The driver escorted him and, he was sure, remained outside the door. The room was fitted with natural pine woodwork. He looked at his watch and was stunned to see that nearly two hours had already passed: it was 5:32. He began to regret not making a run for it in the airport or from the room with the sisal rug.

Beyond the small window was the pine bough he remembered. He studied the window's dimensions. It was small and high—but certainly by standing on the top of the toilet he could reach it. It was wired—no surprise there—and would definitely trigger an alarm. The problems were two. The first was Karen. The second was that he didn't know where this exit led. It didn't face the same way as the garage, and he couldn't see beyond the tree. Even if he could rouse Karen and they both managed to get out, it might lead to a courtyard, for instance, in which case they'd be trapped. He flushed the toilet and went back to drink some more tea.

A woman came into the room, bowing demurely to Obst, to the driver, to himself. She said something in Japanese, and the German barked a reply and nodded. Soon Karen had been roused and the two of them and Obst were padding down a corridor in their socks. Track lights illuminated a fabulous display of Japanese prints. Karen stumbled along next to him, like a zombie. And then they turned right, passed through a door, and were in a large room. At least the Bulgarians were nowhere in sight.

Yotaro Kawai was tilted into a semiseated position on a hospital bed. An IV stand was next to him. The plastic sac containing purplish blood was attached to his arm.

Malone was stunned by the room. It had cathedral ceilings and was mostly glass. One wall of windows faced onto the Japanese garden, and it was in that direction that Kawai had been gazing when Malone entered the room.

"Mr. Malone," the little figure said, inclining his head slightly in Malone's direction. "My Great White Hope."

It was natural, of course, to feel sorry for Yotaro Kawai. His devastated face; his obvious weakness. He was so clearly a victim. Indeed, Malone felt a surge of sympathy, an almost automatic response. And then it turned inside out.

His sympathy became outrage as a shuffle of images and thoughts churned through his mind. The pipe garden, Karen's voice floating up out of the ground: *"Please."* Kawai's gun in the other pipe, the soft pop of the bullet, the gurgle from the ground, the way the Japanese had pulled out the pipe and casually heeled in the dirt. He was looking at a man who buried people alive. Malone thought about the satellite photos of San Diego. He was looking at a man prepared to incinerate hundreds of thousands of people to alleviate his sense of injustice. He was looking at a psycho fuck; that's what he was looking at.

Revulsion spun through him—and it was not Kawai's face or misshapen body that was so repulsive but his soul. His sense of loathing was so intense that Malone was afraid Kawai would be able detect it. And he wanted Kawai to be relaxed. The Japanese obviously believed that Malone wouldn't be here if the red mercury was not genuine. The sample had been genuine, after all. It was important not to show fear or anxiety or any emotion apart from a bored impatience.

A male nurse came in and disconnected the IV. The sleeves of Kawai's kimono were rolled down, and the little man was helped to his feet. His gun, the Makarov, was returned to him with a ceremonial gesture. Malone watched Kawai slide it into a fold of his kimono.

"A little vampirish," Kawai said, "but for a day or two I actually feel quite well."

Malone felt a vein ticking in his temple and realized he was gritting his teeth. He opened his jaw and consciously relaxed. He had to be alert, but he couldn't seem tense or distracted. On the other hand, he did have to *think*. Waiting was fine, but he couldn't wait much longer. He sneaked a look at his watch and saw that it was almost six o'clock. He thought of the transponder, the airplane closing in on the signal. It was not two blips on a radar screen that would converge. What was coming their way was a massive metal container holding thousands of gallons of jet fuel traveling at a velocity that would ensure explosion on impact. Composure was good, waiting for a chance was fine, but pretty soon he was going to have to grab a half-chance, a quarter-chance, any flick of a chance that showed itself.

He walked closer to the window, ostensibly to look at the rock garden. Karl Obst followed Malone and stood next to him. The German cracked his knuckles and a stifled a yawn. Malone saw that the windows were made of triple-glazing. Quite apart from the problem of Karen, that eliminated the notion of hurling himself through the glass: he would just bounce off. He looked out, remembering that the rock garden led to the knot garden; the knot garden led to the stream.

"I thought while we wait," Kawai said, taking Malone's arm as he led him out into the corridor, "you might enjoy seeing my collection."

They all followed him down the hall and stopped at the entrance to a large interior room. Kawai said something to Obst in German, and Obst padded back down the corridor.

The others went into the room. Malone was instantly disappointed. The room offered no obvious means of escape. No doors other than the one they had used to enter it. But it was not just a room, he saw, as he looked around; it was a museum, actually. The soft gray walls were covered in some kind of fabric and had built-in niches for display. The indirect lighting displayed a magnificent collection of Japanese artifacts. Kabuki masks. Rich brocade kimonos that seemed to float on the walls. Woodblock prints. A display of *raku* pottery. Scrolls. Ceremonial chests.

Malone looked and while he looked he thought: *There are just the three of us in here.* There was no sign of the Bulgarians, of Obst, of the driver, of the woman in the kimono, of the male nurse. And Kawai was relaxed, clearly lulled into that state by the fact that he held all the cards. Karen was chemically subdued and Marcus's anger was repressed by self-interest. Still, there was the Makarov. They couldn't just run for it.

"I'm not a well man," Kawai was saying. "As you must have noticed. The dose of radiation I received as a child damaged my bone marrow. This is the case with most of us. Eventually, the blood itself is afflicted. We contract leukemia. The normal course of treatment . . ." Kawai paused and chuckled. ". . . involves radiation. This does seem terribly ironic." He made a gesture, encompassing the room. "I do have the compensation of knowing that when I die . . . others will carry on my work. My collecting and . . . my other work."

As Malone had learned during his first visit and the trip through the gardens, Kawai was didactic; he enjoyed giving speeches to captive audiences. Malone had the glimmer of an idea and wanted to encourage Kawai. He feigned interest in various artifacts, and Kawai took his time, sharing his knowledge of them and Japanese culture.

They stopped in front of one of the ceremonial chests. It was small, and there was nothing spectacular about it; but as with so much Japanese art, there was something about its perfect proportions that made it appealing. The wood was chestnut brown and had the deep resonant gleam of old wood polished often.

"It's beautiful," Malone remarked.

"Pawlownia wood," Kawai said. "Very light, very strong." He stroked the chest. "Most often now it is obtained from the United States. West Virginia, I believe, and Virginia. It grows wild there. Small planes spot the trees—in the spring when they are blooming, with their lavender flowers. And they mark the spots and approach the owners. There are even Pawlownia rustlers, I've heard, who cut down specimen trees by dark. But what do you expect? This is capitalism."

Karen seemed to have gone mute, but she dug her fingernail into Marcus's palm, and when he looked at her he saw, for the first time, in her eyes an awareness, a hint of the real woman behind the fogged consciousness. They were walking now past a display of woodblock prints toward a collection of Japanese ceremonial swords.

"Ah, now, Mr. Malone, your speciality. Weaponry." Kawai gestured at the array of swords displayed on the wall. Each had a similar, slightly curved shape; each was scabbarded. Some of the scabbards were woven reed, one appeared to be finely worked ivory, and some were wood.

"It is a pity what has happened to the *katana*," Kawai said. Malone was revved up into a state of anticipation; his heart bounced in his chest, and he hoped that Kawai would not notice. If only he could manage to get his hands on one of those swords. He was thinking about how he could fell Kawai with an elbow to the face and then grab a sword. He rehearsed the motion in his mind—and then

Kawai reached up and took one of the swords down from the wall.

Malone practically held his breath.

The Japanese removed the scabbard and carefully re-hung it. "Do you know there is only one sword works left in Japan and that it produces only two swords a year?" Kawai said. "It is attached to a larger metal works. The swords are only—oh, a kind of corporate hobby, a kind of advertisement for the company."

This was obviously a lecture and not a discussion, so Malone said nothing. He edged toward Kawai, bending over to get a closer look at the sword. "It's humiliating, Mr. Malone, to see your culture turn into . . . a curiosity. The swords, just like the Nō plays, the Kabuki, the ki-mono—these are mere curiosities now, artifacts, no longer a living part of the culture. That we have ceded to the West. We follow your ways. We adopt your values. And our values . . . are like an oddity to be displayed." He waved his hand, gesturing around the room. "A museum." He laughed. "A theme park. Japanland."

Kawai tried to raise the sword over his head, holding it in his two hands, but the gesture was not completed. The sword was too heavy and Kawai too weak.

"The making of the sword is an art," Kawai said. "There is no handbook. The basic technique is like knead-ing bread dough—get the steel hot; hammer it; fold it over. Do this again, and again, and again. When the sword is complete, it can have as many as ten thousand layers of steel. It is a kind of alchemy."

Malone made appreciative comments and edged a little closer to Kawai. Any minute, someone might come in the door. "That would make the sword very sharp," he stated. "Like a razor."

"Oh, yes," Kawai agreed. "They say that a sharp sword will cut a hair off your arm and that a very sharp sword will make it pop off the skin. But a *katana* is so sharp that if you pluck a hair from your head and let it drift through the air, the sword can cut the hair in half. But the real art is not only in that—it is that the sword, even though quite large, is so beautifully balanced. Here," he said, offering the sword to Malone. "You will see. It is perfectly balanced."

Malone could hardly believe it. He tried to suppress his nerves as he took the sword in his hands, but his hands trembled. He held the blade, hefted it, made admiring noises, lifted it up, and took a horizontal swipe through the air.

"No," Kawai said, shaking his head and smiling indulgently. "It is not used like a French sword, no slashing through the air like the Musketeers. No thrusting and parrying. The traditional stroke is a *vertical* one, a single killing blow. The technique is to—"

But Kawai stopped talking and gaped. Malone stood before him like a samurai, the sword upheld in both hands, ready to strike.

"Very convincing," Kawai commented. "I see you've studied—"

Malone took two running steps toward Kawai and brought the sword down as hard as he could at the juncture of Kawai's neck and shoulder. The weapon *was* perfectly balanced and the motion not even difficult. The flesh, and even the bone of Kawai's shoulder blade, parted like butter under the razor-sharp blade that came to a stop somewhere near Kawai's breastbone. Malone pulled it free. Kawai's arm, nearly severed, hung askew. The little man never said a word. He remained standing briefly and then crumpled. There was a gurgling sound. The blade must have hit Kawai's subclavial vein, because dark, venous blood poured from the wound. Karen made a small wounded noise, a gasp of shock and terror.

Malone put down the sword, took Karen's hand, and stepped out into the next room. He was lucky he hadn't hit an artery, he thought. If he had, he'd be covered with blood.

"Quite a collection," he said to Obst, twisting his head back and forth in admiration. And then, inclining his head toward Karen's white face, "She's not feeling well. She needs to use the facilities," he added, nodding toward the corridor and the lavatory. "We'll be right back."

Once in the corridor, he began running, dragging Karen along behind him. The only way out that he knew was the way he'd come in. He turned through the shoji-screened room into the room where they'd removed their shoes. Tweedle-bang and Tweedle-boom were lounging, against the wall, and so surprised to see him that they didn't react. By the time they began to move, he had pushed through the door, dragging Karen along, and slammed it shut behind them.

Down some steps. An electronic garage door opener. A button on the wall, just in the same spot he had a button at his house in McLean. He remembered from the trip in—blindfolded—that slow, motorized rolling up of the door. He pushed the button and then pulled Karen down so they were crouching on the floor on the far side of the second car—the garage held four—ready to roll out under the door as soon as it was open a foot or so. He looked at Karen and her eyes seemed enormous—but awake. Maybe an adrenaline surge had rocketed through the drug's effects. "Just do what I do," he said. "We're getting out of here." She nodded.

He heard the Bulgarians, shouting at each other, at the head of the stairs. The garage door creaked open with agonizing slowness. He pushed Karen under and rolled out after her, and then they were up and running. They ran down a gravel drive until he heard a bullet gouge into the stones. He yanked Karen into some bushes and pushed through and found that they had emerged on the other side of the knot garden. He heard voices, men running by. He jerked Karen down to the ground, and they curled inside a boxwood hedge. They remained perfectly still.

He heard a car back out of the driveway. Men shouting and running. Another car. After a while, someone walked on the path next to the hedge. Marcus held his breath and clasped his hand over Karen's mouth. The searching man paused right beside them, passing so close that Malone could hear him breathe—a hissing sound.

They lay there, silent and unmoving. He could feel Karen's heart beating. A few minutes passed and she began shivering, hard shudders against him. He couldn't hear anything and, after a while, felt certain that they were alone in the garden. He looked at his watch. Shit! All this had taken longer than he thought. There was less than twenty minutes before the villa went up in flames.

Disengaging themselves from the boxwood seemed to make a tremendous amount of noise—and then they were moving at a crouch toward the entrance to the garden. If

Malone remembered correctly, the way out of the knot garden led to the arched bridge. And the stream.

The stream would run downhill, away from the villa. They moved slowly along the side of the burbling water. Once they were clear of the gardens, the vegetation was underbrush, sometimes so dense that they were forced to walk in the very cold water of the mountain stream. Malone's feet felt numb now, blocks of ice. When he thought they were far enough away to start moving quickly, he pulled Karen's arm and they ran like hell, crashing through the underbrush.

And then Karen twisted her ankle. One moment he could hear her crashing along behind him, her hand grabbing hold of his shirt, and then she was down. She didn't scream, just a sharp little "unh" that sprang from her mouth.

They'd been going so fast, he was twenty yards from her before the meaning of that sound became clear. She was trying to push herself to her feet when he got back to her.

"You all right?"

"Twisted my ankle."

"Can you walk?"

The answer was: not exactly. She could hobble, however, and the two of them staggered onward as fast as they could. After a while, the ankle was clearly hurting a lot and he carried her, piggyback.

It was dusk. He saw dim lights and headed for them. Eventually, they reached what seemed to be the shore of a small lake. Across from them were some buildings—hotels and restaurants perched on the edge, their lights streaming down into the water. There was a footpath that seemed to skirt the lake. They were cold—their feet, particularly, numb and painful. His breath came raggedly; Karen shivered against his back. It was quite tempting to just start moving at a quick jog along the smooth pedestrian path. But it was not yet completely dark and the path was totally exposed and a man with a woman on his back would offer an unmistakable image. He looked at his watch, and they stayed in the trees. He folded his body around Karen's.

"What's going on?" she stammered. "Where are we? Who was that man you—"

Talking was still not a good idea. "Don't talk," he whispered, and looked at his watch again.

Because of the trees, they never saw the plane; they only heard it. Eventually, it got loud enough so that he imagined people in the town coming out to see what it was, the kind of dawning realization that the mind resists: *Isn't that plane too low?* And then there was the explosion. He felt the ground shudder from the impact and then the huge percussive sound. Everything got bright, so bright that he looked up, and, amazingly, there was the pilot in the sky over the lake, suspended from his parachute, sifting down through the air like a feather.

"I'm all right," Karen said suddenly. This was not true. He bent his knees and she got on his back and he began to walk.

They stopped at the first hotel they came to, the Grand Hotel Toplice, a big place, perched on the edge of the lake. He realized he had seen it from the other side. When they went in, squelching along in their soggy socks, there was no one at the desk. Through a series of French doors, half of which were open, there was a vast old-fashioned room with Oriental rugs, a grand piano, a dozen over-stuffed couches, and enormous picture windows along the lake. A dozen people stood there, looking out. One man with binoculars was describing, in a British accent, what he saw. The desk clerk glanced back and hurried toward them.

It was from the look on the man's face that Malone realized the state they must be in, and one look at Karen confirmed it. Their legs were wet up to the knees; Karen's face was scratched and bleeding from the brambles they'd fought through. They had no shoes. The clerk stared.

Malone looked at the man, dumbfounded, for a moment and then found a story that he hoped would explain everything.

They'd been in a taxi, near the lake, and the driver had been so distracted by looking at the explosion that he'd driven into a ditch. The car had rolled over. The driver was fine, and they were both fine—except for the lady's ankle—but the car was not, and Malone and Karen had walked here. In the crash they had somehow parted company with their shoes. And they urgently needed to get to Ljubljana. Could the desk clerk call a taxi?

"First," the desk clerk said, holding up a restraining finger, "you must have blankets and I think a glass of brandy. We are all very puzzled by this . . ." He gestured toward the window and the lake. "We are not on the flight path to . . . *anywhere.*"

He returned with the brandy and the blankets, and they took them gratefully, sitting in the huge room and looking out toward the flames across the lake. When the taxi finally arrived, the clerk insisted that they keep the blankets. "You can return them by post," the clerk said. "You will surely catch a cold otherwise."

He and the driver had a brief discussion about price, and Malone and Karen settled gratefully into the backseat. It only took a hard glance at Karen, while they were making their way from the hotel to the taxi, for her to realize that discussion about what had just happened would be a mistake. His idea had been to get a hotel room in Ljubljana, but about halfway there he realized that several of Kawai's men had been out of the villa when the plane hit it. Some of them might well visit the capital—which was not a large city—and cruise the hotels, looking for wet and tired English speakers, a tall man and a woman with reddish hair. It seemed reckless to risk a return. Even the airport might be a problem.

He negotiated with the driver, who fortunately spoke decent English. Malone told the driver that because of the accident they had missed the flight from Ljubljana. That they must be in Prague in the morning. Would he take them?

The taxi driver said it was impossible. His wife . . . He was tired.

Malone opened his wallet. He offered the driver a thousand dollars.

Some miles closer to Ljubljana, the driver pulled off the road at a gas station. He examined the money at great length.

"No."

"No?"

"How do I know this is real money? No." Only Slovenian money would do; the driver did not trust the dollars.

298

Malone sagged back against the seat as they continued toward Ljubljana.

Perhaps, the driver suggested, the money could be changed? The banks would be closed, but the hotels would change money. And the casino.

In the end, Malone went into the casino, where the cashier looked at him skeptically, taking in the bare feet and the ragged appearance. Nevertheless, the money was cheerfully exchanged, at what Malone was sure was a terrible rate. The taxi driver then called his wife—a very long discussion at a call box. Once all this was accomplished, Malone and Karen took off their sodden socks and wrapped themselves in their blankets.

En route, the taxi driver became incredibly talkative. They proceeded toward the Austrian border. OSTERREICH, the many road signs advised, and pointed the way. WIEN. Along the way, they were treated to a long monologue about the geopolitics of the Istrian peninsula. The Italians wanted their land back. "Now! After fifty years! Ha!" After this subject was exhausted, the driver moved on to his gallstone operation. They went up and down mountain roads at alarming speeds.

They crossed the Austrian border without trouble. Karen fell asleep somewhere near Vienna.

They crossed the Czech border. Malone dozed off. When he woke up, it was dawn and they were on the outskirts of Prague.

31

_____

IT WAS EARLY MORNING AND THERE WAS A COOL MIST IN THE air. Malone directed the driver. When they got out of the taxi outside the safe house in Vinohrady—embraced on parting by the driver—Karen's ankle was swollen to the size of a grapefruit. Malone wasn't much better off. His feet were shredded.

"Where are we?" Karen asked as they staggered toward the door.

Malone fitted the old-fashioned key into the lock and helped her into the tiny apartment. "Home," he said.

Marcus wanted to talk about it—what had happened to them during their separation. He filled her in on Yotaro Kawai's intentions, the transponder, and the airplane. But when it came to her experience, and his questions about it, Karen's eyes filled up with fear and confusion.

She was stunned, first of all, to learn that so much time

had passed. It had seemed to her a matter of days since she had stormed out of the apartment and the men had pulled her into the car. Clearly she had spent most of the time drugged, and her memories were fuzzy and indistinct. He described digging her up, and she was shocked again—she didn't remember it at all. What she remembered was being in a small room that had nothing in it—only a futon and a chair. There was a bathroom, but there was nothing in it but a toilet. She had bits and pieces of memories: a man sitting on the chair, eating an apple, a gun in his lap. She remembered biting someone, trying to get away.

"*Biting* someone?"

She was being taken somewhere, and she remembered a hand on her arm and pulling it toward her and biting it. And then running down a hall. But when she tried to follow the memory, to recall what had happened before or after, it dissolved, and she just shook her head.

Malone backed off. It might all come back to her later—or maybe not. He himself had been through some shit, and to this day there were moments, even hours, of his life buried so thoroughly that if even a fragment of their memory began to emerge, he'd learned to make his mind go completely blank. He would forget for an instant who he was, where he was, what he was doing. It was something like a controlled epileptic seizure. Small, but effective.

There were many who encouraged dredging up those experiences; processing your trauma, they called it, or something like that. During and after his tour with FOG, there were Agency shrinks who wanted that: talk, talk, talk; lay it all out. Obviously therapists thought these things you had done or things that had happened to you were like evil demons—vampires—and exposing them to the light would kill them off. Malone disagreed. He wanted those memories to stay buried. Forever.

So he didn't press Karen. She wasn't feeling well, anyway, and he devoted himself to taking care of her. He stood with her in the shower and washed her hair. He improvised a brace for her ankle. She was nauseated and could not eat; she got sick several times. One minute she'd be sweating, and the next minute she'd be freezing. He thought she was probably undergoing withdrawal from whatever drugs they'd been injecting into her. He had no idea what they were. Certainly more than "a little Xanax," as Obst had put it. Withdrawal could be dangerous, he knew, and he kept a careful watch on her—ready to take her to the hospital if anything alarming happened. He was afraid to leave her, and so they simply stayed in the room and waited.

It was a bad night. Karen was nearly delirious, so restless that her feet and hands were never still, and she begged him to take her outside for a walk—despite her ankle.

"I feel bad, Marcus," she said, and it nearly broke his heart. "I feel so bad."

Karen's withdrawal lasted three days.

Malone did manage to duck out briefly. He went to visit the old couple to tell them that a friend was staying with him, a young woman. This was all quite difficult in a combination of their limited English and his even more limited Czech. The old lady stiffened at the mention of a girlfriend, but the old man shot her a warning look. They liked the deal with Malone. He was almost never there, and when he was, he was quiet. He offered them some extra money, but they actually pushed the suggestion away. He insisted and gave them the equivalent of about a hundred dollars. The old man shrugged and smiled and offered him a beer, which he declined, with regret.

He bought food, some clothes, and a bouquet for Karen. And a *Herald Tribune*.

They read about it. A U.S. military aircraft had strayed off course during support activities for the UN in Croatia and suffered an engine malfunction, crashing into a private home near the resort of Lake Bled, Slovenia. The pilot had survived, but a number of people on the ground had been killed. Authorities were sorting through the wreckage.

Malone suspected that the plane had been a drone, remote-controlled, and that the "pilot" had parachuted from a second plane. Maybe. Or maybe not. It didn't matter one way or the other.

He hadn't even listened for a radio message or called Diamond to say that he'd survived. Some part of his mind was unwilling to engage with all that, but finally, the third evening after their return, Karen began to feel a little better. She even ate a little ice cream. They played a game of chess.

"I'm going to listen to the radio," he told her, after she had cornered him into a sneaky checkmate. "It's the way they communicate with me."

"*Atención, vagabundo.*" He marked down the letters as the message came over the wire. Then he pulled out the

Cadogan and taught Karen how the system worked. They decoded the short message Diamond had sent: "BRAVO. WHERE ARE YOU?"

He finally went out, the next evening, to leave his mark on the abutment at Na Kampa so that Diamond would know that he'd received the radio message and that he'd returned safely to Prague.

The next night, there was another message on the radio: "CALL." And a number. But he wasn't ready to talk to Diamond yet, to set things in motion again. Karen and Marcus stayed in the apartment, playing chess, doing the crossword in the *Herald Tribune*. Karen's ankle began to turn from purple to yellow. She cooked; they ate; they drank wine; they made love. But even though it was pleasant enough, even though the days passed with pleasure, the little room in Vinohrady began to seem small.

He'd long since abandoned his high-profile arms dealer's wardrobe in favor of less conspicuous clothes. He'd also picked up enough Czech to get by in day-to-day dealings with shopkeepers and taxi drivers. His ear and his ability to mimic were good enough that a few words didn't give away his nationality. But he still felt conspicuous and exposed every minute he was out on the streets.

Just because he'd accomplished his task didn't mean anything had changed. He hadn't forgotten the bug in the Mala Strana apartment or the many agencies, from the CIA to the Mossad, who would still be looking for him. It was time to get on with it, to arrange his new identity with Diamond, to begin his new life.

When he placed the call to Diamond's number, something very strange happened, something that had never occurred before. He was used to waiting for long periods while his calls were patched through to Diamond, but this time, after almost ten minutes, a mechanized voice advised him to call back in an hour. He was bewildered.

He called back in an hour, waited, got the same mechanized voice.

And again.

And again.

And again.

And again.

Obviously, the mechanized voice was a default message—to be used when Diamond could not be located. It might be a technical problem of some sort—a computer glitch. Or maybe Diamond's beeper had failed. Otherwise, it meant that Diamond was completely out of touch, and that seemed unlikely—especially now, at this stage of the game, when he was *waiting* for Malone's call. Malone went back to the room and encoded a message: "WHERE ARE YOU. WILL CALL TOMORROW 7AM YOUR TIME."

He left his mark at Liliova and Husova; he bought a packet of Petras, dumped the cigarettes, and went to Stromovka Park and left the drop.

He listened to the radio on the hour, thinking perhaps Diamond had decided to communicate in that way after all despite the fact that he had explicitly instructed Malone to call. There was no message for Vagabundo.

In the morning, he stopped at the newsstand to buy more phone cards—he was going through them like water. He called Diamond's number again.

"Call back," the voice advised. "One hour."

Something was definitely wrong, but he didn't know what to do about it. He could hardly call Curtis Willoughby. You couldn't *call* the director of Central Intelligence. He'd never get past the switchboard. In fact, he couldn't call the Agency at all. As far as the Agency was concerned, he was a criminal and one, moreover, who'd blackened its own reputation. Putting him in prison would do a lot to remove the stain.

So, there was nothing for him to do but monitor the radio and wait. Maybe tonight he'd hear that his message had been received by Diamond. On an impulse, he decided to visit the drop in Stromovka Park.

It was a cool and rainy day. A pale daytime half-moon hung in the sky. Stromovka was all but deserted. A few dog owners hunched into coats, trying to hurry their animals along. He reached the drop and immediately saw that his Petras packet was still there, exactly where he'd left it. Just to be thorough, he hopped on a tram and walked past the corner to see if his mark was still visible at the corner of Liliova and Husova. Normally, whoever serviced the mark would also remove it. That required no more than leaning up against it for a moment or brushing it with the shoulder in passing. But marks were sometimes removed inadvertently—by others or simply by the rain. But not in this case. The mark was still there.

Karen had managed to find some hot paprika that she thought might work as chili powder, and she was standing over the pot, stirring, when he came in.

"It smells good."

"It smells good, it tastes good—but unfortunately, it doesn't taste like chili. The peppers must be different." She paused and looked at him. She was so attuned to his moods by now that nothing as indirect as speech was required for her to sense his frame of mind. "What's wrong?"

"We're in a communications black hole," he said. "I don't know what it means, but it's not good."

Later that evening, there was a knock at the door. They both stiffened. Malone gestured that Karen should go into the bathroom. "Who is it?" he asked.

But it was just the landlady, shyly offering him some slivovitz—homemade by her sister in Cezky Krumlov. The woman couldn't resist edging over the threshold and peering into the room. Malone watched her expression brighten at its extreme tidiness. Karen was fastidious. Karen emerged from the bathroom, and Malone introduced the two. They smiled shyly back and forth. The landlady's nose quivered like a rabbit—smelling Karen's "chili"—and later that evening, after they'd decided it was actually very good, Karen took a bowl of it to the old couple.

There was nothing on the radio for Vagabundo.

Malone went out to call again, and to think about what he might do if he got the same maddening voice advising him to call back in an hour. He decided he would give it one more day. If he failed to get through today or tomorrow, he'd try Diamond's home number—although, come to think of it, he didn't know where Diamond lived. Manhattan? Or was it Greenwich? Still, he might be able to chase Diamond's number down, assuming it was listed. He might even call the Agency and leave a message for Willoughby with the switchboard. From Vagabond. Giving a call-back time. Still, Malone was uneasy. If Diamond was the only link and something had happened to Diamond, Willoughby would have found a way to service the telephone number, to patch it through to himself—or to someone else.

Contingency plans looped through his mind until he stopped at a newsstand to buy the *Tribune*. It didn't arrive in Prague until noon, and the clerk was just slitting the plastic strap that held the bundle together. He handed one to Malone and began putting the others into the rack. Malone glanced at the headlines.

To say that his heart sank would not have been an exaggeration. Certainly there was a plummeting sensation in his chest, a diving swoop. He started reading the story.

CIA DIRECTOR KILLED IN CAR CRASH

Warrenton, VA. CIA Director Curtis Willoughby, 61, was killed early this morning when a gasoline truck jumped the median strip of Route 29 and collided with . . .

"Prosim?"

Malone looked up. The newsstand guy, gesturing at Malone's paper and holding out his hand for payment. Malone shoved some money toward him and continued to scan the article:

Lexus sedan. . . . Also killed in the crash was William Diamond, of the New York brokerage firm Diamond & Bliss . . . and Reginald Farnsworth, 41, of Florence, South Carolina, driver of the truck. . . . apparently fallen asleep . . . alcohol not a factor . . . both men wearing seat belts . . . airbags . . . returning from a celebration honoring the thirty-fifth wedding anniversary . . . President . . . great loss country . . . acting director. . . . Shock Trauma Unit . . . helicopter . . . obituaries page 7.

He read it through two more times. It didn't get better. He had a passing twinge of grief for Diamond—and even Willoughby, whom he had never met—but it was no more than that, a reflexive pang. They had been acquaintances— he and Diamond—no more. The man had not encouraged a personal relationship. He felt the same vague sadness he'd experienced when he heard that someone he knew—but not well—had died. An uncle. A colleague who was not a friend. Mostly, he was thinking about himself, and he was wondering if he, too, was dead.

"What's *wrong?*" Karen asked immediately.

"We're fucked. We are *fucked!* We are totally, completely, and irrevocably fucked." He handed her the newspaper.

It took hours before Marcus could even talk coherently about it. Karen didn't know what to do. He barely spoke a word except to explain to her exactly how "fucked" they were. Finally, he began to elaborate.

For one thing, he was supposed to come out of this with a new identity. The Agency was going to arrange it all: His death would be faked. There'd be a whole life story, with documentation to go with it.

"But you *have* all those passports and driver's licenses and pictures. Don't—"

He cut her off, shaking his head. "No, no, no. No. That's just pocket litter; that stuff wouldn't hold up for a day. No, when the Agency makes you—it's called a legend—they backstop everything; they give you a life, a paper life.''

''What do you mean?''

He sighed. ''Well, pocket litter—now that might include a library card. But when the Agency creates a legend, that library card would have an entire history, that person would have checked out books, paid fines—all that. I mean I have driver's licenses to go with my various passports, but those identities don't have driving *records*; they never ran a red light; they don't have insurance; they don't really *exist*, you see, even on paper. So it's not the same.'' He laughed. ''Not to mention there was to be plastic surgery.'' He stood up and looked out the window, tapping his heel against the floor. ''All that's out the window. Now I'm going to have to spend my whole fucking life—what's left of it—looking over my shoulder. And what I'm looking over my shoulder *for* are various parties that want to bury me— dead or alive. Either way, we're . . .''

''Fucked.''

She made suggestions, which he promptly shot down. Couldn't he get to someone else in the CIA? Surely someone else knew!

Maybe, but who? This was a deniable operation.

He had several passports. Couldn't they just go somewhere very remote? Nazis had disappeared in South America. Why couldn't they? That was fifty years ago. Before computerized data banks, jets, faxes, *America's Most Wanted*, and the Internet. And even those guys—eventually, most of them were found. His cover story made him look so bad, there were at least five different organizations actively looking for him. Of course the two of them *would* go away somewhere—but sooner or later, unless he could figure a way to fake his own death, someone would find him.

He did try. Cold calls, salesmen call them, when you don't have a reference or a gimmick or a way in, when you just call, out of the blue. The calls went pretty much the same way:

"Tim?"

"Who is this?"

"Marcus Malone."

"Marcus. Jesus. If you have any sense, you'll hang up right now."

"No, listen. I was involved in something with the director. . . ."

It tended to go downhill from there. Bill Diamond. The director. Right, they both happened to be dead. It involved this substance called red mercury. "Red mercury? That stuff is supposed to be a hoax. Let me get this straight: it was a deniable operation, your only links to the Agency were two dead men, it concerned a substance that everyone agrees does not exist, and you want me to put you in touch with someone? Have you been drinking? I'm sorry, Marcus . . ." The discussions all followed that general line.

He gave it up. It was time to get out of Prague.

"I do, at least, have an idea about where we can go," he told Karen. "At first, anyway."

"Where's that?"

"Beirut."

"*Beirut?* Why don't we just shoot ourselves?"

He wagged his head. "No. There's nothing happening in Beirut now. The Syrians have it locked down. We need a place where there isn't much of an American presence. So it comes down to either Beirut or Pyongyang or Havana—and I don't think Havana's a good idea right now. And between Pyongyang and Beirut? You don't even have to think about it. And besides, I have a good friend in Beirut, a *very* good friend. Another ex-spook."

"Who's that?"

"Pierre. Pierre Fremaux. New Orleans boy. Strange career path, but anyway, he ended up like this"—he held up two fingers—"with Syrian intelligence. I already talked to him, and he can fix it at the airport. All we have to do is get on a plane and get ourselves there. And we'll be all right . . . for a while."

"And he'll help?"

"Yeah. He owes me." Marcus fell back on the bed, exhausted.

Beirut. Four days later, they were there.

32

THEY'D BEEN IN BEIRUT FOR THREE MONTHS WHEN THE world exploded again.

Pierre had seen to it that their arrival went smoothly, and they'd enjoyed a month of pure euphoria. They were alive, and they were together: it seemed greedy to ask anything more. They were even unimaginably rich. Bill Diamond's final payment to Malone had not been made. But neither had the banker, before he died, sent instructions for the transfer of the $4 million that Yotaro Kawai had paid into Malone's account. And so, it was still there.

No, money wasn't the problem, time was. And the sense that, once again, Marcus was running out of it. No one had dropped out of the search for him—which meant that the Israelis, the Agency, the U.S. Marshals' Office, Interpol, the bail bondsman, and anyone who might have survived the Kawai business were still hunting.

Pierre, who was wired into Syrian intelligence, reported every new rumor about Malone. The most disturbing rumors concerned the Iranians. Somehow, they took it personally that he'd dropped out of sight. They wanted to buy what he wanted to sell. What was his game? Why didn't he want to sell? Whom was he aligned with? Even the Syrians were a problem—the Assad government would like nothing better than to trade Malone to the U.S. for a political favor. "A little more pressure on the Israelis in regard to the Golan, maybe?" Pierre had mused. "You've got to keep your head down, my friend. My influence only goes so far."

And since the disappearance of Malone from Prague and the sudden appearance of Declan Yates in Beirut were nearly simultaneous, it was only a matter of time. The Yates identity wouldn't hold up forever. Malone did have one more passport, one more unused identity. But only one.

He was beginning to feel paranoid. Every knock on the door seemed a threat, every trip to the souk a risky exposure. Malone had initiated some inquiries, through Pierre, about finding a good plastic surgeon who would not be too inquisitive about why he wanted to alter his face. Even there, the preliminary meeting with the man gave Malone the creeps. The doctor wanted to photograph him and play with the image on the computer—and Marcus had been reluctant to permit the photograph. He'd backed off—and said he wanted to think about it.

In other words, it was a claustrophobic life he and Karen were leading, an existence badly constrained by the fear of discovery.

And then it happened.

It was an impossible sound, a sound without meaning, a huge concussive wallop in the night. Before she was actually conscious, Karen began to scream, although her voice was lost in the din.

It wasn't so much the sound itself that was terrifying, even though it was literally deafening, a roar that seemed to fill up all the space in the room, a dense boom that annihilated thought. There was something worse, the feeling that the air itself was sucking at her, as if her skin were being pulled away from the flesh, as if her flesh were detaching from the bone.

Then it was over.

First the feeling that her body was going to fly apart stopped. Then the roar receded, replaced by recognizable noises: crashing objects, a rain of lighter debris, the splintering of glass. Through it all was a fluctuating ribbon of sound, a somber and muted wail that she suddenly recognized as her own voice. She closed her mouth, and it stopped. Marcus put his hand on her shoulder for a second and then went to the window. He stood there silhouetted in the shuddery light from outside.

"Car bomb," he said finally.

She thought, *It's the kind of light a fire makes.* Then she noticed the strong smell of acrid smoke in the room. Then she observed that the windowpanes were empty of glass. Then she saw that the glass had fallen onto the floor. Each one of these thoughts occurred in isolation, as if the mechanism in the brain responsible for linking thoughts had been damaged by the explosion. Finally she noted that

Marcus was standing on top of shards of glass and that his feet were bleeding.

"Your feet!" She started to get up and look for shoes and then saw that, in fact, there was glass several feet back from the window, some shards of it sticking up from the floor almost vertically, as if someone had been playing that game with them, that game where you throw knives into the dirt. Although it was a game from the past, one she never played but only read about or saw in movies, it annoyed her that she couldn't think of its name. It seemed urgent to remember, and she was relieved when it suddenly snapped into her mind: *Mumblety-peg*.

Outside, people were shouting; people were screaming; people were weeping.

His feet were not badly cut. Still, she spent quite a bit of time picking the glass out, little needles of glass that she pinched between her fingernails and extracted. It took longer than it might have because the lights were out. They were used to that; the supply of power in Beirut was still not always dependable. Taking an elevator, especially after 6:00 P.M., was a calculated risk, and no one went without a supply of flashlights, candles, batteries. But it was really hard to see, by the beam of the flashlight, the tiny spikes of transparent glass. She ended up doing it mostly by feel, running her fingertips over the soles of his feet until either he winced or she felt a sharp little extrusion.

Outside, someone was yelling, "Fouad! Fouad! Fouad!" on and on, in an escalating tone of terror.

Finally Marcus said it was good enough, although once they were dressed and headed out the door she saw that he walked in a gingerly way, almost with a slight hesitation before he set each foot down.

They lived on the rue Madame Curie. Their first thought was to go and see their friends Pierre and Monique, who had an apartment across the street, closer to where the bomb went off than their own place. To see if their friends were all right. But even without this concern, they would have gone out. Disaster was an almost irresistible magnet, Karen thought. There was a compulsion to check, to assess, to witness the extent of catastrophe. She felt it, this slightly perverse excitement, and castigated her self. *Voyeur!*

Marcus had seen it out the window, so he was not so shocked, but Karen sucked in her breath once they stepped out the door, stunned by the devastation. On their side of the block the buildings had shattered windows and minor damage, but across the street two buildings were nearly reduced to rubble; huge chunks of concrete lay scattered around, looking far too large to have been moved by anything less than a crane. There was an amazing amount of twisted metal. A bedroom stood revealed, the front wall gone, looking like a room in a dollhouse. There was something so forlorn about that bedroom, Karen thought, the floral wallpaper, the rumpled blankets, the two pairs of shoes waiting tidily at the foot of the bed. She didn't see the people, so they must have gotten out all right.

Over it all hung a pall of corrosive smoke that smelled like burnt hair. And dust. Grit in Karen's mouth; her eyes watered. Fires burned here and there in the wreckage, looking oddly festive. The exploded car gouged out a crater; all that was left of it was a snarl of smoking metal. The air was filled with shouting and talking; there were dozens of people in the street, mostly in small clusters. Apart from

317

the fires, the only other illumination was provided by the bobbing, unsteady light of flashlights.

A group of men used long boards, trying to lever a block of concrete off a moaning figure. Marcus stopped, detaining Karen with his hand. The sight of the helplessly pinned man commanded Marcus to *do something*, but it was apparent that there was nothing he could actually do. There were already a dozen people doing nothing more than shining their lights, spare men on the periphery of the working group. A terrible feeling of uselessness squirmed through him.

Pierre and Monique's building was not too bad, although the door was blown off the hinges. Karen and Marcus picked their way up the stairs over big hunks of plaster.

Pierre opened the door, his face speckled with pinpricks of blood where he'd been hit by flying splinters of glass. Monique was on the couch shivering violently; she tried to laugh about it, but she kept on quaking. Pierre attempted to administer brandy, but her teeth tapped wildly against the glass. Karen swept the floor; Monique shook; they all congratulated one another on being alive and speculated about whether this meant the old days were coming back. Bombs were a rarity in the city now. Everyone was having to adjust to it: peace and the new, prosperous Beirut. Marcus and Pierre talked for a while about which group was likely to claim responsibility for the bomb. And then there was nothing to do but say good-bye.

Outside, the scene was much the same except that the fires had subsided to smoldering. In the absence of the firelight it was quite dark except for the two ambulances, lights whirling, at the end of the block—which was as close as the vehicles could get because of the rubble in the street. The location of the wounded was marked by the dimming beams of flashlights.

No one dead. Ten wounded.

That was the toll so far according to the paramedics, who turned down Karen and Marcus's offers to help.

"A miracle," Marcus said.

One paramedic, perhaps thirty years old, his eyes bright under heavy brows, leaned against the driver's door. He shook his head and curled his lip in distaste.

"Maybe," he said, in a tone that made it clear he didn't believe in miracles. "What I think? The bombers fuck up."

"What do you mean?"

He shrugged. "Car bomb at night. No." He wagged his head, his mouth turned down in disapproval. "Car bomb is *made* to kill people. They go off when man-y people on the street. This one?" He chopped his head down decisively. "Mistake. Maybe a bad timing device."

"You're probably right," Marcus said.

"I think many amputations," the man went on. "One little girl going to lose one of her legs to here." He chopped toward his body at midthigh. "One man—a piece of the car somehow enters his window and cut off his both hand." He held his arms out, wrists together as if shackled, hands in fists, and then opened his fingers out in a gesture of loss.

From the interior of the ambulance came a shout, and the man opened the door and got into the driver's seat. He nodded his head at them. "Inshallah."

"Inshallah."

It was difficult to see because their flashlight batteries were so low. They were forced to proceed very slowly on the way back home. Karen followed Marcus, but she kept seeing a mental picture of the man with no hands, his wrists gushing blood. She shook her head, trying to dispel the image. It made her own hands feel funny, a kind of sick tingling sensation in them. But she couldn't stop seeing it: wrists, gushing blood. She tried to concentrate on Marcus, who was ahead of her, walking in the strange hesitant gait that made it quite clear his feet hurt him. But it was all she could see: hands severed at the wrist, spouting blood. Finally, she squeezed her eyes shut, hoping that would dislodge the image, and of course she tripped, stumbling over something. Her flashlight fell out of her hand, clattered, and rolled. And there, illuminated by its dim glow, caught in the orangish disk of its beam, was: a hand.

Karen felt a swoop of panic, a terrible arrow of fear. A strangled scream came from her, and then Marcus was at her side.

Of course, it was not one of the disembodied hands, one of the hands cut off the wounded man; it was attached to a body. Marcus played his disk of light over the man. He wore khaki pants and a tattered blue shirt. The light lingered on the face. It was a European face, a sandy-haired man, with jug ears. His hair was dirty and matted. His eyes were blue and open. The sightless gaze, the blank contemplation, made her shiver.

And then she knew who he was. They called him Billy, but no one really knew his name or even his nationality. He was half-mad; he talked only to himself; he was said to live in an abandoned building near the Opera House. She remembered Monique saying he was supposedly a Dane, a relief worker who went over the edge and never recovered.

Once or twice Karen had tossed money into the grimy cup he held out—shyly, his head averted. When she gave him money, although he wouldn't look at her, he acknowledged it with a cordial little dip of his chin. Billy. The fact that she knew him, the fact that she'd seen him walking down this very street, the fact that she'd put money in his cup—somehow this made the sight of his lifeless body worse.

Marcus was taking his pulse. "He's dead."

"I don't see a mark on him. He looks *perfect*; he looks . . ." Her voice was ascending, getting hysterical.

Marcus put an arm around her.

"It can happen that way," he said. "Didn't you feel the pressure in the air during the blast? What happens is that the explosion creates a vacuum. If you're close enough, it can crush the alveoli in the lungs. Basically, you suffocate—that's what an autopsy would show."

They were crouching over the body. Now Marcus stood up and lifted her up with him. He stepped back, looked around. "For some reason he was coming down this walk. Maybe he knew somebody who lived in this building."

It was easy to see why no one had spotted the body in the dark. It was uncanny, the way it fell, nestled into the curve of the low wall that embellished the beginning of the short walkway up to the front door of the apartment block.

Karen felt very cold. And then an idea vaulted into her brain.

"What do you think?" Marcus asked. "Should we run and tell them before they take off?" He gestured toward the remaining ambulance.

"I don't think so," Karen said slowly. "I have an idea. But first . . . I have to know how you feel about . . . about organ transplants."

What Marcus thought was that, obviously, she was losing it. Shock, maybe. They were standing on a bombed-out street in Beirut, with a dead man, and she wanted his views on transplant policy. Wait a minute. Now he saw what she meant. "I think it's too late," he said. "It's been a couple of hours at least. Anyway, I'm not sure they do too many transplants in Lebanon. They don't even have the equipment to take fingerprints."

"What? Oh, no, I . . ." She paused, looking almost embarrassed. "What I mean is do you believe that the dead can rescue the living? Do you believe it's *right*?" She tapped her flashlight against her palm. "I think *I* do."

"Well, I'm a donor," he said in a wary, uncommitted voice, "so I guess—"

"Good, because I think I see a way that this guy can save your life."

Their car, a used Mercedes sedan, happened to be parked around the corner, a good thing, because their block of the rue Madame Curie was now impassable. Luckily, the dead man was not too big and Marcus was able to fireman-carry him the block and a half to the car. They did not meet anybody. If they had, they were prepared with a story: the dead man was a friend, a colleague; they were taking his body to the authorities.

At first, they tried to put him in the backseat, but it was amazingly difficult to maneuver what amounted to a dead, segmented weight. Then they put him in the front

322

seat, but he flopped over alarmingly and Karen wondered out loud about how smart it would be to drive around with him like that. Someone might remember, for one thing. Or they might be stopped, questioned, detained; the authorities might take over responsibility for the body. There'd be a lot of questions, at least.

Finally, they decided to put him in the roomy trunk. Marcus opened it; Karen helped him lift. The body fit without any problem.

It wasn't until Marcus had both hands on the smooth curve of the metal of the trunk lid and he was about to slam it shut that the irony of the moment occurred to him.

"What?" Karen said in an urgent tone, because after all, it was going to be light in a couple of hours.

Yet Marcus just stood there, hands poised, shaking his head. "That's weird," he said and finally slammed the trunk shut.

"*What!?*"

"That's how it all started."

"No," she said. "I don't. I don't know what you mean."

His eyes didn't really focus on her. He was remembering it: the Staten Island Ferry, Diamond's voice in his ear telling him the story. He shook his head in a grim little gesture of recognition. "I mean it all started with a dead body in the trunk of a car. A long way from here."

33

AFTER THE DEAD MAN WAS SAFELY LOCKED INTO THE TRUNK, they went back to their apartment to get the camera and Karen's makeup bag. Returning to the car, their eyes adjusted to the darkness; they picked their way over the scattered debris quickly.

The violence was localized. By the time the Mercedes was three blocks from the rue Madame Curie, except for the receding bleat of the ambulance it was as if nothing had happened. Well, nothing recently: there was little of West Beirut that did not have scars from the long conflict. Instead of neat cables, a strange spiderwebbing of wires came out of each building, jury-rigged electrical and telephone lines. And there were the marks of shells and bullets everywhere.

Malone turned onto the Corniche, the beautiful road that ran along the Mediterranean Sea. It was a cliché to bemoan the fate of Beirut because of its reputation as a beautiful city, "the Paris of the Mideast." In fact, in Malone's opinion, Beirut was far more beautiful than Paris. The beauty of Paris was man-made; the city itself set in a vast plain, with only the Seine and its islands as natural assets. Beirut, on the other hand had a spectacular setting, perched as it was on a promontory jutting out into the Mediterranean, the land behind it rising up precipitously into the Chouf mountains, which were crowned with snow most of the year. In early summer, it was possible to go windsurfing in the Med and then drive for forty-five minutes and go skiing.

"I hope I can figure out his equipment," Karen was saying. "I hope it's not too different." She looked out the window and shook her head. "It's a little surreal, isn't it? I mean driving around with a corpse in the trunk?" She gave a shaky laugh, and Malone feared she was going to lose it. When he glanced over, she looked white-faced but determined.

They were passing through the the bombed-out center of the city now, the ruin of the elegant opera building and the site where the exploded wreck of the American Embassy stood until recently, when it was finally levelled.

East Beirut was the Christian sector and crossing into it was immediately apparent because it was less afflicted by damage, because there were pots of flowers out in front of the buildings, because everything looked well kept. They turned a corner and pulled up in front of a small building. A small white sign with black letters hung from a wrought-iron arm. It was just visible in the light from a street lamp halfway down the block. The information was in Arabic as well as in English:

FADI CASSIS, D.D.S.
Dentist

It was in this little office where the continuing battle for Malone's dental health had been waged in recent months. The Mercedes looked enormous, as conspicuous as a white whale, sitting in Fadi's driveway, and as soon as they got the body out Malone planned to move it a few blocks away.

Malone felt very bad about breaking into this nice man's office, especially since they would have to steal something in order to make the break-in resemble a robbery. There wasn't even time to pick the lock. Malone pulled his shirt down over his sleeve and drew his arm back and punched the window—hard and precisely, with a karate-style chop. The glass cascaded to the floor: an avalanche of sound. Malone stopped, listened, and looked. But he did not see a light go on in any of the surrounding buildings or hear a door open. He pulled his shirt up around his head and covered as much of his flesh as possible before crawling through the window. He still managed to scrape his cheek on a piece of glass in the window frame. There was that cold feeling of sliced flesh and then the wet seep of blood.

The door was a simple dead bolt, and he unlocked it and rushed out to the car. He looked at his watch: 4:45. They had perhaps an hour and a half. He and Karen managed to dump Billy onto the ground, and Marcus dragged him inside, his lifeless feet bumping and rolling over small obstructions. Together Marcus and Karen maneuvered him into the dental chair.

They shut all the blinds and pulled all the curtains and

turned on the lights. But the office was hardly designed to be light-tight; it was definitely a risk.

In the bright fluorescent glare Malone felt as exposed as if he were standing in a spotlight. If any alert neighbor happened to be looking out the window . . . The thought made him remember. He touched Karen's arm.

She jumped. "Your face is covered with blood!"

His fingers went to his cheek, and he was surprised—because of the lack of pain—at the amount of blood.

"Good," he said grimly. "I'm going to need some blood. Look; I've got to move the car."

The dead man lay in the chair, and between his loose-limbed sprawl, the way his clothing was bunched up to reveal his pale skin, his staring eyes, he looked somehow *so* dead, so lifeless. *And yet,* Karen thought again, *there's not a mark on him.* She moved quickly around the office to get what she needed; it wasn't difficult. There was a certain logic to where things were kept in dental offices. She found the X-ray materials and then she approached the corpse. She pushed the foot pedal and raised the chair and pushed another lever and tilted him back. She adjusted the light. She stopped, put some rubber gloves on, and then tried to open his mouth and insert the first film—she intended to take a complete set of X rays.

But it was almost impossible. She hadn't realized how much she relied on the patient's help—to move the tongue, to bite down. She couldn't do it alone. Not only that, but the man's mouth was actually getting stiff; she had to yank open his jaws. She was standing there, tears beginning to come into her eyes, when Marcus returned, his face half-covered with blood. The situation suddenly seemed so surreal that she started laughing, a silent body-

327

shaking hysteria that finally subsided when Marcus put his arms around her and pressed her to him. "Come on, Karen. Come on."

With rigor mortis setting in, with Marcus's, inexperienced hands, with the problems of a dead tongue, with a world of slippery spit—still, they did it, Karen positioning the film and holding the man's tongue aside with a depressor, Marcus pushing the man's jaws shut. Finally it was done: two full sets of X rays of the dead man's mouth. Marcus went to get the car while Karen developed the film.

By now, the sun was rising, a pink radiance behind the skyline. The streetlight flickered off as Marcus pulled the car back into the dentist's driveway. People would be getting up now; anyone might look out the window and see the car in the driveway. Anyone, in fact, might be watching him drag the body out, crouch down, heave it into the trunk. The body was getting stiffer by the minute; it was difficult to maneuver it into the trunk. Malone gritted his teeth and wrenched the man's knee aside to force it inside. This caused a disgusting sequence of liquid pops and tears, the ligaments and tendons giving way. Two doors down, a man came out of his house with a little dog. Malone hurried inside.

"Hurry up, Karen! It's almost light out."

This time, he looked around before he ventured outside. He didn't see anyone. He'd "stolen" the copier and the fax machine and, one by one, put them in the backseat.

Finally, Karen was finished and they were in the car and leaving.

"I put one set of X rays in the Declan Yates file,"

Karen said. "I took the old ones out and cut them up and put them in a trash bag with the gloves and stuff. I tried to clean up the office so you couldn't tell what we were doing in there."

"Nobody would guess," Marcus replied. "They might think we were playing with the laughing gas or something, but nobody would guess. Not in a million years."

They passed a small blue sedan. Malone lifted a hand to the driver in a kind of salute, but the man looked horrified and Malone realized that his face was still covered with blood.

"I think I scared the shit out of that guy."

The blood had dried. It felt stiff and hard when he tried to smile at Karen. He felt it crack and flake.

They crossed what used to be the Green Line and entered the bombed-out center of the city. Malone left the car running and ran to the kiosk near the Hotel America—the one that opened at dawn—and bought that day's paper. It still smelled of ink and seemed slightly damp to the touch. Then they retraced their route, back toward East Beirut and up the mountain toward Beit Mary. There was a Syrian checkpoint up there, but before they reached it Malone stopped the car alongside a fairly dramatic rock outcrop.

"You know, we're not ready," Karen said, a sudden desperate tone coming into her voice. "I don't have a Magic Marker! I don't have any paper! And it seems to me we should rent another car."

She was right, of course. They stopped and she bought a bottle of water and with some napkins that were in the glove compartment cleaned off his face. Karen imagined she smelled the body in the trunk but knew it must just be her imagination. They drove back to the apartment, where Karen promptly ran into the bathroom and got sick.

The day was difficult—seeing their friends and neighbors, discussing the car bomb, the damage to the block when all the time, one thought was screaming in Karen's head: *there's a body in the trunk. You know, Billy* . . . that panhandler . . .

She made a sign to dangle around Malone's neck, using a shirt cardboard and black Magic Marker and shoelaces to suspend it:

DEATH TO CIA PIG

Finally, night arrived—a gorgeous night, the stars strewn against the sky, the moon dripping onto the Mediterranean.

They drove to the airport, and Malone rented another car. Karen followed Malone downtown. Next to the destroyed Opera House was an abandoned apartment building. It wasn't totally abandoned, as there were a couple of families living in rooms there. The front walls were constructed of sandbags, but the families had, of course, chosen areas in the less devastated section of the building. Karen and Malone trudged up the stairs of the badly damaged sector with their newspaper, with their sign, with Karen's makeup kit. In the hallway, Karen applied makeup to Marcus by the inadequate light of an upended flashlight. She blackened one eye with eye shadow and eyebrow pencil; she rubbed foundation mixed with blue eye shadow on his lips to give them a deathly pallor. And then Malone took her makeup mirror and a razor blade and reopened the cut he'd received when entering the window at Dr. Cassis's office. Then he cut a slit in the very corner of his mouth.

"Oh, God," Karen said, squeezing her eyes shut. "How can you do that?"

Blood oozed from the cuts and then dripped down effectively, especially when Malone squeezed the flesh to encourage it. His cheek was drenched; another thick trickle oozed from the corner of his mouth. Malone slumped against the stairwell, eyes rolled up, limbs arranged in oddly contorted and uncomfortable positions, the sign around his neck, that day's copy of *Al Nahar* pinned to his shirt as a date marker. Karen took ten shots of him, the flash winking in his open eyes.

"Jesus, Marcus, you *look* dead. Is this bad juju? OK, that's it; I'm done."

He couldn't see; his eyes were shot through with after-images of the flash. He pulled her down into his arms and kissed her, and there was blood on her lips when he looked at her, and a smear on her cheek.

Karen followed him in the rental car as they drove through East Beirut and then up into the mountains. They passed Beit Mary and the curving drive up to the Hotel Al Bustan and then arrived at the Syrian checkpoint. The guard emerged from his sandbagged enclosure. Malone was nervous, but the Syrian just looked at him and waved him on. He watched in the rearview mirror. The Syrian waved Karen on, as well.

About fifteen minutes later, they were still in the mountains, but the Bekaa valley was visible, a strewn glitter of lights in the distance. Malone pulled the Mercedes off the side of the road. They were at the top of a rise, with good visibility on either side—they would be able to see any approaching car ten minutes before it reached them. And yet the site was not so remote that the explosion of the car would go unnoticed. There were dozens of houses within a half-mile, their lights winking.

Malone opened the trunk and the smell—the sweet, rank smell of putrefying flesh—assaulted him. He dragged the body from the trunk and checked the pockets for identification. He found a wallet, removed it, and put his own passport, house keys, wallet, and so on,. in the pockets. He also removed a chain and a pendant from the corpse's neck—an Egyptian ankh symbol. You never knew what would survive a fire. The most difficult part was wedging the stiff body into the front seat. He fastened the seat belt.

He closed the trunk. There were some shirts in there, which had been destined for the cleaners, and he used one of them, stuffing it into the gas tank. He threw the gas tank cap into the car. Just as he was ready to light the rag in the gas tank and push the car over, a light appeared, sweeping up the mountain. He hesitated but then realized that the car would not arrive for some minutes. It was perfect.

"Let's do it," he said. He drove the car to the precipice, put it in neutral. The alarming part was lighting the rag before pushing the car. How long would it take to reach the gas tank? There seemed a possibility it would explode and incinerate them. The car was heavy, and even though it was perched on a downward slope, just overcoming inertia took all of their combined strength.

The big white car began to roll slowly, as if it might stop and explode right in front of them. But then it picked up speed, gravity took control, and finally the back wheels were over the edge.

Malone resisted the temptation to watch. It either exploded or it didn't. He and Karen jumped into the rental car and and took off. The lights of the approaching car stuttered off and on depending on the terrain. They'd gone about a quarter-mile, maybe, when they first sensed the illumination of the explosion, and then, a split second later, came the sound of it, a sequence of concussive bangs that richocheted around the odd acoustics of the terrain in such a way that explosion seemed for a moment to be chasing them.

He drove back, toward the airport. When they passed the spot where the car had gone over, the air was still full of smoke. There were emergency vehicles—a police car, an ambulance, a Syrian army vehicle. They slowed down, but they were waved on by.

They stopped at the Al Bustan for a drink. Karen took the dead man's identification and the ankh chain and wrapped them in a clean Kotex pad purchased from a machine in the incredibly ornate ladies' room and discarded the result in the little metal bin designated for the disposal of intimate refuse. The leather wallet she kept in her purse and planned to get rid of at the airport.

"Well, I'm dead now," Malone said solemnly when they got back into the car. "I'm dead and I think I like it!"

"You're not dead yet," Karen said. "You're not dead until we get this film to *Al Nahar*. But I don't want to take it in there; that's too risky. Let's mail it—" She shook her head. "No. We'd have to spend the night somewhere."

But then she thought better of it. "I think we'd better risk it."

They spent the night at the Al Bustan. In the morning, Karen got sick again, throwing up violently in the hotel room's luxurious bathroom. Marcus worried over her, but she insisted she was OK.

She spent what turned into almost an hour on a pay phone at the central post office, calling the United States and reserving a room for herself at the Radisson Hotel in Alexandria, Virginia. She inquired about sending mail to a guest and obtained their mailing address. She bought two padded mailers from a stationery store. Into one she put the undeveloped film of the dead Marcus Malone slumped in the stairway of the bombed-out building near the Opera House—which she would send to *Al Nahar*. Into the other she put the set of X rays of Billy's teeth which she would send to the Radisson. Then she bought food, some "tan-in-a-can," blond hair coloring (they had Clairol), and sunglasses. It seemed worth the effort to her to disguise Marcus just enough so that no one at the airport would—if *Al Nahar* printed the photo in a day or two—associate that slumped man with anyone spotted departing Beirut.

He submitted without complaint, although when she was finished he studied himself in the mirror and winced.

"God, Karen, my hair is *orange*. My *skin* is kind of orange, too."

She winced. "You do look a little strange."

"I look like a golden retriever."

She started giggling. "I'm sorry, Marcus. If you could just leave your tongue out and *drool*. Don't worry. I can fix it. I'll just get some, I don't know, Grecian Formula or something and dull it down."

The end result was less garish, and he really did look different. "Let's see; I guess I could be . . . an entertainer kind of down on his luck, maybe an international bowling star."

He held up his final virgin passport. "Chandler Bailey. Kind of a nice name, don't you think?"

"Chandler," she said in a brittle voice. "Chandler. *Chan.*"

He sank down on the bed and grabbed her hand. "I don't like this last part of your plan," he said. "I don't think it's absolutely necessary."

"It is. I'll be careful."

"I hate it."

"It will be easy," Karen said, with far more conviction than she felt.

An hour and half later, they were aboard a Mideast Airlines flight to London. They did not take seats together, nor would they talk to each other again until their planned reunion in Ireland. When Karen waited at the back of the plane for a vacant rest room, Malone came up behind her and risked kissing the back of her neck, just below and behind her ear.

"Well, this is it," he whispered, "the wild blue yonder."

She got sick again, in the airplane lavatory. It took a long time to clean up the mess.

34

At Dulles, she approached the barrier at Passport Control with some degree of nervousness, which was justified when the clerk did not stamp her passport and wave her through but asked her to wait.

"Oh, Jesus," said the impatient man behind her. "I always pick the slow line. It's a talent, really, if I could just learn to control it."

Ten minutes later, Karen was strip-searched by a humorless matron. This involved the humiliation of having her anal and vaginal cavities probed, a procedure that left her in a combative mood when she was once again dressed and sitting in a utilitarian room across from three men in suits. She demanded their identification and wrote down their names in the back of her magazine.

At first, she was sullen and uncooperative: "I haven't broken any laws. I don't have to answer any questions."

"Well, actually, you do. . . ." There were threats (obstruction of justice, accessory to this and that, ambiguous hints of "serious trouble," and promised escape routes from same), then sympathy, intertrio arguments, food, coffee, an unending barrage of questions. They counted the money that had been in her purse ($9,000) and suggested that they might seize it. They dished out a good deal of information about Marcus, where he'd been, what he'd done. The aliases he'd used. They showed her photographs of both of them, taken outside their apartment in Prague and on the balcony of their apartment in Beirut.

Finally, she allowed herself to break down. "I think he's dead," she said. She was not actress enough to make herself cry. She had rehearsed this story in her head, but she found herself embellishing it. The car bomb that she was persuaded was aimed at Marcus but missed. Then, the next morning, three thuggish Iranians hustling Malone into a car just as the two of them came out the front door of the building. Later that day, someone had been in the apartment and searched it. "I was frightened," she said. "I thought they might come after me. That's why I left."

They seemed to believe her, but she couldn't be sure. By the time they let her go, it was morning. She rented a car. Everything seemed utterly familiar, as if she had only been gone a day or two.

The hotel was tall, a cool aquamarine glass building of perhaps twenty-five stories. No, they had no mail for her. She hadn't expected the package to be there, really, but still, she was disappointed and worried. And in her pleasant room she collapsed on the bed and she couldn't have said why, but for at least an hour she did nothing but cry.

After a shower and three hours of sleep, she felt better,

strong enough, even, to phone her parents. Her mother was "delighted" she'd be coming to visit.

Karen went to a used car lot on Route Seven and bought a green Subaru station wagon for $1,900. She drove to the DMV and registered it, using her old address. She thought a gray sedan was following her, but there were so many gray sedans—she wasn't sure. She checked at the hotel. The package hadn't arrived.

She returned the rental car to Dulles and then caught the shuttle to the metro stop at East Falls Church and took a taxi to the Radisson. She was fairly certain that a man sitting in the lobby was familiar. Hadn't he been at the DMV? The desk clerk handed her the package from Beirut, and she just resisted turning around to see if the man was watching. Could he see it from there? The telltale foreign stamps. That would be total disaster—if they got this package, somehow, if they opened it and saw the little square dental X rays. She picked up a booklet, *This Week in Washington*, and covered the package with it, then removed her purse from her arm and clasped it against her body.

She stayed in her room, ordering from room service. She peeled the stamps off the packaging and burned them, making sure to remove and burn the postmark as well. In the morning, she tore one leg off a pair of panty hose and twisted the X rays inside it and pinned it to the waistband of her underpants.

This was the part she was dreading, actually, confronting Dr. Pratt. After all, she had left without giving notice, and with his passion for order he would not be forgiving. He had treated her well, and she'd left him in the lurch.

Someone was following her, but she had the classic

advantage: familiarity with the terrain. She could easily lose this bozo in a neighborhood she used to use as a shortcut. The twists and turns remained as familiar as if she were still doing this every day. She executed a loop and turned back the way she'd come. He'd be stuck in there for a while. Whoever had designed the neighborhood realized that it lay between two major thoroughfares and didn't want it to be used as a shortcut. She parked a few blocks from Dr. Pratt's, in a grocery store lot, just to be safe.

Doreen was happy to see her, but Dr. Pratt was cold, at first. He didn't look up from his computer keyboard for at least five minutes. She sat, surrounded by his diplomas and tasteful paintings, until finally he stored whatever he was working on and looked at her. He pursed his lips.

"I must say I never thought I'd see you again."

"I thought I owed you an apology."

He swung his head from one side to the other and looked at the wall, shaking it. He sighed. "It was total fucking chaos. You didn't give me time to train anyone else; it was hard *finding* someone else—" He threw his hands up. "I couldn't believe it!"

She did not defend herself. "That's why I'm here," she started. "I felt bad. I—"

But he wasn't finished yet. "*You* felt bad. I felt *betrayed!*"

"Dr. Pratt. *John. I'm* sorry. That's why I'm here. I just wanted to explain. I was depressed. I had—well—what they used to call a nervous breakdown. I wasn't myself. And it's been weighing on my conscience." She almost believed herself. "I was hoping I could take you out to lunch. Doreen, too."

"Let's leave Doreen out of it," he said.

They shared a bottle of Chardonnay and ate pasta and she listened sympathetically as he went through the list of his problems, his triumphs, his worries. He made a pass at her, of course, but she managed to deflect it in such a way that he ended up flattered. ("I've always been attracted to you, but my therapist tells me that I can't afford to get emotionally entangled now. Especially if it would make me feel guilty, and, John, it would.") The news that she found him attractive, however, seemed to turn him on and he still tried to kiss her in the car, but she dodged it and it landed on her cheek. ("It would be a mistake, John. Trust me.")

They returned to the office and she hung around Doreen's desk, catching up on the details of Doreen's life and waiting for Doreen to go to the file room or the bathroom so she could steal Doreen's office keys. The conversation was definitely dragging, but Karen worked hard to keep it alive. Finally, Doreen had to pee.

Doreen kept her keys on a huge key ring that reposed along with her sunglasses in an oblong ceramic dish on the desk. Despite the establishment of this steady location, Doreen was always losing her keys and her sunglasses. It was an office joke. As a consquence Doreen had several sets of keys, at least one spare set at the office, another at home, another with her mother. All this had been described to Karen in tedious detail more than once.

Karen stuffed the entire key ring into her pocket. She left soon afterward, fearing Doreen would notice the missing keys.

Karen drove around for a long time before she was satisfied no one was following her. She wore black and she had a package of garbage bags and some duct tape and a flashlight in her backpack. She parked at a shopping center almost half a mile away and worked her way to the building, taking a long time hiding in the bushes before approaching Dr. Pratt's town house door. She waited until the night watchman came by, shining his flashlight around, whistling the tune to the song "Lean on Me." She disarmed the security system, tapping in the passcode on the keypad. She worried they had changed the code, but then it worked.

She taped the garbage bags over the windows before she turned on the lights. Karen found Marcus's file and took out all the X rays. The cardboard mounts used in Beirut were different, so she had to actually remove the film and insert it into Dr. Pratt's mounts. It was tedious, exacting work because she wanted the results to be as indetectable as possible. The night watchman came by, and she prayed none of the light was filtering through the garbage bags. She waited for the glue to dry, refiled Marcus's folder, and dropped Doreen's keys on the floor, under the front desk. She turned off the lights, took down the garbage bags, and took off, disposing of Malone's old films in a Dumpster behind McDonald's. Just as she had slung the garbage bag up and over, a voice said: "Hey!"

She probably should have stayed and brazened it out, but it scared her so much, she bolted. Her heart slamming in her chest, she didn't stop running until she got in her car. Even then she sat there in the dark for at least twenty minutes before she was calm enough to drive.

She visited her parents. For once, she did not feel threatened by their crotchety concern, their judgmental disapproval. It was just their way, she supposed. She would manage to stay in touch with them, one way or another. There were mail services that basically laundered mail. She might even phone once in a while.

She abandoned the green Subaru in Montreal. Of course, it would be found sooner or later and traced back to her. But it would take a while.

She took a circuitous route, just in case. She flew to Vienna to muddy her footprints, took a train to Paris, an airplane to London. She called Marcus from the airport with a phone card, the first time she'd spoken to him since he'd whispered in her ear on the Mideast Airlines flight. She took a train to Folkestone. Along with others, she retched and heaved her way across the choppy Irish Sea. She staggered off the ferry, and there he stood, in a brown leather jacket.

Big as life, as they say, with his strange orange hair. She had engaged in elaborate fantasies of this reunion, but the reality was different. It was a terrible, cold and rainy day. The only way she'd been able to stand it on the boat was to stay out on the deck, and she was badly chilled, almost shivering. The taste of vomit in her mouth was still so strong, she couldn't even bring herself to kiss him. She averted her head and just let it fall against his chest.

"I missed you so much," he said. She looked terrible. She'd lost weight, and her face was drawn and thin. The whole ordeal had been too much for her; it had been too much to ask.

He led her to the car. Of course, she tried to get into the driver's side and he gently steered her around to the passenger's seat. She made him stop the car after about half a mile so she could get out and be sick again. She was hunched over on her hands and knees, and he felt entirely helpless as he watched her, crouched there in the rain, vomiting into the grass. His heart lurched as she flung herself slightly to the side and collapsed, her face in the grass now, her whole body shaking. She was weeping uncontrollably.

"Are you all right?" he asked. He put his hand on her back. "I'll take you to a doctor. Usually the seasickness is over when you get onto the land. It's exhaustion; you must—"

But then she stood up and he saw that although her eyes were wet with tears, in fact she was laughing, not crying.

"Oh, Marcus," she said finally, when he'd got her into the car and she could speak again. "I'm a bit of a hypochondriac, you know. I thought after *all this*—I mean I was thinking, wouldn't it be just like me to get something now? *Now.* Stomach cancer. A bleeding ulcer." Cars were rushing by. The rain picked up. The wipers were beating furiously across the windshield. Malone merged into the traffic, and he earned a complaining bleat from the car behind. "I'm an idiot!" she suddenly exclaimed.

"Karen, you're not. I'm taking you to the doctor, immediately. Obviously, you're sick."

"Marcus—I mean *Chan*—I'm pregnant."

He pulled off the highway again, earning another angry honk from the car behind. He stared at her.

"Well, I left my pills behind in Mala Strana," she started, "and then . . ."

"Wonderful!" he said and threw his arms around her. "Karen, that's *fantastic*." He looked out at the awful day, at the sullen sky, at the traffic rushing by, at the raindrops sliding down the windshield. He felt surprisingly happy, if a little nervous about the future.

"I have my own news," he said, an hour later, in their hotel room in Kinsale. "Not quite so spectacular." She was in bed, doing the *Tribune* crossword puzzle. It was an old copy that she'd found on the bedside table.

"What?"

"You're not even paying attention."

"What's a six-letter word for rich fabric? It's not *brocade;* it's not *satin;* it's not—"

He took the paper from her.

"Hey!"

He rearranged the paper and folded it. The headline read: "Fugitive Found Dead in Lebanon."

She read the story through three times: "Forensic odontologists confirmed the identity of Marcus Horatio Malone through dental records." She looked up at him. "Well, how about that?" She hesitated. "Horatio?"

"Family name," he said.

"We won't pass it on," she said.

He threw back his head and laughed.